A SEA SO CRUEL

· STACEY FOSS ·

TABLE OF CONTENTS

For the ones who stand back up, even when their legs shake

Author's Note

This book contains subject matter that might be difficult for some readers, including strong language, graphic sexual content, violence, physical abuse (not the main couple), death of a parent (off-page), injury to animals (in combat), death of secondary characters

Alternate Chapters

Alternate chapters have been created for readers who do not prefer graphic sexual content. These alternate chapters are not "closed-door romance," but "door ajar romance." As important emotional and informative plot points occur during sexual chapters, the alternate chapters were created so that information can still be read. Chapters where alternates are available are clearly marked within the novel and the alternate chapters can be found after the epilogues.

PART 1

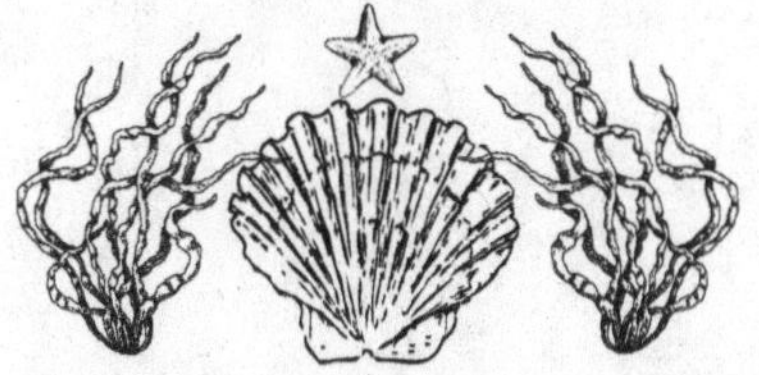

THE SEA

Stealing from the moon.
Absorbing the sun.
Molding rock.
Taming lava.
Lives forgotten beneath the surface. But also life born within.
She is immovable. So much so that the rest of the world forms around
her.
She can be gracious, quelling her currents and granting reprieve.
But she can be barbaric.
Some of her creatures possessing a bloodlust so insatiable, so unforgiv-
ing.
A sea so cruel. So, so cruel...

CHAPTER I

The vision was always the same. Veins of lightning pulsing across the onyx sky, a flame-haired woman kissing the crown of his head, men shouting, the roaring of lapping waves. Over the years, he'd had the same daydream countless times, never understanding if it were real or a fantasy.

Thump. Kaid's eyes refocused on his best friend, dragging him away from the mirage once again.

"Focus. We're here." Halsten wore a smug smile as he tucked the news scroll back onto the bench beside him.

Kaid narrowed his eyes toward his friend. "You can't abuse me. I'm royalty."

Halsten sat back and crossed his arms, flicking stray strands of his dark hair over his shoulder. "Not yet. I have a whole month left until you're officially a prince."

Kaid rolled his eyes, looking out the carriage window as they approached a massive gray castle. The grounds were covered in flowers of every shape, size, and color, and they reminded Kaid of his manor back in Haalberg—his home.

The somewhat bumpy ride changed to an easy roll as the roadway transitioned from unkempt dirt to smooth stones. Large horse sculptures flanked the large iron gates as they officially entered the capital grounds. He found it peculiar that the horses had strange, fishlike tails, but figured it was just a trick of the weary eye. Who would depict horses with fins? He didn't know much about Orntali aside from it being the capital of Salendron, home to a small seaside village and the large castle ahead.

Kaid's heart beat rapidly and he placed a palm on his chest, pushing down the nerves. In his twenty-two years of life, he had never left his father's side. Well, aside from when he was socializing with his best friend-made-chief courtier, Halsten.

He and Halsten met when they were younger after Halsten had moved to Haalberg from an Eastern kingdom. They had gotten into a fist fight over a girl, but once they realized that they were a fair match, the boys instantly became inseparable, forgetting about the girl entirely. Kaid appointed Halsten as his chief courtier once they were old enough, since he was the only person willing to set him straight.

"Check it out!" Halsten pressed his face to the window of the carriage, leaving a smudge. "I think we're going to like it here, Kaid. They worship women as much as we do."

Kaid leaned forward, noticing the statues of women that covered the castle walls. But they weren't human women. No, they had fishlike tails in place of legs, just as the horse statues had, and their torsos were wrapped in what looked like seaweed and jewels. The peaks of each of the many towers held a sculpture of a strange three-pronged fork.

The castle was oddly shaped, as though it started as a quaint structure but kept having new additions built, taking on an abstract shape that gave the fortress a life of its own. The strangest part was the tower built at the end of a rock bridge jutting out into the sea. Kaid watched as the waves broke against the tower's walls, and he shivered.

The carriage came to a halt and Kaid silently looked to Halsten, nodding before Halsten slipped out. Kaid followed him, the briny air violently punching into his nostrils and spreading throughout his lungs.

A small man with curly golden hair and pale, freckled skin came rushing forward. "Good evening, Lord Kaidian. I hope your travels from Haalberg went smoothly. My name is Niklas, and I've been appointed by King Botmar to assist you with anything you may need."

The skinny man bowed, and his glasses slipped down to the tip of his nose. He pushed them back up and gave a toothy smile, his eyes hardly ever making direct contact with Kaid's for more than a second.

Kaid's face twisted into mild disgust. "Gods, do I hate the name Kaidian. I go by Kaid. Can you show me to my rooms so I can freshen up before the party?"

Niklas blanched. "Sorry. So sorry, my lord. It won't happen again. No one mentioned—"

Kaid breezed by Niklas as he was mid-sentence.

Halsten nodded his chin toward Kaid, who was already sauntering toward the castle entrance without the rest of the group. "Better luck next time, mate. The rooms?"

Kaid turned to watch Halsten clap Niklas on the shoulder before he too passed by him.

Niklas sprang forward, running to catch up and lead the way.

In the entry hall, there was a grand staircase with a landing in the middle that split to more stairs going left or right. The walls were equipped with floor-to-ceiling windows, sandy shore visible through the glass, similar in color to the dark marble Kaid stood on. The sunlight from the ocean reflected on the golden accents lining the white walls, causing shiny tendrils of light to dance along the surface. Kaid had been to castles before, but never any this naturally bright. The nobility in Salendron liked their quarters dim and mysterious, so this was a refreshing change.

The rumble of a crowd caught Kaid's attention and he started walking toward it, Halsten falling into step behind him.

"My lord!" Niklas cried from the center of the foyer. "Your suite is upstairs!"

Kaid chuckled to himself when he heard Niklas sigh in defeat as he and his friend continued down the hall, leaving their tour guide behind. They came to a grand set of doors, the sound of the crowd bustling within, and a blonde woman pacing to the side of the doorway.

Kaid walked past her and she halted. He peered into the ballroom and observed the massive crowd, staying back to remain out of sight.

"Are you an attendee?" the blonde woman asked, startling Kaid from his spying.

Kaid cleared his throat and ignored her question. "Quite the grand party for a couple who has never met."

The woman's eyes narrowed slightly. "It's not every day that a princess gets engaged. Though I'm not sure it will last."

"You don't think the engagement will hold?" Kaid asked, his curiosity instantly piqued.

He tilted his head, observing the woman from head to toe. Her looks were pleasing to the eye—fair skin, blonde waves and captivating emerald eyes. Her figure was small but not weak. If she wasn't so ill-tempered, Kaid likely would have tested the waters with a seductive remark or two.

She nervously pressed down the front of her high-necked lilac gown. Kaid couldn't put a finger on it, but something about the soft color didn't fit her. One of her hands clenched into a ball. "Well, you said it yourself. They have never met. The Enrathi line has standards, and as I'm sure you know, the lord has a notorious reputation for seeing women as pieces in his game." The woman peeked into the doorway and observed the crowd. "He hasn't arrived yet, but I don't think he will stick around once he realizes that marriage means being tied down, and being tied down means he can't bed any woman he meets. I'm also quite positive that the princess doesn't want to wed such a problematic partner."

"I've heard the man is a real prick," Kaid mused.

The woman made a noise that was a combination of a laugh and a scoff. "I don't need to meet him to determine that. I've heard enough. A selfish child is what he is. A spoiled brat who lets his father do the hard work while he reaps the benefits."

Kaid laughed and looked over his shoulder at Halsten, who was monitoring from down the hall. Halsten gave him a knowing smirk, then grabbed Niklas's shoulder to hold him in place and stop him from his incessant pacing.

"What if Lord Kaidian is different from the rumors you've so willingly believed?"

"He's not," the woman said curtly, tugging at the high neckline of her dress.

Kaid had no problem internally admitting that she was correct. He and Halsten had slept their way through Haalberg and all the surrounding dukedoms. They liked to party, and most of the time, did not give a single fuck about anything other than that. But why was that such a terrible thing? Until now, Kaid hadn't any responsibilities. He was just a duke's son. The parties were happening regardless of his attendance and the women were willing, so why not seize the moment?

Kaid took her cold stare as his cue to exit. "Enjoy your party. I have a feeling I'll see you again soon."

Before she could respond, Kaid walked back to Halsten and Niklas, letting the latter lead them to his suite.

CHAPTER 2

Niklas unlocked the finely carved oak door with a golden key, then pressed it into Halsten's palm.

"I'll wait in the hall for you. When you're ready, I will escort you back to the engagement party." Niklas began slowly closing the door, but then it swung back open quickly. "Not that there is any rush, of course! I didn't meant to imply—"

"You're a worry-wart, aren't you, Niklas?" Kaid chuckled. "We will come out once we've cleaned up."

Niklas bowed, once again catching his glasses, and then backed out of the door and closed it behind him.

Halsten nodded a head toward the entrance of the washroom and made his way there, closing the door behind him. Kaid looked around his common room, taking in the fluffy sofas and chairs, lush fur rugs, and paintings of the coast. He ran his hand over the cherry oak bar, which was set in front of a floor-to-ceiling window that overlooked the beach below.

It was similar in decor to his home, aside from the oceanside location, so Kaid immediately found the room comfortable.

The young lord peered out the large window and watched the waves crash against the sand, seaweed and driftwood floating about. The shores were lined with evergreens and large boulders, aside from the stretch of sandy beach directly in front of the castle, which was likely finely groomed for the royals to enjoy. At the edge of the castle, there were multiple terraces with stairs that led directly down into the water below, and he made a mental note to steer clear of those particular entryways.

He wasn't going to touch the water. His father had warned against it his entire life. Kaid had never known where his father's fear of the sea originated from, but it was severe enough that he took it seriously. Haalberg, the territory of Salendron where Kaid's father was duke, was landlocked, so throughout his entire life, Kaid had never actually seen the ocean—until today.

Kaid ran his fingers through his dark hair as he considered the warnings his father had repeated during his last weeks in Haalberg.

The sea is filled with dangerous creatures. Things you can't imagine. Don't touch them.

The sea will lure you in, call to you. You must not answer it.

The sea will swallow you alive and it will be as though you never lived at all. Don't let it.

*The sea will know and crave you once you touch it. You must
resist.*

The advice was eerie and vague enough that Kaid didn't desire
learning if any of it was true. Even though he would be living here in
Orntali for the rest of his existence, he would never touch the mysterious
waters of the ocean. Never.

But even now, watching the waves, he understood what his father
meant by the calling. It was as though the settling waves seductively
whispered his name, beckoning him to caress them, even just once.

Kaid pried himself away from the window and walked over to the
other open door, discovering his bedroom. It was exquisitely decorated
in blacks and silvers, all glistening from the sunlight streaming in from
the massive wall of windows. Kaid sat on the fluffy bed and ran his manicured fingernail along the headboard carved with seashells and coral. The
crackling fireplace warmed a small sofa in front of it, and a bookshelf
crammed with texts of various colors and sizes sat in the far corner.

"Grand, isn't it?" Kaid startled at the sudden sound of Halsten's
voice. "The washroom is insane. I'm coming to your suite for all my
baths."

Kaid huffed a laugh. "Like you ever planned on leaving my suite
anyway? You can't get enough of me. Sixteen years later and you still seek
me out daily."

"True. If Maren turns you down, I might propose." Halsten sauntered over to the bed and threw himself onto the thick, dark comforter,
landing facedown. A crisp, clean scent wafted up around them. "Sweet
Knud, any woman you bring to this bed is the luckiest female alive."

"Don't mention the god of love in this sacred space. There's no
room for that emotion here." Kaid smirked.

Love wasn't one of Kaid's interests. Though he'd been sent to Orntali for marriage, it was arranged. And it was only orchestrated to save

the people of Haalberg. Their crops had been less abundant over the last few years and the farming territory was on the brink of poverty. Though Kaid's father didn't want to accept King Botmar's offer, Kaid urged his father to embrace it for their people. Kaid would move to Orntali and marry the king's eldest daughter, Princess Maren. Begrudgingly, his father ended up agreeing to the terms.

Kaid wasn't one to get involved in politics and didn't care much about what was happening around him, but he did care about his father and could see how heavily the future of his territory sat on his shoulders. He didn't cherish much in life, but he cherished his father. It had only been the two of them since his mother died when he'd been too young to remember. Everything Kaid's father did was for him, to ensure his future was steady and bright. This sacrifice was the only way to begin returning the favor.

Halsten sighed. "The love bug will bite one of us someday, unfortunately. Speaking of, ready to attend your engagement party?"

Kaid's face tightened into a begrudging expression, but he nodded, staring out the window, his gaze instinctively drawn back toward the ocean once more.

Kaid felt much better after freshening himself up from traveling. He donned his finest formal wear to the party—a white tunic accented in silver seams with a thick, forest green sash over it to represent the colors of Haalberg. Halsten wore a similar style, except his tunic was gray and his sash much thinner.

Niklas guided them down the halls of the Orntali castle, his golden curls bouncing from his springy steps. They passed a large tapestry in immaculate condition and Kaid paused to observe it. Depicted was a finned woman, nearly identical to the strange statues built into the castle's structure. What strange obsession did Orntali have with replacing legs for fins?

Niklas stepped beside Kaid and folded his hands. "Ah, yes. Queen Else's beloved siren tapestry. Beautiful."

Kaid side-eyed the courtier and noted the sparkle in his eye as he became lost in the tapestry. He shot Halsten an *Are you hearing this?* glance. "You're saying this is a siren?" Kaid asked skeptically. "As in the mythical creatures that are half-human, half-fish?"

"Well, my lord, she is certainly too humanoid to be finfolk, so obviously she is a siren!" Niklas snorted as though Kaid's confusion was the most amusing joke he'd ever heard.

What the *hell* were finfolk? Did Niklas believe these beasts were real? "So I suppose the statues scattered throughout the castle are also sirens? Why such fascination?" Kaid asked.

"Great question, my lord!" Niklas's voice was filled with joy, which made Kaid feel guilty for being so doubtful. "The royals who built the castle thought that displaying images of sirens would make it seem as though we worshiped them, deterring them from preying on our people. According to the history texts in the south wing library, each addition to the castle was outfitted with the same busts to continue to discourage the sea folk from coming ashore. Looks like it's worked so far. I've never seen a siren attack recorded within the castle grounds."

Kaid's eyebrows shot up. "Don't you mean never seen one recorded at all?"

The appointed courtier shook his head. "Oh no, we have stacks of reports. Sailors claiming they heard voices at sea. Women swearing their husbands were lured to the shore. The hard part is picking through them to see which are true, which are exaggerated, and which are a hoax. Most are fake, but I've found some very convincing reports with evidence."

Kaid stopped walking. "Evidence?"

What possible evidence could someone collect from a siren, even if they were real? A scale? Who was to say it wasn't from a very large fish?

Niklas wrung his fingers. "A fang, and a lock of hair. We've got them in the archives below the castle."

Kaid barked a laugh and wagged his finger at the man. "You are good, Niklas. Very good. This is a joke, is it not? Are you going to have someone spring out of the water wearing a paper fin to scare me?"

The young lord's attention turned toward the windows overlooking the coast. Even on such a sunny day, the swell remained merciless.

"It's no joke, Lord Kaidian. *Erm*, Lord Kaid." Niklas's face reddened. "We take our myths and folklore very seriously here. There is so much about the world that we do not know. Do you believe in air?"

"Air?" Kaid questioned.

"Yes. Do you believe that air is real?"

"Of course I do. But what does that have to do with sirens?"

Niklas smiled. "Just because you cannot see something, does not mean it doesn't exist. You cannot see air, yet you believe it is present. Who are we, as simple humans, to decide what is real and what is not?"

Kaid couldn't disagree with that. He was shocked that this argument had come from Niklas. He figured the man was more of a logical being. Clearly, he had read the courtier incorrectly.

The walk down the halls was silent until they were outside the ballroom once more. Niklas mumbled to one of the heralds flanking the doorway, and the man slammed his large golden staff to the ground. The crowd quieted as he announced, "Presenting Lord Kaidian Poulson of Haalberg, accompanied by Sir Halsten Seung of Haalberg."

The few murmurs in the crowd completely dissipated. Kaid hated the amount of eyes that were locked on him, the pregnant silence filling the massive ballroom, but noticed a pair of familiar green eyes through the onlookers. It was the same blonde woman he had met in the hall, though she was now casting him an icy gaze. Kaid gave her a complacent grin and nodded to the crowd.

The guests resumed conversing, eating and dancing a moment later. King Botmar approached from across the room, so Kaid and Halsten walked to meet him. Kaid bowed to the white-haired king, Halsten bowing a moment later, then returning to ogling at the surrounding women.

"Welcome to Orntali, Lord Kaidian. We are pleased to have you here, and pleased to have you join our family," King Botmar said as he gestured around the room.

Kaid held in his laughter. He was amazed that the king so willingly threw around the word "family," as though the scandal with his eldest daughter hadn't nearly torn his family apart. To the public eye, the king was a man who made a mistake and conceived a bastard child with an unknown woman, but had done the honorable thing in taking in his daughter and treating her as full royalty.

To the nobility, they could see the rest. That he had hurt his wife so deeply they slept in separate suites for months. That they only conceived their own child to put on a united front for their kingdom. That the salvation child was what had killed Queen Else during the baby's birth. That the king had drunk himself into oblivion most nights since, permanently damaging his memory in the process.

Reigning in his amusement, Kaid replied, "It is my greatest honor, your majesty. I would like to thank you personally for providing such generous accommodations for myself and my chief courtier."

Halsten's gaze snapped to Kaid, clearly realizing that the mention of his position was Kaid's way of reminding him to at least *act* like he was paying attention.

The king grinned widely. "Now, what you've been waiting for. Come, meet my daughters."

King Botmar marched back across the dance floor and Kaid and Halsten followed, ignoring all the eyes that were now locked on them. When Kaid realized who they were walking toward, he halted abruptly, causing Halsten to crash directly into him. He prayed to every god and goddess he could think of that the blonde woman was not his betrothed. He distinctly remembered his father describing Princess Maren as copper-haired.

Kaid felt Halsten push him, urging him to continue on. Luckily, the king didn't notice the slight stumble. However, now that Kaid's attention was on the blonde woman, he could tell that she had witnessed his hesitation by her smirk.

King Botmar stepped to the side and to Kaid's relief, a petite ginger-haired woman appeared. She smiled kindly and stepped forward, holding out her gloved hand. She spoke softly. "Princess Maren Enrathi."

Kaid gently pressed a kiss to her fingers, then bowed. "Princess Maren, words cannot express how appreciative I am that you have agreed to this arrangement. I hope I will live up to any expectations you have for a partner."

The blonde woman scoffed, and Maren flashed her a wide-eyed glare. Kaid stared at the woman, wondering who she was to the royal family. There were multiple women surrounding the princess and king. Was she a courtier? A lady-in-waiting?

Maren slipped her hand away from Kaid's grip. "I look forward to getting to know you more over the next few weeks, Lord Kaidian." She stepped back and placed a gentle hand on the blonde woman's shoulder blade, nudging her forward with a dainty grunt. The blonde woman leaned her weight backward, allowing her slippers to skid on the floor. "This is my sister, Princess Asta."

Even though Kaid wanted to let his jaw drop to the finely polished floor, his face remained indifferent. This cynical woman was to be his sister-in-law, not some employee that he could hopefully be rid of someday.

Asta whipped her hand out and Kaid grasped her fingers, kissing them briskly before letting go. Kaid put on his most charming grin and was pleased to see Asta scowl in return as she wiped the back of her hand on her gown.

"It is a pleasure to meet you, Princess," Kaid said. "I have a feeling that we will get along just fine."

Pleased with how the introductions had gone, King Botmar excused himself to speak with one of the dukes. Asta watched the king, waiting for him to be out of earshot before she spoke. "Then you, Lord Kaidian, are not only a prick, but also an idiot." She threw him a fake smile and Halsten covered his mouth to hide his laughter.

"Sister!" Maren interjected, and Asta winced. "Please go get Svanhild and let her know I will be in need of a short retreat soon. But first, I will dance with my husband-to-be."

Maren smiled, holding out her hand for Kaid. He contemplated the dynamic between the sisters. Asta had such strong, blunt words, but winced when Maren reprimanded her. He found that peculiar, but pocketed the information for later.

Kaid gently took Maren's delicate hand and led her to the dance floor.

Even though Kaid was usually quite charming, he was struggling with Maren. He had never had to charm a woman he didn't exactly want to

pursue. Most of his charisma was utilized on women he wished to bring back to his rooms or fellow nobles he was trying to manipulate.

Nobility was a game, and Kaid was a star player. Duke Aerik, his father, handled the paperwork, the residents and the politics. Kaid, however, handled the social interactions. Even with his notorious reputation, he found that everyone he encountered seemed to love him.

Everyone except for Princess Asta, apparently.

Kaid spun Maren to the melody, her mint green dress billowing out in a circle around her, and he used that moment to glance over at the jade-eyed she-devil standing at the edge of the dance floor. She seemed to be chuckling at something Halsten said, but she kept her eyes pinned on Kaid and Maren.

Maren smiled fully, a small gasp escaping her as Kaid pulled her back to him. That was what he needed to finally get her attention. He seized the opportunity in the song to dip her dramatically, his strong hold on her never wavering as she fell back, and then pulled up again. This time, she wasn't smiling. But her large, brown eyes were locked on him, a fire burning within. At that moment, Kaid knew he had her, and could easily keep this up for a few weeks. But could he do this for his entire life?

He supposed he might grow to love her. Someday. A very, very long time from now. But he didn't want to love anyone. He didn't want his happiness to rely on anyone but himself.

Kaid saw the struggles his father still went through regularly for having to live out the rest of his life without his true love, Kaid's mother. He sometimes felt guilty for his father's sorrow, even though he couldn't have stopped his mother passing away during childbirth.

Kaid's gaze drifted to Asta again, the other person in the room who had unintentionally killed their own mother. He wondered if she ever felt that same guilt.

Likely not, he thought to himself. *She seems too heartless to care about such a thing.*

"It is customary that you dance with my sister as well, Lord Kaidian," Maren stepped back, "I will send her to you. Thank you for the dance."

Before she could walk away, Kaid pulled her fingers to his lips once more and lingered seconds longer. He pulled his eyes up and saw that her face was rosy, accentuating the freckles peppering her nose and cheekbones.

"I look forward to our first date. Tomorrow?" Kaid asked.

"Tomorrow," Maren replied, trying not to look too eager.

She floated off toward her sister, her steps weightless. Her face turned serious as she spoke to Asta, and then Maren was escorted out by a brunette woman. Kaid assumed the woman must be Svanhild, her lady-in-waiting.

Asta stalked toward Kaid, leaving Halsten standing with a woman with light auburn hair in a sky blue dress. The two were awkwardly shifting on their feet and not speaking.

Kaid was shocked when Asta grabbed his arms and placed one of his hands in the proper position on her waist and his other hand in hers. He was even more shocked to feel the well-developed calluses of her grip.

"No spinning, no dipping, no frills," Asta mumbled through gritted teeth.

Kaid gripped her tightly and pulled her closer to him as he began leading their motions. He dipped his head down to her, keeping his voice low. "As you wish, Princess."

Asta rolled her eyes but let him take the lead. Kaid was amazed at the amount of muscle he could feel through the fabric of her dress, the delicate lilac color hiding what fury lurked within. How did a princess become so strong? They danced quietly for a few moments, the air thick between them.

Kaid gestured toward Halsten with his head. "Who have you left my chief courtier with?"

"Linnea, my lady-in-waiting." Asta glanced over at the odd pair. "I made sure she knew exactly where to kick him if he tried anything with her."

Kaid barked a laugh. "He would probably deserve it."

They danced mutely for a few moments.

"Why didn't you say anything?" Asta blurted.

Kaid acted clueless, though he knew where this conversation was going. He wanted to see how much further Asta could dig herself into a hole. "Say anything about what?" He quirked up an eyebrow.

Asta stopped moving with the music. "When we first met in the hall, obviously. Why didn't you mention who you are? Why didn't you stop me?"

"What better way is there to learn what people think about you than hiding your identity? Though you didn't teach me anything new." Kaid smirked.

"You won't be marrying her." Her voice was stern and unyielding, her face expressionless.

"I most definitely will. And I'll win you over, too." Kaid pushed on Asta, a reminder for her to keep dancing.

Asta howled a humorless laugh. "Not even when I'm dead will I have an ounce of respect or liking for you. Go back to Haalberg and drink yourself to death, as you seemed so fit to do before my father made this ridiculous arrangement."

"Drinking seems to be more of your father's hobby, is it not?" Kaid smiled, keeping his voice light, but he knew how much his words stung.

Asta used the long skirts of her dress to conceal her foot as she stomped on Kaid's toes, and pain shot up his leg. Her voice remained innocently sweet as she said, "Oops, it seems I forgot the steps for a moment."

Kaid held back a wince and tightened his jaw. He had never met someone so challenging, so absolutely infuriating. But he needed to go through with this to keep Haalberg from desolation. "I've never met someone who dislikes me so strongly before," Kaid admitted, though he wasn't sure why he said it.

Asta smiled, a gleam of victory glowing in her emerald eyes. "I'm honored to be the first of what I suspect will be many in your lifetime."

CHAPTER 3

Asta stalked down the halls of the castle, her feet aching from a long night of dancing. She passed by rooms booming with laughter, by couples tucked away in shadowed corners, by mumbling noblemen making business deals. When she was finally safe in the west wing, she sighed in relief as she passed Tova, the female guard at the end of the hall. No one was allowed in this part of the castle except those whose suites were here, which was, to her great relief, currently only her.

The doors to her suite were slightly ajar, and she could see Linnea bustling about, preparing the rooms for her return. Asta tapped the doorframe twice, then entered her suite. Dyri, her large goofball of a dog, greeted her right away. He nudged her hand for pats, and Asta obliged.

"You're back earlier than I expected. Let me go prepare your bath." Linnea departed for the washroom in a hurry.

Asta lazily waved a hand while she pulled off her slippers and released her hair from its combs. "No rush, I'm not tired anyhow. Can you make the water a little colder than usual?"

Linnea displayed a confused expression, but said, "As you wish. Give me a moment."

Asta was aware it was the end of summer and she shouldn't call for a chilled bath, but she needed it tonight. Lord Kaidian had her so worked up that she needed more than a mental cooldown. He was worse than she expected. Sweet Absolon above, she could throttle him.

Asta had disliked people before, but never loathed someone as quickly as she had Kaidian. He'd caused her to break down every filter and wall she had strategically built all her life.

The wind whistled outside and Asta watched the evergreen trees bend to its will. She let out a sigh, pressing her palm to the cool glass. It had been a very, very long day, and she was drained. Movement in the waves caught her eye, and she could have sworn she spotted a woman wrapped in a blanket step into the water. She rubbed her eyes and saw that the water was clear. The exhaustion was really wearing on her.

Asta heard voices coming from the hall, which peaked her interest, since her suite was the only one occupied in this wing. She dipped her head into the hall, expecting to find conversing guards, but she was gravely disappointed at who she observed sauntering down the passage.

"Didn't anyone tell you the stables are off the north wing? That's where the animals sleep," Asta mused.

Kaidian jolted, clearly shocked from her sudden appearance. He and his chief courtier must have been drinking heavily since she had left the party, based on the way they were leaning on each other.

Dyri slipped by Asta's legs in a flash of copper, black, and white, running to greet the men. The dog's massive body slammed into Kaidian in excitement, and Asta scowled over the fact that Dyri seemed to like him.

Traitor.

Halsten pointed at Asta, a brown dress shoe in his grip. "You're funny, Princess. I like you. Say something mean about him again."

Asta glanced over the swaying men, noticing that it was Kaidian's shoe that Halsten was holding. Kaidian caught her glance and wiggled his toes, wriggling his eyebrows in tandem, and Halsten let out a loud hiccup. If she didn't despise the men so much, she would find the sight quite humorous.

"Why are you in this wing?" She asked, narrowing her eyes. She could hear Linnea behind her, shuffling around and keeping herself busy in the common room.

Kaidian splayed his arms out, gesturing to the hall around them. "Haven't you heard, blondie? This is where we live now."

Who would put them in her wing? Her father knew that she liked her privacy, and seemingly everyone knew how she felt about Lord Kaidian and his friend.

"Fantastic," Asta's voice dripped with sarcasm, but the intoxicated men likely didn't notice. She cracked a few of her knuckles until it felt right to stop. "Safe travels from here to your door. Or not. I honestly couldn't care either way, Kaidian."

Asta heard Halsten burst into laughter as she started closing her door, but then she heard a faint voice through the wails of amusement.

"Kaid."

She looked up and her eyes locked on Kaidian's. For the first time, she noticed the unique turquoise color of his irises, like the sea on the brightest of days—which were sparse in this part of the world.

Kaidian gave her a half smile, which made her stomach somersault in an unfamiliar way. "I don't like being called Kaidian. My friends call me Kaid."

"We're not friends," Asta snapped.

Kaid grinned. "Yet." He gave her a mock salute. "See you around, neighbor."

Asta enjoyed watching the tides fluctuate and had each tidal pattern memorized. She had been watching the waves since she was born, playing in them during the warm summer months. She and Maren used to spend hours splashing each other and playing sirens, seeing who could best mimic the finned sea creatures' swimming.

"Have you noticed the change in the tides today?" Asta shouted from the washroom to Linnea, who was preparing her bed.

"Hmm?" Linnea grunted in response, clearly distracted.

Asta stalked from the washroom in her nightgown, tapping the door frame as she exited and sat at her vanity. "The tides. They came up farther than I've ever seen. Nearly covered the terrace steps during the party. Peculiar, is it not?"

"Mmm," Linnea responded.

Asta was ready to sass the woman for not paying attention, but then Linnea came up behind Asta in the mirror, the lady-in-waiting's gray eyes surrounded by rings of purple. The sight made Asta crack her knuckles again, this time having to do both hands until she could stop. She hated seeing Linnea look so exhausted, so frail. But she had looked that way since she arrived in Orntali years ago, after enduring abuse from her mother, Asta's aunt. She wanted to wring that woman's neck and dump her body deep in the forest for the beasts to consume.

Asta noticed Linnea rubbing the white bracelet of a scar on her wrist. "Have you eaten today?" *Is it bad today?* That's what that question meant between the two of them.

Linnea nodded. "Two meals. I'm just tired."

"Stay with me?"

Linnea nodded again, the corners of her eyes glistening with moisture.

Asta loved having her closest cousin as her lady-in-waiting. Her father had brought Linnea to Orntali a few years ago when he discovered how his late wife's sister had been treating her only child. The sole reason Asta hadn't marched straight to her aunt's manor to murder the woman was because Linnea begged her to let it go. Asta's only vengeful satisfaction was her father cutting off the royal funds to her aunt, leaving the woman completely broke. No one had spoken to her in years, and no one planned to ever again.

"Go lay down, I'll be there when I'm done." Asta waved her hand toward her massive bed, the deep purple comforter calling to her as drowsiness took over.

Asta picked up her mother's comb and began dragging it through her hair.

One, two, three...

She counted each stroke, the tension in her shoulders relaxing more and more with each pass.

"What do you need for tomorrow night?" Linnea asked, her head gently nestling into the plush pillows beneath her. She yawned loudly and her eyes closed. Dyri jumped up onto the bed and settled close to Linnea's petite figure. The big oaf took up half the bed.

Nineteen, twenty, twenty-one...

Asta paused her counting. "I haven't been able to bring bread in a while. Think we could get our hands on some by sundown?"

The counting continued.

Linnea's voice was soft, and Asta rotated on her vanity stool to see that her cousin was almost asleep. "Of course. I'll go and see Mikkel in the kitchens tomorrow. Just the normal supplies other than that?"

Before Asta could answer, Linnea's breathing changed and Asta knew she had fallen asleep.

Asta finished combing her hair.

Twenty-seven, twenty-eight. Done.

CHAPTER 4

Asta patted the pleats of her maroon dress to smooth them as Linnea stood behind her, tying a ribbon to the end of her braid.

"Must we go? There are horses to ride, books to read, and so many other more enjoyable things to do!" Asta pleaded. Dyri nudged Asta's knee with his wet nose. "See? Dyri doesn't want me to go. He needs someone to play with."

Linnea gave a small laugh. "It is only breakfast, cousin. Eat quickly, then excuse yourself. You just have to make an appearance." She made her way to the suite doors, her light auburn hair swishing behind her. "Plus, I'm starving, and Mikkel told me yesterday that there would be bacon."

Fine. Asta would attend the stupid breakfast. But only for the bacon.

The pair of women made their way to the dining hall in the west wing, which was reserved for smaller, more intimate meals. It was typically where Asta, Maren, their father, and their closest courtiers ate breakfast and lunch.

Asta preferred the small dining hall rather than the grand one in the heart of the castle. This room was warm, the sunshine pouring in through the massive windows. They were propped open all summer long, so the scent of salt water and pine drifted through the air.

Passing through the doorway, Asta tapped the threshold. Kaid was in her usual seat and Halsten was in Linnea's. Disgruntled, Asta took up a seat opposite him, next to Svanhild.

Maren gave the women a soft smile and nod. "Good morning, sister."

"Morning," Asta grunted out as she piled fruit onto her plate.

The platter at the center of the table was much more extravagant than usual, filled with fruits Asta hadn't seen in months.

She peeked at Svanhild through the corner of her eye. Her sister's lady-in-waiting had always intrigued Asta. She had never seen the brunette smile, nor had she ever seen her eat more than a few bites of a meal. But somehow, Svanhild was quite muscular. Maren's lady-in-waiting was hired by their father when Maren turned sixteen, which was six years ago. Asta had never seen a sign of aging on Svanhild since her arrival, but she guessed she was in her late twenties. She never bothered asking the woman anything about herself because, frankly, she was frightening. Asta could ask Maren, but their sisterhood had been fading over the last two years.

Asta noticed the empty seat at the head of the table. "Where's father?"

"Not feeling well after last night's activities. He says he will see us for dinner, as his day is filled with meetings starting this afternoon." Maren gestured to a maid in the corner, summoning more orange juice to her glass.

Good. Asta didn't feel like dealing with their father and Kaid at the same time. She knew her father loved her; he always had. But Asta had heard so many terrible things about how he had treated her mother during the last year of her life, and it was something she could never let go, even when they were sharing delightful moments together.

Since she died giving birth to her, Asta never had the pleasure of knowing her own mother, Queen Else. Maren couldn't tell her anything either, since she had been about a year old when Asta was born. But Asta would stare at the paintings of her mother around the castle daily. Sometimes she would even talk to them, asking advice that a daughter would ask her mother, had she been alive.

Asta listened to the breakfast conversation as it manifested. Kaid and Maren asked each other questions that, in Asta's opinion, children would ask when they first met. It made her stomach churn, causing the bacon to be far less enjoyable than she anticipated.

"What's your favorite color?"

"What's your favorite food?"

"What's your favorite animal?"

Maren was only doing this because their father wanted her to. Asta knew that without even needing to ask. Kaid was not the man for Maren, and everyone knew it.

Linnea, being the extremely polite and docile creature she was, had engaged in pleasant discussion with Halsten. To Asta's surprise, the man was not a terrible conversationalist. She enjoyed watching Linnea's eyes light up as Halsten described the Poulson manor in Haalberg. Linnea seemed especially excited when he told her about the gardens, the ivies climbing the stone walls and the bubbling fountains. Asta made a mental note to go on a walk through the grounds with her sometime soon. She couldn't even remember the last time she had done something Linnea wanted to do.

Selfish, Asta scolded herself.

Halsten Seung wasn't horrid to look at, Asta admitted to herself. His warm beige skin complemented his dark, shoulder-length hair. He had it pulled back the first few times she had seen him, but today he let it flow freely, the locks being tugged in every direction as the sea breeze swept through the room. His dark tendrils framed his high cheek bones and accentuated his deep brown eyes. Yes, he could stay here.

Asta interrupted Kaid and Maren's painfully awkward chat about their favorite flower. "Have you ever had a girlfriend before?"

Halsten's fork clattered on his plate and Maren cast Asta a warning glare, but Asta just returned the gesture with a sweet smile.

Kaid cleared his throat and the cogs in his mind were clearly at work, pondering what the correct answer was. Asta tried to hide her amusement as she imagined smoke billowing from his ears due to his brain overexerting itself.

"I have before, yes," he said.

She raised her eyebrows and stabbed her fork into her eggs. "I mean girlfriends that lasted more than one night."

Kaid clamped his mouth shut and Halsten choked on his juice, a small orange drip slipping from his nose. Asta was proud that she could make her enemy's best friend laugh at her snide remarks.

Maren snapped at Asta. "Sister! I'm not sure what your foul attitude is driven by the last few days, but I suggest figuring it out. Perhaps you need to start taking more naps, since you are acting so childish."

Asta blanched. Even though Maren was only a year her senior, her older sister had always been much more mature. Likely because neither of them had a mother, so someone had to take on that role, especially since their father had always kept them at arm's length. Asta kept her mouth shut after that, but noticed Kaid's glances and hidden smirks each time Maren was distracted.

After another thirty minutes, Asta caught herself cracking the bones in her fingers and decided it was time to excuse herself. Everyone else began rising as well when they realized how long the breakfast had lasted.

Linnea escorted Asta down the halls, making their way back to the west wing. Asta could hear two sets of footsteps behind them and knew they were Kaid and Halsten. She ignored them the entire walk back, only making small comments to Linnea to make it seem as though she was busy.

Asta lingered outside her doorway, hoping to catch a glimpse of exactly which suite Kaid was staying in. Linnea was clearly tired of her cousin's antics for the moment, so she stepped inside and began helping the maid tidy up the rooms a bit.

Halsten led the way, opening the suite door directly next to Asta's and stepping inside. Kaid turned to Asta before he entered. "Waiting to see where I'm staying so you can kill me in my sleep?" he mused.

Asta grinned. "Now all I have left is to count the windows so I know which is your bedroom. Then you're gone."

Kaid shook his head and laughed—actually *laughed* at Asta's joke about murdering him. "If you want to know where my bedroom is, Princess, you need only ask. I'll gladly show you." He winked, a corner of his mouth turning up.

The way he could make her royal title sound so belittling set Asta on edge.

"You sat in my seat," she snapped.

His brows furrowed. "Excuse me?"

Asta placed her hands on her hips. "My seat in the dining hall. I always sit between Maren and Linnea, right where you decided to plant your ass today."

Kaid cocked his head to the side, his dark hair sliding down his shoulder. "I didn't realize we had assigned seats. We didn't think you would show up, anyhow. Next time, I'll make sure there are place cards on each chair."

"I only showed for the bacon."

"Ah, so you like meat. I was beginning to think you were a prude altogether." Kaid smirked, crossing his arms in front of his chest, the hard edges of his muscles capturing Asta's stare for a beat.

Her face tightened at his implication. "You're despicable."

"You're the only one that thinks that."

"You're to marry my sister and do what? Have affairs the entire time you're married?"

Asta had meant for those words to slice through the air, but instead, they sounded as though she were in pain. Was that why she hated him so much? She didn't want what happened to her own mother to happen to Maren?

The corners of Kaid's mouth turned down, his posture loosening. "It won't be like that. I don't want to be miserable the rest of my life. I need this marriage to work as much as Princess Maren does."

When she surveyed his face, Asta could see no sign of deception. "This doesn't mean I'll instantly stop hating you."

"I would expect nothing less from you, blondie."

Her teeth gritted at the nickname, but she didn't feel like arguing anymore. She just wanted to read and forget about this stupid breakfast. She could feel the bones in her hands starting to ache, that familiar tight ball in her chest coiling by the second.

Asta placed one hand on the handle of her door and the other on the frame of it. She caught Kaid assessing the hand placement, but she didn't move them. "Goodbye, neighbor."

Asta tapped the frame and opened the door, about to step inside when Kaid asked, "Why do you do that? The tapping?"

The color drained from Asta's face. He had been watching her, observing her habits. She couldn't explain them. "I don't know what you're talking about."

Asta rushed into her suite and slammed her door behind her.

CHAPTER 5

Kaid was bored. So, *so* bored. He and Halsten could only keep themselves so busy in a suite, but where were they to go? He didn't want to wander too far in case Maren requested his company, and he also couldn't exactly head into town without being recognized by villagers.

Asta had struck a sore spot this morning during their argument in the hall. He didn't want to be the unfaithful husband, and he surely wouldn't be. Which was why he now decided to fall in love with Maren as quickly as possible.

But that would be harder than he had hoped. First, he had to remold his brain into realizing love was actually a good thing. Second, he needed to actually feel a spark with Princess Maren. She was pleasant enough, but there was no fire in her. He had met many redheads before and they were always plucky and fun, but the princess was different. She was mature, of course, but almost as though she had been alive far longer than anyone in this castle altogether—stoic and ethereal. He hoped that it was a front, and that behind closed doors, he could hear her laugh and let loose.

It was almost dark now, and Halsten had taken to drinking hours ago to pass the time. He had been bouncing a ball against a wall, but Kaid realized the noise had stopped. He turned to see that Halsten had passed out on the chaise in front of the hearth, the ball rolling across the glossy wooden floor.

Kaid laughed quietly, thinking his friend was a fool for drinking so much that he passed out before dark. But that had been their life until this last week, hadn't it? Eat, drink, socialize, sleep. Over and over and over. He had never wanted anything more than that for his future.

Kaid never felt like he belonged in politics. He never felt like he belonged anywhere, really. He felt like a black sheep, but was not treated as an outcast. Instead, he was a prize to be won. His wool was the rarest color, everyone loving him without even really knowing him.

He walked to his bedroom and stared through the window at the crashing waves. He never imagined the ocean would look so vicious. Everyone had told him how calming it was, how peaceful. All Kaid had seen since his arrival was nearly flooding tides and large, foamy waves. But still, it called to him. He couldn't explain the pull he felt, the need to run his hands through the briny water. The tug was there while he ate, while he exercised, even while he slept. There was a murmur in his ear, but no words were distinguishable. Like a babbling brook, but louder. A screaming sea.

The sunset over the water tonight was incomparable to any he had seen. Kaid thought the sunsets in Haalberg were the most magnificent, but he now knew he was wrong. He'd never seen such a vibrant array of purples, pinks, and oranges. And those colors reflected onto the grounds around him, causing the world to look as though it were on fire. Like the air itself was ablaze.

There was movement on the castle wall far off to Kaid's left, and after a few hard blinks, he realized it was a cloaked figure climbing down. He thought he was hallucinating. Who would be crazy enough to do such a thing? Scaling down the castle couldn't be an easy task, let alone a safe one heading toward the rough waters below. He tried to guess the area of the castle, and though he had only been here a few days, he deduced that it was the north wing.

Kaid stalked back into his common room to find Halsten still passed out, so he swung his cloak over his shoulders and made for the hall. Finally, something interesting was happening around here.

When he got to the stairs, he dipped his chin toward the raven-haired female guard, who he was pretty sure was named Liva, and walked on.

He had to go on the beach to find the cloaked figure, but that meant going near the ocean. The ocean his father had warned him so fiercely about. The ocean that had been mysteriously calling to him. He just wouldn't touch the water.

Kaid took a wrong turn a time or two before finally finding glass double doors that led to a terrace. Luckily, he had found one that stepped down onto the sandy beach instead of directly into the water.

He crossed the terrace, feeling the warmth from the stones radiating up his legs. Osmond, the god of day, had put his all into giving the seaside capital one final moderately tempered day of the summer season.

Kaid hesitated on the last step, staring at the sand below. He looked up to the wall where he had seen the climbing person, but they were no longer there. He had taken too long. He turned back toward the castle, defeated that he lost the figure, but relieved that he didn't yet have to face his fear of the mysterious blue beyond.

Kaid nearly walked right into Niklas, his appointed courtier. The man had been so quiet that he hadn't even noticed he was behind him.

"Niklas!" Kaid clapped a hand on the man's shoulder. "Where have you been today?"

The blond man folded his hands together. "In meetings with the king, my lord. To fill you in, so you can start learning how everything will work once you are prince of Salendron."

Prince of Salendron. Kaid knew he was here to wed the princess in order to save his home, but sometimes he forgot exactly what that meant. Politics, responsibilities, work. All things he didn't exactly enjoy.

"Right. Can we talk about it tomorrow? I'm not prepared tonight."

Niklas nodded, catching his glasses and holding them on. "Of course. Were you about to go for a walk on the beach? I could join you, if you do not wish to be alone."

Kaid turned and observed the shore again. He had to do it at some point. If he was to live in Orntali for the rest of his life, he couldn't avoid it forever.

"Come, Niklas. Tell me about Orntali."

Niklas's blond curls bounced as he waved his arms erratically, gesturing to various parts of the castle. He knew the history of every wing, every addition, every room. If Kaid wasn't so bored, he would be amazed by how much information he was receiving.

Kaid couldn't help but let his mind wander to the person he'd seen crawling down the castle walls. Were they in danger? Was the king? The princesses?

He wasn't trained enough to survive the attack of a skilled assassin. Kaid could probably hold his own until his guards came to help—or Halsten, he supposed. But someone with the capability to scale a fifty-foot wall had clearly undergone extensive training, whether it be as a spy, assassin, or soldier.

"...which, again, sirens are not to be confused with finfolk."

Niklas was still happily rambling about anything he could read in the archives, breezing over his mention of finfolk once again.

"As intrigued as I am about how sandstone forms, can we go back to finfolk?" As much as he didn't want to believe in the mythical beings, Kaid couldn't help but wonder.

Niklas eagerly obliged. To Kaid's surprise, the sirens weren't the original inhabitants of the sea. There was another species—the fin-folk—who were far worse. Finfolk looked to be half-human, half-fish, having an eel fin instead of legs. They had a mouthful of fangs meant for ripping human flesh. Humans were their prey, and they ate human blood, flesh, or bone.

The villagers of Orntali had fallen victim to finfolk lure since the beginning of time. But only humans foolish enough to be drawn to the ocean would be eaten, because finfolk could not come on land unless they were breeding. Their breeding shifts were only allowed to happen twice—once to conceive a child and once to birth a child. They could never access their human form again after that.

Apparently, centuries ago, finfolk bred with fae, a land-dwelling mythical humanoid. It was another pointless tidbit of imaginary information to take up space in Kaid's mind, but what else did he have going on right now?

The finfolk's goal with this union was to create a lesser breed to enslave and use as their servants, and the fae hoped to gain better access to the sea and all the resources it held. Their plan backfired when they accidentally created the sirens.

Niklas explained that sirens were more powerful than the finfolk. They were far more beautiful, allowing them to lure humans to the ocean depths more easily. And though they relied on blood to survive, it didn't specifically have to be human, so their survival was more assured. A siren's song could be used to hypnotize people and force them to do whatever they wished, and they could shift to human form at will, thanks to their fae heritage. Unbeknownst to them, the finfolk had created their greatest competition.

"Hold on... fae?" Kaid jumped to the side, narrowly avoiding a drifting wave. He had been so caught up in Niklas's stories that he had forgotten that they were on the beach altogether.

Niklas laughed as Kaid sprang away from the water. "Do you really want to get into land folklore right now?"

"No. This is hurting my head enough already. I should have drank myself to sleep like Halsten did." Kaid rubbed his eyes. "But go on."

So, Niklas continued his "history" lesson.

When the fae realized that the sirens were better predators than the finfolk, they refused to continue breeding with finfolk and opted to return back to the mountains where they would be unbothered. They took the easy way out, abandoning the mess they had made.

After a century of enslavement, the sirens rebelled and broke free of their owners. Euphemia, the goddess of the sea, favored the sirens and their superior humanity and allowed them to separate into a different kingdom. She also dubbed them their own crowned royalty and left the sirens to take charge of all the Northern Seas, the same Ventarin Sea that was mere inches from Kaid's boot.

Finfolk. Fae. Sirens. Did everyone in Orntali actually believe this, or was Niklas the last enthusiast descended from a long line of lunatics? Either way, Kaid wasn't convinced, though he would be intrigued to see the supposed evidence stored in the castle's archives.

Kaid stared at one of the statues on the side of the castle. The woman's torso was elongated, flanked by irregularly long arms tipped with slender fingers. Her ears came to a very small, almost invisible point at the top of the helix.

Kaid understood what Niklas was talking about. They really were quite captivating.

He compared it to how he felt when observing Asta. How he knew something was so dangerous and off-limits, yet he couldn't help but to stare. To get sucked into her lure.

"Magnificent, isn't it?" Niklas said. Kaid turned to see the young man staring out to sea.

Kaid huffed a small laugh through his nose, wearing a smirk. "'Magnificent' is one word for it, I suppose. How can a sea so cruel also be so captivating?"

Niklas's voice was hardly more than a whisper. "That's what makes it cruel. It is a beauty we cannot ever fully appreciate, because we will never truly and completely understand its depths."

CHAPTER 6

It had been about a week since Lord Kaid's arrival, and to Asta's surprise, she hadn't heard of him being involved in a single scandal. *Yet.*

She had hardly seen the philanderer or his chief courtier. They had either been too busy attending dates with Maren or hiding away in their suites. It was a relief, honestly.

Asta and Linnea were walking through the gardens on a brisk afternoon when they heard music coming from the northern tower. The location itself wasn't odd, because that was where the music room was. What *was* odd was that someone was actually playing an instrument. No one had dared set foot in the room since Queen Else's death.

Asta stalked toward the tower, Linnea struggling to keep pace behind her. She often forgot that her cousin was permanently weak from her malnourishment during her childhood—at that memory, Asta slowed down a bit so the lady-in-waiting could keep up.

"Who do you think it is?" Linnea's voice squeaked.

"Dunno. Can anyone on staff play piano?"

Linnea shook her head.

If it wasn't anyone on staff, that left only two options. But that couldn't be possible. How would either of those beefcakes from Haalberg know how to play so well?

Though Asta was walking briskly, she knew how to keep her footsteps quiet. She couldn't stop herself from speeding up now, figuring Linnea would meet her there anyway. She was almost to the north tower—the part of the castle that jutted out over the ocean, surrounded by water aside from the stone bridge.

As she approached the outside entrance, she opened the door, tapped the frame, and began climbing the stairs. When she swung the music room doorway open, her stomach flipped.

Kaid was alone, sitting on the piano bench with his eyes closed as he built the most powerful crescendo she'd ever heard. Asta didn't even know a solo musician could draw such a lovely melody from a piano.

The lord tilted his head back, his eyes remaining closed as the bridge formed. The notes were building higher and higher. This was the first time Asta had seen him in the direct sunlight, which was coming off the ocean from the windows, and she realized that his hair was not in fact black, but the deepest cherry red she had ever laid eyes on. His chiseled jaw and the strong muscles of his body tightened as the music escalated.

If she hadn't hated him, she would look at this man, in this moment, and mark him as one of the most beautiful men in the world. Hell, she would admit it even though she *did* hate him.

As the bridge reached its peak, Kaid hit the deepest note, causing Asta's stomach to spiral to her toes. His eyes snapped open and his turquoise gaze met hers. He smirked and continued playing. Something pulled at her, urging her to stay. Urging her to get closer.

Kaid watched Asta while she walked around to the other side of the piano and sat next to him. Asta saw motion in her peripherals, a person standing in the archway, and knew it was Linnea.

The doorway. Asta hadn't tapped the threshold twice before entering. She had been so caught up in Kaid's song that she had forgotten all about it. And once she realized it, she still didn't get that usual feeling of the world crashing down when she didn't complete one of her rituals. The ball in her chest wasn't coiling in on itself, strangling her from the inside.

All she could think about was his song—needing to hear more. Needing to step into the keys and live within the depths of the melody. She would follow this song to the pits of the sea.

Kaid kept his eyes locked on Asta while he played, and she worked through her emotions of victory and confusion. His song was like a current pulling her under, and she did not want to come up for air.

When the melody ended, neither of them said anything. They sat in strained silence, Asta taking quick glances around the room she hadn't been in for years.

Her father had always told her that he felt her mother's spirit the strongest here. Queen Else was an exceptional instrumentalist, spending all her free time in this music room creating art from thin air. Asta liked to think that her mother used to play her songs while she was in her womb.

Asta jolted when Kaid grabbed one of her hands and positioned it on the keys, then did the same with the other. He covered her hands with his and began pressing the keys using her fingers. At first, there were some unpleasant notes reverberating through the room. Asta's face reddened, but Kaid kept his focus on the keys before them.

After a few more adjustments, Kaid figured out how to play using her hands. The tune was light and simple, nothing nearly as complex as the one he had just been performing. But the song was still mesmerizing.

Asta didn't know why she didn't pull away. She couldn't understand why the silence between them wasn't uncomfortable. Why wasn't she repulsed by his touch?

She watched their fingers work together, pressing down the ivory and black keys. He had shockingly rough palms—rougher than she expected a rich, spoiled brat's hands to feel. But they gently wrapped themselves around hers, despite the uneven skin.

Asta couldn't break the trance she was in, even though she knew she should. This was her sister's soon-to-be husband. But all she could focus on was his forearms resting on hers, the heat of his breath so close to her face as he leaned to reach her hands, his cedar scent wrapping around her, his—

The music stopped as Kaid quickly pulled his hands away, resting them on his thighs. Asta didn't understand why until she looked up and saw her sister standing in the doorway.

"Princess," Kaid stood, making his way to Maren, "come in."

Maren gently placed her hand in Kaid's and entered the music room, her eyes sweeping over the various instruments and decorations. Now that Asta had broken from whatever spell she had been under, she took in the room at the top of the tower. It was round, half the walls completely glass to observe the sea below. The waves were particularly angry today, coming in ten-foot walls and crashing brutally onto the beach below.

The deeply colored tapestries were dusty, but intact. They depicted various sea creatures, but one caught Asta's eye. It was of a horse with a fin for a tail, much like the statues at their front gates. She would have to come back later to observe it more closely.

What was she doing in here, anyway? What strange moment had she just shared with Kaid?

Linnea was standing in the doorway next to a particularly irritated Svanhild, and Asta took that as her cue to leave.

As she walked out the door, she looked back to see Kaid guiding Maren to the bench and sitting next to her. He positioned her hands on the keys, but he didn't hold them as he had Asta's.

She tapped the doorway and left, Svanhild regarding her with a foul eye roll as she passed.

Stupid. You are so stupid.

Asta scolded herself as she walked back to her suite. But what was she scolding herself for? All she had done was play the piano. Simple as that. At least, that's what she tried her best to convince herself.

For all Asta could tell, it was Kaid playing a trick on her, using his womanizing ways to string her along and then crush her. But something within her had felt empty ever since that music had ended.

At the bottom of the grand stairs, Asta saw Niklas.

"Nik!" She waved to him, pausing for Linnea to catch up. The scholarly man smiled at the princess in greeting. "I've hardly seen you since the lord's arrival. How is it going?"

Asta rested a hand on Niklas's shoulder, and he started shaking his head. "Oh, no you don't. I'm not gossiping with you."

The princess's nose crinkled. "You say it like I've *forced* you in the past. You indulge in the whispers nearly as much as I, and you know it."

Niklas nervously removed his glasses and cleaned them with the hem of his tunic, his eyes shifting around to make sure no one could hear. "There is... something. It's an odd tidbit I noticed. Hardly anything, really."

Asta smiled maliciously. Niklas was so quiet that people simply forgot he existed half the time. He was a fly on the wall, noticing all the little details that members of the castle and nobility never wanted discovered. But Niklas needed someone to tell his secrets to. And luckily for Asta, that person was often her.

"Put away that cruel smile or I won't tell you."

Asta folded her lips inward, but amusement still danced in her green eyes.

Niklas sighed. "It's about Lord Kaidian."

Asta's heart skipped a beat. After the moment she and Kaid had shared, she needed news about him that would remind her just how much she despised him.

"Go on," Asta said sweetly.

Niklas twisted his fingers anxiously. "He seems to be frightened by the ocean. Like, won't-touch-the-water kind of frightened."

Hmm. Niklas may be right with this one. Kaid had been here for over a week, and she had never once seen him down on the beach. She had seen Halsten doing his morning exercises in the sand, but never Kaid. But how could Asta use that to her advantage?

Asta thanked Niklas for the information and beckoned Linnea to keep following her as they made their way to her suite in silence. Linnea didn't say a word, but Asta knew she would receive a full, but soft-spoken, lecture regarding the music room incident once they entered those doors.

Tap, tap.

The princess took a step back when she saw a member of the royal guard in her common room. But all panic extinguished quickly when she realized who the tall man was, his long braids swinging freely.

Asta shoved herself into his arms. "Gyrial!"

He caught and spun her so her legs kicked out in the air before gently returning her to the floor. His grin was infectious, and Asta couldn't help but return it.

Dyri was jumping around them, barking. He had no idea what the excitement was about, he just wanted to be included. Asta patted his large head, and he trotted off.

"I didn't expect to see you here." Asta lightly punched his arm.

Gyrial walked over to one of the many sofas in her common room and plopped himself down. "Had free time for my lunch. Figured I'd see my favorite girl while I had a minute."

Asta joined Gyrial on the sofa, Linnea taking up a plush armchair across from them. The crackling fire in the hearth made Gyrial's golden eyes flicker.

"Will you be in tonight?" he asked as he threw an arm over her shoulder.

Asta nodded, nestling into his chest. "Plan on it, unless something goes wrong. Hasn't yet, thanks to Linnea."

Linnea gave a sweet smile to Asta and blushed when Gyrial saluted her.

Her cousin had been helping her sneak into the village for months now, ever since she caught Asta climbing out of a window one night. When it first happened, Asta expected Linnea to go straight to the king. But she took a few days to think about it, then agreed to help cover for Asta with each break-out. After all, what else was there to do while locked away in a castle? It was the only rebellious thing Asta had ever known Linnea to play a part in.

Gyrial pulled his black braids back into a loose tail behind his head, some plaits drooping to cover his ears. Something about him had always been otherworldly to her, between his aureate gaze and his deep toned complexion, he also moved like a wildcat.

"How's the promotion? Father working you to the bone?" Asta tapped his nose lightly. He had recently been promoted to major in the royal guard, now running his own command of over one hundred men.

It filled Asta's heart with pride to know that so many relied on her best friend. He deserved it.

"Loving it. Though I do wish I had more time to visit a certain princess more often." Gyrial winked, causing Asta to roll her eyes.

Their friendship had always been complicated. A little more than friends but a little less than lovers. They were in a gray area and Asta always felt guilty about it.

The doors to her suite burst open and Gyrial was on his feet instantly, a hand on the pommel of his sword. A flash of black, copper, and white zoomed in from Asta's bedroom, and Dyri began barking at the two guards in the doorway. Not that the canine would do anything. Dyri's only form of defense was his booming bark. If there was a real threat, he would hide behind whatever ally he could. *A giant baby*, Asta thought to herself. Dyri was the largest dog she had ever encountered, yet she'd seen him run from his own shadow on multiple occasions.

"Burning Dagmar, you two! Knock next time." Gyrial's gesture to the goddess of war was in hope that she would set her soldiers straight.

Liva and Tova smirked, the twin guards sauntering over to the other sofas and spreading out across them. Gyrial sat back down, his shoulders relaxing.

Tova let out a laugh, her long sheet of black hair swaying. "Don't get your undergarments in a knot, Major. Who else would be coming into Asta's suite in the middle of the day?"

"A poorly trained murderer," Liva mused, but her face remained stony while she picked her nails with a dagger.

The Nagi twins were members of the castle guard, and Asta had befriended them over the years. They were always assigned to her wing, and she couldn't pass them every day without stopping to say hello. Saying hello turned into small conversations. Small conversations turned into them stopping by at the end of their shifts. And stopping by turned into the type of friendship where they could barge in unannounced, apparently.

Tova looked at Asta and grinned. "Think daddy dearest will ever let you out to come to the pub with us?"

"Not a chance," Asta stated. Tova had been trying to bring her out for a girls' night for years now, and King Botmar refused every time. The longer-haired twin was the less uptight of the two, always indulging in everything life had to offer.

"Any updates?" As the words left Asta's mouth, the mood in the room shifted drastically.

Liva's mouth formed a flat line. "Three more orphans showed up, two of them with symptoms. Seven more fishermen are missing."

Asta had only been out of the loop for a week, and seven more villagers had gone missing. She couldn't believe it. The villagers of Orntali had always disappeared mysteriously, but not nearly at the same rate that they had been this past year. She had brought it up to her father multiple times, but each time she pushed the subject, his eyes would gloss over and he would grow quiet. So quiet that Asta had no other choice but to leave the room and try again another time.

It was another reason her father infuriated her so much. He did not possess a single fragment of backbone. His people were going missing and he shut down any time someone wanted to address it, as though he were in a trance and unable to speak on the matter. So, Asta had started investigating months ago, but she always came up empty-handed. The men and women simply... disappeared. Orphans had been appearing more and more. Orntali had always had full orphanages, but they were bustling now.

The villagers whispered that the orphans were cursed, but Asta disagreed with their harsh language. Their town bore an unusually high number of children who were nonverbal, deaf, or a combination of both. But lately, that number had also been increasing. The disabilities didn't mean they were cursed, but the fact that so many had been born with the impairments was of concern and did not seem like a simple coincidence.

Asta rubbed her temples. "I'll look around more tonight."

"Be careful," Gyrial replied quickly.

"I am."

"I mean it."

She knew he meant it, and she was always cautious when she investigated. Maybe not as careful as a princess should be without her guards, but she still checked her surroundings.

Asta observed the crowd in her room, noticing that Linnea was only watching, but seemed relaxed. The princess cracked one finger. *Nope.* Another. *Nope.* Then another. *Done.*

She let out a long exhale in satisfaction, the pressure in her chest unfurling.

She had to figure something out tonight, even if it was small. Even if it didn't make sense yet.

They just needed something to work with.

CHAPTER 7

K aid took a cool bath, needing the icy water to free him of his nerves. After Asta had left the music room, he had found it rather difficult to focus on the song he had been teaching Maren.

The copper-haired princess picked up on the tune easily enough, but the music didn't feel the same as when he and Asta played together. He hadn't felt drawn to put his hands on hers, to breathe in her scent, to watch her every move. With Maren, he simply went through the motions.

Maybe that was because Maren was far more self-assured than her younger sister, Kaid thought. Her face didn't heat when she hit the wrong key, she just corrected it and moved on. She was so proper that she often came off as stoic. Maren was certainly a king's daughter.

Asta, however, was something completely different.

The youngest princess of the Enrathi line had a fire in her that Kaid wanted to continuously stoke, even if his only way of doing so was to rile her up. She had been challenging him constantly since his arrival—considerably more than Halsten ever had.

There was a knock on the door.

"What?" Kaid barked.

He heard Halsten laugh. "I'm retiring to my own suite, you grouchy old crone. Don't know what got you all heated but make sure you sleep long enough to forget about it by tomorrow. I don't want to deal with you having a pissing contest with everyone we encounter."

Kaid simply grunted in response and heard his friend leave.

He rested his head back on the lip of the tub and closed his eyes. He thought about how he found the music room accidentally while he was looking for the library. This castle was so enormous and mazelike that he took one wrong turn and ended up in the complete opposite wing he was looking for. But when he saw the disconnected tower, he had to look within. To his surprise, he found a room with a vast array of instruments and he couldn't help himself.

Kaid had always been drawn to music, whether he was listening to it or playing it himself. A melody was the only place where he felt like he belonged. Kaid had asked his father on multiple occasions to attend music lessons, but he was always refused. So he resorted to teaching himself in secret at the playhouse in Haalberg, having to sneak in to do so.

Kaid found it incredibly easy to learn how to play a new instrument. He could play the violin, the cello, the harp, even the trumpet. But his favorite was the piano. The music came naturally to him, and he knew he was a fairly satisfactory player when it always seemed to put an observing Halsten in a trance.

But the trance he had seen with Asta today was something different. Kaid felt it in return. It was like the music was a tether between them, yanking them closer with each note. He knew Asta wanted to cut the rope, to will it to fray. But Kaid hadn't wanted that. He *still* hadn't wanted that, even now as he reminisced. He wanted to wrap his hands in the ties and hold them tightly, pulling her closer until his palms bled.

He was an idiot, and this whole situation was bad. He was engaged to a princess, hated by her sister, and hopelessly caught between the two of them.

Kaid lifted the pitcher and poured icy water on his face.

He pulled himself from the tub and dried off, dressing in a loose shirt and cotton pants for sleeping. Maybe Halsten was right. Maybe he just needed to sleep for a long while and then he would forget about whatever strange phenomena happened between him and Asta.

Kaid stepped into his room and went to pull the curtains closed when he, once again, saw a figure cascading down the castle walls with ease.

He wouldn't lose them this time.

He threw on his boots and cloak, rushing out of his suite. As he dashed through the halls, he stopped at a window that overlooked where the figure had just been and he could see them sneaking along the stone of the castle. He sprinted, getting outside in time to see a horse galloping down the roadway in the distance, the cloaked figure atop it.

Kaid went for the stables. When he got there, he chose a well-tempered chestnut gelding and threw on tack as quickly as he ever had. Once he was sure the leather straps were secure, he swept his leg over the horse and took off.

He knew he was far behind the figure, but they were heading in the direction of the village below the castle, so Kaid headed that way. Maybe he would luck out and that would be the end of his search.

The gelding he selected was fast, and seemed to enjoy the freedom of the speed as much as Kaid did. He hadn't left the castle grounds in over a week and wondered how often the horses had an opportunity to leave, as well. The only inconvenience was that his night clothes did nothing to block out the balmy chill in the air.

When they approached the outskirts of the village, Kaid slowed the horse to a walk and entered town.

Kaid slipped the hood of his cloak up over his head so he wouldn't be recognized by anyone. He was now realizing how dangerous and stupid it had been to take off after this person while he was unarmed and alone. He was to be the next prince of Salendron in a few weeks and was sure there was some small group of locals that didn't agree with that, as there always was with any royal marriage.

Shaking off his nerves, Kaid dismounted the gelding and tied him to a post outside of a pub before walking down the main stretch of village.

Orntali was quaint, but had everything a town could need. A pub, a church, a marketplace. There were some buildings tucked back from the main road that Kaid easily recognized, though he never utilized their services. Brothels, opium dens, black market dealers. Kaid knew these businesses were normal occurrences in any kingdom, but he hadn't expected to find any quite so close to the castle.

As he searched the streets, weaving between the carts selling everything from flowers to fish to dried herbs, he spotted the black horse. The tack was too expensive to belong to common villagers in a fishing town, so he knew this was the horse he had seen escaping the royal stables. The dark mare was tied to a post outside of a building with no signs on it to indicate what it was.

Kaid remained in the shadows across the street, casually leaning against a wall. There was only a sliver of the sun over the horizon now, and soon the dark would hide him completely.

"Looking for some company?" A voice like honey slithered across Kaid's skin.

He startled, turning to see a black-haired woman behind him. She reached out and gently stroked a hand down Kaid's arm.

He shook his head. "Not tonight, I'm afraid."

She held him in place with her nearly white irises as they bore into him. The courtesan brushed her fingertips along the deep vee of her blue velvet dress. "Honey, you look stressed. Let me help you. I know all sorts of tricks to release—"

"You'll find no business here, miss. You're wasting your working hours on me," Kaid snapped.

Something about her was... off. It wasn't simply her stunning beauty. Something about her felt wrong, like her existence clashed with his. Even if he did choose to pay for a courtesan, it certainly wouldn't be this one despite her preternatural beauty.

She huffed. "Suit yourself, Bright Eyes. Come find me if you change your mind." She pointed to the brothel down the alley before winking and sauntering back toward it, the hips of her hourglass figure swaying side-to-side as she walked.

From what Kaid could guess, another thirty minutes passed and the sun had set completely, leaving the town in a dark shadow aside from the lanterns in shop windows that were still open for business.

Kaid's attention was drawn to the mysterious building when he saw a person in a dark cloak exit and mount the horse he had been watching. What was the business within? Why was someone from the castle sneaking out to go to an unmarked shop?

His mind raced as worry took over. Were they making dark dealings? Was the royal family somehow involved in nefarious businesses? He worried that maybe he made the wrong choice to marry a woman he had never met, but then he remembered his father. Duke Aerik, the most genuine and respectable man he had ever met. Kaid could endure whatever this was if it meant Haalberg would be saved and his father could know peace.

Kaid followed the slow walking horse down the road, making sure to stay several feet away so he blended in with the crowd. The person atop the mare steered toward another unmarked establishment and hopped off, leading the horse around the back of the building. When the person came back around the side, he could see that they were cracking their knuckles.

He had seen this habit before. But that person would certainly have no need to sneak out of the castle in the dark, would they?

They approached an angled basement entrance and heaved the dense metal door open, stepping down into the ground. Kaid made a run for it, hoping to catch a glimpse inside before the door closed. He poked the top of his head over the angled door enough to see the person tap the door frame before stepping into the well-lit basement, then the solid door at the bottom of the stairs slammed shut behind them. Now, he most certainly knew who this cloaked figure was.

Asta. But what in the world was she doing?

Kaid needed to learn more. He was desperate to. He circled the building and saw a whisper of light behind a large stack of grass at the base of the building. Ah, a window. Exactly what he needed.

He dove down and spread the fronds enough to see what was happening within when he heard a sound behind him. When he turned, he found the dark-haired courtesan from earlier guiding two men down a forest path and out of sight. *Guess she doesn't mind dirt and bugs*, Kaid concluded.

He faced back to the basement window and his heart thumped so strongly that he could feel it in his fingertips as he watched a blonde-haired, sage-eyed princess duel with a full-grown man, wielding a sword with such familiarity that she could be mistaken for a warrior.

CHAPTER 8

S weat slid down Asta's back as she hoisted her leg up over the windowsill and climbed into the art room of the north wing. Linnea was there, nervously rubbing at her scar on her wrist.

"I made it, Linnea. I'm fine. I'm okay." Asta reassured her cousin, patting her on the shoulder.

Linnea nodded. "Let's get back to your suite. I have a bad feeling about tonight."

Asta wasn't going to argue with that. Linnea was usually quiet and didn't have an assertive bone in her body, so if she was giving Asta an order, the princess knew to obey it.

When they got to the suite, Asta stripped off the black pants and tunic she was wearing and slipped into a purple nightgown. She knew she should bathe, but she was just so tired. Her trips to the village always left her exhausted between the climbing, the riding, and the training.

Gyrial had worked her hard tonight. Her arms and legs felt like jelly. But she hadn't been to training in over a week and had to make up for it, so she embraced the pain. She walked out of this session without a scratch or bruise, even after she fought three opponents simultaneously during her final match. Asta smiled. She was getting better.

Her doofus of a dog came barreling in, ducking into a play bow. Asta stomped at him to taunt him and he ran off in a flash. She could hear him knocking down various items throughout the rest of the suite and she laughed. Dyri was a bull in an antique shop.

"Did you see anything?" Linnea asked, trying to keep such a heavy question as light as a feather.

Asta splashed her face with water from the basin in her room and patted her skin with a cloth. "I think so. There was a woman who left the village with a married couple while I was leaving my session. Something about the woman seemed strange, like she was coaxing them into going with her, but I couldn't get close enough to hear. I trailed them to the path that cuts through the forest and down to the shoreline, but I lost them in the dark. I turned around and came back before I was caught."

Linnea contemplated Asta's words but didn't respond, which Asta was relieved about. She was too tired to dissect that information tonight. They could talk about it with Gyrial and the twins tomorrow.

"The new orphans are sweet. Everyone was quite happy that I brought paints and bread this week." Asta looked to her cousin. "Any trouble here?"

"None," Linnea shrugged. "There are extra guards on duty tonight, though. The castle is swarming with them. I was sure you'd be caught when you returned."

There was a knock on the main door and Linnea walked through the common room to answer, Dyri hiding behind her legs.

Linnea's voice was raised—alarming Asta immediately. "You can't just—"

She turned to find Kaid standing in her bedroom doorway, dirty and panting. Something about him looked so primal, far from the clean-cut, finely pressed appearance he always presented himself with.

"What the hell are you barging into my room for?" Asta approached the lord and pushed him back into the common room with a swift shove of her palm to his chest.

"Do you want to tell me why the fuck you're wandering around the village and swinging swords in the middle of the night?" Kaid snapped. "And don't lie to me. I know it was you, blondie."

Asta's blood went cold as the color drained from her face. How had Kaid caught her? She had been doing this for years by herself, only having Linnea's help starting a few months ago. She had never been discovered.

But she knew there was no sense in acting confused. Kaid would see right through it.

"Why do you care? It's not hurting you. Unless you would like me to demonstrate my blade skills on you," Asta smirked, and she was relieved to see that the joke made Kaid's shoulders loosen a bit.

His turquoise gaze swept over Asta's body and she realized she was only wearing her nightgown—her short, tight nightgown that barely covered her legs—and she immediately felt very exposed.

"Wait here," Asta gestured to a sofa in her common room, "I'll be right out."

After dressing in the longest robe she could find, Asta returned to the common room and sat in a chair opposite the sofa. Her traitor of a dog had joined Kaid on the couch and laid his head on the lord's lap, enjoying the ear scratches the man was giving him while his ridiculously long tongue flopped from the side of his mouth.

Kaid leaned forward, bracing a forearm on his knee. It reminded her of earlier that day when those same forearms had been resting atop hers.

He spoke softly. "I won't tell anyone. Just tell me what you're doing. Tell me, so I know what kind of family I'm getting involved in."

Asta laughed harder than she thought she would. A family. Maren had hardly socialized with her in two years and Asta still held a grudge against her father for his unfaithful acts and insistence to ignore the happenings in his closest village. They weren't a family. They hadn't been for a long time.

"You're marrying a polished, proper princess. That's what you're getting involved in. The rest of us don't matter."

Kaid's brows furrowed. "Look, I know enough now where I could keep tailing you to find out, or you could confess. Your choice, sweetheart."

The dark-haired lord leaned back now, crossing one leg over the other. He had collected himself and returned to his usual charming form once more.

"Fine," Asta said curtly.

She told him about the missing villagers and the increasing number of orphans. Asta explained that she started going to the village to try and investigate the cause of it all, but then Gyrial suggested she should know how to defend herself if she was going to keep putting herself in dangerous situations. Kaid listened intently, and Linnea had made herself a ghost in the room, straightening piles of books and clothing strewn about.

"So the first place you were visiting was the orphanage?" Kaid's eyes wandered back to the canine's face that rested in his lap and he patted Dyri's head.

Asta nodded and explained that she brings gifts to the orphans and has grown to love them. She mentioned that she even learned sign language so she could play with the nonverbal and deaf children.

"Why do you do it? Why do you go there and risk it so often?" Kaid asked through narrowed eyes.

Asta couldn't quite read his expression. It was stuck somewhere between curiosity and disbelief. "Don't you ever want to be something more than a title? Don't you want to make an impact on the world?"

He rubbed the back of his neck and Asta took in the sight of his flexing arm muscles. "Sometimes, I guess."

Asta sat forward in her seat. "Well it's not just sometimes for me. It's always. It's fate. I am going to make a damn difference in this world one way or another, whether it's something small like bringing more funding to the orphanages or something large like apprehending whoever is responsible for our missing villagers. Either way, I will be more than just a princess. I'll be a savior."

Asta would live up to her title of the "salvation child," as the nobles ironically called her in secret. But she would change the meaning. When her kingdom remembered her, they would not remember her as the child born to symbolize unity, but the princess born to wield it.

Kaid was quiet for a long while. Asta simply watched him, wondering what he was thinking. Wondering what he was doing with all the information he had learned. A small part of her hoped that it was finally the moment he would decide to return to Haalberg and call off the engagement, realizing that he was taking on more than he wished by helping rule the chaotic Salendron, but another small part of her didn't want to see him go. She tried to stomp that part out, kicking and shoving at it to leave her mind, but it remained.

"I want you to teach me sign language," The lord said.

Asta stared blankly. That wasn't quite the reaction she expected from all this. "I—You what?"

Kaid smiled, clearly pleased that he caught her off guard. "I want you to teach me how to speak to those children, so I can go with you."

"And if I say no?" Asta sat back and crossed her arms in front of her chest.

The lord held a hand to the side of his mouth to intensify the volume of his voice. "Oh, King Botmar-r-r-r!" He elongated her father's name. "You would never guess what your perfect princess daughter does at night!"

Asta took off her slipper and threw it at him, which he deflected and sent flying to the side. "Oh, shut up, you prick! I'll do it!"

He wanted to go with her to an orphanage in the middle of a dirty village. He wanted to learn something that had no advantage to him. Maybe, just maybe, there was more to the lord than Asta had first assumed.

After about an hour of teaching, and a whole night of signing before that, Asta's hand muscles were throbbing. She led Kaid to the door for his departure.

He stopped in the doorway, a hand lingering on the handle. "You're not as stealthy as you think, Princess. This was the second night I've spotted you climbing down the castle wall since I got here."

Asta's brows furrowed. "You must be delusional. Running a fever?" She placed the back of her hand to his forehead and he swatted it away. "This was the first night I've gone since your unfortunate arrival. It must be all the alcohol you consume. It's finally killing your brain."

Kaid rolled his eyes. "I saw someone climbing out of the same window you did just a few nights ago. I swear it. Why must you argue with me?"

"Why must you say stupid things?"

Asta felt quite accomplished as Kaid sighed in discontent.

"Fine, fine. I'll keep an eye out for your imaginary friend." Asta waved an arm lazily, "Maybe we'll bump into each other on one of our climbs and I can ask them what fairytale they're from," Asta laughed. She could irritate him all day. The memory of what Niklas had told her about his fear of the ocean surfaced in her mind. She would store that information and utilize it at the right moment when she knew it would send him reeling.

A little trick, Asta told herself. *Nothing that would scar him for life.*

Kaid narrowed his eyes and flicked her nose. "They're real." He turned and opened the door, stepping into the hall.

Asta popped her head out of the threshold as he walked away. "I'll ask them what their magical powers are!" She shouted.

Kaid shook his head and glared over his shoulder as he continued down the pristine hall.

"Maybe they can teach us how to fly! Oh, or talk to animals!" She mused.

Kaid never looked back as he held a middle finger up over his shoulder and disappeared into his suite.

CHAPTER 9

Even though it had been days since Asta was in the music room, she couldn't stop thinking about it. Something about seeing that small glimpse into her mother's life had been tugging at her, a pull so strong that she once again found herself standing in the doorway of the music room at the top of the tower, her hand resting on the cool wooden doorframe.

The musty air filled her nose, settling heavily into her lungs. Flecks of dust danced in the sunlight beaming through the wall of windows, but Asta peered through the floating debris to the tapestry straight ahead. A large, emerald horse was wading in chest-deep water, its golden bridle a vivid contrast against the darkness surrounding it.

"Kelpie."

Asta nearly jumped out of her own skin at the sound of a man's voice behind her. She turned to see Niklas, whose face was now a deep shade of red as a coy smile bloomed. "Niklas, you really should give a warning before sneaking up on someone!"

He took a step back and turned away. "Sorry, I—I saw you enter the tower and wanted to make sure you were all right, since this was primarily your mother's room. Then I saw you staring at the tapestry and, well, you know I can't help myself when it comes to folklore."

Asta stared back at the kelpie depiction. She knew the basics of Salendron folklore, but not much artwork had been rendered of the beasts. Or, if it had, it was destroyed for fear of calling on the creatures. She tapped the threshold then stepped into the room, echoing footsteps behind her indicating that Niklas joined her. She approached the tapestry and ran her finger down the cloth, noticing that some parts were moth-eaten and faded.

She looked around at the other decorative fabrics lining the walls. Illustrations of half-human, half-fish beings, spotted seals and massive dragons with fins surrounded her. They were all quite basic, just the creatures with a nautical background.

Niklas cleared his throat. He pointed to the human-fish, "Siren." Then shifted his finger to the spotted seal, "Selkie," and then, to the dragons, "Water dragons. I do find it odd that your mother never displayed any works of finfolk, though she may have done that for good luck. Surely, of all the beasts out there, finfolk are the most dangerous to tempt."

Asta silently nodded as she continued caressing the fabric on the wall. When she gripped the edge, she noticed that the tapestry was also embroidered on the opposite side. Where there should be rough material, her fingertips met soft threads. Tapestries were hardly ever double-sided. There was no point in putting so much work into a side that would never be seen. Knowing this made Asta all the more curious. She flipped the corner up and found that there was a neatly depicted scene facing the stone wall.

"Help me turn this," Asta called to Niklas. "There's something on the back!"

Niklas's brows furrowed but he grabbed the opposite end and helped Asta turn the tapestry around, the rope holding it up creaking as it stretched and twisted. They coughed as dust engulfed the air, but once it settled, Niklas and Asta stood frozen while they took in the new portrait. The kelpie from the front was mirrored on the back, but there were additional images. A child was being dragged behind the kelpie, their hand seemingly adhered to the kelpie's flank. The emerald, horselike beast had sharp teeth and glowing red eyes, its white mane knotted and unkempt. Floating in the water surrounding the kelpie were bodies, facedown—all of small stature and presumably children.

Asta covered her mouth, "Gods." She took a step back and peered around the room at the other tapestries.

As though reading her mind, Niklas walked to the next one where she met him and they turned the fabric together. One-by-one, they revealed the horrors on the reverse sides of the fabric. A human man dragged the selkie back to shore by its tail. The water dragon held a finned humanoid in its mouth, its body bloody and mangled. The siren held a man's hand, his face blue, as he was dragged down into the seafloor. However, in its other hand, the siren held what looked to be a golden pitchfork.

"What do you think that is?" Asta pointed to the pitchfork. She didn't need explanation for the rest of the portraits. It was glaringly obvious that the artist's intent was to emphasize despair.

Niklas pressed a finger to his chin and stared silently for some time. "I think your mother was one of the few to actually procure a rendering of the Lost Trident."

Asta expected to hear admiration and curiosity in his tone, but she only heard concern. Was it odd that her mother had collected these double-sided tapestries? Certainly. But at the end of the day, it was all folklore and nothing more. Right?

"I was actually hoping the siren portrait would contain evidence of—" Niklas shook his head. "Nevermind."

Asta rolled her eyes. "Well, now you *have* to tell me, Nik."

Niklas sighed. "I just thought maybe there would be evidence of the comb and mirror. They're only written about a handful of times, usually in side-margins or random scraps of parchment tucked between pages of tomes."

"And what is the significance of a comb and mirror?" Asta asked. It seemed strange that such inanimate objects could be of great importance.

"Erm, that's the thing," Niklas brushed dust from his chest and straightened his tunic. "No one really knows. The comb and mirror are some sort of siren relic, but no scholars could discover the purpose. Like the Lost Trident, no one has seen the comb and mirror for a very long time. Longer than the Lost Trident, actually. Thousands of years. I was hopeful that they would be on this tapestry and I would be the first to gain an inkling of their use."

Of course Niklas was upset that there was no breakthrough information on the eerie tapestries. Asta understood why his mood was so dampened now.

She took a step back and stared at the tapestries as a whole, the horrors of the sea on full display. Gone were the sweet smiles and vivid colors from the front sides. They had been replaced with gore and teeth and death. But why would her mother keep these? Especially in her music room where she had created so much joy and beauty.

"Queen Else was deeply involved in folklore research," Niklas stated. Asta hadn't realized she'd voiced her question aloud until he answered. "She believed that Salendronean folklore was all very real. I've read some of her research journals and she was quite meticulous. She likely enjoyed these tapestries so much because they portray both sides of the lore, the mesmerizing and the cruel. Having them in this room, while she played her music, probably made her feel connected to the sirens since they use song to lure their prey."

Asta knew that bit of information from the locals. It was common knowledge that sirens and music went hand-in-hand. The song entranced their victims to follow them to the depths of the ocean where the sirens drowned and ate them. A vicious thought came to Asta, only for a second. *Kaid's music pulled me to this room with an unstoppable force.* She pushed it away. She would know if Kaid was a siren. He would have eaten someone by now and, more noticeably, a fishtail would be quite difficult to conceal.

Her thought process was, thankfully, cut short as she heard footsteps rushing up the stairs. Gyrial and Tova appeared out of breath in the doorway.

"Oh sweet Knud, you're safe!" Tova let out an exasperated sigh. "We thought you'd gone missing as well. We searched the entire castle."

Asta's eyes narrowed on the pair, "What do you mean, 'as well?'"

Gyrial's golden eyes sharpened as his panic dissipated. "Three guards have gone missing. Abandoned their posts and vanished completely. Whatever is preying upon Orntali has infiltrated the castle."

CHAPTER 10

"You don't need to come," Asta said sternly as Kaid trailed her and Gyrial to the stables. "I have Gyrial."

"But what if she's dangerous?" Kaid asked, struggling to keep up with the pair of warriors.

Asta stopped walking and spoke in a deadpan tone, throwing a thumb over her shoulder. "I have Gyrial."

Kaid knew the major could handle whatever trouble they may encounter, but he still felt uneasy letting just the two of them go.

"You said it yourself. If she sees you, she'll recognize you, *'Bright Eyes,'*" Asta mocked. "So if you insist on coming, stay out of sight and keep an eye on our surroundings."

Kaid had tried to talk Asta out of it, but she insisted on learning more about the white-eyed courtesan. The second he had told Asta about her, he had regretted his decision. He knew she wouldn't let it go, but he also knew it would possibly be dangerous to confront the courtesan, so he had gone behind her back and involved Gyrial. Now that he witnessed how the two of them interacted with each other, he was regretting his decision.

The group mounted their horses and took off for the village, cloaks billowing out behind them. When they arrived in town, they pulled their hoods up and Kaid split off, walking down the opposite side of the street. It was particularly windy tonight and he had to keep adjusting his hood while he waited.

Upon their arrival to the alley holding the brothel, Kaid's teeth ground together as he watched Asta and Gyrial move closer to each other. Not that it took much effort seeing as they were nearly glued to each other the whole night so far.

Asta reached down and interlocked her fingers with Gyrial's, causing Kaid's stomach to churn, the rumble of an odd feeling he had never experienced before burrowing deep within his chest. He knew the parts they had to play to get the courtesan's attention, but he certainly didn't anticipate how uncomfortable it would be to see them act it out.

Kaid stood across the alley, watching the pair as Gyrial backed Asta into the side of a building and began whispering into her ear. Asta's genuine laughter was a punch to Kaid's gut.

He had come up with the idea to lure the courtesan out with a bait couple and then corner her for questioning. But in his original plan, he was one half of that couple.

Somehow, the plan evolved into this. Evolved into him watching Gyrial lean in closer to Asta, their hoods concealing what was happening between them. Evolved into him watching Asta's hand slide up Gyrial's back while the soldier pressed his hips closer to hers.

Thank the gods for what Kaid saw next, because the skin on his face couldn't heat anymore without melting off completely. A woman with luxurious raven hair was gliding down the alley directly toward Gyrial and Asta. Kaid crossed the street and leaned against the corner of the building, picking at his fingers to remain inconspicuous.

"Do you two share, or are you territorial?" A satin voice rolled down the alley.

To Kaid's relief, Gyrial finally pried his head away from the princess so he could look at the courtesan. Kaid inspected what he could see of Asta's face beneath her hood and only found swollen lips. He would curse himself until the end of time for being talked out of his own plan.

Gyrial's thickly accented voice—the Spellid mountain dialect—echoed through the alley toward the woman, who was merely three feet away from them now. "We only share if she approves." He nodded a head toward Asta. "What do you think, my love? Can she play?"

Asta walked a circle around the courtesan, the former assessing the woman like a slab of meat from the butcher while the latter was nearly devouring Gyrial with her gaze. "Hmm. She could do," Asta smiled. "Do you have anywhere for us to go besides the brothel? I'd like to have you all to ourselves, away from all of this." She clung to Gyrial's side and her arms wrapped around him, eyes trailing up the surrounding walls with feigned disgust.

They played the part well—too well. They surely had to be together based on the tension he was witnessing between them. But how had Kaid missed that? He always had an impeccable knack for reading situations and hadn't picked up on their relationship at all.

The woman walked to the other side of Gyrial and draped her body across him, laying a hand on his chest. "Oh, I know just the place." Her hand brushed over Asta's, which was resting on Gyrial's abdomen, then traveled farther down, thankfully bypassing his manhood and caressing his thigh.

Gyrial stepped back from the women and placed a hand on each of their hips, pulling them closer to him. "Show us then, beautiful."

This was it. This was the moment when they would get the courtesan alone and finally figure out if she had anything to do with the missing villagers.

Kaid trailed a good distance behind the three of them as the woman directed where to go. They were walking down the path he knew led down to the shoreline, but they were still quite close to town.

Gyrial's hand slipped from the women's hips and landed on each of their buttocks.

He's playing a part. He has to make it believable. Kaid tried to reason with himself, but nothing could stop the boiling in his blood, the heat that infiltrated his entire being.

He noticed Gyrial and Asta slow their pace, so Kaid tucked behind a tree, suspecting that this was the moment.

The woman stopped and gestured around them. "This isn't where I was thinking, but if you can't wait any longer, then by all means, let's begin."

In one swift movement, Gyrial lunged forward and had the woman pressed against a tree with a forearm across her neck. It was faster than Kaid had ever seen any human move. Gyrial's teeth were bared, something barbaric radiating in his golden eyes.

"What do you do with them?" The warrior snarled.

Asta was beside him, a dagger in each hand, and Kaid came out from behind the tree with a dagger of his own just in case.

The woman coughed against Gyrial's grip. "Who?"

Gyrial pressed harder, his other hand holding a dagger to her abdomen. "Do not play games with us, female. What are you doing with the villagers?"

A tear slipped down the woman's face, the whites surrounding her pearly irises turning bloodshot. She let out a sound that resembled a sob mixed with a gasp and spoke with a raspy voice. "I'm a courtesan. Please. I'm just a courtesan."

Asta looked over her shoulder toward Kaid, but he couldn't see her eyes under her hood. He wondered if she, too, was having doubts that this woman was guilty.

Kaid approached the three of them, holding his dagger pointed at the woman. A strong gale from the nearby shore burst through the air, pushing his hood back and revealing his identity.

He reached to tug the fabric back up but was distracted when the woman opened her mouth and started singing.

All is well, my humans. Come with me, and I will show you
peace. Come with me, and I will guide you to a dream land.
Come with me, and you will meet the gods and goddesses.

Her serenade sent goosebumps down Kaid's neck and arms, but the thing that set off every alarm in his mind was that Gyrial had lowered his arm and weapon, and so had Asta. They stared blankly at the woman as she continued her song, holding her hands out and removing the daggers from their grasps, tossing them deep into the forest. What the hell was she doing? What was wrong with Asta and Gyrial?

Her eyes began to glow, like white paper lanterns cast into a night sky, and a second set of canine teeth appeared in her grin, sharp and long. He didn't know what she was, but Kaid knew she was not human. He used the only thing he knew—brute force. He walked up to the woman and punched her directly in the face, causing her to fall backward into the tree she had been pinned against.

Instantly, Gyrial and Asta shook from whatever spell they had been under. The major once again pinned the woman to the tree and an animalistic growl escaped his throat. Why hadn't Kaid fallen victim to the woman's song as his company had? No matter the answer, he was grateful for it.

"Oh, Bright Eyes, I'm delighted you're here. If you changed your mind about wanting company, you only needed to ask," the woman mused. Kaid noticed a drop of blood leaking from her nose, likely from his punch. Her tongue darted up and licked it away, then a wicked laugh erupted from her. "You're all in over your heads."

"I've had enough. What are you? A witch?" Asta rushed over and grabbed Kaid's dagger from his hand before returning to the woman, lifting the blade, and plunging it directly into the woman's shoulder before removing it swiftly, blood smattering the ground.

Kaid flinched. He knew Asta was ruthless with her words, but he had no idea she was so merciless with her blades as well. Though, he did feel a bit ridiculous that he hadn't been the one to impale the courtesan with the steel. He had completely forgotten that it was in his hand when he punched her.

The light flickered out of the woman's eyes and she shrieked. "I'll tell you! I'll tell you if you spare me!" She pleaded.

Asta looked between Gyrial and Kaid before nodding her head. Kaid flanked her side, just in case the woman decided to use her enchanting song once more, since he apparently was unaffected by her spell for reasons Kaid would rather not question until they were safe.

Again, Gyrial moved with an unnatural speed and switched out his forearm against the woman's throat for the dagger that had been in Asta's grip seconds ago.

"Speak," Asta demanded in a voice colder than the gale coming off the ocean.

"You won't be getting your missing villagers back. They will keep disappearing and you cannot stop it. We will keep taking more until there are none left, and then we'll move on to the next village. And the next, then the next, then the next, until we've wiped out Salendron. And then we'll move on to the next country." The woman looked into Kaid's eyes as she cried, "Hail Yrsa!"

She lunged forward with the same speed Kaid had seen Gyrial move with, and pinned the major to the ground. She crawled on top of him and pinned his wrists above his head, hissing in his face to reveal her elongated canines. Gyrial hissed back and curled a knee between them, using the force of his leg to throw her into the air.

Asta charged at them but Kaid caught her shoulder and pulled her back, moving her behind him. She fought against him, trying to get around his large body in order to get to her friend, but Kaid held her in place. He couldn't even think about what might happen to Asta if she got involved in this fight if this woman was giving a formally trained warrior like Gyrial a hard time.

"Gyrial!" She bellowed, the desperation in her voice breaking Kaid's heart in more ways than one.

Gyrial and the woman moved in a blur of limbs, but Kaid knew the soldier still held the dagger because he could see the flash of silver glinting in the moonlight.

The movement stopped and Kaid's heart skipped a beat when his vision focused to see Gyrial pinned against a tree, the dagger now in the woman's hand and held to his throat.

The courtesan sneered. "Say goodbye to your friends, creature. You should have stayed in the mountains where you belong."

It was like time had slowed in Kaid's mind. He watched the woman's muscles in her arm tighten as she prepared to slide the blade across Gyrial's throat. At the same moment, Gyrial's palms pushed into the courtesan's chest, sending her stumbling backward. Then, a flash of golden hair raced past Kaid, and Asta placed a hand on each side of the woman's face and twisted. The woman fell to the ground, her neck mangled, causing her head to lay at an unnatural angle.

"*Shit,*" Kaid muttered.

Asta stepped away, continuing her steps until she backed directly into Kaid. She was shaking uncontrollably and he wrapped his arms around her as she shouted in anger. In agony. In defeat. They had rid the world of this demon, but they now knew there were many more to come.

Gyrial stalked over to Asta and cupped her face in his hands. "You're okay." He pressed his forehead to hers and Kaid could see the line of dried blood on his throat from where the dagger had rested a moment before. "You're okay, Asta. Everyone is okay."

Asta pulled out of Kaid's embrace and approached the woman's body before gesturing an arm toward it. "*She's* not okay. I *killed* her!"

"And if you hadn't, she would have killed *me,*" Gyrial countered. "You saved me, Asta. You saved whoever else she was going to kill."

Asta cracked her knuckles multiple times, then grabbed the woman's foot and began pulling her across the forest floor.

Though he was frozen in shock, Kaid understood what she was doing. They needed to get rid of the body. Quickly. They had made a lot of noise out here and someone could have heard them.

Gyrial ran to Asta and put a hand on her shoulder, stopping her motion. "I'll take care of it, Asta. Go home with Kaid."

Her eyes shifted to Kaid as she wiped a trail of tears from her cheek. She sucked in a deep breath and dropped the creature's foot before pressing her palms to her eyes.

Kaid stood beside her and placed a hand on each shoulder. "Let's get you back. We can get Linnea and you two can have a sleepover. Okay?"

Asta nodded and leaned into Kaid's chest. "Okay."

He steered her away, bringing her back down the path without another word to Gyrial, who surely wanted to make quick work of the body disposal. By the time they got to their horses in the village, Asta was once again walking with her confident swagger.

"You had to, Asta. There was no other choice." Kaid mounted his horse and she mounted hers.

She looked over to him from atop her black mare, her dark hood again pulled up over her head. She was the most beautiful grim reaper, lady of death, collector of souls. A collector of hearts, beating or still.

"I did what needed to be done. I know that. But it's not her death that bothers me," Asta admitted.

Kaid cocked a brow, though it wasn't visible from under his hood. "What is it then, blondie?"

Her grip on the reins tightened. "I would do it again. I would end any life to protect someone I love. To protect my people. I now know what I am capable of, and I *like* it." Her legs squeezed her mare and in a black flash, the heart collector was gone.

The sound of bones crunching reverberated in Kaid's mind, over and over, long after they returned to the castle that night.

CHAPTER 11

Kaid and Maren walked together down the beach, but he found it hard to concentrate on the princess when he knew they had an audience trailing behind them, even if the company did hang back quite a bit.

Every date had been chaperoned. Kaid knew they would have eyes on them often, but he thought they would occasionally have some alone time to get to know one another. He would never get used to having so many people around.

Kaid looked over his shoulder to the crowd down the beach. It consisted of Halsten, the twins who were part of the royal guard, Svanhild, Linnea, and Asta, who was repeatedly throwing a stick over and over for her massive, galloping dog.

He and Asta had met twice since the courtesan incident to continue their sign language lessons, once in the garden and once in the library. They hadn't mentioned what had happened in the forest since, but Kaid knew it was something they wouldn't soon forget.

He had suggested they have their next lesson in the music room, since no one really went in there anyway, but Asta downright refused. He didn't push it, seeing as the last time they were in there alone, something between them changed. He just wasn't sure if she had felt it, as well.

Kaid once more turned his attention to his betrothed. Maren really was beautiful. Her copper hair was luminous in the bright afternoon sun and her freckles were the color of the sand surrounding them. He learned that she and Asta used to be much closer growing up, but coming of age had separated them. Kaid wondered if that was the full story, but he didn't ask. It wasn't likely that Maren would tell him anyway.

It seemed that the more he tried to get to know Maren, the more he learned about Asta. Or was that subsequently the only information his brain remembered? Their relationship was still nothing more than bickering and poking at each other, which was good. He needed to keep his distance from Asta, even if they did share a monumental secret between them regarding the missing villagers. No matter how intriguing she was, that was not the princess he was to marry.

"May I ask you a personal question?" Kaid kept his gaze forward, the essence of casual.

Maren's brows furrowed, but she replied, "Yes, Lord Kaidian?"

He flinched at the use of his full name. He still hadn't told her his preferred nickname, but he wasn't sure what stopped him from doing so. "Have you ever tried to find your mother?"

Maren paused for a moment, but then continued walking. She let out a long exhale before responding.

"I suppose I could answer yes to that. But I'm not sure if it counts as a true 'try.' My father foiled my plans before I even left the castle, warning me that I might not like who I find if I really do seek her out. He explained that she is an influential woman and it could cause complications should she ever lay claim to my birth. So I never tried again."

Maren picked at her gloved hand, adjusting one of the fingers. Kaid had never seen her fidget before and felt bad for asking such a question. He hadn't even had a legitimate reason for asking aside from pure curiosity.

So Maren's mother was a lady of the nobility, perhaps? A royal from a neighboring country? Really anything was possible, seeing as they always had guests coming and going for parties and meetings.

Before Kaid could respond to Maren, or try to apologize, she spoke again. "I'm not feeling well. I'd like Svanhild to escort me back to my rooms."

Kaid bowed, quickly kissing Maren's gloved fingers. "Of course. Feel better, and I will see you for dinner."

Maren smiled sweetly then turned to face the crowd behind them. Svanhild did not need any more than that gesture to know it was time to go. The navy-eyed lady-in-waiting approached the couple and placed a hand on Maren's back, guiding her back toward the castle.

Over the last few weeks, Kaid had realized Maren fell ill quite often—usually in the middle of the day. He wondered what kind of condition she had, but he couldn't just ask that. Not when they were still mere acquaintances.

He watched Maren and Svanhild approach the closest terrace and disappear toward the castle, one of the twin guards trailing a few feet behind them.

Kaid's lips curled into a grin as Asta approached him, Dyri clumsily trotting behind. He observed the princess's outfit and laughed to himself—one more time—before he had to hide it.

When they had stepped onto the beach this morning, Kaid and Halsten couldn't hold back their howls as they took in Asta's outfit. She wore a flowy white blouse, black pants, and brown leather boots.

It wasn't her choice of clothing that was entertaining—Kaid couldn't care less if women decided to wear pants or dresses. They could wrap themselves in curtains, if they pleased. No, her attire had been hilarious for an entirely different reason—she and Kaid were matching. And gods, did he love the way her face heated immediately. She didn't speak a word to him.

Until now, apparently.

"You couldn't have gone and changed? I was out here first! You must have seen me from the terrace." Asta's arm gestured back to the castle.

Halsten stood behind her and shrugged as he shot Kaid a look that said *I have no idea how to help you, mate.* Useless. Kaid's chief courtier was bloody useless. That was his fault for hiring his best friend for the job.

Asta ball her fists at her sides.

He pinched the flowing sleeve of her blouse then let it fall. "What if I wanted to match you, Princess? Though I do think I wore it better, if there's a competition."

The lord held his arms out wide and spun in a circle before striking multiple muscle-displaying poses. He swore he saw the corners of Asta's mouth twitch up then quickly turn back down.

Asta looked to the remaining group of people behind them and waved a hand. "Leave us."

Linnea lingered for a moment and Asta whispered something to the auburn-haired woman that had her following the previous order, taking Dyri with her. Halsten clapped Kaid on the back as he left and the second twin gestured that she would be watching from afar.

As soon as they were alone, Asta commanded Kaid to show her everything he remembered from their lessons. He fumbled with some of the words and Asta helped correct them, noticing how quickly she pulled away every time she touched him to fix a finger placement or wrist angle.

After about thirty minutes, Asta was pleased enough to allow him to stop. To Kaid's surprise, she sat in the sand and started removing her boots. He watched in curiosity as she rolled up her pant legs as high as they would go.

"What are you doing?" he asked as she approached the water.

Asta peered over her shoulder and smiled, something wicked in her grin.

The princess stepped into the waves until the water was halfway up her calves. "The water hasn't yet cooled from the turning seasons. Figured I'd let myself enjoy it one last time before I'm forced to avoid it for the entirety of winter. Join me?"

Kaid shook his head. "Not much of a swimmer. I prefer land."

"Afraid of getting wet, like a pampered pussy cat? That makes sense."

The lord narrowed his eyes at her and crossed his arms over his chest. Asta shrugged and turned away.

Kaid watched her as she kicked her legs around, the seawater rippling against the tide. The water was so tempting, but he remembered his father's warnings.

Danger. Evil. Death.

But how? How could the sea be filled with such cruel things and yet feel so enchanting? It called to him, like an instrument yearning to be played. Could he resist the song of the sea for the rest of his life?

Asta was so stunning as she meandered about in the clear blue water. Her blonde, wavy hair cascaded down her back like a waterfall and her sage eyes glistened from the reflection of the mirrorlike substance below her. This version of Asta was far different from the warrior he had seen the other night, but still as captivating. She was just so—

Water smacked Kaid on his face, his chest, his legs. Asta burst into laughter as he stumbled back, then she doubled over and held her stomach.

Irritating. She was just so *irritating*.

Emotions ran through Kaid. Worry from the ocean water touching him, something his father had warned him to avoid. Relief that nothing detrimental happened immediately, even though it had been embedded into his brain since childhood. And annoyance, because Asta was finding so much amusement in his discomfort.

Kaid took a step back, worry coursing through him. He couldn't feel an earthquake, there wasn't a tsunami on the horizon, hail wasn't falling from the sky. No, the thing that worried him was that he wanted more. So much more of the ocean that it was causing him to grind his teeth. Causing every muscle in his body to seize.

The ocean was pulling him in. Whispering to him. A flash of white glowing eyes flickered in his mind. The courtesan's eyes.

Closer, young male. Come closer, and you will discover your fate.

The faint hushes were all Kaid could hear, as though something long asleep inside of him had finally awoken. The waves carried the voices of the sea to him and he couldn't step away.

Return, Lost One. Return to sea.

Every spot where the water had touched his skin warmed and tingled. It felt familiar, yet new. Young, yet old. Welcoming, yet harrowing.

"Kaid!" He felt his body shake and he snapped from his stupor. He was face-to-face with Asta, her sea glass eyes frantically darting all over him. She was panting, her grip on his shoulders so tight it would surely leave a bruise. Was she worried?

Kaid looked down to see that he was a few inches from the water and he jumped back.

What the hell was that? His conversation he'd had with Niklas during their beach walk one night came back to him, pouring into his thoughts like a current sweeping him away. Was that a siren trying to lure him in? Or was that how it felt to be called by a finfolk?

Kaid shook his head. Neither were real. None of it was real. It was folklore, wasn't it? But the courtesan...

Asta shook her head and stepped forward toward Kaid. "I'm sorry. I didn't—"

Did she know? Was she aware of just how terrified he was of the deep depths beside them? It couldn't be possible, seeing as his father was the only one he had ever discussed such manners with.

He once again stepped back, lengthening the distance between himself, the water, and her. She reached an arm out toward him. "Kaid, don't. I'm truly sorry. I didn't know you were this terrified."

So she *had* known. Somehow, someone had figured out his greatest fear and reported it to her. That part wasn't a shock, he supposed. Asta seemed to have everyone in her back pocket.

It was what she had done with the information that bewildered him. She had chosen to taunt him with it. He knew they were playing a game of cat and mouse, but he never would have exploited her most serious terrors. And besides, he thought they were getting closer, moving past the seriousness of the game and more so using it as amusement in a dull moment. Oh, how wrong he had been.

Kaid's lips formed a flat line and he subtly shook his head. "I thought we were past this, Asta."

He had been there for her no matter how far she pushed him away. He had comforted her after the courtesan encounter. But right now, he felt stupid for doing so. He had been a fool to think it was not a one-sided friendship.

Her shoulders sagged, but Kaid did not feel guilty. It was her turn to feel such a thing.

He noticed Asta cracking her fingers, then her knuckles. Her breathing quickened and the color drained from her face until she cracked her wrist and the tension uncoiled. It took everything in him to not reach out and comfort her.

Maybe he would never understand her. Maybe they would never be friends. The only thing he knew for certain was that he needed space.

Kaid lifted his hands and knew he didn't fumble over his words as he signed, "Leave. Me. Alone."

CHAPTER 12

Since arriving in Orntali, Kaid had hardly attended any parties and actually found that he didn't miss them as much as he expected. With the wedding being about a week away, he'd been too distracted with planning, dance lessons, and dates to notice.

Kaid had been successful in skillfully avoiding Asta for almost a week now, aside from being in each other's presence during meals and the dates that Asta was sent to chaperone. But she had kept her distance as well, not speaking a single word to him since that day on the beach.

Though his anger had simmered a bit now, Kaid found joy in making Asta live in her guilt. She deserved it for a few more days. Then he would cave and speak to her again and they could return to their bickering, sign language lessons, and investigation. He didn't have much to hold against her since he hadn't been dragged to the ocean or attacked by seafolk.

However, he did find it easier to concentrate on his dates with Maren since he distanced himself from her sister. He had even managed to coax a laugh out of the copper-haired princess, which was an amazing feat.

Kaid was feeling excited for the party tonight. Though he wasn't quite sure of the theme or reasoning for having a celebration the second week of autumn, he didn't object. The monotony of meetings, planning, and dates had started to feel quite boring, but this was his life now. Politics until he died.

Halsten stumbled into Kaid's suite, smiling and holding up an amber bottle.

"Pre-party drink session?" The dark-haired man jostled the bottle and the liquid inside sloshed.

Kaid laughed and grabbed the bottle from him, taking a long swig.

The pair of men sauntered into the party fairly buzzed and ready to mingle. Halsten approached Svanhild, which seemed like a poor decision, yet Kaid was curious to see how it would play out. The untamed brunette with midnight blue eyes was probably the first woman to ever truly strike fear into Kaid.

The bad choice became evident when Svanhild slapped Halsten across his face. Even over the murmur of the crowd, Kaid could hear the impact. His best friend wandered back over, rubbing at the massive red spot on his cheek.

"Maybe not that one, friend." Kaid clapped him on the back.

"Yeah, well. It's not like my Little Flame is interested." Halsten nodded a chin toward Asta's fire-haired lady-in-waiting, Linnea.

An upbeat song began playing and Kaid couldn't resist the dance floor, so he found Maren and tugged her into the crowd. To his surprise, she didn't object and Svanhild didn't stop him from leading her away. It seemed like the lady-in-waiting was usually around solely to ruin Maren's fun, so he was relieved when she didn't step in. He hoped he was finally gaining both of their trust.

Kaid pulled Maren close—their bodies flush—and her breath whooshed out of her. He searched her light brown eyes for any sign of discomfort, but he couldn't find a drop of it. So he continued on, spinning and dipping her, taking part in the partner tradeoff but never keeping his eyes off her ginger hair as it bobbed and weaved through the movements.

He had almost been enjoying himself. Almost. But his thoughts were unintentionally caught on a blonde maned, emerald-eyed princess observing from the edge of the dance floor. She was wearing a long, black gown, the bodice tight around her toned torso then loose at her hips as it cascaded toward the floor. The back of the collar was high, but the front cut open into a sweetheart neckline and her hair was swept away from her face, making her eyes glimmer from the intricate jewels embroidered onto her shoulders. Her sleeves were an exaggerated length, nearly touching the floor, but her hands poked out from small slits in them. She was cracking her knuckles.

If she hadn't been displaying a nervous habit, the young princess would easily be mistaken for a queen. Her appearance was both fierce and inviting, like her personality. She was the princess who visited orphans and death's angel who would kill for them. The tiara atop her light locks shone against the flames on the chandelier, and she lit up the room.

The partners switched back and Kaid was once again holding Maren. He smiled, taking in the princess in front of him. Gods, the sisters were so different. If he hadn't known they had the same father, he would say they weren't related at all.

They both had queenlike ways about them. Maren was refined and perceptive. She took in her surroundings and adapted to them. She was the kind of queen that ruled next to a king.

Asta, however, was not. She was opinionated and calculating. She didn't mold into her surroundings, they adjusted to her. She was the kind of queen that did not need the assistance from anyone to rule. She *made* the rules.

Thank Absolon the song ended, because Kaid needed a break. The fast-paced dancing did not complement the alcohol he had ingested before arriving. He found Halsten sitting at a table near the king's throne and plopped into the chair next to him.

A server walked up to them and offered a tray filled with wine glasses. Before Kaid could wave him on, Halsten reached up and grabbed not one, not two, but four glasses and thanked the man. Mischief made its way into Halsten's gaze, romping through a field of bad choices and hangovers. Kaid knew it was ill-advised, but he grabbed a glass, tipped his head back, and drained it. After all, he hadn't any plans tomorrow, anyway.

After the two men emptied all four glasses, they felt much more relaxed. Kaid didn't want to think about his wedding, or his father, or a certain blonde princess who made him want to scream every time she looked his way. He didn't want to think about missing villagers, or whatever creature the courtesan was, or Gyrial running his hands down Asta's body. He just wanted a break, and the alcohol gave him that.

Before he knew it, he was lying on the floor petting Dyri. The pup had wandered into the ballroom and immediately found Kaid.

Kaid liked this dog. It was a good dog, he thought, as far as dogs go, though he hadn't met many. Dyri was happy and carefree, much like Kaid used to be before moving here. Here... What was here's name again? Orange tail? Ore and tally? He'd think about that later.

Right now he needed to figure out where this glass in his hand came from, and how to safely place it on the table without breaking it.

A figure stood over him, or maybe five figures. Nope, it was one figure again. A shapeshifter, perhaps?

"You're a bloody idiot for getting this drunk here."

Kaid knew that voice, but he didn't know she had magical powers. He squinted, forcing his vision to focus. Asta looked down with a disapproving glare as she rhythmically stomped the toe of her slipper on the shiny wooden floor.

"Witch!" Kaid shouted.

Asta barked a humorless laugh. "Not the first time I'll hear that from you, and certainly not the last, I'm sure. Now, get up."

He reached out a hand and stroked a finger across the wooden floor panel. So, so shiny. Like glass. Or the ocean. Kaid shuddered. The ocean was scary. He shouldn't touch it. It tried to lure him to his death, didn't it? He retracted his finger and began petting Dyri again, who was now presenting his belly for rubbing.

Asta rolled her eyes and tucked her hands under his arms. "I'm going to stand you up, but you need to help me. My father can't see you like this."

Oops. His fiancé's father was here, wasn't he? Why did Kaid still have this blasted glass in his hand? He held it out and looked at the shining crystal, but it was yanked away as he watched Asta place the cup on the table.

Her hands went back under Kaid's arms again and he grabbed the side of the table, pushing as hard as he could to steady himself.

"The great King Botmar! Father of two princesses of different mothers!" Kaid bellowed.

A hand clapped over his mouth, but it wasn't a female hand. Halsten was now helping Asta heave the young lord to his feet.

"*Weeeee!*" Kaid exclaimed behind the fingers clamped over his lips. He flew through the air under Halsten's strength. Finally, he was on his feet.

Kaid watched as Halsten swayed a little and braced himself on the table.

"Can you walk?" Asta asked Halsten and he nodded in response. "Great," she said through gritted teeth as she dragged Kaid toward the exit.

A familiar curly-haired man stepped to Asta's side.

"Niklas!" Kaid bellowed. "Come, have a drink with us. You need to loosen up anyway. You're coiled tighter than a cobra ready to strike. Always so worried isn't he?" Kaid threw a thumb in Niklas's direction.

The courtier and princess spoke in hushed tones and Kaid looked around the ballroom at the metallic accents and blinding lights surrounding him. So shiny, like Asta's hair. He reached up to touch her golden locks but felt a hand smack his away before it reached its destination.

"Stop that. We're going back to your suite," Asta seethed.

Kaid laughed loudly. "Aren't you going to woo me first? Though, this dress is doing a fine job of doing that on its own. I hope at least one person told you how magnificent you look tonight." He gestured to Asta's black gown, his gaze wandering up and down her body.

Her face heated, color trickling from her cheeks and spreading down her chest. Her grip under his arm tightened. "You're drunk, and an imbecile. Niklas, let's go."

Niklas led the group, peering around every corner like they were involved in some secret mission. The halls were always winding and confusing, but Kaid was downright lost with his mind this addled. For all he knew, they were leading him in circles. Asta would stop frequently to readjust her hold on him and then they would continue. Niklas was on Halsten wrangling duty, steering the man in the right direction whenever he strayed.

Finally, they were at Kaid's suite door. Asta sighed in relief as she swung the door open and tapped the frame before pulling the prince-to-be inside. Why did she always do that? Kaid had noticed it for a while now. He opened his mouth to ask, but only a groan came out. His tongue felt strange in his mouth, like it was somehow getting in his way. He wondered how Asta's tongue would feel in his mouth, on his skin. Not that he could ever find out. Tongue. Strange word, wasn't it? *Ton-gue.* Kaid smirked.

"What's so entertaining in your mush of a brain?" Asta asked as she guided him to his bedroom.

Kaid could hear crashing in the common room behind him and knew he would be waking to Halsten sleeping there.

Asta stepped into his bedroom, looking around, and Kaid guessed she had never been in this suite before. From what he had seen when he bursted into her rooms a few weeks ago, both were grand, but in different ways. Kaid's bedroom was regal and impersonal, and he hadn't done a single thing these last few weeks to fix that. Probably because he didn't ever really know who he was, where he belonged. Nothing ever felt right. That was, until he had felt the water of the ocean the week prior. *That* had felt right. Which was also very, very wrong.

Kaid fell face first into his puffy black comforter and he moaned.

"All right, you lush. On your side. Your death doesn't matter much to me, but I'm sure it's destined to be far grander than choking on your own vomit," Asta crooned.

She hoisted Kaid's body so he was lying on his side and then began removing his boots.

"I am not a lush," Kaid insisted, "It's the wine here. It's been enchanted."

Yes, this night was infused with magic. How else had Kaid let himself get so out of control? He hadn't drank like this since two years ago, during a party where he and Halsten competed to see who could handle their liquor best. They ended up being so drunk that neither of them remembered who won.

Asta disappeared into the common room and emerged a moment later with a waste basket. As she placed it near the headboard, she said, "You could have really embarrassed Maren tonight. I don't think anyone saw you, though. Father was too involved with nobility and Maren left early. So, unfortunately, you're safe to stay for another day."

Kaid crumpled his face. "You can't poke fun at me when I feel this ill."

"It's your own fault you're this sick in the first place."

No, that's your fault. If I was not thinking about you *all the time, I wouldn't have to drink myself into oblivion.*

Kaid shook the thought away and rubbed his eyes while letting out a yawn. He was so, so tired. The room began spinning and he jolted, grabbing Asta's arm.

"Are we in a tornado?"

"No, we're in your room," Asta said through a laugh.

When the tornado finally released the castle, Kaid focused on Asta. On her blonde hair falling out of the combs it had been swept into, her eyes dancing with the flames of his oil lamp, her skin so fair even though she grew up on a beach. She was his anchor while enduring the storm. Something so delicate, yet so strong.

"Why do you hate me?" Kaid sighed as he nestled into his pillow.

Asta waved a hand in front of her face, donning a disgusted expression. "Because your breath is rancid."

Kaid laughed at that. Surely, she was right.

He wasn't sure why the words came out, but he couldn't stop them in his drunken state. "Stay with me."

Asta stared at him for a long moment. Her eyes shifted all over his face and a glimmer of hope began to bubble in Kaid's chest that she may actually surrender. She turned and looked over her shoulder at the doorway, then back to Kaid.

She reached up to his face but hesitated, her palm lingering just inches from him. Whatever intrusive thought she was having won, and she reached forward and brushed his dark red hair from his forehead.

Her eyes locked onto his as she answered, "I can't, Kaid."

He wanted to taste his name on her lips, to hear her say it over and over as he brushed his mouth against her neck. To let her taste her name on his lips, as well. Not blondie or neighbor or princess. Asta.

Kaid reached up to caress her cheek but she pulled away, standing up fully and taking a step back.

"Goodnight," she said breathlessly.

Asta walked over to the door and paused in the threshold, her fingers curved around the wood of the doorframe. The tips of her fingers tapped the wood silently as she took one last look at Kaid over her shoulder, then left.

CHAPTER 13

Young Kaid stumbled to the shore, his small legs not accustomed to trudging through sand. This was his first time ever seeing the ocean and he wanted to take it in as best as he could. With the way his father spoke of the sea, Kaid figured he would never lay eyes on it again.

He watched the waves ebb and flow over the sand and pebbles, wondering if the salty liquid felt any different than the lakes and rivers he usually played in. As he bent down to touch the water, a jolting sensation like lightning struck up his arm and he reeled back, clutching his fingers. Kaid reasoned that it was his mind's way of reiterating his father's warnings, transpiring physically like an alarm.

From observing the sea, he couldn't fathom what would be so dangerous. The sun was caught in a delicate dance atop the glossy surface, gulls squawking above while heat radiated from the sand and stones below Kaid's boots, warming his toes. There was nothing that told him to back away. It was quite the opposite, actually. As though he could hear whispers coming from the ripples.

Come, child. There is no danger here. Only joy. Only power.

Kaid bent down once more, stretching his fingertips toward the foamy waves. The tingling jolt struck him again but he pushed through it. As his shaking fingers were mere inches from the water, he heard a shout.

"Stop!" Kaid's father was sprinting toward him, Halsten at his heels. "Back away, son!"

Kaid glanced back and forth between his father and the sea at his fingertips. The lightning was becoming stronger, impossible to fight. Kaid pulled his hand away and fell backward, landing on his rump. He cradled his wrist, taking in the streaks of white skin that ran from his three middle fingers, through the back of his hand and up his forearm. The skin throbbed and flashed a handful of times before the marks disappeared completely. The stinging sensation was still there, however, the skin tender like it was freshly healed.

His father and best friend were at his side a moment later, just a few seconds too late to witness the odd pale skin that had now vanished. His father knelt down next to Kaid. "Are you all right?" He smoothed down the top of Kaid's windblown hair. "I've told you to never, *never*, touch the sea. What got into you?"

What had gotten into Kaid was mere children's curiosity. He had snuck away from his father while he was in a business meeting in a coastal territory and used the opportunity to make his own judgments of the sea, not opinions that had been forced onto him.

"I only wanted to see what was so bad about it. It looks fine from—"

"Kaidian Poulson, you listen to me right now!" His father snapped, a tone Kaid rarely heard. Halsten shifted nervously on his feet. "I only warn you because of what lies below the surface. There are things down there that dream of eating up small children like you." His father's gaze shifted between Kaid and Halsten now, extending the warning to his best friend. "Your mother went to great lengths to make sure you would stay safe and far away from the sea. You owe it to her to honor her sacrifice."

Kaid hated when his father brought up his mother. The only thing Kaid knew of his mother was that she passed during childbirth. His father wouldn't even share her name, as though it was too painful to recall anything about her. But Kaid and Halsten had done some digging in his father's study one day and found a locket with the initials, "A. A." engraved on a golden seashell. The photos inside had withered and crumpled to dust by the time Kaid had discovered the locket, but he found some comfort in knowing his mother's initials.

"Maybe she was wrong! Maybe it is not so bad! I can hear it, you know... It has been whispering to me all day. It sounds friendly. It tells me that I will be happy." Kaid's voice faded away when he noticed the distressed looks from both his father and Halsten.

Halsten cleared his throat. "You hear the sea talking to you, mate? Like voices in your head, or—"

"I'm not mad! Listen!" Kaid shouted. Once again, he could hear whispers rolling toward him from the deep.

Return to me, boy. You were so close to solace. So close to your full potential.

The three males stood perfectly still as Kaid took in the sea's latest murmurs. "See! Can't you hear it?"

Kaid's father slowly shook his head. "No, son. I think you need to lie down. Come back inside."

Begrudgingly, Kaid stood up and turned toward the manor. He found no reason to fight or argue further. Why would anyone ever believe that he heard voices inside of his head without accusing him of insanity? If Halsten had been saying such things, Kaid would be calling a mender straight away. He knew how bad it sounded, but he couldn't help but stare back at the sea one final time. One particularly tall wave held steady for a moment before breaking, as though the sea were gesturing a goodbye.

Kaid sat straight up in bed, drenched in sweat and tangled in his sheets. He pressed a finger to his temple, instantly regretting how much he had drunk the night before. He remembered getting to the ballroom, but not returning. Well, aside from knowing Asta had been here. But why? What had they said to each other?

And then he had the dream. The same dream Kaid had every time he was trudging through emotional turmoil. The dream was a memory, down to every last detail. He never understood why this specific memory surfaced when he was going through troubling times, but it was almost a comfort at this point. A reminder that it was all real—the whispering waves, the dangers, the skin on his arm that would become tender each time he had the dream.

Kaid ran his thumb over the back of his hand, a tickling sensation of fresh skin causing goosebumps to surface. He untangled himself from the bedding and stood up, approaching his wall of windows overlooking the shoreline. He stared into the waves as high tide came in, swallowing up the beach and almost brushing the castle walls. An object washing back and forth caught his attention—a seaman's hat. He watched as the fabric floated atop the tide, not yet soaked enough to sink into oblivion. Either it had just blown off someone's head or something very terrible had just happened to a fisherman.

Then Kaid saw it—the large, maroon fin glowing beneath the water's surface. Kaid was too far to see more detail, just that it seemed to resemble an over-sized eel. He rubbed his eyes, his vision going blurry from the excruciating headache he now suffered. When his hands fell away from his face, the fin and hat were gone.

CHAPTER 14

Asta nervously paced in her common room as she watched the time tick by. Any minute now and Kaid would be in her suite for their lesson.

With royals from neighboring countries and nobility from all over Salendron arriving every day in preparation for the wedding, security around the castle had tightened and no room was a secret anymore, not even the music room. So, Kaid suggested having their lesson in Asta's suite, since no other suites in the west wing would be occupied per Asta's request.

It wasn't a request, really, but more like a scolding. Asta had reamed her father out weeks ago when she realized that Kaid and Halsten were taking up rooms in her wing and King Botmar had heard the message loud and clear, and not simply because of the volume of her voice.

Knock, knock. Pause. *Knock, knock, knock.* Pause. *Knock.*

Asta rolled her eyes and opened the door, wisps of her light waves blowing back from the motion. Kaid stood in the hall with his cloak hood up. "I told you a secret knock wasn't necessary. We're the only ones here." She snorted, taking in his appearance. "Also, you're wearing a cloak indoors. Not very inconspicuous. You're literally just walking one door down the hall."

Kaid stepped inside and closed the door, turning the lock behind him. "I'm the husband-to-be in the upcoming wedding. Surely, I cannot be seen entering my fiancé's sister's suite without trouble."

The overly cautious lord pulled his cloak off, revealing a white blouse with a black button-up vest over it, the fabric clinging to his back muscles as he reached up to hang his cloak on a hook. Her eyes traveled lower, observing the curves his pants hugged, admiring the view from behind before he turned back to face her. Asta only allowed herself to look because she knew nothing would ever happen between them. If she was stuck with this man for the rest of her life, she might as well enjoy the little things.

Luckily, Asta didn't match him in her white flowing dress and black underbust corset. She had inspected every one of their outfits as they approached each other since that day on the beach. The day when she broke what little trust they had finally built between them. She had sacrificed it all for a silly prank.

She hadn't asked Niklas for any gossip since.

Asta had made up for it when saving Kaid from his own embarrassing antics at the party a few days ago, but things had still been awkward between them. This was the first time they were meeting like this since their argument. Well, since their first real, emotionally-charged argument. Asta hated the weight of the silence as he continued into her chambers.

"Where do we start?" Kaid smiled as he sat on the sofa.

The pair focused on the sign language lesson for about an hour before somehow trailing off to the real reason as to why they began lessons in the first place. Asta had been to the village a few times since the killing of the courtesan creature. Luckily, the number of new or-phans had slowed over the last week or so, but the villagers were still going missing at an alarming rate, and the majority were not just sailors anymore. Many were townsfolk who never approached the coast in fear of such fate. That female *thing* had not been lying when she said the disappearances would worsen.

"Maybe the answer is in one of these thousands of books." Kaid lifted his eyebrows as he toyed with the leather cover of the book on top of a stack next to the sofa.

Asta cocked her head to the side and arched an eyebrow. "Are you making fun of my reading habit?"

His head swung back-and-forth. "Not that you read. But I am definitely poking at your ability to collect books."

"Sometimes life is too heavy. But no matter the size of the book, it is always lighter than reality." She knew that all too well. Asta had done a remarkable job at pretending that the whole night in the forest had never happened, but that blood would be stained on her soul for eternity. She shrugged as she snatched the book from Kaid's hands. "Don't you ever feel that way?"

Asta's heart raced as the echoes of footsteps and voices sounded in the hall outside of her suite door. *No one was supposed to be here!* But she supposed the castle was open ground for guests, so maybe they were just passing through. She turned to say as much to Kaid, but before she could, he grabbed her wrist and pulled her into her bedroom with a finger pressed to his lips.

"What in the—"

Kaid gently shut the door behind them. "We can't risk it, blondie. I'm serious."

And he was. He was as serious as Asta had ever seen him. Maybe he really was taking his marriage to her sister seriously. But still, something tugged at her, reminding her that he can't marry Maren.

Oh, sweet Knud, god of love above, not now.

Asta excused herself to the washroom before she imploded, tapping her doorway on the way in. She pointed at her reflection in the mirror. "You are *not* falling for him. You hear me? That is your sister's husband, to be king of Salendron someday. He is *off limits.*"

After a few minutes of scolding herself, she emerged to find Kaid picking up various items on her vanity and investigating them.

"Will you ever tell me why you tap them?" Kaid gestured to the doorframe where Asta had just exited. "Is it a nervous habit?"

Asta wasn't sure why, but she didn't feel like hiding it anymore. Not from Kaid, at least. Something about him being in her room made her give in, made her want to just have someone to talk to without secrets.

"It's not exactly a nervous habit, but similar."

Kaid listened tentatively as Asta explained her rituals she had been doing since the beginning of her memories. The tapping, the bone cracking, the hair brushing. There wasn't an easy way to explain that she simply could not move on with her life if a ritual wasn't fulfilled. If she tried to skip over one, a tugging in her chest would eat her alive to the point of a breakdown. If she didn't complete her ritual, something bad would happen to her or someone she loved and it would be all her fault.

It was hard to put into words, but Asta described it as a giant fly, buzzing around her head, and the more she ignored it, the closer the fly would get until it burrowed deep into her ear and drove her mad until she cracked a knuckle or tapped a threshold. She knew it made no logical sense, but she still couldn't let it go once it was in her mind, until she completed the task. Well, except for one time, when she passed through the doorway of the music room to listen to Kaid play.

"You didn't tap the threshold that day?" It was the first and only question Kaid asked throughout the entire explanation. He didn't look at Asta like she had lost her mind, like she needed to be locked up. Instead, he looked to be in awe.

Asta shook her head in response.

"And you live through this every day and keep it to yourself?" he asked.

Asta nodded. "Every day."

Kaid sighed. "Don't ever see this as a weakness or flaw. You fight something internally that others may never understand, and that makes you a warrior. Your greatest battles may be within your own mind, but you do not have to fight them alone." Kaid grabbed Asta's mother's comb from her vanity and held it up. "Do you think if I combed your hair, it would work that way?"

Asta didn't know how to respond to that. No one had ever offered to do it for her. She supposed it made it difficult because only her father truly knew how important her rituals were to her, but the people around her had seen it enough to know. No one had ever bothered to help, they simply avoided the topic.

"I don't know. I've never had someone try."

Kaid gestured to the stool in front of her vanity and Asta rested on it, her back as stiff as a board. She was nervous, to say the least. Kaid was so close to her, and not only was brushing her hair intimate enough to begin with, but knowing that it may fill an emotional gap for her made it feel worse.

He is your sister's betrothed. He is your sister's betrothed. He is your sister's betrothed. Asta chanted to herself over and over as she pulled her hair from its braid, breaking it free.

"Twenty-eight, right?" Kaid asked as his turquoise eyes met Asta's in the mirror before her.

She simply nodded, her heart swelling at the thought that he remembered the number she had said during her rambling. He began combing through her hair and with each stroke, Asta's nerves vanished more and more.

Thirteen, fourteen, fifteen...

It was working. She might easily fall asleep tonight without needing to re-comb her hair. A small ball of guilt settled in her stomach for sharing such a moment with Kaid, but she pushed it away. He could break her rituals.

When Linnea was first appointed her lady-in-waiting, she had combed Asta's hair, and the princess would secretly redo it once she left her bedroom. But Kaid... His combing had satisfied the clawing monster within.

The two didn't speak. Kaid strictly concentrated on the comb going through Asta's blonde locks and Asta concentrated on watching him in the mirror, the way his muscles shifted with each stroke.

Twenty-seven, twenty-eight. Done.

He was done, and she felt... *free*. Although her ritual had still been completed, it was the first time in her twenty-one years of life that Asta hadn't had to do it herself, and it was liberating.

Asta let out a happy sigh and ran over to her bed, jumping on and propping herself up against the mound of pillows there. Kaid hesitated for a moment, shuffling his feet.

She patted the top of the comforter. "It's only a bed, and I'm just a friend. Surely you can sit in bed with a woman without anything further happening." Asta gestured to the room around her, challenge in her tone.

Taking her challenge to heart, Kaid stalked over to the other side of the bed and sat down, resting against the pillows like she had. "Is there anything you do to distract yourself from your—what do you call them? Rituals?"

A surprisingly astute question for a pretty rich boy.

Asta explained to Kaid how difficult it had been when she was younger, the crippling feeling that came with each ritual. When she was a child, it was difficult to express the distress it caused to her father. He was never knowingly cruel to her about it, he just simply hadn't understood the importance. But as she aged, he began to empathize to the best of his ability. Her brain was unfixable, but they needed to find ways to help comfort it.

That was why she took up reading at first. She could disappear into the world of a book and not feel the need to crack a knuckle. The imagery of other worlds bringing her mind temporary peace. But after a few years of burning through nearly every book in the castle, she needed something else. That was when Gyrial offered to teach her how to fight, which in turn helped her learn how to defend herself on her outings.

Her mind felt healed when she fought, whether hand-to-hand or with blades. She could kick men through doorways and step through them to continue her attack. She could duel for hours before feeling the need to snap a finger.

Asta's words trailed off as she felt her eyes close, watching Kaid's posture relax more and more as she spoke. She was so comfortable, and so tired. She would close her eyes for a minute. Just one minute...

CHAPTER 15

K aid's eyes fluttered open as he took in his surroundings. He was lying atop a plush purple comforter in a brightly colored room lined with stacks of books. The oil lamp on the side table flickered as it came close to extinguishing. And lying on her side next to him was a silhouette of what he thought must be the most beautiful woman he had ever seen, her figure outlined by the flames of the roaring fireplace behind her. She looked so serene, countering her usual guarded demeanor.

Kaid turned onto his side facing Asta and took in the sight of her. Her ample chest was moving up and down with each breath, her lion's mane hair was draped on the pillow behind her, and the hem of her dress shifted high enough for Kaid to admire her muscular thighs.

Why? Why must Maren be the eldest of the two?

Asta had made her thoughts of Kaid's existence clear, anyway, but he still pined for her. It was like her clear disfavor of him made him want her more. He had never met a woman so ready to knock him down at any chance she got. So ready to humble him. What kind of sick game was Knud playing in this castle, anyway? And why did he like it so much?

The princess stirred next to Kaid, as though she sensed his change in consciousness even in her own state of sleep. Her eyes opened slowly, blinking a few times to clear her vision. Shock and regret didn't overcome her face as Kaid suspected it might.

"I missed guard change," Kaid gestured to the clock on the mantle.

They had planned for him to sneak out when the guard at the end of the hall switched with another, just in case any of them had a desperate need to make a copper on selling a scandalous story to the papers.

Asta craned her neck to peer at the clock over her shoulder and let out a sigh.

Guessing the exhale was fueled by discontent, Kaid suggested he move to the chaise in the common room.

Asta lazily waved a hand. "You're stuck in here now, and we were already sleeping. No sense in you having a sore back for the next three days from sleeping on that thing. Just stay here."

Kaid didn't know how to respond to that. Didn't know how to respond to the fact that his heart skipped a beat as her green eyes looked into his, willing him to stay.

He settled down onto the bed further, subconsciously nudging closer to her as he did so. Asta adjusted her lying position as well to be face-to-face.

He knew it wasn't right, and yet, he couldn't stop it. He and Maren were marrying out of obligation. They hadn't even discussed the wedding with each other, only with the staff who needed answers—answers to questions that Kaid, quite frankly, gave no fucks about. Maren was as uninterested as he was, but did that make what he was doing any less wrong? It was her sister, afterall. So, why didn't it *feel* wrong?

Kaid didn't let the argument in his mind conclude as he reached up and brushed stray hairs from Asta's face, tucking them behind her ear.

Her eyes searched his face and her mouth twisted, the gears of her mind nearly visible as they turned.

Her breathing changed, becoming more shallow. Her gaze was heavy-lidded as she bit her lip and, gods, did he want to be the one biting it instead.

"You're awful, you know that?" Kaid said, his voice for more husky than he anticipated.

Asta faintly smiled. "You're not so great yourself, neighbor."

Ah, neighbor. So she was still convinced nothing would happen if he remained lying in this bed.

Kaid couldn't stop his next words. "Tell me something you hate about me."

At first, Asta looked confused. Even a little curious. But she answered, "I hate that you can charm your way out of any situation."

Kaid knew her answer was part of whatever game they were playing right now. That she was asking him to use those charming abilities on her. He reached up and brushed his thumb across her bottom lip and her breathing hitched, but she remained motionless; frozen.

Kaid whispered only inches from her face. "Now tell me, Princess. Would you hate me more if I kissed you right now?"

Her tongue darted out to lick her lips as she responded, "It would make you my greatest enemy."

Kaid understood her answer. He dove forward, catching Asta's mouth with his. She tasted exactly as he had imagined, sharp and strong. Unyielding.

Asta adjusted her position on the bed so she was lying on her back as they breathlessly exchanged one frantic kiss after another. His tongue grazed the seam of her lips and they parted, allowing their tongues to collide. Kaid let one hand roam her side as the other held her face. He stilled for a moment when he realized one of her hands was running through his hair, but continued kissing and caressing her soon after.

Kaid brushed the rolling plains of Asta's side, every dip and beautiful curve she had. Was he delusional, or was she leaning into his touch?

She let out a faint moan, so quiet that he could tell she was fighting against its escape. She was *absolutely* leaning into his touch, then.

Their kissing became deeper, each one lasting longer but still just as hard. Gods, he never wanted to let this woman go. She hated him and he fucking loved it.

He let his touch begin slowly tracing Asta's front, lightly grazing the fabric of her dress and corset. At first, he brushed her stomach, sometimes letting his touch stray down the path of her thigh then back up. When Asta didn't object, his fingers lightly circled her breast. Her back arched against his hand, but Kaid didn't want to do anything she wasn't ready for, or anything they both may regret.

Up until this moment, their relationship had been that of unfriendly friends. At least, that was what he had convinced himself. A pair thrown together by a twist of fate, now forced to endure each other for life. They had merely been making the best of a terrible situation.

Well, they were certainly making the best of it now.

Kaid pulled his lips from hers, though it pained him to do so. He needed to see her face, to see her approval of his touch. At first, her eyes were filled with desperation, begging him to return to her, but his hand stilled on her abdomen as he watched her gaze turn to uncertainty.

"Asta," Kaid whispered.

She blinked a few times, as if being freed from an illusion. She suddenly sprung out of bed.

"What about Maren?" Asta snapped. "What am I to tell my sister?"

Kaid saw the thoughts running through her head, tearing her apart. He had put her in this position because he couldn't control himself around her.

He stood and made his way to her, but Asta jumped back.

"This night didn't happen." Her tone was demanding and cold.

It hurt Kaid to hear her speak to him that way, to know that she wanted to forget this, and his stomach twisted into a tight coil. But right now, agreeing to forget was the only thing he could offer her. Though it was torturous, he knew it was the only option for himself, for Asta and Maren, for his father and his kingdom.

"I'll find a way to my suite unseen," he said as he left the bedroom.

Kaid grabbed his cloak from the hook near her entryway and began fastening it around himself when the front doors burst open, their handles slamming into the walls behind them.

Gyrial burst in and his golden eyes darted toward Asta's bedroom door where she stood, covering her mouth.

Of course he *shows up. What are the bloody odds?* Kaid's jaw clenched. Even at this ungodly hour, Gyrial still managed to appear and make things worse for him.

Gyrial's fierce stare turned to Kaid as he growled, "Get out."

"I'm trying to," Kaid snapped, "if you would stop barging into places like a charging bull."

Kaid wasn't in the mood, and he would pick a fight with anyone right now, especially *this* specific person. Not that he could win without Halsten at his side, but then again, maybe being beaten into oblivion would make him feel better.

Gyrial grabbed Kaid by the front of his shirt and pinned him to the wall, and Kaid couldn't help but let out a cold laugh. This whole thing was typical. He was the one who fell for the girl and now he was also the one who would be painted as the villain.

"Stop!" Asta shouted as she ran toward the men. "You," She pointed at Kaid, "to your suite, now! And Gyrial, to my bedroom." Her arm flung behind her as she pointed to her bedroom door.

Kaid continued to stare into Gyrial's eyes, his unhinged laughter echoing through the silent suite. Eventually, Gyrial let go, storming past Asta and disappearing into the bedroom.

She stared at Kaid for a long moment before shaking her head and retreating as well.

CHAPTER 16

Asta awoke in her bed the next morning, eyes puffy and cheeks tear-stained. She stretched and realized she was still wearing her clothes from the day before, but that was the least of her worries.

She walked over to her bedroom door and cracked it open enough to see that Gyrial was still sleeping on her chaise in front of the fire. Not only did she feel guilty about kissing him during that night in the alley—even though it was part of their plan—but now she felt worse because she had told him what happened with Kaid.

Asta rubbed her eyes, still unable to process all the events of the night before.

She had wanted him. She couldn't stand him, but she had still wanted him. How incredibly broken did her mind have to be to let something like that happen?

When she thought of Kaid, she thought of his infuriating charisma—his ability to make light of nearly any situation and never take anything seriously. She saw a man not fit to be a king, not fit to marry her sister.

But that was the problem. There were never any thoughts of a man not fit for *her.*

Kaid was infuriating, challenging, and often annoying. And yet she didn't want to go a day without bickering with him.

Asta had spent the whole night crying over a spoiled philanderer, who was also betrothed. To her own sister. To be married in less than a week. How despicable was that?

In determination, Asta dressed in fresh clothes, opting for a thick velvet dress after observing the dark clouds brewing on the horizon. The storm at sea looked to be particularly nasty, the lightning already visible from the coast.

When she exited her room, she gave into the urge and tapped her threshold. It made her wince, her own ritual becoming a bad memory that she would now have to relive each time she entered a new room. She had told Kaid of her compulsions, her inability to refrain from them. She had laid herself bare willingly.

Had it all been a game to him? That was the thought that worried her more than anything. She had played a trick on him on the beach and this was his revenge. To lure her in, get her to confess her embarrassing secrets, then seduce her and claim control of this dance. What other explanation was there?

She was so damn stupid for falling for it all.

Gyrial was awake by the time Asta was done getting dressed, his expression light and filled with sunshine as always. "Care for a walk before the storm rolls in?"

Gyrial looped his arm with Asta's as they peacefully walked down the beach, letting her choose when to talk. He always knew what to do to make her feel better, and Asta didn't deserve him. After everything she had confessed, why was he still being so kind to her?

They had tried once, years ago, to act on those emotions. Gyrial had done nothing wrong during that time. He was the perfect gentleman on every date, holding doors for her, giving her his undivided attention, loaning her his cloak when it got too cold. He was an attentive lover, gentle and sweet. Everything she had read about in romance novels, Gyrial had done. But when it came down to it, something was missing for Asta.

Ending the romance between them had not been an easy decision, but her choices were limited. She could have let it continue until she blew up and ended the relationship terribly, with no chance of reconciling their friendship afterward. Or, she could have ended things right away, before their relationship developed further, and hoped Gyrial could find it in him to remain her companion.

Though he never spoke of it since, Asta had suspected he remained in love with her. It was why she never spoke to him about romantic interests or dates. Avoidance was her best tactic—one Asta had mastered.

That was, until their plan to confront the courtesan. Asta had been selfish in insisting that Gyrial pose as her lover instead of Kaid, not thinking of her best friend's own well-being. She knew the kiss they shared in the alley that night had hurt him, but he would never complain. He would do anything for her.

Last night was proof of that. Gyrial claimed he was making his rounds and had heard sounds in Asta's suite late at night and believed it to be an intruder. He had burst in and when he saw Kaid there, he knew exactly what had happened. Or so he thought.

It wasn't as bad as Gyrial originally believed, Asta had explained to him the night prior. She had stopped it before it escalated. She would never forget the relief that shown in his golden eyes at that. The confirmation of his everlasting feelings for her.

"I'll be fine," Asta sighed.

Gyrial smiled at her, his perfect teeth shining despite their cloudy surroundings. He planted a kiss atop her head. "You always are," he said.

Loud thunder cracked through the air and in front of them, a dapple gray horse reared up on the beach. She could see the shine of the mare's golden bridle and assumed it was a horse that escaped from the royal stables due to the storm spooking her.

Asta, having grown up in the stables, rushed over to the horse despite Gyrial's objections as he followed.

She had never seen such a wild horse. The mare was bucking, snapping at the air around her. When she spotted Asta watching her, she charged.

Asta didn't step back, and didn't display any uneasiness in her posture. She simply held up a hand and let out a demand.

"Stop!" she bellowed at the horse.

The mare stopped charging a whisper away from Asta, ready to rear up, but the princess grabbed the golden bridle.

Asta walked the horse in a few tight circles before lightly stroking down the mare's face, delighted that she was not head shy. She was definitely from the royal stables, then. The horse's white mane was unkempt and she needed grooming, but otherwise, she was unharmed.

Gyrial approached Asta and the horse carefully. "Asta, back away from it," he whispered, his hands held out cautiously as he lightly stepped in their direction.

"*It?*" Asta snorted. "She's clearly a horse, Gyrial. She's just frightened from the storm. She must have ran off from her handler in the stables. What has gotten into you?"

Gyrial shook his head, narrowing his eyes at the mare. The horse was fidgeting, stepping from side-to-side, but no longer showing signs of aggression. "Nothing. Let's return her to the stables, if that's where she belongs."

Asta kept a hold of the horse's golden bridle as she and Gyrial walked the mare back to the north wing. The horse seemed discontent, her ears slightly turned back, and Asta couldn't help but notice the little tugs the mare pressed against the bridle.

The princess stopped abruptly and looked into the horse's brown eyes as she spoke. "*I know*. I know how it feels to taste the freedom that you can't have. But Orntali is too dangerous for a wild horse, do you understand? I will come check on you."

The mare kept her ears back, but didn't tug against Asta's hold for the rest of the walk.

When they arrived at the stables, Asta approached the stablehand nearest to her, a young, black-haired girl no older than fifteen.

"I'm here to return this mare," Asta said, holding the reins out for the girl to grab, "She seems to have escaped."

The young girl looked the dapple mare up-and-down, circling around her. She reached a hand up to pet the frost-white mane and the horse side-stepped out of reach, keeping an eye on the girl. After she gave a long stare at the bridle, she shook her head. "Not one of ours, Your Highness. No idea what crest is on that bridle, there, but it isn't the Enrathi family crest."

Asta looked closer at the bridle and noticed the small crest engraved into a gold coin. It was a conch wrapped in kelp. She had never seen it before.

Frustrated, Asta turned to Gyrial for any type of advice but he only shrugged, his long braids sliding off his shoulders as he did.

Asta looked around at the well-kept stables. "Can we house her here until we know who has misplaced her?"

The girl bowed and took the reins. "Of course, Princess Asta. I will find her a stall."

The mare tensed, every muscle of her powerful body visible. She turned her head back to Asta.

"Are they turned out daily? Will she stretch her legs?" Asta couldn't help but ask. She felt like the mare needed to hear the answer, as if she understood.

"Yes, daily, Your Highness. So long as I can find her a herd she tolerates enough to be in her presence." The girl gestured to the stalls around her, all filled with gorgeously groomed horses.

Even though the dapple gray horse was wildly stunning, Asta could see that it was not the same kind of beauty as the royal herds.

The mare finally allowed the girl to lead her down the hall. Before they left, Asta asked the girl if she could keep the golden bridle with her so she could research the crest that was engraved on it.

On their walk up to the castle, Asta ran a thumb over the cool gold token. She had never seen a crest so plain. She figured it was the symbol of a small coastal village somewhere nearby.

"I wouldn't go visit that horse, Asta," Gyrial said. He had hardly spoken a word since they caught the mare on the beach.

Asta's head whipped toward her friend, her acid irises burning his golden stare. "I'm going to visit her. She trusts me. What is your problem with that horse?"

Gyrial sighed, scrubbing his face with his palm. "She's wild. I don't want you getting hurt. And I don't want anyone in the stables getting hurt, for that matter." He glanced over his shoulder, back toward the north wing. "Some horses can't be fully tamed. I can tell she is one of them."

So Gyrial is some master horse trainer now? Asta had never even seen him interact with one except for when he was on patrol.

"I'm going to see her, and I'm going to make sure she is safe if we don't find her home." Asta's tone was stern and unwavering.

He held up his hands in surrender. "Fine, fine. But always take someone with you. Preferably myself, if I'm available. But Tova or Liva if I'm not." His eyes narrowed at her in thought, "You've already gone and named her, haven't you?"

Asta laughed, and could not deny it. "Her name is Thurs."

CHAPTER 17

Two days had passed and Asta had successfully managed to avoid Kaid even though they lived in the same wing. It frustrated him to no end.

Kaid just wanted to see her, to talk to her, to explain that his actions were true. Though he would admit they had poor timing, he did not regret the moment they had shared in her bed.

He was pleased to hear that Asta had been selected to chaperone his and Maren's lunch today. Even if he couldn't talk to her, at least he could see her.

What was she even avoiding him for anyway? *She* was the one who had hurt *him,* insisting that they forget the whole thing. She had thrown him out like a wet dog while she remained in her bedroom with Gyrial. This was why he had never seriously dated anyone. This was why he kept to himself. It was too messy.

Kaid had told Halsten everything that had happened between himself and the princess, and Halsten only laughed. He knew it, he had told

Kaid. Though others may not have been able to pick up on the tension between them, Halsten could slice straight through it with a knife. It had made Kaid feel the slightest bit relieved to know that he may not be completely imagining their spark.

Halsten would be at lunch today as well, so Kaid sent him on a mission. Asta liked Halsten—for some odd reason—so Kaid asked that his chief courtier subtly hint around and uncover as much as possible. Why was she avoiding him? Why had she kicked him out that night? What had she and Gyrial done that night?

The last question lingered in Kaid's mind. Gyrial's reaction to Kaid being in Asta's suite was far more severe than a best friend protecting a best friend. Had the two actually been involved and Kaid wasn't aware? He had been wondering that since he watched them kiss in the alley, but he hoped to the gods it wasn't true. Ruining one relationship with a kiss was a mess, but ruining two was disastrous. He didn't need more ingredients added to the pot of scandals he had brewing.

Kaid sucked in a deep breath, displaying the cool exterior he had mastered. His posture relaxed, a lazy smile graced his lips, and a slow saunter emerged all at once.

He and Halsten strode onto the terrace, loose and laughing, just as the two of them had always been. Kaid took up his seat on the iron chair across from Maren at the small bistro table while Halsten went to the fountain, taking a seat on the edge next to the brooding, blonde princess.

The lord of Haalberg looked over the water at the gloomy horizon. It had been looking like a storm was on the way for days now, but it remained at sea. Not the best day for lunch on the terrace, as it was breezy, but everyone had put on a thick cloak to endure the chill.

Maren watched where Kaid's gaze wandered. "Sometimes the storms just remain at sea until they've run out of ambition."

Kaid looked into her brown eyes. They seemed colder than usual, somewhat detached. "You speak of storms as though they have a mind of their own."

She offered a sweet smile, then looked back out to the unruly waters. "Doesn't everything in nature? The storms, the forest, the sun, the moon, the sea." Kaid's thoughts wandered to that day when he had felt the pull of the ocean, had heard it beckoning him to step into its trap. Maren continued, "We would not believe in our gods and goddesses if it were not true."

Not totally wrong, Kaid admitted to himself. They had the normal gods and goddesses—Absolon, the ruler of the gods, Dagmar, the goddess of war, Knud, the god of love, and Gylla, the goddess of afterlife. But their traditions believed in environmental rulers as well—Osmond, the god of day, Inga, the goddess of night, Huldrik, the god of the forest, and Euphemia, the goddess of the sea.

Kaid had known they were believed to rule over their realms, and he had often prayed to them, but he had never actually given them life in the context that Maren had.

"Who is your favorite?" Kaid asked. Though it didn't seem terribly intimate, it was a far more personal question than they had been asking each other all these weeks.

For the first time since Kaid had met her nearly a month ago, Maren looked caught off guard. Her eyes were wide and her breathing slowed, as though she were holding the air within her lungs prisoner. She was so, so still, almost unnaturally so.

Had Kaid offended her somehow? He couldn't think of a reason as to why the question would startle her so much. Surely, she knew that they needed to become closer at some point if they were to wed in a few days.

"There's no pressure," he added, "You can pick a random one if you don't have one you favor."

Maren's eyes drifted to Svanhild, who was standing near the terrace entrance with Linnea should either princess need assistance. When the copper-haired princess's gaze returned to Kaid, she leaned forward, as though her answer was a great secret.

"Euphemia," she whispered. "The sea is where I belong."

Kaid wished he could be as sure as she was. He still hadn't felt a sense of belonging, though the ocean had whispered to him. But it was the spell, the hypnotic state the sea had put him in. The calling of the creatures of the deep that Kaid was sure existed now. They had made a believer out of him.

The lord dared a glance over at Asta, who was speaking quietly to Halsten with a smile on her face. The charcoal-haired male was laughing, running his fingers through his locks. Something in Kaid's stomach twisted at the sight of them together.

"Knud is the one I find most interesting, I suppose," Kaid proclaimed loudly enough for everyone to hear, "For his ability to hide his true intentions until one figures them out themselves."

He turned once more to look over at Asta and his eyes met hers, her green irises laced with venom. She lightly placed her hand on Halsten's forearm and turned her torso to face him more, all while keeping her eyes on Kaid.

Fine, if she wanted to play another game, he could play. Kaid spent the rest of the lunch laughing, caressing Maren's fingertips, flashing his swoon-worthy smile. He noticed Asta had put her book on the edge of the fountain and surrendered her full attention to Halsten, finding any excuse to touch him—a hand on his shoulder as she laughed, fingertips brushing his hair as she complimented it, a caress on the bottom hem of his vest as she inquired about where he purchased it. That one made Kaid's blood boil.

He couldn't fault Halsten for any of it. The man was a natural flirt and likely had no idea what he was doing. But Asta knew. Goddesses, did she know.

When the lunch was over, Kaid stood and took Maren's hand, placing his lips to her gloved fingertips and let the kiss linger. He knew it would have had more of an effect if Maren hadn't been wearing gloves, but the princess had always covered herself in layers of fabric no matter the occasion or weather. Likely something to do with her mystery ailment.

Maren left with Svanhild at her heels, the pair always running off together after every date. Was he really that awful that Maren needed to hide away in her room after every encounter? He supposed she would have said something to King Botmar if it was that bad, seeing as their wedding was in four days.

Kaid looked to Asta, who was once again staring at her book intently. He nodded to Halsten, who found an excuse to bring Linnea away from the terrace. The quiet lady-in-waiting made no effort to object, likely understanding that Kaid was asking for a moment alone.

As he strode over to the reading princess, he could see that the fair skin on her ears and cheeks was bright red, and a rash was spreading on her chest. The kiss to Maren's hand must have made him the winner, her anguish displayed for all to see.

But it didn't feel like a victory. No, it felt much the opposite.

"Jealous, are we?" Kaid crooned with his best attempt to lighten the mood.

Asta's gaze whipped toward him as she clapped her book shut. Kaid could see her emotions battling on her face, trying to think of which approach she would like to take in this exchange.

Instead, she smacked him in the chest with her book. Hard.

Oof. The air whooshed from him, the blow far more impactful than Kaid had anticipated it would be.

He rubbed his chest. "I deserved that, I'm sure," he said through a raspy breath, "but if you would just talk to me, at least I would know *why* I'm being beaten."

"Are you daft?" she blurted. "You seriously don't know why I'm this angry with you?"

"I'm sure I could make some guesses, but I don't want to remind you of any extra reasons to resent me, in case they weren't already on your list."

A corner of her mouth feathered, but she quickly hid it. "You kiss me a week away from your wedding to my sister, and can't figure out why I'm angry?"

"And you tell me to forget it right away, even though I know you felt something between us. Don't you think *I'm* angry?" Kaid waved his arms. "Don't you think it's driven *me* mad, not being able to even find you and talk about it?"

The unspoken questions rang through him. *Don't you think I'm angry that I must marry the sister I do not love? Do you not see that I'm being torn apart from the inside, with no rightful solution?*

Asta stared at him breathlessly for multiple agonizing heartbeats. She placed her book on the edge of the fountain and curled her hands into fists. Kaid could tell that she was resisting cracking her bones.

Maybe she was right. Maybe they should forget the entire thing. Maybe, just maybe, Knud had made a mistake. Had his cherub aim his arrow at the wrong sister, entrapping Kaid in eternal misery.

Asta bit her lip, deep in thought. He wished she hadn't grazed her teeth on her supple lip, the same way she had the night they kissed. There was an ache in his chest at the sight.

Finally, she said, "I've been thinking about what you said, about someone else sneaking in and out of the castle. We need to find them. For my sister and father's safety. It may have something to do with the missing villagers and increasing number of orphans, like the courtesan did."

Kaid knew her change of subject meant that she was done talking about what had happened between them. That was her method, ignore it until it went away. He had known that for a while now, but it had never infuriated him until this moment.

If she wanted to forget, he would forget. But he couldn't get her to say the words. To say she *wanted* to forget, not only that they *should*.

"What's the next step?" he asked.

Asta planned for the two of them to meet on the terrace that night for a watch. With the wedding approaching quickly now, and the castle filled with so many extra bodies, she had a feeling that the figure would choose tonight, during the welcoming dinner, to slip in and out of the castle once more.

Kaid insisted that they would never be able to miss the dinner without being noticed, but Asta had an answer for that, too. She had already planted the seed two days ago, telling everyone who would listen that she hadn't been feeling herself and must have an impending ailment brewing. Now all Kaid had to do was mention to a few people that he had the same symptoms as the princess and needed a night to rest before the big day. They both could excuse themselves from the dinner and no one would think twice about it.

Clever. She was so gods damned clever.

Asta had told him once that she wanted to be more than a sit-still-look-pretty princess, and in this moment, he knew she would. She could do whatever she desired, and no one would be able to stop her. The heart collector, adding his own to the top of her list.

CHAPTER 18

Linnea stood in front of Asta tucking stray strands of hair up into the princess's black hood.

Asta gently placed a hand on her cousin's scarred wrist. "I'll be okay, Linnea. There will be plenty of guards around to hear us should anything happen. Plus, Kaid might not be heavily trained in fighting, but the sheer size of him will likely prevent any type of physical attack." Asta threw a thumb toward Dyri, who was lounging on the fur carpet in front of the fire. "He's like Dyri, all bark, no bite. But the bark will be enough to scare them away."

Asta allowed her mind to indulge in the mental image of Kaid for a heartbeat. His deep red—nearly black—hair, his turquoise eyes, his severe facial features, the perfect cut of his tall, muscular body. And the things he could do with that body...

Linnea still continued fussing over Asta's cloak, being sure to tuck in anything that could easily identify her. Asta felt her pat the daggers she had hidden in each sleeve, then the hilt of the sword that was concealed by fabric at her hip.

"You'll stop this nonsense if anything seems awry?" her frail cousin asked as she rubbed at the white band of skin on her wrist.

Asta couldn't help but watch her cousin fidget with her only visible physical marking of the abuse she had endured. She understood why Linnea wanted her to be careful. Her lady-in-waiting knew how it felt to be held somewhere against her will.

"Nothing will happen. I'll be back in no time. Remember the plan?" Asta smiled at her cousin, the only reassuring thing she could do.

Linnea's eyes shifted around as she ran through the plan in her head before listing it aloud. "Go to the dinner, tell the king you are unwell but not enough to need the mender, come back and distract Tova in the hall so you and Lord Kaidian can sneak past her, meet Halsten at the terrace entrance and help him stop anyone from going out there."

Asta nodded. "Good, now let's do this."

Linnea slipped from the door and made her way to the grand dining hall while Asta paced in her common room. So many things could go wrong tonight. She may very well be putting herself and Kaid in danger, but what if catching this person saved so many others? It was worth it, so long as they made it out alive.

Asta cracked her door open a little while later, figuring Linnea should be back soon. She watched as her thin, auburn-haired cousin approached Tova, who stood guard at the top of the stairs, and began inquiring about a missing earring.

She had to give her cousin credit; her years of observing her friends had paid off. Tova was definitely the twin to be just as concerned about a missing earring as she was. If it was Liva, she would have told Linnea to move along. Tova began searching the ground, stepping down the stairs with Linnea.

Asta slipped from her door and gently closed it behind her before running to Kaid's suite. She knocked on the door and heard a whispering response from behind the oak.

"What's the magic knock?" a voice crooned.

Asta ground her teeth, annoyed that Kaid would play a game at a time like this. But jokes were his way of diverting his worry.

Knock, knock. Pause. *Knock, knock, knock.* Pause. *Knock.*

The door opened and Kaid slipped out, amusement glinting in his turquoise eyes. She could throttle him right now.

They snuck down the hall as briskly as they could while remaining undetected, passing the staircase where the raven-haired guard was thoroughly investigating every golden detail on the carpet. They would have to take the hall to the staff's quarters, then use those stairs to make their way down to the terrace. Asta knew her way around because she was a frequent flyer in the staff quarters since she often visited it to see her friends who worked in the castle, including the twins.

They treaded lightly down the stairs, still not wanting to call too much attention to themselves. They were two people dressed in all black with their hoods up while the castle was filled with royals and nobility. Surely, they would look like assassins or thieves if they were seen. The pair blew out a breath of relief when they had passed by the guard and entered the staff hall, sneaking down the narrow stairs until the terrace door was in sight.

Asta nearly jumped out of her skin when a man rounded the corner in front of them, blocking their way to the glass doors. But—wait—she knew that dark hair and mischievous grin.

She smiled and approached the courtier, punching him in the arm when she got to him. "You nearly gave me a heart attack!"

Halsten quietly laughed in response. "Just getting your adrenaline going for this little adventure," he mused.

Asta and Kaid shook their heads and moved past him and onto the terrace. They sat at the iron table and chairs that Kaid had used earlier for his date with Maren.

Kaid played with the intricate designs on the iron surface as he asked, "So, you and Halsten? Are you two... interested in each other?"

Asta froze, her eyes wide, and then she burst into laughter. "Gods, no. Though he seems like a fun time, I'm not the type to jump around."

Kaid blinked a few times then averted his gaze. It was dark, making it hard to confirm her suspicions, but Asta thought she could see his cheeks filling with color. Couldn't he just ask Halsten that himself? Though, the courtier may think he was romantically involved with everyone if you asked him.

The lord kept his attention on his finger, which was still picking at the table, when his next question escaped his lips, the lips Asta resentfully couldn't take her eyes off of. "What is your type, then? Gyrial?"

He's your sister's betrothed. He's your sister's betrothed. He's your sister's betrothed.

She repeated it to herself, but couldn't take her eyes off of his mouth.

Asta did, however, feel a prickle of self-defense building within. "Not that it's any of your business, but no. Gyrial and I dated and it didn't work out." She cracked a knuckle, remembering how much she had hurt her best friend the day she ended their romantic relationship. "He's a good man, but not what I'm looking for."

Kaid's entire posture seemed to loosen, his brows unfurling, and he stopped fidgeting. Asta kept her eyes on the castle walls around them, but watched the lord in her peripherals as he leaned back and locked his fingers behind his head in a relaxed pose.

"You didn't answer my other question. What is your type, blondie?"

Asta's jaw tightened. "I don't know, a man with purpose. One who isn't afraid to make sacrifices for what he wants. Who can make me laugh and keep me busy."

You.

Oh, gods. Yuck. Why had that thought even popped into Asta's head? She shivered.

A flash caught her eye and she whipped her head toward the north wing, where a black dot was cascading down the stone wall.

"Run!" she bellowed as she took off.

Kaid was right behind her.

Asta sprinted down the beach, her thighs burning from the resistance of the sand. The crunching sound behind her let her know that Kaid kept pace with her. Her eyes remained pinned on the cloaked figure, who had almost dipped out of sight behind the brush around the shore.

She darted up a path leading to the north wing, grabbing Kaid's wrist behind her to swing him in the same direction before she ran again. She had to get there before they left. She had to get there to get answers to at least one mystery in her life.

Kaid's breathing was labored since he was not as in shape as Asta was. She was thankful for the hours of work she had put in, thankful that they had a purpose.

They made it to the north wall to see not one, but two cloaked figures hurtling back toward the beach. Asta heard a groan of displeasure behind her, surely Kaid realizing they had to run back toward the shore they had just come from. If she hadn't been so worried about what was yet to unfold, she would have stopped to laugh at him.

The figures were in her sight the entire race to the beach. They were extremely fast, about the same speed as Asta. That rattled her nerves, knowing they were likely as well-trained as she was. Maybe more.

When Asta's boots hit sand once more, she lost sight of the others and she felt something strike her stomach so hard that it knocked the air from her. She fell back into Kaid, who had caught her and held her up. They had thrown a log of driftwood at her and kept running.

She took a moment to catch her breath, not nearly as much as she needed, but she couldn't let them slip away. Asta and Kaid continued chasing them down the beach until they came to halt at least a mile away from the castle. The coast had turned to crushed stone, the sandy shore forgotten behind them.

The two cloaked figures were pacing back-and-forth in front of them, like predators circling their prey. They had lured them away from the safety of the castle grounds. They were clearly female, their figures small yet sturdy, but Asta couldn't see under their hoods. She hoped that they couldn't see under hers or Kaid's, either.

Asta pulled a dagger from her sleeve and tossed it to Kaid, then unsheathed her sword from her hip.

She heard a snarl from one of the beings in front of her—the noise was very, very inhuman. She noticed the glint of metal against the moonlight in each of their hands.

Shit.

Shit, shit, shit. They could turn back. They could run. But how much of a head start could they get from these things, these... creatures?

Asta felt the pressure of Kaid's hand on her lower back and knew what he was voting for. Stay here and fight. Stay here and find answers.

Asta dared to step forward and her step was met with multiple in return by one of their opponents. She thrust her sword up in time to block the blow coming at her face, her arms straining against the sheer force of her assailant. The other dove for Kaid and he pulled a sword from his cloak, one Asta had not noticed on him before. She watched as he used the sword and dagger to block, parry, and swing, still keeping her wits about her enough to block her own partner's strikes.

The four were caught in a dance, all fair opponents for each other. None had managed to strike an injury as they all attacked. They spun and spun and spun, and Asta was completely unaware of what direction she and Kaid were facing now, unaware of their surroundings, and she hated it.

Was that their tactic? Keep them busy enough to confuse them and get the upper hand?

After blocking a particularly strong blow, her arms shook, and she dared a glance around and saw that the castle was now at their assailants' backs, the attackers standing between her and Kaid's protective fortress.

Absolutely a tactic, Asta concluded.

The glance around had cost her and the cloaked figure in front of her managed to slice her shoulder. The pain seared through Asta, causing her knees to buckle, but it was superficial enough that she fought through the burn. At the same time, she heard a yelp from Kaid and he was now clutching his thigh.

His partner attacked him again in a storm of steel, more forceful and skillful than before. Kaid was a moderately skilled fighter, but an amateur compared to that.

"Go!" Asta shouted to him. "I'll hold them off!"

Kaid ignored her and went for his opponent again, favoring his injured leg. She couldn't wait to witness the scene because her cloaked figure made a dive for her again as well.

She was strong, this creature. Every one of her attacks made Asta's bones reverberate within her flesh. Asta spun out of the way of a straightforward jab and managed to slide her sword along her opponent's ribs as she passed.

A growl broke from the cloaked figures mouth, feral and, honestly, terrifying. That solidified Asta's thoughts that these were creatures and not people. Maybe the same thing the courtesan had been.

Kaid's wail echoed across the sea as his opponent drove her heel into his already bleeding wound. Lightning cracked through the dark sky, charging the energy between them. His turquoise eyes locked on Asta's and she just nodded before blocking the next strike. He needed to get out of there. They both did. Asta knew that, she just didn't know how to do it.

The least she could do was get Kaid out before it got worse. She had dragged him into this mess and he didn't need to die with her for it.

Asta snarled through gritted teeth as she plunged her sword forward, narrowly missing her opponent's abdomen as they parried. "You need to go!"

She could take them both on long enough for him to escape. Long enough for him to live. Asta, however, wasn't sure what her own fate would be.

Without having to warn him again, Kaid took off in a limping sprint down the beach, his cloak billowing out behind him. He couldn't run past their attackers and live, so he ran the opposite direction. Asta jumped to his place so she was facing both figures now.

The wound on her shoulder was throbbing, but Asta held her ground.

What do you do if they hurt you, Asta?

Gyrial's voice echoed through her thoughts. What do you do? You don't run, you don't hide, you don't surrender. She remembered the answer as she bared her teeth and let out a growl.

Let it fuel you.

Asta's sword slashed out in a fury of calculated combinations. It was like training, when she had taken on two sparring partners at once. She ducked when one swung high, using the position to sweep their legs. She jumped when the other swung low, using the momentum to kick the creature in the chest.

She was wild. Unleashed. An uncontrolled chaos, ruthless and devastating. She was not a princess sitting on a throne, but a warrior fighting for her kingdom. There was no knight to rescue her. There was no army to back her up. She didn't need it. There was no stopping her.

She whirled like a hurricane and slammed the pommel of her sword into one assailant's head. Even through the fabric of the thick hood, she could feel the crack of their skull. That opponent staggered back, clutching their temple.

The next charged her, but Asta was ready. She parried, twisting her own sword around her opponent's and shoving it to the ground. Asta managed to drag her dagger through the attacker's torso before they lifted their sword again.

She was so shocked that they were still able to fight that she wasn't able to block the next strike. The blade landed on her forearm, lacerating the same arm that bore her shoulder injury.

Asta needed to plan her retreat. She knew it when the assailant with the head injury hadn't been knocked out. They should be incapacitated by now with the strikes she had been making. Whatever they were, they could withstand injuries far worse than humans could, and she needed to live to warn others about them.

The next time the still-fighting creature attacked, she took a cheap shot and pushed her heel as hard into their abdomen as she could, sending them flying and landing on their back.

Asta turned and sprinted, taking off in the direction that Kaid had gone. Hopefully he had found a safe place to hide, or someone to help, or a shortcut to the village where they would be shielded by the crowds.

She didn't hear running behind her until she was quite a distance down the beach, her attackers clearly needing time to gather themselves before they could chase her.

Good. She had done some damage, then.

Asta was running at full speed, pushing the pain in her left arm aside and focusing on her legs. She could feel the blood trickling down her fingertips, but she wasn't losing it fast enough to bleed out as long as she could tuck herself away and make a tourniquet soon.

She turned a corner, temporarily out of sight from the things pursuing her.

Suddenly, Asta was being pulled backward, a hand pressed firmly against her mouth and her back pressed against something hard. She kicked and elbowed as she was dragged back into a dark cave, so far back that she could no longer see the opening.

Asta felt warm breath caress her ear, causing the hair on her arms to stand up.

"Stay quiet, Princess."

She knew that voice. It was Kaid. Thank the gods.

Asta did as he said and waited, quietly. They heard footsteps rush past the cave, sand kicking up in their wake. When they passed, Asta began breathing again, not realizing she had been holding air within her lungs the entire time.

Kaid's palm finally dropped from her lips and he stepped away from her. She could hardly make out his face in the faint moonlight as she turned to face him.

The pain in her arm was coming back with a vengeance, the throbbing worse than ever. "My arm." The only words she managed to get out.

Kaid pulled her a little closer to the light of the cave entrance but remained far enough back so they could easily disappear into the shadows again if needed. He assessed the lacerations under the moonlight, then used his dagger to cut the bottom of his cloak.

He wrapped the strip of cloth under Asta's arm at the top of her shoulder and nodded to her. "This will hurt."

Asta gave a sharp nod in response and readied herself. When he pulled the cloth tight, her vision turned clouded and her knees buckled. *Sweet Dagmar, that throbbed.*

When Asta came-to again, she rested against the cool cave wall. Her eyes had adjusted to the darkness and she could now see that the structure wasn't completely made of rock; the ceiling was made up of a tree trunk, the tree itself growing directly over the opening in the shoreline and creating a cave below.

If they had discovered this from adventuring and not from hiding from things who wanted to kill them, Asta would consider returning here and passing some time reading within the peculiar structure.

Kaid got to his feet from where he had been resting at the opposite side of the cave. He sat down next to her and tucked his legs up, resting an arm on his knees.

He scrubbed his face with his hand. "I vote we stay here, in case they're waiting us out. You?"

Asta ran through their options, which were few. Stay here and potentially face being attacked in a cave with nowhere to go. Try leaving and potentially be attacked on the beach, still with nowhere to go. At least those creatures didn't know where they had disappeared to and maybe they could get some rest and heal before their next potential battle.

"Here will have to do," she whispered.

They talked quietly for a while, the conversation being cathartic after what they had endured. They discussed how the king needs to know that there were vicious, murderous creatures slinking in and out of the castle. Though they hadn't actually had the chance to confront the creatures and demand answers, Asta knew they were the reason that more villagers had gone missing. She could feel it deep in her gut. But why hadn't they taken anyone from the castle? Why were they sneaking into it so often?

The royal army would have to figure that out when they captured them.

CHAPTER 19

ALTERNATE CHAPTER AVAILABLE

Asta stretched and let out a yawn. The tourniquet had done its job and stopped the bleeding. Her injuries were not deep, but certainly had made an impact. Figuring the cloth had been tied on for multiple hours now, Asta released the knot and let it fall. The bleeding didn't seem to start again.

Kaid watched her and did the same with the tie he had made above his thigh wound. In her daze, she hadn't remembered to ask him about his injuries, but he had remembered and treated hers, and guilt bloomed on her cheeks. To her relief, his leg injury seemed to be clotted now as well, no thanks to her.

"I can't sleep sitting up like this," Asta said.

Immediately, Kaid took off his fur-lined cloak and laid it on the ground, patting it down.

Asta unbuttoned her cloak and slipped it off. "We can use this as a blanket," she murmured as she laid down between layers.

"We?" Kaid asked.

Asta huffed a laugh, amazed that she could smile even under such circumstances. "We. I need you down here with me. For warmth purposes."

It wasn't a lie. It was autumn now and there was a brisk, salty breeze coming off the sea and making its way into the cave. They would freeze to death before the night was through if they didn't use each other to stay warm.

Kaid didn't object and slid between the cloaks, lying close but not touching her. His breath wheezed slightly as he settled.

"Do you have to breathe like that?" Asta huffed. He drove her mad.

"Oh, sorry, Princess. I'll just stop breathing to please you," Kaid quipped.

Asta hid her faint smile. "That would please me very much, thank you."

They rested in silence, Asta trying to not think about how cold she truly was. She couldn't stop her body from trembling, between the cold air and the last of her adrenaline draining from her.

Kaid's closeness became very apparent to her, and she remembered that the last time they were in such tight proximity was that night in her bedroom. The night where he kissed her as a part of his torment.

His warmth slid closer to her, forming to the shape of her body. The heat he was letting off instantaneously made her shivering stop. The cold was still nipping at her, but it was much more bearable.

"For warmth purposes," Kaid mumbled.

Asta tried to push away how right it felt to be up against him like this. How she wished he would wrap his arms around her and pull her in snugly.

A familiar, tight ball formed in her chest.

Kaid's fingers dove into Asta's hair, brushing downward to the tips and starting back at the top.

One, two, three...

"What are you doing?" she snapped, but couldn't stop her instinctive counting.

Eight, nine, ten...

He chuckled. "Relax, Princess. I know you can't sleep without."

Fifteen, sixteen, seventeen...

Asta had been subconsciously counting his strokes already, but now she was focusing on them, hoping they would help relieve some of the tension in her chest.

Twenty-two, twenty-three, twenty-four...

Four more. Four more strokes and she could breathe. Four more strokes and she would be able to focus on the world around her again.

Twenty-eight.

Twenty-eight. The age my mother was when she died. When I killed her.

The ball in her chest released its grip on her thoughts. She didn't know why it worked when Kaid did it, but she couldn't help but let a tear slip from the corner of her eye at the thought. They had just been through something terrible and he still remembered. He remembered her ritual and didn't tell her to forget about it for a night; to let it go. He didn't remind her that it wasn't important in comparison to the current danger they were in. He helped her.

Asta closed her eyes, wishing away the comfort it brought. She shouldn't feel this way. Not about him.

A strong arm wrapped around her abdomen while another nudged her head to lift off the cave floor. When she set it back down, she realized that Kaid was providing her with a pillow using his own arm.

The emotions were undeniable now. There was no stopping them. At least not tonight.

Asta allowed her courage to take one final stand before it disappeared completely. "Was it all a game? Was *I* a game?"

Kaid's body went rigid, his voice unsteady. "You're the first thing in my life that hasn't been."

Asta swallowed loudly and scooted back so her body was pressed against Kaid's. At first, he didn't react to her movement and she worried that she had crossed a boundary. But his fingers start brushing against the fabric of her shirt, tracing lazy circles across her torso.

Kaid respectfully avoided any intimate areas within his path. He traced a long line starting at her hip, gliding up her side, breezing past the side of her chest, tracing her collarbone, and running up the corner of her jaw. Asta's breathing hitched under his touch, all thoughts leaving her mind besides him. He continued to trace the contours of her body, dipping his hand down to outline her thighs.

She backed into Kaid as hard as she could, unable to stop her hips from moving in a circular motion. What did it matter? They may die, anyway.

At first, Kaid paused when he felt her hips rocking, but then his fingers continued their circles with more purpose.

He leaned down, his warm breath coating the skin of Asta's ear. "You're safe," he whispered.

Asta let out a small laugh, her skin mottling with raised bumps. "That simply can't be true when I'm stuck in a cave with my greatest enemy."

Her proclamation didn't stop him from pressing his lips to her neck, each kiss deeper than the last. Asta craned her neck to allow him more access and he chuckled.

Kaid's teeth grazed Asta's earlobe before he asked, "Do you still hate me?"

"Yes," Asta replied breathlessly.

She realized that was the answer he had wanted when Kaid's lazy circles quickly turned to a grip on her abdomen.

"Tell me why," he growled.

What was the reason? Because of his reputation? Because of his uncanny ability to show up everywhere she was? Because he matched her challenges and pushed back?

There was only one real answer which summed everything up.

"Because, Kaid, you are... insufferable. You drive me absolutely mad. And I *hate* that I enjoy it."

Asta concluded that the sentiment was reciprocated when Kaid slipped his hand under her shirt and began palming her breasts. She rolled onto her back and captured his mouth with hers, their kissing feverish and determined, much different than the kissing they had done in her bed.

Gods, she had wanted this for so long and refused to admit it. She might be able to tolerate him if he never spoke again and they lived in this moment for eternity.

One of Kaid's fingers lightly brushed under Asta's waistband and he pulled his mouth away from her, looking into her eyes with his turquoise gaze glistening in the moonlight, glowing like the bioluminescence of the sea.

"Will you hate me more if I keep going?" His finger continued tracing a line across her abdomen, back and forth.

"Yes," Asta replied.

Kaid's too-perfect-for-this-world smile slid across his lips and Asta nearly passed out from the sight of it.

He pressed a kiss to the corner of her mouth before asking, "May I proceed anyway?"

Asta didn't need a moment to think about her answer. She knew what she wanted. Damn the consequences—she would deal with them in the morning.

Her voice was hardly more than a whisper. "Yes."

Kaid kissed Asta as he unbuttoned the clasps on her pants and slid them down. She reached down and shucked them off completely, warranting a smile from Kaid as he continued kissing her. She couldn't help but smile in return, their teeth grazing each other's as their lips collided.

His hand dipped between her legs once before pulling back up. Asta whimpered, needing more. But his mouth was gone, and so was the heat of his body next to her. Actually, the heat of the cloak that had been on top of them was gone as well.

Asta opened her eyes to see Kaid centering himself between her thighs, his palms now resting on her knees to spread them further apart.

"You wickedly cruel, beautiful thing. Please, hate me forever," Kaid whispered.

She could hate him forever if this was what it meant. If this was what it led to.

He dove forward, and when he pressed his mouth to her center, it only took a few minutes before she drifted away to oblivion, her body quivering from release and pleasure. Bursting stars clouded her vision as heat flushed throughout her body.

She could do this every day. That was, if her sister wasn't set to marry this man in less than a week.

Now that the lust was leaving her body, her mind cleared and reminded her of that. But in that moment, she didn't care. Kaid helped her get dressed, knowing her arm was still sore from its injuries, and then nestled in next to her.

Tomorrow, she would be the pretty princess in the seaside castle who was happy for her sister for finding a husband.

Tonight, she was the warrior, fighting for what she wanted and seizing it.

CHAPTER 20

Kaid awoke next to Asta, who was still using his arm as a pillow. The sore neck was worth it. It was all worth it to spend the night with her. He could still taste her essence on his lips, that same addictive taste he had been craving since that night in her bed.

The lack of sleep should have been clouding Kaid's judgment, but he was thinking more clearly than he ever had. He would call off the wedding with Maren and offer his hand to Asta. Consequences be damned.

They would find another way to save Haalberg from financial crisis. Kaid's father would understand if it was for love. Duke Aerik had always been a firm believer in the emotion, saying it could overcome anything.

Even if Asta rejected him, even if she banished him from the castle for offering her his life, it was worth it to try. If this was what it felt like to be hated by her, he could only begin to imagine what it would feel like to be loved by her.

The blonde princess lying next to him stirred, her heavy-lidded eyes meeting his as she smiled, yawning lightly.

"Good morning, Princess," Kaid murmured.

Asta smiled mischievously. "Good morning, prick."

Kaid chuckled. Yeah, he could get used to this.

They got up, exposing themselves to the chilled air before taking their own cloaks back and dressing in them once again. The pain in Kaid's leg shot up to his chest with every step, but Asta seemed to be managing well with her injured arm, though she was clearly favoring it. They just needed to get back to the castle to see the mender.

They had successfully survived the night, which was the most difficult feat of their adventure. Now began their trip home.

Kaid exited the cave, his eyes watching Asta as she emerged into the sunlight next to him and the rays kissed her blonde locks, setting them ablaze. But she didn't return his gaze. No, she looked forward in horror.

The lord turned to see the crowd before them, some on the sandy beach and some lurking in the waves. Among them, at their center, stood Maren and Svanhild. They were wearing dark cloaks with slashes through them— the same injuries Asta had inflicted on their enemies the night before.

Kaid side stepped so his body was mostly blocking Asta's but, naturally, she stepped out of his cover. He could see multiple figures in the water, but where their legs were supposed to be were strange fins instead.

Kaid's head began to spin. Were these sirens? Was this who had called to him that day on the beach? Did they know the courtesan?

Maren prowled forward, her unbound copper hair whipping around her in the winds from the brewing sea storm. Her red strands looked like her own personal hurricane, ferocious and unforgiving. The clouds were much closer now, the lightning striking the small islands visible from the beach.

The redhead princess smiled wickedly. "Many of you may know, but for those who do not, this is my sister, Princess Asta, and my sweet, loyal future husband, Lord Kaidian."

The crowd around them cackled as Maren observed Asta and Kaid. Maren's hands were not gloved for once and her skin was riddled with scars from her fingertips to the sleeves at her wrists. The gloves hadn't been an act of modesty—they were to hide her true self. He risked a glance toward Asta, who was calmly assessing, calculating. The wheels in her brain ever-turning.

Maren continued, "It's so nice to finally introduce my separate families. Kaidian, Asta, these lovely finfolk are my courtiers." She gestured to the creatures wading in the waves.

So they were finfolk, the worse of the two merfolk species. *Perfect*.

Maren's voice echoed as she announced, "Except for the queen, of course."

A chill rattled through Kaid as a royal blue-haired woman swam forward, a crown of golden bones atop her head. Her eyes were black like an abyss at the deepest depths of the ocean and her skin was cobalt hued. The queen's cheekbones stuck out so sharply that they reminded Kaid of the cliff overhangs in the forests of Haalberg, and her ears... her ears were long and pointed, sticking out inches away from her head. Her black lips parted in a cruel smile, displaying her mouth full of sharp, flesh-ripping fangs.

"Queen Yrsa of Ryktarva, the finfolk kingdom of the Ventarin Sea," Maren's thunderous voice boomed over the beach. "Also known as my mother."

"What the—" Asta lunged forward, but Kaid whipped out an arm and held her back. Multiple finfolk in the water hissed as Svanhild stepped closer to Maren with her sword drawn.

"Ah, ah, ah," Maren waved a finger in the air, "No picking fights with family, dear sister. Is that really how you want to earn their trust?"

Asta was panting, her anger mirroring the storm looming above. Maren was finfolk, and not just common finfolk, but a finfolk princess. All of the myths and legends were real. Kaid wished he had heeded his father's warnings and never left his hometown, remaining as far away from the sea as possible. But it was too late now.

Maren laughed, a wicked sound so different from the reserved woman she posed herself to be all this time. "Oh sister, your emotions really do control your actions. You should get a handle on that. Maybe if you stopped cracking your knuckles and combing your hair long enough, you could play in this game with me, too."

"Fuck you," Asta snarled.

The finfolk princess only waved a hand in the air, as if swatting a bothersome fly away instead of her own sister. "Now, Lord Kaidian, if you'll come with me, we have much to discuss."

Kaid stepped back and grabbed Asta's wrist. "What do I have to do with your kind?" He tried to sound merely curious, but his voice shook as he asked.

"We have a wedding to move forward with, silly. Have you already forgotten about me after one lust-filled night in a cave?" Maren gestured toward Asta as she kept her focus on Kaid. "Now, say goodbye to Asta. She will stay safe, so long as you obey orders. You are coming with us."

Kaid gestured to his body. "Clearly, I cannot go with you. I am not an ocean dweller."

"But aren't you?" Maren's question lingered in the air like smoke.

Kaid was human. Born of two human parents. His mother passed during his birth. How could he possibly be anything but human without knowing? But if he was a merperson, it would explain the calling he felt toward the waves. Explain the warnings his father gave him. Explain why he never felt like he belonged.

He looked between the sisters, each of them pleading for him to go with them. He knew what he had to do.

Kaid released Asta's wrist and stepped forward. Maren waved a hand and Svanhild and placed a firm grasp on his shoulder. "You come with me now, Lord Kaidian, or you watch as she dies at the hands of the finfolk."

A sob escaped Asta as she pleaded with her sister. "Maren, please! I'll forget all about this. We'll never speak of it again if you let us go and come home with us."

The princess of Ryktarva's voice was cold as she responded, "Orntali has never been my home, not since the moment I was born, and it never will be. You live in a delusional world, Asta, if you cannot see that. I was only sent here for one purpose—to find him." Maren pointed a scarred finger directly at Kaid.

He didn't know what any of it meant. He just knew he had to go with them in order to protect Asta.

"I will go with you, Your Highness, if that is what I must do. I will go with you, and I will marry you. Please, let her return to the castle safely," Kaid begged, his own desperation engulfing him.

Asta sniveled as Svanhild dragged Kaid toward the water, sand kicking up with each heavy foot step. He looked back at the blonde princess, her cheeks tear-stained and eyes bloodshot. He plastered on his most charming crooked grin for her before he turned away from her pleading eyes. He wanted that face to be what she remembered of him. Always smiling even in the face of evil. The evercharming prick.

Svanhild shoved Kaid forward with a splash and Maren stepped to his other side as he stood knee-deep in the ocean. A sting shot through his body, but it wasn't from the salt water spraying into his laceration on his leg. This was a strange sensation that was painful but welcomed.

Kaid heard a gasp behind him as he fell to the water, unable to control his legs, because he no longer had legs. A royal blue fin replaced his lower limbs, small swirls of silver dancing between the scales.

Before he could observe the changes further, Maren gripped his arm so tightly beneath her sharp nails that she drew blood. She opened her mouth and a horrific, ear-piercing screech erupted from her while the world around Kaid went black.

CHAPTER 21

Asta's vision was blurry as she attempted to take in her surroundings. She could hear thunder in the distance, and there was sand under her palms. Gulls cried from above and a salty pine scent seared into her nostrils, causing her sudden headache to worsen.

The beach. She was on the beach. But what was she doing there? She blinked hard a few times, forcing her eyes to focus.

It was just Asta, the sand around her, the crashing waves inches from her boots and a storm circling above the shore.

Kaid.

Her thoughts cleared in unison with her vision. Where was Kaid? Why had she passed out?

Then, she recalled the shrill sound her sister had made and her memories turned to black after that. Her sister, who was a finfolk princess. Who had been lying to her this whole time. Asta racked her brain for any evidence that could have led to solving the puzzle before now, but she couldn't think of anything. She didn't know enough about the mythical beings to actually know what the signs would have been, anyway.

And then there was Kaid. He was some sort of sea folk, but what kind? His tail didn't match the finfolk tails, which resembled more of an eel shape. Kaid's tapered down to a fork at the end. A siren, perhaps? Could the statues around the castle be an accurate depiction of what they looked like?

Asta pinched her own arm—convinced she was hallucinating—and yelped.

This is crazy. Last week these creatures weren't even real and now I'm related to one? Asta gritted her teeth and let out a growl of frustration.

She cracked one knuckle after the other, grains of sand dropping from her fingertips. There was a faint throb in her left arm from the injuries, but she didn't care about that right now. She needed to find her father. He had produced the heir to the finfolk kingdom, and she needed answers. It was as good a place as any to start, since there was no one left on this beach to interrogate. Her father *had* to know something.

Her palms pounded on the threshold of the east wing as she entered from the terrace, and Asta did not stop to properly greet every guard and staff member she passed. She didn't have the patience for formalities currently.

She had a two mile walk down the beach to think about how to confront her father, each rehearsal playing out differently except for one factor—she was unbelievably angry with him. Her fists curled into tight balls at her sides as she stomped through the halls.

A light set of footsteps approached her side and Asta knew it was Linnea without looking.

"What happened?" Her cousin's usually soft voice a bit on the harsher side.

Asta didn't look at her lady-in-waiting as she hissed, "That's what dear old father is about to tell me."

Linnea gasped at Asta's tone, which made the princess glance at her. Her cousin had purple bags under her eyes and the whites around her irises were bloodshot.

Asta stopped walking, stifling her fury long enough to speak to her cousin in the soft tone she deserved. "I'm sorry. Linnea, so much happened last night, and I need to talk to my father before I speak with anyone else about it." Asta grabbed Linnea's hands and squeezed them. "I want you to go back to my suite and eat, then take a nap. I'm going to see the mender after this, but I promise I'll be there when you wake up. Okay? Then, I'll explain everything I can."

Linnea rubbed her wrist, but nodded and drifted away without another word.

As Asta continued stalking down the halls, she stopped a maid to ask that a fruit platter be sent to her suite for Linnea. The maid had scurried away to complete the mission in a hurry, clearly nervous of Asta's current physical state.

The blonde princess paused outside of her father's private office, staring at the mahogany double doors that towered over the foyer. She still wasn't quite sure what she would say to him but decided she would figure it out as she went.

The guards beside the office doors glanced wearily at each other as Asta stepped past them and tapped the doors before flinging them open. In front of her, a man with hair as white as snow sat at a desk, writing on various papers spread before him. The windows behind him displayed the main garden, which was now browning from the autumn frosts.

King Botmar removed his glasses and placed them on the desk before him. "Asta, my dear. What is it?"

She waited for the doors to shut behind her, thankful that the guards had stepped in and pulled them closed. "What is Maren?" Asta snapped.

Her father's eyes went glassy and he stared straight ahead, not *at* her, but *through* her. After a long moment, his vision re-focused as he asked, "What were we talking about, dear?"

Asta stepped forward to assess the king. "Maren. Your bastard daughter. *What. Is. She?*"

The emphasis on the last words caused a ringing in the glass of the oil lamp on the desk.

King Botmar pressed his green eyes shut, the same green as Asta's. It made her want to ease up, release the invisible death grip she had around her father's throat, but she couldn't. He reached his hands up and squeezed his head, like he was fighting something inside his own mind.

Asta asked her final questions in desperation, understanding that she may never know the answer. Something was not right with her father's memories. "How is it that Maren is finfolk, father? How is it possible?"

There was a stagnant silence in the room. The thickening air caused Asta to breathe heavily. Her father began shaking uncontrollably in rhythm with the quivering flame of the lamp.

The king's eyes snapped open and his gaze shifted around the room as though he were seeing it for the first time. He covered his mouth with an unsteady hand and began weeping softly.

Asta took a cautious step forward. "Father?"

His wide stare slowly turned to her, sorrow flooding them and overflowing down his wrinkled cheeks. "I remember... something. The finfolk... they are real?"

Asta waved a hand through the air. "Well I would say so since I just fought for my life against them! What do you remember? Tell me. *Now.*"

King Botmar inhaled deeply multiple times, though it did nothing to diminish his shaking. "I have these dreams. Well, nightmares." He forced his eyes closed once more, exhaustion visibly taking over him. "The finfolk are real. They storm the castle and take Maren away from me over and over again. She gets swept into the sea as she reaches for me and I can do nothing about it."

"And you just so happened to keep these nightmares to yourself all this time? You never wondered what they meant?" Asta's face felt hot and she couldn't help but pace. Her knuckles begged for relief and she cracked each one.

"I couldn't remember them each time I woke up, until now. It's as though they were wiped from my memory until you confirmed their existence. There's so much missing. There are black holes in my mind." He gasped, "Oh gods, the things I've done. The things people believe I've done."

The king's hands shook as he searched his pockets and pulled out a cloth to dab his eyes.

"What do you remember? Is it about Maren?" Asta reeled in her anger at the sight and tried to approach the situation more gently, not fully understanding what was happening.

"I'm so sorry, my sweet, for what lies you've been told. For the life you've had to live because of me." The king spoke through rattled breaths, his whole body trembling.

Asta didn't know why, but she trusted him. She trusted this reaction—that it was genuine. "Tell me everything."

And so, King Botmar Enrathi told his tale.

Over twenty years ago, he had met a strange navy-haired woman during a royal ball and approached her to inquire about her bold style. They exchanged pleasant conversation throughout the ball, the king always checking in with his wife to make sure she was faring well on her own—which she always had. But then someone approached him and sang a strange song to him, and he felt an undeniable need to follow the blue-haired woman out of the ball and up to his suite. The more the stranger sang, the harder it became to resist the advances of the blue-haired woman. She seduced him fully, taking him to his own bedroom where they conceived Maren. When they emerged, she told him who she was, Queen Yrsa, ruler of the finfolk.

A strange song came over him again and he listened as Yrsa explained that she would leave during her pregnancy, but return to pass the child to him to raise when she was born. On Maren's birthday, the finfolk queen returned, as she promised, and abandoned her child with King Botmar. Through song and a strange liquid the queen made him drink, the king's memories were altered once more, so that he would think Maren was the child of a noble. A bastard child that he was claiming to his royal line. The scandalous rumors spread from there, and Botmar had spiraled with them. His entire memory became addled, not solely his ability to remember Maren's conception. He hardly remembered making any decisions during the last twenty-two years. It was a miracle the kingdom wasn't in complete ruin.

But hearing what Maren was from someone who knew with absolute certainty broke him free of his spell, allowing his thoughts to solidify and make sense once more.

Asta didn't know how to react, aside from dropping into the nearest chair she could find. Her father wasn't an unfaithful git. He wasn't so dependent on alcohol that his brain was permanently damaged. His memories had been tainted. He had been spelled to believe those things of himself, and she had treated him terribly because of it.

Her conception was an act of putting on a united front, but it never should have happened. Her mother never should have died birthing a child that was only brought into the world because of the trickery of a ruthless sea creature.

"She is a sea witch, Asta," King Botmar admitted, shaking his head. "She can do more than an average finfolk. She possesses magic of electric currents. Queen Yrsa is not only dangerous, but living death itself."

The hair on Asta's arms stood up and a tingle ran over her body. She took a step toward her father's desk and spoke softly. "Maren has returned to sea and taken Lord Kaidian with her. What do we do, father?"

It was the first time Asta had ever asked advice from her father. He must have realized it, too, because despite the overbearing weight of truth that had just fallen over him, he smiled.

King Botmar's voice was gentle, like a father reassuring a daughter's should be. It was a tone she was entirely unfamiliar with. "I will send out rescue ships. I have rough knowledge of where the Ryktarvan kingdom hides. We'll find them."

Them.

Asta didn't have the heart to tell her father that Maren was never coming home.

CHAPTER 22

Awake, but too comfortable to open his eyes yet, Kaid rolled over in the softest bed he had ever slept in. He felt weightless, drifting through the air like a crinkled leaf in the autumn breeze.

But there wasn't a breeze. The air around Kaid felt thick and strange. His eyes flung open to reveal a dimly-lit suite of some sort, the dark green walls containing patches of swaying grass growing from them. The only other things in the room were a vanity and two closed doors.

Kaid sat up quickly, remembering what he had last seen before blacking out. He looked down at the bed underneath him and saw that it was some sort of sponge and the blanket crossing his legs was tethered to the posts.

No, not legs. He curled the blanket back and saw the blue fin. Kaid thought he had dreamed the whole thing, his imagination helping him escape from whatever had actually happened to him. He worked his muscles as he would to make his legs wiggle and the fin rolled in response.

When Kaid reached down to his fin, his right arm snagged backward and he saw the black cuff. The thick bracelet around his wrist was connected to a chain bolted to the wall near his headboard. However, it wasn't the shackles that caught the majority of his attention, but the tattoo on his hand. A long staff extended from the center of his wrist up onto the back of his hand, then forked into three prongs that spread up his three middle fingers. A trident.

Kaid didn't know where he was, but he knew he needed to get out of here. His head was pounding, and he remembered Maren's shriek on the beach. She had known what he was, so how had he not ever figured it out?

He dug through his memory, thinking back on the times his father had warned him to never touch the water. Had Duke Aerik known that his son was some sort of merperson? And why had he kept it a secret if he had known?

He was underwater, breathing in liquid instead of air. He had a fin instead of legs. He had a tattoo on his hand that had not been there before his transformation—that he had only seen in dreams, and maybe once, a very long time ago, when he reached for the sea. Now that he was thinking about it, his torso, arms, and fingers certainly seemed longer than he remembered.

There was a knock on the door and Kaid stilled, not daring to respond.

When the stone hatch crept open, a red-haired being was observing him.

Maren watched from the doorway, or what Kaid believed was Maren. She still had the same copper hair, the same brown eyes and freckles.

But her ears were long and pointed, her cheekbones were sharp and pronounced, and her teeth were that same terrifying shape that he remembered her mother's being.

She smiled wryly and entered the room, her burgundy eel fin pushing her through the water, keeping her hovering a few inches from the stone floor. The silver foil wrap she wore on her torso accentuated her blue-tinted finfolk skin. At least whatever Kaid was, he had a human skin tone still.

Maren took up a seat at the vanity near the bed and drummed her long, sharp nails on the mirrored glass surface as she stared at him. "Did you sleep well?" Her tone was relaxed, almost bored.

Kaid didn't want to admit that the strange sponge he slept on was actually quite comfortable. He didn't want to admit anything—he simply wanted answers. He shifted to face her, the chain clanking against the side of the bed as he did so. "Where am I? What do you want with me?"

"Hmm, someone woke up on the wrong side of the sea sponge," Maren mused, wearing a fake pout.

"No more games, Maren. Tell me what's going on." Kaid's voice was curt, a tone he didn't typically let surface.

Maren's deep red fin flitted slightly in a soft current that swept through the room, her hair brushing back from her face. It was at that moment that Kaid noticed the silver crown of bones resting atop her bright hair. It was nearly identical to the golden one Queen Yrsa had been wearing during their beach encounter.

The finfolk princess sighed, "You're lucky Mother isn't around to hear you address me without my title. I'll let that one pass, just this time. I'm a forgiving host." Her brown eyes caught on the chain holding Kaid in place. "Apologies for the iron, but we can't have you using your magic. You should be grateful, you know. I fought for you to have a suite instead of a cell. We can certainly make the chain longer once we know you will cooperate."

Kaid hissed, an animalistic sound he had never made before. He caught his reflection in the mirror behind Maren and froze. His canine teeth were fangs, sharp and long, and his ears came to a small, delicate point at the tip.

Maren laughed, her entire body jostling with the movement. "My poor, naive husband-to-be. You haven't figured it out yet, have you? Everything you know has been a lie."

Kaid's emotions felt heightened in his new body, his inability to stifle his rising anger confusing him more than anything. Why did everyone seem to know more about his own life than he did?

"Tell me," his voice boomed.

To his shock, Maren did.

She started with Duke Aerik, explaining that he was a siren and not fully human. He was married to Queen Arielle Andreassen, leader of the Ventarin sirens and empress of all Northern Seas. But the empress status was only reliant on her ability to produce an heir to take up the throne when she abdicated. That was when Kaid was born. He was in line to be the next great ruler of both the sirens and finfolk, including rule over Maren's mother, Queen Yrsa.

Kaid interrupted bluntly, "But that would mean that I'm..."

"A prince," Maren stated. "Prince Kaidian Andreassen."

Kaid swallowed loudly. Not only was he a prince, but he was a *sea* prince.

"My mother grew impatient, wanting to control the seas and bring them back to the old ways when we ruled over humans. But the only way she could claim ownership to the empress status was if the entire Andreassen line—your line—was exterminated. So, Queen Yrsa gathered her army and attacked your mother's castle with hopes to rid the sea of your entire family. But your mother used the power of Ventarin royalty to summon whirlpools, rip currents, really any powerful natural occurrence she could to weaken our army before they reached their destination.

"By the time the forces stormed the siren castle, you were gone, along with your father, King Aerik Andreassen. He had been sent into hiding with you to keep you safe—to keep your lineage safe—until it was time for your return. Queen Arielle had sacrificed the power of her siren song to the gods and goddesses to keep you concealed so even my mother couldn't find you. It was very foolish on her part.

"And so, I was conceived and raised to be a spy and assassin. I was sent to live with the humans, to search for you and anyone who may know where you were being hidden. When I learned your name, I insisted that my father bring you to the castle as a 'prospective husband,' but I was really trying to figure out if you were *the* Kaidian. There was seemingly a lot of faith put into the protection spell if no one bothered to change your name, which worked to our favor. It was also a senseless move, on your father's part, to allow you to reside so close to a seaside town. But he stupidly came to care for the people of his territory, so he agreed to the marriage, not knowing what was waiting for you in Orntali. That *I* was waiting for you. It was as though the fates aligned and blessed me with the very thing I had been searching for."

Svanhild entered the room, her murky eyes matching the color of her eel tail. The smile on her face told Kaid that she was likely far more brutal than she had allowed her human form to be.

Kaid's mind was racing, so he asked the first question that came to his mind. "Is that how you can walk on land then? You are half human?"

Maren nodded. "I am, and so are many others in Orntali. Being half human gives us the ability to have a human form, which our purebred parents lack. But many of our young have been birthed with hearing and speech deficiencies over the last two decades or so—since about the time you'd gone missing—so their parents discarded them on the shores.

Many of those beloved orphans that you and my sister fuss over are abandoned finfolk offspring."

Gods, the increasing number of orphans was because the finfolk were ridding themselves of their children with disabilities. Scum. These creatures truly were the refuse of the sea.

"The missing villagers?" Kaid questioned, though he was quite sure of the response.

"Our lunch," Maren sneered, a feral grin spreading as Svanhild snickered. "The finfolk's hunger has been insatiable ever since we noticed the change in tides and the whispering currents that the lost prince was near. Our people have been feeding more often, becoming stronger with hope. Queen Arielle has been sending her forces to try and stop our feedings, but fails each time." The princess tapped a finger on her chin. "That may have something to do with our siren spies we have planted in her court and the human land."

Kaid's realization struck him like a slap to the face. The dark-haired courtesan must have been a siren spy, luring humans to the finfolk as meals. He shifted in his seat, lightly tugging on the iron chain bound to his wrist. "So your ailment. What was that?"

"Oh, my grand act!" Maren proclaimed, "All the times I excused myself were because I couldn't stand being in a room full of humans anymore without ripping their throats open and licking their bones clean. Svanhild always took me to find a satisfying meal during my absence."

Kaid shuddered, his nerves completely on edge. All the answers Asta had been searching for laid within her sister. The sister that Asta had trusted and loved despite their differences.

The siren prince shifted his gaze between Maren and Svanhild. He had been living with them for nearly a month, two people who clearly wanted him dead. But why hadn't they done it? Why hadn't they killed him?

Kaid swallowed loudly. "How did you know it was me? That I am the lost prince?"

"Your protection only lasted as long as your avoidance of the ocean. We've known since the day my clueless sister splashed you with sea water."

Kaid narrowed his eyes at the princess, his fists curling into balls. "And once you found out, you graciously decided to spare me? Imprison me in a life of unwanted wedlock instead?"

"Our matrimony has nothing to do with you, sweet prince, but everything to do with Queen Arielle. She has made our life such hell since your disappearance, making it nearly impossible for us to properly feed. That's why I started bringing villagers to my people to help them sustain life. We can only eat so much fish and crab before we *need* to consume human. Whether it be blood, flesh, or bone, we cannot survive without it in our systems. Your mother instated a law in the Northern Seas that we were no longer to kill our prey, only feed from them. But that's not the finfolk way of life, so we haven't exactly been willing participants.

"So what better way to punish our tyrant empress than ensnare her only son in a binding union with the princess of the finfolk? Together, we will find the lost Ventarin Trident and rid the sea of Queen Arielle and King Aerik's existence, leaving the throne open to us. You will be my puppet for the hundreds of years we have together. And when the time comes, we will produce our heir, the first of mixed merpeople blood. We will restore the Northern Seas to the chaotic glory they were before the sirens ever came about!"

Someone cleared their throat in the opposite corner of the room and Kaid whipped his head around to find Queen Yrsa floating in his doorway, her dark hair dancing around her head like tentacles. Kaid sat up straighter than he had been, all of his senses on high alert as the queen pushed into the room using her gray eel tail.

The finfolk queen smiled superficially toward her daughter before turning her attention to Kaid, who was still helplessly shackled to the wall. He immediately felt more aware of his vulnerability than he had before.

"My sweet daughter, you have forgotten one small part in your story," The queen displayed her mouth full of fangs in a twisted smile that resembled more of a snarl. "Me."

The sharp nail Maren had been using to caress the vanity surface scratched along the top of it, leaving an indented line in the glass. She averted her gaze to the smooth stone floor.

The queen approached the side of Kaid's bed before she spoke again. "You will have your turn to rule together, but first, once we kill your parents, *I* am the rightful empress of the Northern Sea. And *you* do not get your turn until I abdicate or die. Neither of which I plan to do for a long, long while. But need not worry, I will allow you both to enjoy the perks of royalty until then. Though I still think it would be far easier to exterminate the entire Andreassen line, Maren was quite persuasive with her proposal to wed and control you. And a mother only wants her child to be happy."

Kaid couldn't stop the scoff that escaped his throat. He was in a room of deadly females who wanted to ruthlessly kill his entire family for a crown, and yet they were acting like it was a favor to spare him. But he had a mother. The mother he believed to be dead, the mother his own father had mourned over his entire life. But Kaid now realized that the mourning had never ended because Duke Aerik had known his wife was still out there, alive, awaiting the day he could safely return to her with their son. Kaid's heart ached. He had a mother, and he may never get to meet her.

Through gritted teeth, Kaid snapped at the copper-haired princess next to him. "I will fight you for the rest of my life, I swear to the gods and goddesses. I will defy you in any way I can. I will never make this easy for you."

Queen Yrsa barked a wicked laugh as she said, "Fight all you like, dear prince. But if you try to run—or worse—I'll have your little human girlfriend dragged to the ocean floor where I can play some delightful games with her, giving her hardly enough air to keep her alive to partake in the fun. Then, I'll have her neck snapped and force her flesh down your throat."

Kaid was too shocked to speak, to move. Asta's life was in his hands, reliant on his cooperation. He had no choice but to obey their orders until Asta's hair turned as white as King Botmar's, until she crossed over to goddess Gylla and found her peace in the kingdom in the sky. He couldn't save his parents, but he could save her.

The queen swam out of the room, followed by a sneering Svanhild. Maren took her time getting to the door, her shoulders uncharacteristically sagging. She turned to Kaid as she floated in the doorway and something he had never seen from her glinted in her brown eyes, vanishing as quickly as it came. Desperation. The princess of the finfolk sucked in a deep breath, squared her shoulders and left without another word.

CHAPTER 23

Asta's patience grew thin when all three rescue fleets failed to return. It had been three days since Kaid's abduction. Three days of silence with no trace of him to be found. Three days of him at risk of being tortured, beaten, and the gods knew what else.

The blonde princess paced in front of her hearth, a wide-eyed Linnea sitting on the sofa next to Halsten, who buried his face in his palms.

"We need to send another fleet. We need to do something," Asta announced.

Linnea shook her head, not allowing her eyes to meet her cousin's. "Three ships of men have been sacrificed, Asta. Nearly one hundred sailors never to return home."

"And I will sacrifice one hundred more to find him!" Asta snapped, her voice raspy from lack of sleep.

Halsten ran his hands down his face. "Unless either of you know some magical sea creature who can rescue him for us, I can't think of another way."

She had stayed awake day and night watching the sea. Hoping to see a change in pattern, a creature lurking too close to shore, anything that would give her answers. But all that had come was a vicious storm, fat rain drops pelting the stone of the castle and lightning striking the ground as thunder boomed loud enough to rattle the windows.

Linnea stood up and made her way to the rack near the doors, lifting a cloak off a hook. "Maybe it's time you go see Thurs, cousin."

Dyri, the goofy canine, perked up at that. He had been going with Asta to visit the wild horse each time she went to the stables, the visits now becoming a part of their regular routine. Progress with the beast had been slow and grueling. The mare was wildfire but begrudgingly obeyed Asta's commands, never fully willing to please her new partner. Asta remained hopeful and determined that she and the horse would ride together someday.

Asta approached Linnea by the door and wrapped herself in a fur-lined cloak, gesturing for Linnea to put hers on as well. Halsten excused himself to his suite. The courtier had not been himself since Kaid's abduction.

Asta patted her thigh and Dyri sprang up, running to her side as they began their descent through the castle.

When they got to the stables, the energy within was charged. All of the horses were on edge because of the multi-day storm that had engulfed Orntali. Dyri shook the rain drops from his short coat and sauntered down the path in front of them, running ahead and sniffing various stalls along the way. When he got to the one tucked in the far back corner, he sat in front of the gate.

"Good boy," Asta said as she and her cousin approached the dog guarding the stall. Within was the dapple gray mare standing in the back corner, her ears pulled back as she stomped a hoof on the floor.

"Yeah, yeah. You hate me. Get in line," Asta threw a thumb over her shoulder, thinking about Maren's betrayal and the harsh words they had exchanged on the beach, "But you won't let anyone else touch you, and I can at least bridle you, so I'm your only option."

The stablehands had turned the mare out the day after Kaid's disappearance and she had refused to let anyone catch her and return her to her stall. Asta had been summoned to come down and escort the horse inside, which she had succeeded in, but not without the mare giving her a fight.

Asta grabbed a curry comb from the bucket hanging on the gate and stepped inside with the horse.

"Be careful," Linnea whispered.

Asta only nodded in response. Thurs didn't scare her, though she probably should. She was quite positive the horse's previous owner had probably released her on purpose after giving up on taming her. Either that, or Thurs had taken it upon herself to end her previous owner's life, which would not shock the princess one bit. Asta still couldn't track down any information on the crest that was on the horse's bridle and the horse seemed to have chosen her, so for the time-being, she would care for her.

The princess got to work on grooming the horse, picking her hooves, brushing her body, combing and braiding her white mane. The process took a little longer since her arm was still healing, but she was able to get it done regardless. As Asta started to relax, she watched Thurs's posture loosen. The anxiety never fully relinquished, but her ears were no longer turned fully backward and she had ceased her rebellious stomping.

Finally, once she finished up her horse's grooming, Asta felt calm enough to go speak with her father once more.

Asta strolled into her father's study composedly and found him where he always was, scribbling away at his desk.

"We need to send more fleets," she declared.

King Botmar sighed and pushed back in his seat, crossing his arms over his chest. "We cannot lose any more men to find them."

He rubbed at his eyes and Asta noticed how irritated they looked, the corners damp and puffy. Had her father been crying? She wouldn't be surprised if he had. Over the last three days, they had to unravel the last two decades of his life. The sea witch's curse on his memory had leaked to all parts of his brain, blackening much more than the existence of the finfolk.

"But he's still out there!" Asta gestured to the wall which held the shoreline on the other side. "A member of your nobility has been abducted by another kingdom and you just give up?"

"And how many of my loyal army members would you be willing to sacrifice to save him? Would you send Major Bohr into the depths of the ocean to find the lord?" Asta's father snarled, his tone laced with command only a king could conjure.

Major Bohr. Gyrial. How dare he use her best friend as an example. How dare he guilt her into changing her mind.

"Do not bring him into this. You know he would depart immediately if asked. They are here to protect our people, and Lord Kaidian is one of them!" Asta slammed a fist on her father's desk. "We must bring him back!"

"Your sister is out there, too, Asta. Believe me, I am sacrificing everything I can for their rescue. I cannot lose more good men. I cannot lose anyone else." Asta watched the king rub his temples as he mastered his breathing.

Something washed over her, dulling her frustration. He had lost a daughter during all this. She had lost a sister. Even if their relationship meant nothing to Maren now, Asta held onto the belief that their childhood together wasn't a complete lie. With that realization, she excused herself, knowing there was no arguing with the king. If he could sacrifice more men to find his daughter, he would. But that wasn't what a king would do. That wasn't what a princess should want to do, either.

Asta was exhausted, having hardly slept in days since Kaid had been taken, but she couldn't fight her weariness anymore. When she returned to her suite, she called Dyri to bed with her and fell asleep straight away, the large pup delighted to take a midday nap.

She had no knowledge of how long she had been asleep when she heard a whisper of her name.

Asta.

At first, it felt like a dream. A woman's voice as smooth as sea glass winding its way through her thoughts.

Asta.

The more she heard the woman call to her, the more awake she became.

"Asta."

The princess's eyes sprung open and she screamed when she saw a black-haired woman with golden eyes staring at her from the threshold of her bedroom door. Asta grabbed the dagger she kept under her pillow and pointed it toward the woman, who did not flinch at the sight of the blade.

"Who are you?" Asta snarled as she stood. Dyri was barking loudly beside her on the mattress, but backing up with each vocalization.

Cowardly clown.

The slender woman swept her long obsidian locks back behind her shoulder.

"Your presence has been requested for a meeting, Princess Asta," the woman said. "If you could please come with me, I will escort you."

Oh sure, walk off with the complete stranger after a man has been abducted by the finfolk queen and a Salendreon princess has been revealed as a spy for said finfolk. This sounds very safe.

Asta scoffed, somewhat toward the woman's vague request and somewhat toward the cowering Dyri, who had spooked himself by backing his rump into the headboard.

"Why would I go with you? How do I know this isn't a trap?"

The stunning woman let out a soft chuckle. Her beauty was the kind only seen in paintings, where women's features had been vastly over-exaggerated.

She stepped forward gesturing to the room in a sweep of her arms. "Do you think one would be so foolish as to enter their enemy's territory unarmed just to request an audience?"

She has a point, there. Besides, what more did Asta have to lose? She knew the finfolk would never let her live a peaceful life from here on out. She knew too much; had seen too much.

Asta turned back to her massive whimpering canine. "Stay, Dyri. Linnea will be here soon." She kissed his head and ran her thumb over his velvety ear before turning back to the woman. "Lead me."

The woman of indescribable beauty sauntered down the castle halls as if she had been within hundreds of times, which made Asta uneasy. None of the guards stopped her or questioned the female because, Asta now noticed, she was wearing a royal maid's uniform.

Asta was stupid for following this mysterious person. She knew that. But something deep down told her it was okay; that she was to be trusted.

They walked across the eastern terrace and stepped onto the beach. Asta silently followed behind the woman as they strode farther and farther away from the castle, quickly approaching the bend that held the cave she and Kaid had slept in the night everything had changed.

The woman's pace slowed and she approached a strange spotted lump lying in the sand. At first, Asta had thought it was a seal carcass, but when they got closer, she could see that it was a blanket of seal skin. She shuddered. Who would make a blanket of seal skin?

As the woman lifted the blanket and draped it over her shoulders, she looked back to Asta and gestured to a rock about twenty feet off the coast, "It was nice to meet you, Princess Asta. The queen will see you now."

Asta didn't know where to look between the woman silently walking into the water with a seal skin blanket draped over her or the fire-red-haired woman sitting atop a rock.

At first, Asta's heart skipped a beat when she thought the female was her sister, but when she observed the woman more closely, the similarities were scant. Her hair was a far more vibrant shade of red, like a cooked lobster shell, and her eyes were a shade Asta knew well—a turquoise as bright as the waves crashing around her. Kaid's eyes.

Asta watched as the obsidian-haired woman disappeared under the waves, no sign of her once she fully submerged herself. The princess's gaze bounced back to the woman on the rock once more and discovered the female's gentle smile.

She waved a hand, beckoning Asta closer, so she toed off her slippers and pulled up the skirts of her dress as she stepped into the water, the icy temperatures of the autumn ocean making her toes numb immediately.

From her new angle in the water, Asta could see the female's royal blue fin containing golden outlines of each scale that matched her gold crown made of coral and crystals. Her elongated torso was covered by a pearly seashell-shaped corset.

Asta went to take a step back, fear roiling through her from the memory of the last finned creature she met on these shores. As she leaned away from the woman, her back collided into something hard.

CHAPTER 24

Asta felt the breath of something casting a warm breeze atop her head. She let the dagger she had hidden up her sleeve slip down so the hilt was in her palm. Maybe this had been a bad choice.

She whirled toward whatever beast awaited her, ready for battle, but froze at the sight of the massive red dragon standing behind her.

Its large, scaled body glistened with remnants of sea water sliding down its hide. Where a painting would usually depict wings for a dragon held large pectoral fins instead, along with a powerful tail containing a fin at its rear. The beast's talons were so long that the arches peeked out of the waves, an observation that made Asta swallow loudly.

But the dragon made no effort to attack. It remained still as it stared down at her, as though it were an old friend coming for a visit.

She prayed no one would gaze out a castle window and have a heart attack upon seeing a dragon.

Asta turned back toward the finned female and found that an identical beast in all aspects except color swam behind the crowned woman, its olive green hide the perfect color to camouflage within seaweed.

The female smiled once again, nodding her head slightly as if to say *It's okay.*

"Who are you?" Asta tried to hide the waver in her voice.

The woman shook her head and laid a palm on her throat.

Asta barked at the woman. "What are these beasts? What do you want with me?"

Again, the woman shook her head, caressing her neck once more before pointing to her ears, which Asta now observed were delicately pointed at the helix.

It was as if fate had guided Asta to this moment, prepared her all her life for the skills she needed for whatever situation was unfolding before her. A puzzle piece in Asta's brain locked into place as she held her hands out in front of her and signed to the woman. "Can you understand this?"

The crowned female nodded.

She signed again. "Who are you?"

The woman signed back. "Queen Arielle. Leader of the Ventarin sirens and empress of the Northern Seas."

Asta couldn't stop her jaw from swinging open like a gasping fish out of water. This female, the one who bore the same eyes as Kaid, was the empress of their ocean. Queen Arielle's eyes glimmered at Asta's reaction, which reminded the princess to collect her composure once more.

Asta asked even though she knew the answer. "Are you Kaid's mother?"

The empress nodded, her deep pink lips forming a flat line. The two massive water beasts circled around them. Asta took a step forward with the intent of forming a little more distance between the eerie creatures and herself, but it only pushed her closer toward the queen, which also made her hesitant.

"Can you tell me where he is?" Asta signed.

Queen Arielle again nodded, and began signing hurriedly.

She told Asta the story of Kaid being sent into hiding, how she had been born deaf but with a beautiful voice and gave up her siren song in an agreement with Euphemia, Knud, and Gylla—the water goddess, god of love, and goddess of afterlife—in order to keep Kaid masked and protected. She hadn't realized that giving up the song meant giving up her voice altogether, until it was too late. Kaid was supposed to only return to the sea once the empress had found a way to put a stop to Queen Yrsa's assassination attempts, but he had touched the water before she was ready for him and broken his protection spell.

Asta covered her mouth with her hand. *She* had forced Kaid to touch the sea. *She* was the reason he had been abducted. If it wasn't for her silly little prank, Kaid would still be safe. Regret washed over her as quickly as the frigid waves washed over her bare legs.

Queen Arielle continued, ignoring Asta's reaction. She explained the finfolk queen's intentions, wanting to turn humans into their chattel once more. But the empress could not understand why they took her lost prince captive instead of killing him, could not understand what more they could want from him besides his death. The empress was not sure what the finfolk were planning, but she knew they were overfeeding to gain strength. They were also over-producing to create more spies and soldiers, just as Maren had been, but abandoning any offspring they didn't deem worthy of finfolk lineage. Nature had been attempting to balance the sudden overpopulation by creating more beings like Arielle—clean souls.

Asta rubbed her temples, needing a moment to process everything. Kaid was the lost prince of the sirens, taken by the rival finfolk who wished to restore chaos amongst humans. They must have been the reason for her missing villagers and rising orphan population. At least she had gotten some answers out of this, but still no solutions.

Asta's head was filled with so many questions but for some reason, the only question Asta could manage to sign was probably the least important at the moment. "What are these water beasts?" she gestured to the dragons.

The empress of the Northern Seas looked upon the circling reptiles. "They are water dragons, an extremely rare shifting ability that can be gifted to a siren from Absolon himself. Before this pair came to life, the last known water dragon had died about two centuries ago. I think, however, you may recognize these water dragons as a familiar set of twins you've befriended."

Asta stared into the purple eyes of the dragons patrolling them. The green one playfully dipped its fins into the water as it passed, while the red one kept an eye on the royals between them and the other on the surrounding waters. They were Tova and Liva.

"Why have they been in the castle for years?" Asta asked.

Arielle grinned. "We discovered a tidbit of information implying that an ancient siren artifact was within the Orntali castle, and the twins accepted the assignment to locate the item. They have been searching to obtain the relic for years."

It was all too much for Asta. Until a few days ago, these creatures had been folklore. A storybook of myths passed down through generations. Something imaginary that she had listened to Niklas drone on about time after time. But, no—they were real. And now a subspecies of them threatened the people of her kingdom.

Once more, Asta turned her gaze to the empress who was basking on a rock. Queen Arielle gave her first full-toothed smile, and Asta's stomach turned at the sight of her elongated, disturbingly sharp fangs.

The blonde princess paced in the water, the splashing waves and screech-ing gulls fading as she was deep in thought. She could rally the royal army, have them guard the border. Maybe they could stop the slaughter of her villagers.

That wouldn't work. Not against the dizzying screech of the fin-folk. Not against the preternatural strength of them. Not against the half-breeds who had the ability to come on land and drag the men right into the water, like Maren could. The odds were not in the humans' favor. Not while the finfolk were so strong. Not while they had leaders like Maren and soldiers like Svanhild.

The memories of growing up with Maren flooded Asta's mind. The games of hide-and-seek they played in the castle. The hidden laughter during formal dinners. The siren game they used to play in the waves. It had all been a lie, and it gutted Asta. She had thought they were growing apart these last few years because of their differences as they matured, not because Maren was living a double life. It made sense now, why everything had changed when Svanhild was hired as her sister's lady-in-waiting. She was one of her royal subjects, her finfolk heritage secretly taking precedence over her human lineage. Rage roiled through Asta. She hated her sister, and she would tell her as much when she found Kaid.

"How do I find him?" Asta signed to the empress. She would send out more rescue fleets, and she would join their ranks if she had to.

Queen Arielle's hand motions were sharp—determined—as she answered Asta's question. "He is being held in the finfolk kingdom, Ryktarva. Your sister and her courtiers will not be leaving the safety of their fortress willingly any time soon, now that they have what they want. I offer you my sea dragons, as well as my best soldiers, to accompany you.

I cannot go there myself. I cannot leave my people unprotected." The empress patted a trident tattoo covering her right hand, the prongs inked up her middle fingers. "I must remain in Naltania to guard them from the continuous attacks."

Asta blew out a frustrated breath, one obvious problem looming over her. "In case you haven't noticed, I'm human. I can't go to Ryktarva unless I'm floating atop it on a ship."

"Would you like to be a siren, Princess Asta?" the empress asked.

Asta stilled, unsure if she read her signing correctly. Could she do that? Could she simply become a siren?

Asta cocked her head to the side and noticed how Tova and Liva seemed to freeze in place. "How?"

Queen Arielle's tail slapped the water and the sea dragons continued their patrol. "Sirens have the ability to turn humans, a scarcely used power. No other merspecies holds such a gift. It is as simple as you enduring my venom when I release it from my fangs into your bloodstream. There is a risk, however. Some humans cannot handle the turn and do not survive it. Only those who truly want it can complete the change. It's the magic's way of maintaining balance, creating a failsafe so sirens cannot simply turn any human they encounter."

Take the empress's venom into her bloodstream and survive. That was the only way. Asta's mind whirled. She needed to be sure she wanted this.

"Why would someone *not* want to become a siren?" Asta asked.

The empress looked down toward the waves in front of her and ran her fingers through it, the water responding to her touch and climbing up her arm like ivy. "The bloodlust. It can be irresistible, even more so for newborn and newly turned sirens. We require blood to survive, human being our favorite because of our finfolk heritage. But we can survive so long as we drink any blood, and I have been working diligently during my reign to fully transition my people to fish or land-dwelling prey. We do not need to kill in order to feed, only drink enough to sustain, but sometimes the craving takes over and causes a complete drainage of the donor. That is why I abolished human feedings."

Great, another piece to add to the list. Make sure she doesn't eat her family or friends once she's turned. Well, at least Asta didn't have to worry about accidentally killing Tova and Liva, since they were already sirens. That comforted her. Sort of.

Queen Arielle tried to offer assuaging words. "I turned my bonded, Aerik, and helped him through the transition. He has never drank an ounce of human blood and he's been a siren for nearly ninety years. I can help you, too."

Asta knew there were probably different ways to rescue Kaid. She knew there were likely other people more trained to sneak into enemy territory and retrieve him. But she wanted to be there, wanted to bring him back. So she would do this, *could* do this, to save Kaid.

"Do it. Turn me."

CHAPTER 25

Asta paced her room, dropping random bits of clothing into her small pack. Queen Arielle agreed to meet her back on the shore in one day's time so she could get her affairs in order before making the change. But that day was almost up, and soon, Asta would be a siren.

It was not lost on her how insanely mad this all was. She'd had Linnea—much to her objection—pinch her several times throughout the day to ensure she hadn't dreamt the entire thing.

Gyrial slid through the door of her suite, his expression grim. "Are you sure you want to do this?"

Asta had told her best friend everything. Every last detail her addled brain could churn up. He had taken in the news with a surprising calm, that preternatural stillness he possessed taking over as he listened. She couldn't tell if Gyrial's unbothered reaction was his own personal form of shock, but he was still here, ready to help her.

The princess nodded. "Thank you for always being here, for always believing in me. I can never repay you for teaching me what it means to have someone truly care about you. Before I go, I have one more favor to ask of you. I need you to watch over my father. Make sure that bitch of a finfolk queen doesn't come for him. And if Maren dares to return…"

"I will do what needs to be done," he said sternly.

Asta closed her eyes and sucked in many deep breaths. She cracked her knuckles while she crossed her bedroom. When she got to her vanity, she stared at her reflection judgingly. She would have a second form soon, this one only being half of her existence. Her torso would become longer, her ears would bear a delicate point, and her legs would be replaced by a fin.

This is crazy. You can't do this.

No, she couldn't have those thoughts. She had to be sure she wanted to turn. She needed to survive the change for Kaid.

Asta emerged from her bedroom to find Gyrial lazily lounging on the sofa with Dyri.

Her tone was sharper than she intended as she said, "How are you so okay with all of this madness? How are you not questioning your sanity as I am?"

His gilded eyes swept over her before turning back to the roaring fire in front of him. "I've always sensed the presence of the mythical creatures in and around the castle, I just never truly knew what exactly I detected, or that there were so many. And I never expected one of them to be the heir to the savage finfolk line."

"What exactly do you mean by 'detected?'" Asta sat in the chair opposite Gyrial and folded her shaking hands in her lap.

"I don't know if you're ready for more surprises right now," Gyrial said.

Her eyes narrowed and Dyri perked his head up in curiosity, glancing at his mother. "I think I can decide when and if I am ready for something. Plus, I'm not sure I could feel any more surprised at this point."

Gyrial held his hands up in surrender. Sighing, he answered, "I am not human, Asta."

Asta stilled, her blood running cold. If he wasn't human, what was he? Siren? Finfolk? She stood corrected; she was shocked. Asta felt lightheaded. Just a few months ago, she had been searching for her next great fantasy novel to escape into, and now she was living on the pages.

Gyrial leaned forward to press his palm to Asta's knee but she turned out of his reach. He let out a long sigh before speaking again. "I am fae."

Fine, maybe Asta didn't exactly need *that* news at the moment. She pinched the bridge of her nose and closed her eyes. "Prove it," Asta urged. It would be poor timing for Gyrial to play a joke on her but she held out hope that he was poking fun.

Gyrial brushed his braids back behind his ears—which he always kept hidden by his hair—to reveal the delicately pointed tips. Before Asta could react, he opened his mouth and a second set of canine teeth snapped down from his gums, the new ones much sharper and larger than the others.

As she gaped at him, Gyrial decided to finalize his proof by extending a hand toward a flower bud that sat in a vase on Asta's coffee table. She watched with wide eyes as the flower bloomed to full maturity, the pink petals vibrant against the dimly lit room.

Asta should have had more of a reaction to Gyrial's big reveal, but she was so tired.

Tired of the secrets. Tired of the lies. Tired of the curses and spells and creatures. The entire world as she knew it was an illusion.

She reasoned with herself. If she could handle the existence of sirens and finfolk, what was one more mythical creature added to the list?

Gyrial took Asta's hand in his as he whispered, "I'm only going to ask one more time. Are you sure you want to be turned?"

Yes. No. Someone decide for me.

Asta remained silent while her best friend's gentle touch still lingered, his thumb smoothing over the back of her hand. She had to want it. She had to make sure that her mind was made up when the siren venom entered her bloodstream or else, death. But of course she wanted it. She wanted to save Kaid. She wanted to avenge her father. She wanted to confront Maren. But did she want it for herself?

Maren. Her sister. The one she had grown beside all these years, laughed with, played with. Not only a sister, but a best friend in their younger years. Was that humanity still in there? Would Maren's heart find weakness when it came to her own sister? No matter the answer, Asta needed to know. She needed to know if her sister was well and truly lost to her.

The blonde princess sharply nodded her head once. "I'm sure that I need to be turned in order to do what I need to do."

Asta walked over to her desk and pulled out a rolled piece of paper, handing it to Gyrial.

He took the paper gingerly, his golden gaze never breaking eye contact with Asta's. "What's this?"

"For my father. I need him to read it, just in case..."

In case she doesn't live through the turn. In case she does live, but death finds her another way once she begins searching for Kaid in the merciless Ventarin Sea.

Asta had written the letter to her father the night before, knowing she needed to get the words out before she left. She needed to tell him how sorry she was for arguing with him about sending out more rescue fleets. How sorry she was that she blamed him for her mother's final grueling days. How sorry she was that she had never built the relationship they were meant to have, for not having more time.

"I'll bring it to him." Gyrial tucked the rolled paper into his pocket and Asta pulled him into a tight hug.

"Make sure Dyri is played with. And Thurs needs grooming. And Linnea... make sure she eats." Asta listed her top priorities as if they weren't emotional burdens.

Gyrial didn't balk, only held Asta tighter to him. He kissed the top of her head. "Of course, Asta. Anything for you."

Asta's pack was heavier than expected for only containing a few articles of clothing and her mother's family signet ring. She only brought the Blomvin ring to remind her of home, her mission, and—optimistically—her humanity in case of bloodlust frenzy.

She and Gyrial stalked toward the water's edge hand-in-hand as rain beat down on them in heavy drops, instantly soaking through their clothes. The two massive water dragons emerged from the crashing waves and between them, a head of bright red hair bobbed in the water. Asta looked to Gyrial and kissed his cheek lightly, but his palms rested on her face as he placed his lips to hers.

For the first time, something fluttered in Asta's chest at his touch. But was it drawn out by a hard goodbye, or did it mean more? She pulled away and stared into his golden eyes, only to find them welling with tears that disappeared into the rain.

With a nod, she turned and walked toward the sea. Queen Arielle swam closer, matching each step Asta took, until they were hardly ten feet from each other.

Asta had to be sure. She had to be at peace with leaving all this behind—possibly forever. Whether Gyrial had kissed her out of love, out of loss, out of a need to say goodbye, she didn't have time to wonder. She needed to be willing to let it go no matter his reasoning.

Water lapped against the toe of Asta's boot, the predictability of the waves being the only constant in her life right now. The ocean never stopped, never relented. It was always a force with no weakness. Cruel and beautiful.

"I'm ready," Asta signed to the empress of the Northern Seas.

The corners of Queen Arielle's lips tilted upward. "Then come forward, and we will begin."

Without allowing herself a second thought, Asta stepped into the water and pushed through the waves until she was a few feet from the empress. She turned and granted herself one last look back.

Through the sheets of rain, she could see Gyrial standing on the beach, one hand on his sword hilt and the other pressed against his chest—a gesture of his promise to protect what she left behind. Her cousin, her beloved animals, her father, him. Her kingdom.

The castle behind her best friend was shining through the constant thunderstorms that had been cursing their land since before Kaid's capture. The stones were illuminated with hope, the siren statues grinning wider than ever before.

Maybe it was her imagination showing her such things, but Asta took in the sight and let it fill her with warmth and assurance that she was making the right choice.

Asta nodded to Gyrial and placed her hand over her own heart to return his gesture. After sucking in a deep breath, she stared into the deep turquoise eyes of the female before her.

"The bite will be agonizing, and then the searing venom will scorch its way into your heart. But everyone's reaction is different after that, so this is the only warning I can give you, Princess Asta."

Queen Arielle's hand reached out, beckoning Asta to hold out her arm.

The siren queen's grip was firm but not unfriendly, her fingers cold to the touch, which caused the skin on Asta's arm to pebble.

The empress opened her mouth and revealed her sharp fangs, two mini daggers that could end a life as fast as a full-sized weapon. Asta made the wrong choice of observing the fangs too closely and saw the silver venom start to drip from the points. The sight made her stomach churn, wanting to step back in retreat, but it was too late.

The fangs plunged into Asta's wrist before she could object. At first, she only felt the pain from the bite itself. She jostled against the discomfort, but the empress grabbed her shoulder and held Asta still.

When the pain of the bite subsided, the venom began its slow ascent to her heart. The siren queen had certainly down-played the sensation by saying it was a sting.

A fierce burn swept over Asta's body like someone had set it ablaze from within, and the wildfire would burn until she was nothing. There was a loud ringing in her ears, but through it she could hear two male voices shouting. But her vision turned white, the otherworldly flame within blinding her.

Asta couldn't see or hear properly. It felt like she had been turning for days, maybe even years. The pain was so agonizing that she couldn't feel her own body anymore. She could only focus on the obscured voices, so faint that they seemed to be in another dimension.

Until the world went quiet and the white in her vision turned to black.

CHAPTER 26

Asta's head was pounding like someone had slammed a stone into it, but she managed to open her eyes. Her vision adjusted to the dimly-lit room as she took in the bright orange walls surrounding her. Her head was resting on a spongy pillow and her hair kept floating up into her line of vision.

Floating?

Asta sat up quickly in a plush bed filled with sponge pillows, topped with a very heavy red comforter. Her movements were easy and sharp, but she concluded she must be underwater by the movement of her hair and the fabrics of the bed.

Go to the surface. Everyone will love your song. Sing to them.

Her head was squeezed in an invisible grip so tightly she felt like it would pop, but Asta pulled back the blankets to emerge from the bed and look around the room.

Call them to you, call them home to the siren kingdom.

The beastly thoughts were flooding Asta's mind as she continued taking in her surroundings. There was a tight ball in her chest, but it was much different from the one she had become accustomed to with her rituals.

*Show them the beauty of the depths. Allow them the honor
of seeing what humans cannot.*

A flash of purple caught Asta's attention and she dragged her gaze to her fin—not her legs—her large, deep purple fin. She couldn't help but smile as it moved where she willed it to.

*They want to play. Let them join your games. Everything
you want is at the surface, in their veins.*

Well, that was enough for Asta to feel a chill skitter down her spine.

As Asta reached up to steady herself on the headboard, she noticed the scabbed over bite mark from where Queen Arielle had turned her. She ran a thumb over the mark, surprised that it was almost completely healed. Now that she thought about it, her entire arm was healed of the injuries she'd had from her previous fight with Maren and Svanhild. Had she been sleeping for that long?

As the princess was about to try her first swim again, Queen Arielle entered the room. Her royal blue and gold fin moved gently as she made her way to the edge of the bed and sat.

"How are you feeling?" the empress signed.

A spotted seal came floating in through the doorway and laid on the bed next to Queen Arielle.

Asta rubbed her head then answered, "My head aches, but it is bearable. How long have I been sleeping?"

"Just a day," the siren queen signed, then rested a hand on the seal in front of her.

Asta looked down at her scabbed bite wound again, her brows furrowing and a corner of her mouth turning up. "How am I nearly healed?"

Queen Arielle smiled. "Accelerated healing. Now that you're a siren, you'll find that healing comes faster in water. You're also stronger, so please take care when touching breakables in my castle until you adjust."

Asta laughed, until the realization that she was in Naltania—the siren kingdom—overtook her.

"The headache is from your bloodlust. All newly turned sirens experience it. We need you to feed before we can continue."

The blonde princess started. She knew this was part of becoming a siren, but she hadn't actually thought through her need to feed. It wasn't going to be like eating food or drinking wine. This was entirely different and the thought made Asta's stomach turn.

> *They want to give you their life. They want you to feast on*
> *them. Sing to them and they will tell you as such.*

The empress continued, "That is why Annika is here. We're in agreement with the selkie population that we may feed from them so long as we offer them protection from the finfolk." She smiled at the golden-eyed seal lying across the blankets. "Many vow to work as messengers to help repay the favor, like Annika does for me. Now, whenever you're ready, your royal highness."

Asta knew she shouldn't be surprised that selkies were real, but she had really hoped that her growing list of not-so-mythical creatures had ended with Gyrial's fae reveal. She stared deeply into the seal's eyes and saw a familiar gold within. Not Gyrial's gold, but the gold from the woman who had brought her to meet Queen Arielle for the first time. The woman she had watched wrap herself in a seal's skin before walking straight into the ocean and disappearing. She didn't quite understand the magic behind selkie transformations, but her headache was too strong to care. She needed blood before she burst.

> *There is a ship just above, filled with men and women. Their pulses are bounding, blood warm from a hard day's work. Drink, siren. Drink.*

Before she even realized what she was doing, Asta lunged forward and bit into the seal's side. It gave a quick huff of discomfort but settled soon after. The warm blood coated Asta's mouth and, to her shock, was not revolting. The more she drank, the more she seemed to crave the metallic taste as it smoothly ran down her throat.

Something sharp dug into Asta's temples and forehead, breaking her concentration on her feeding. She pulled her mouth away from the seal to find Queen Arielle gripping her head with her sharp siren nails. The seal swam off the bed and through the door, a faint trail of blood dancing through the water but dissipating quickly.

The empress released her grip. "The first few feeds are the hardest. You must always have someone who can stop you until you know you can control yourself."

Shame roiled over Asta. Had she been about to kill Annika if Queen Arielle hadn't been here? Would she have enjoyed it? Maybe turning wasn't such a good idea, if all she would be able to think about was feeding. She needed to focus on why she had come here in the first place—to save Kaid.

"So, I sneak in and find the royal suites. And you think Kaid is there? It can't be that simple," Asta signed, her brows furrowing.

Queen Arielle's mouth formed a flat line, avoiding Asta's stare. "He is likely chained in iron, which is the difficult part. If he isn't chained, he can easily use his royal magic to escape. But since he hasn't, I can only assume they have him restrained with that blasted metal."

"I'll break the chain. I'll snap the hinge and he can get us out from there."

The empress shook her head and sighed. "It's not that simple. Once iron is placed on a magical being, it can only be removed with a key, all of which haven't been seen in centuries. We've never found another way to break the iron since magic courses through our veins and the metal naturally deflects it. You can likely free him from whatever he's held down by, but the iron cuff will be stuck on him, rendering his magic useless."

Magic was stupid and had too many rules. But Asta would figure all of this out to get Kaid back. Did Kaid even know he had magic?

Every time she looked at the empress, she saw Kaid's eyes staring back at her. It helped her stay grounded and fight off the longing need to drag a human to the deepest depths of the ocean and turn them into her personal puppet. Though, for some reason, that actually sounded fun.

Asta shuddered. "I'll get him back."

The violet-finned princess pushed into an upright position and threw the strap of her bag over her head so it crossed her torso. She reached in and dug out her mother's signet ring, placing it on her forefinger. If she died while trying to save Kaid, she would not go down without a piece of Salendron on her.

Asta fastened her sword sheath at her hip and swam past the empress, stopping to gently squeeze her fingers before she exited by tapping the threshold. Annika, who was waiting in the hall, guided her through the castle and directly out the front gates. The seal continued swimming forward, but Asta turned to fully observe the kingdom of Naltania.

The sun shining through the reflective surface above illuminated the opalescent walls of the castle, the bright colors reflecting off the coral reefs surrounding the structure. Fish, seals, crustaceans, and other sea animals swam carefree around the fortress, an emblem of Queen Arielle's accomplishment of imbuing humanity into the sirens.

When Asta turned back toward Annika, she was swimming alongside an enormous, green sea dragon, followed by two sirens completely covered in blades of various shapes and sizes.

"Are you my rescue crew?" Asta asked, her gaze catching on the sea dragon in curiosity of which twin this one was, though she suspected it to be Tova based on its playful nature.

The male siren with a deep orange fin and a large scar cutting diagonally through his face bowed his head, his brown hair lagging behind his movements. "We're at your service, land princess. My name is Soren and this is Revna." He gestured to the pastel blue-haired female siren at his side and she stared Asta down with her icy gaze. "We're in the empress's highest ranks and swear our blades to you for this journey."

Asta observed the warriors and took in their various scars. "Have you been to Ryktarva before?" she asked.

Revna scoffed. "Of course we have. We wouldn't be accompanying you if we didn't know where we were going. Do you land princesses have working brain cells or do you just hire other humans to think for you instead?"

Soren threw a hand in front of Revna, pushing her back. "Please excuse her. We haven't had a newcomer in quite some time," he turned and spoke through gritted teeth while glaring at Revna, "especially one of such importance. Revna would do well to remember her place."

"Oh, it's no problem," Asta waved a hand and her elongated fingers still shocked her as they passed, "I don't expect respect nor trust simply from having a title. But I will earn it."

The group suddenly parted as a flash of emerald and white darted behind the crew and stopped next to Asta. A large, emerald horse was beside her with a fin in place of its tail. The mare swished the fin, causing a small current to jostle Asta's hair. She looked closely into the horse's gaze and her eyes widened.

"Thurs?" Asta reached out and ran a hand over the golden bridle containing the conch crest.

Soren swam forward, a wicked grin on his face. "You didn't know?"

Thurs nudged Asta with her nose. "Know what?"

"'Thurs,' as you call her, is the alpha of the northern kelpies," the scarred siren gestured to the horse. "Her entire herd has been at your command since you captured her. We even heard about it here in Naltania. The kelpies allegiance is to you. They haven't been tamed in centuries."

A mass of emerald green emerged from the clouded waters around them, nearly one hundred kelpies, from Asta's quick count, and they all answered to her.

Asta grabbed Thurs's bridle and ran her thumb over the crest on the golden coin. She grinned as she announced, "Then I guess we know how we're traveling to Ryktarva."

Annika swam in circles around the group, clearly eager to get moving. Revna pulled her light blue hair back into a tight knot, the strands of hair matching the color of her fin. But her nearly white eyes bore into Asta, which made her heart skip a beat.

No, Asta wasn't a trained soldier. She couldn't make someone's stomach turn with one glare like this siren warrior could. But Asta could fight, and she was damn good at it. She already held off Maren and Svanhild by herself. Surely, with this group, she could free Kaid.

"Let's bring the lost prince home."

PART 2

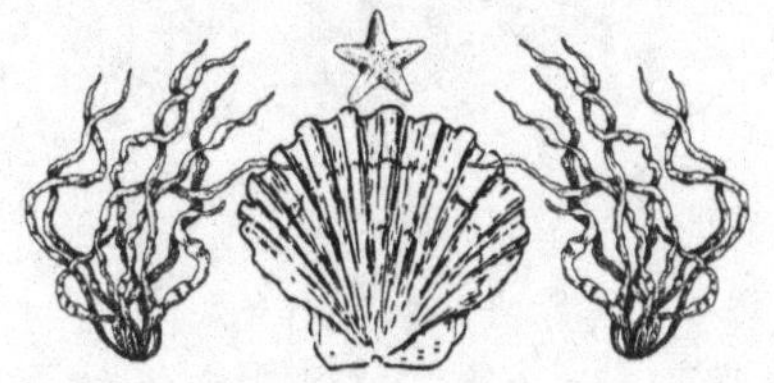

CHAPTER 27

Linnea felt the air completely depart her lungs as she watched Asta crumple into the ocean, landing in the arms of a finned female with flaming red hair. She sprinted—something Linnea hadn't done in years—toward her cousin who was being pulled under the currents, but she was too far.

Linnea's perpetually frail body was no match for the storm winds. She had wasted precious moments frozen in fear on the terrace and it had cost her the minutes she needed to reach the shoreline in time.

Why did her cousin always have to play the hero? Asta insisted on saving everyone, even if they didn't deserve it. But Linnea knew that the sacrifice her cousin had made was not for one person. No, Asta had done this for their nation; for her kingdom. And though Linnea could not fault her for that, she still felt a pang of betrayal at the sacrifice.

Linnea's weak body only ran so far until she was exhausted and had to slow to a brisk walk. She heard heavy steps behind her and turned to see Halsten trudging through the wet sand at a jog. His long, charcoal hair was plastered to his high cheekbones and if Linnea wasn't so enraged, her legs may have turned weak at the sight of him.

Linnea turned back to the sea to find that her cousin was gone, completely swallowed by the deep water, and she fell to her knees.

"No!" she bellowed. Her breaths came quickly and she felt like there wasn't enough air in the world. Not without Asta.

Year after year, her cousin had breathed life back into her slowly and that was something she could never manage to repay. Now, she may never get the chance to try.

The warmth of a hand pressed itself to Linnea's back, seeping through the soaked fabric of her dress. "Breathe, Linnea. You have to breathe," Halsten begged, his voice straining to be heard over the deafening downpour. "In... and out, *slowly*." Linnea sucked in a deep breath and let it out steadily. "That's it. Again," he pressed.

After a few more breaths, the tightness in Linnea's chest began to ease. Halsten kneeled in the sand in front of her, grabbing her wrists to pull her hands away from her face. She stared into his soft brown eyes and blinked away her tears that camouflaged into the rain. But Halsten knew the tears were there.

"Asta wouldn't want to see you like this, right?" Halsten asked.

Linnea shook her head.

He gave her a gentle smile and ran his thumbs over her stark white scars on her wrists. "What would Asta want you to do?"

She looked around, taking in her surroundings. To one side, the crashing sea. To the other, the castle—a beacon in the storm. Her voice shook as she murmured, "Stand up."

Halsten leaned in closer to Linnea, his face hardly a few inches from hers. "You're going to have to say that louder, Little Flame. I couldn't quite hear you."

Little Flame. The strange name Halsten had been calling her since his first few days arriving in Orntali. Though she never understood the meaning, she presumed it was due to her light auburn hair. Linnea was thankful for the horrid weather because it hid her now hot, rosy cheeks. She sucked in a deep breath and repeated herself a little louder. "Stand up."

Halsten let go of her wrists and stood to his full height, extending a hand toward her in support. "One more time, for me. What would Asta want you to do?" he shouted.

Normally shouting made Linnea flinch and revert to her old self. Obedient. Quiet. Unremarkable in every way. But something about Halsten's encouragement sparked a light in her. A little flame.

Linnea reached out and firmly gripped Halsten's hand. Through the rain, the worry, and the defeat, she shouted, "Stand up!"

As the words escaped her mouth, Halsten heaved her up to her feet with one swift tug of his arm and caught her hip to stabilize her. He pointed at her with a stern finger. "You always stand up, Linnea. From here on out. It's okay to fall, but you need to get back up. We're in some serious shit and Asta is going to need you."

Linnea nodded, understanding that he wasn't scolding her. This certainly wasn't the proper way to speak to women but Halsten was accustomed to pep-talking his male best friend, not a feeble woman with no confidence. However, for some strange reason, it worked for her.

The pair turned toward Gyrial who was still standing at the edge of the water, but there was another figure with him now. An argument had clearly erupted based on the tense postures and waving arms. As she approached the situation with Halsten, Linnea recognized Niklas.

"How could you let her go?! Oh, Queen Else is probably seething from up above!" Niklas shouted as he waved a hand toward the sky. "A siren? You let her change into a siren!"

"You know damn well that no one was going to stop her, Niklas," Gyrial answered in a booming voice that cut through the storm effortlessly, "and if I couldn't stop her, the least I could do was be here while it happened to make sure she was okay."

Niklas pressed his palms to the sides of his head and squeezed his eyes shut as he paced along the murky shoreline.

"Queen Else? As in Asta's mother?" Halsten asked, startling the arguing pair who hadn't noticed their approach.

Niklas's chest heaved in a deep breath. "She knew about all of this. She knew and kept it to herself. And I can guarantee you that the last thing she wanted was for her daughter to be involved in this never ending war." The young courtier looked pale and unsteady on his feet. "*Ooooh* this isn't good. Not good at all." He turned away from everyone and began mumbling to himself. Linnea could only pick out key words like "doom" and "chaos."

Linnea wrapped a hand around Niklas's bicep and gently turned him toward her. "How is it you know? You weren't even a year old when Queen Else passed away."

Niklas pushed his glasses up to the bridge of his nose. "Journals. She kept meticulous journals recording any information she discovered about the merspecies and their lives. I found them in the castle archives, tossed aside in a box as if they were trash. I could tell they were important, however, due to their impeccable condition. They are quite informative. Riveting really. Her recording style is something to be envied by—"

Gyrial held up a hand to stop the courtier from rambling. His Spellid mountain accent was strong as he spoke. "I do not care about *how* she took her notes, Niklas. I care about what they say. Tell me anything that can help bring Asta home safely. Anything to end this war for good."

Niklas gave a quick nod. "Of course, let me think. There is the lost trident, but no one has seen that for centuries. Rumored to be last seen in a nondescript fae territory somewhere north, but there is no solid proof. Well, erm, there isn't really solid proof of any of this, I suppose." He pressed his index finger to his chin. "And there's a side note that the queen scribbled in a margin. I'm not sure what it truly means but I don't think you," Niklas gestured to Linnea, "will like it."

Linnea's heartbeat skittered. She had nothing to do with sirens, or finfolk, or any other mythical being out there. If she had any magical powers hiding within her, surely they would have surfaced during years of abuse, triggering some sort of self preservation against her mother.

Halsten placed a gentle hand on Linnea's lower back and asked the question she couldn't voice. "What won't she like?"

"We have to go to Queen Else's old manor. We have to go to your mother's home, Linnea." Niklas wrung his hands, an apologetic look sliding over his face.

Linnea's blood ran cold. She hadn't returned to her mother's manor since her uncle Botmar rescued her years ago and she planned on never returning as long as she lived. Her hands began shaking and she soothed herself by rubbing the smooth scar on one of her wrists. It reminded her that she was free of the shackles she had worn time and time again, both physical and emotional.

Am I strong enough to see her again? To see the rooms I'd been beaten and starved in? I can't, I can't, I can't.

But if she didn't return to her old home, what would happen to her cousin? A vision of Asta wearing chains on her wrists flashed in Linnea's mind and she felt her body begin to heat back up. Her cousin could be in danger even as she stood on the beach contemplating. She would not allow it. She would do anything to prevent her cousin from enduring torture similar to that she had experienced herself.

Linnea stood tall as she yelled through the deluge of rain. "When do we leave?"

CHAPTER 28

Annika swam around the band of warriors, which Asta learned was her usual signal for "we should rest here," so the princess dropped her pack from her shoulders, watching it drift to the seafloor beside her. She still wasn't accustomed to the lag of being underwater, which was why she practiced her swordwork every night that they rested. She needed to be ready when her team finally reached Ryktarva to save Kaid. It would have been easier if she'd had the twins with her, but Asta was glad that Liva chose to return to Orntali to continue gathering intel instead. At least her family would have one more warrior to protect them.

"Yeah, yeah," Revna drawled. "We're settling down, pup." She waved a lazy hand toward Annika, who was still frantically zooming circles around the group.

Asta ran through her exercises while Soren sharpened a particularly jagged looking dagger with a rock. "Practice up, Princess," he said. "We'll be there tomorrow."

She froze mid-swing, her arms locking up in a way she had never experienced before. This was what she had always prepared for, but it still felt surreal that she was in this situation.

They had been traveling for a few days now, which Asta was grateful for since it gave them time to learn how to work in unison in the most basic ways so they stood some chance of survival. Asta had learned that Annika was best as a scout with her speed and ability to blend in with other sea animals. Thurs and the other kelpies had terrifyingly long fangs that they, luckily, kept concealed unless they were eating or fighting. Soren had muscle for stronger opponents, but tended to leave his back open, which Asta took a mental note to keep watch of during a fight. Tova—who Asta was still having trouble believing was a massive green sea dragon—seemed to enjoy rounding up her victims before attacking, like a pack of wolves with a flock of sheep.

Somehow during sparring practices, Asta, Soren, and Revna always ended up back-to-back as Tova circled them like a predator herding prey. And lastly, there was Revna. Asta could find no weaknesses with the icy warrior, only pure ferocity. She still got a shiver down her spine whenever she witnessed Revna wield a blade, so hopefully their enemies would do the same.

Humans are above, Princess. Feed. Feed!

Asta still fought the impulse to drink human blood hourly, having complete faith in Queen Arielle's promise that it would weaken over time. The fish that they had been eating on the journey had suppressed the urge enough to be tolerable, but it wasn't sustainable forever. Asta would need to feed from *something* soon.

Thurs glided over to Asta, stomping her hooves in the sand a few times and forming a hollow for Asta to lay in like she did every night.

Asta laid in the soft sand, resting her head against Thurs, and drifted off to sleep one last time before they rescued Kaid.

"So, that's not ominous at all," Asta quipped as she stared at the black, spiky castle. The stone looked like it was made of igneous rock, which would make sense based on the red glowing pit positioned beside the fortress. If Asta weren't underwater, her palms would definitely be sweaty.

She tapped the stone in front of her multiple times, the tightening in her chest beginning to unfurl. Thurs chuffed and nudged Asta's hair, the kelpie already attuned to when Asta needed comforting.

Soren laughed. "Finfolk are a little gaudy, if you ask me. Couldn't be more of an opposite species if we tried."

Annika swam by, lifting her right fin twice.

"Coast is clear," Revna barked. "Move out."

What happened next was a blur for Asta. She waited with Thurs and Soren as Revna took out the guards near the door. Tova waited behind the hill surrounding the castle, the dragon sure to give their presence away if she entered too soon. Annika was instructed to keep watch and if they didn't return to her before nightfall, she was to return to Naltania and alert Queen Arielle of their capture.

Revna took the guards out with ease using her long sword. Within seconds, three finfolk were limp and being dragged to the side of the entryway by the ruthless siren.

Could Asta do this? She had only killed once, and it unleashed something within that she never wanted to surface in the first place. But just as she had killed to save her friends the first time, she would do it again if need be to save Kaid or any member of the rescue team. She hoped it wouldn't come down to that again.

Soren nodded to Asta, his deep scar cutting through his face aglow from the lava pit not far from them. She wondered how he earned that scar, but that would be a story for another time. She knew to trust him, because whatever he had gone up against in the past, he had won.

It was time.

CHAPTER 29

Asta, Soren, and the kelpies rushed into the castle after Revna, where she was already in combat with multiple finfolk at once. Soren pulled his sword out in time to block a spear careening directly toward Asta's chest. Thurs and her fellow kelpies immediately began using their sharp fangs to rip finfolk flesh apart, latching onto anything that moved around them. Asta used her sword to block a finfolk wielding a jagged, dark blade as she backed up to Soren, remembering he always left his behind open.

Asta leaned into the numbness she felt taking over her, thankful for the reprieve. Back-to-back, she and Soren were a tornado of blades, cutting down anyone and anything that attempted to infiltrate their circle. A quick glance at Revna told Asta she was doing the same, just on her own without help from a partner. *Showoff.*

As they were gaining the upper hand, which was an amazing feat considering they were only three warriors and a herd of kelpies against an entire castle of finfolk, a door at the top of the grand staircase burst open and a massive horde of finfolk poured in.

"There are too many of them!" Revna shouted. If *she* was saying that, then they were absolutely fucked. Asta remained collected, not batting an eye at the onslaught. If this was how she died, this was how she died. At least she would go doing the one thing that made her feel free.

The moment that Asta accepted her fate, a loud crashing sound erupted behind her and before she could process what had happened, an enormous sea dragon had at least twenty finfolk herded. Tova's movements were swift, each strike and recoil a blur, and all that was left was a pile of finfolk bodies, their putrid black blood floating in the current.

"About damn time you showed up!" Soren bellowed as he shoved a finfolk female back using his sword against hers. "Bloody dragons, always doing things their way."

Tova's head jerked toward Soren, her maw stained with black blood as she hissed in his direction.

"Princess, take your alpha and go! Quickly, while they are distracted!" Revna shouted and Soren nodded in agreement.

Revna smoothly swapped with Asta, guarding Soren's back as if it were her own. Asta had thought her and Soren made a great team, but it was nothing compared to watching Soren and Revna work together in tandem. It was like a dance, where you had to have a partner you trusted with your life to not drop you in the dangerous lift. Except this was much deadlier than dance. This was war.

Asta swam as fast as she could toward the grand stairs, Thurs and two other kelpies not far behind. Thurs cut in front of her, the alpha seeming to know the way. Turn after turn, the hallways blended together. All she could focus on was the kelpie gliding in front of her at top speed, guiding her to Kaid.

Thurs stopped in front of a door and dug her hoof into the bottom of the threshold. This was it, but it was too easy. There were no guards lining the halls, no duels along the way. Something was not right, but Asta needed to move forward. She tapped the threshold twice—for good measure—then did something to let Kaid know she was here to save him. *Knock, knock.* Pause. *Knock, knock, knock.* Pause. *Knock.* Asta burst through the door, and there was Kaid, lying in complete stillness.

"Kaid!" Asta held back a sob. He was there, but he was either unconscious or... or he was...

"He's not dead," an all too familiar voice came from behind Asta. She turned to face Maren, fury overtaking her panic. Maren sneered, "Oh *sissy*, you always were the more dramatic one."

"If he's not dead, then what's wrong with him? What have you done to him?" Asta demanded.

Maren swam to the other side of Asta, blocking her way to Kaid. Movement to Asta's side caught her attention and she locked eyes with Svanhild, who was emerging from the shadows of the room. Asta was surrounded with only her kelpies on the other side of the door, awaiting her command.

"It's a little sleeping potion that I slipped him when I heard you had breached the castle stronghold. Maybe I should send some home with you. You know, so you don't have to do your silly little hair brushing in order to fall asleep." Maren unsheathed a short dagger. "On second thought, I hear significant blood loss is another way to fall asleep quickly. Would you like to try that, sissy?"

Maren dove forward, her blade in a direct path for Asta's chest. Asta pulled out her own dagger from its sheath at her hip, parrying the attack and sending Maren's blade toward Svanhild instead. Maren barely missed the other finfolk's wrist, to Asta's disappointment. Asta grabbed Maren's wrist and knocked her hand against the door, causing her sister to drop the blade.

The moment Svanhild noticed, she unsheathed her long sword, swimming directly toward Asta with it raised high above her head. Before she could swing down, Thurs slammed her body against the beastly finfolk and knocked her sideways. The other kelpies burst into the room, biting and kicking with everything they had, but the room was so small, and three massive horses took up so much space that it was impossible for them to move the way they needed to.

A kelpie let out a pained whinny and Asta noticed the green liquid wisps floating through the water before she saw the deep bleeding gouge in the creature's side.

"Get yourselves out of here!" Asta commanded. "Return to the grand hall and help the others! This room is too small for you all."

Without hesitation, Thurs did as she was told and got her herd members out. Asta grabbed the dagger Maren had dropped, giving herself a second weapon to take on two opponents. This duel felt familiar to the last time, yet different. Asta hadn't fully felt the betrayal of her sister during the last fight, but now, it fueled her.

Maren stole Svanhild's dagger from her sheath and gripped it tightly, her eyes darting between Asta and Kaid. During the kelpie attack, Asta had managed to position herself back between the finfolk and the prince.

Asta sucked in a shaky breath, but when she released, it was steady.

CHAPTER 30

S vanhild's blows were the hardest to block. The female had such power behind her attacks that Asta was pushed back each time their blades met.

Maren mostly sat back, watching her body guard do her dirty work. That made Asta more disgusted with her sister than before, the princess unwilling to even fight her own battles. Every time Maren went in for a strike, it felt half-hearted. That pissed Asta off more—knowing that even now, her sister could not be bothered to give Asta her full attention.

Asta's mind ran rampant while she held off her opponents, trying to calculate a way out of the situation. All she was doing was tiring herself out by continuing to fight them off without a plan. She couldn't stop fighting them to free Kaid, especially since he would need to be carried in his current sleep state. But she also would not be leaving this room without him, so retreating to find help wasn't an option.

While weighing her options, Asta managed to land a nasty gash to Svanhild's cheek. If only she was one step closer, the finfolk female would have lost her jaw. Svanhild drifted back to steady herself just as Maren was shoved from the doorway by an orange-finned siren.

"Soren!" Asta cheered. She had been growing fond of the warrior during their travels, but now, he was definitely her favorite.

"I didn't take you for the damsel in distress type of princess," Soren chuckled as he swam next to Asta, "but here I am, saving your ass."

"I was figuring it out," Asta retorted.

"Yeah, it sure looked like you had everything under control. I'm mistaken," Soren said dryly.

Maren swept her blade low, hardly missing Soren's fin as he jolted backward. Svanhild screeched in that horrific way the finfolk could and swung from above. Soren blocked with his own, twisting the blades together until Svanhild withdrew to strike again. The way he didn't shake from the impact of Svanhild's sword was a testament to his strength.

Asta rapidly swam to Kaid's bedside. She touched his face gently as he slept peacefully. When she flipped back the tethered blanket, she saw the large iron chain and shackles. As she reached to free him, she was yanked back by a tight grip in her hair. Long nails scraped against her scalp, then she felt the coolness of metal against her throat.

In the very farthest corner of her vision, Asta could make out Maren's red hair as her sister rested her chin on her shoulder. Maren yanked Asta's head back using her hair, leaving the column of her throat wide open to Maren's black dagger that now rested firmly against her jugular.

Maren spoke in a voice that was much too calm for the mayhem surrounding them. "Everyone drop your weapons, or she dies."

Svanhild grinned wickedly, keeping her sword pointed toward Soren as he tossed his sword and dagger to the floor. Asta dropped her sword onto the bed in front of her, trying not to lean forward into the sharp edge pressed to her neck.

Maren gripped Asta's hair tighter. "Good little sirens. I feel like playing nice today, so I'll make you a deal. Withdraw your fighters and leave the prince with us and you will all leave unharmed. Or, choose to continue to fight, and get yourselves thrown into the dungeons."

Soren stared at Asta, the warrior awaiting command. Since when was Asta in charge? She was definitely in no position to be making decisions.

Movement in the doorway had everyone in the room turning their heads. Revna slowly centered herself in the threshold, two swords stretched out to either side of her. Her head tilted forward and she stared through her eyebrows menacingly. Revna would not be choosing either of those options.

As Revna swung a sword back, time slowed in Asta's mind. Through all the hate and resentment, something in her begged the sword not to kill Maren. Begged the sword to spare her sister, just in case there was a small chance at redemption for them. Because at the end of the day, when her life was on the line, Asta loved Maren and always would.

Revna's sword speared through the air, its target locked in.

Please don't kill her. Dear gods, please save her soul.

Asta pleaded with any god and goddess she could think of to save her sister not only in this moment, but in life.

The sword landed directly into the side of Maren's hand that she was holding the dagger to Asta's throat with. The point of the blade cut clean through Maren's hand and grazed Asta's shoulder. Maren dropped her dagger, letting go of Asta's scalp in the process.She was *alive.* They both were.

Asta turned around in time to see another sword swinging directly for Maren, but this time, it wasn't from Revna. Kaid hovered above the bed, one arm outstretched from releasing a blade toward the finfolk princess and the other pulled taut against the chain binding him to the wall.

Asta's fin buckled at the sight of him, his deep crimson hair almost black in the dark castle's ambiance. But despite the poor lighting, his turquoise eyes shone brightly, and they were looking right at her.

Maren ducked, avoiding the sword Kaid had thrown in her direction, but the distraction had cost her and Svanhild greatly. Before Maren could stand straight again, Revna was on her, smashing her face into the stone wall and knocking her out cold. At the same moment, Soren finned Svanhild in the face so hard that she passed out, her black blood settling in a cloud above her face.

Asta rushed to Kaid and he pulled her into an embrace as best he could with one arm. She didn't know how he was awake, but there was no time for questions.

"Where do they keep the key?" Asta blurted, her eyes darting around the room looking for anything to help break him free.

Kaid shook his head. "They don't have one. These are iron chains and iron keys have been lost over time. They put me in these on purpose, so I'd never be able to use my magic; Never be able to fight back."

Soren and Revna came to Asta's side and picked up the chain. "Grab on, Princess. If we can't get it off of him, we'll take it with us," Soren said with a grin.

Asta held onto the chain along with Kaid grabbing with his free arm. Asta could see substantial bruising around the wrist that was cuffed, and her heart ached.

All three sirens pulled back in a heave, the iron nails in the wall groaning against their strength. If the anchor hadn't come flying from the wall with all of their strength combined, it was no wonder Kaid couldn't break himself free.

Multiple heaves later, the anchor came blasting from the wall and fell to the floor with a thud.

Kaid bunched the chain up into his arms and nodded. "Thanks. Now how the hell do we get out of here?"

"Follow me," Revna said curtly as she exited the room.

Soren threw a thumb over his shoulder. "Sorry about that one, Your Highness. She needs a bit of work with royals," he bowed. "Right this way, sir."

Kaid made eye contact with Asta then followed the orange-finned warrior, Asta following closely behind.

CHAPTER 31

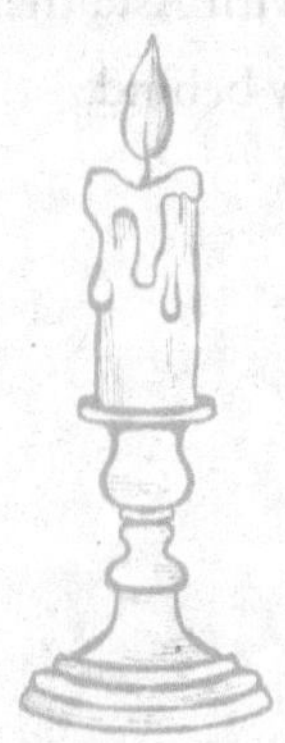

After days of packing and preparing, Linnea still could not confidently say she was ready to return to the Blomvin manor. Her lack of self-assurance had nothing to do with the items she was bringing—it had to do with the fact that she would be returning to the place where she was mercilessly tortured for so many years.

Linnea read over the letter she planned to leave for Asta once more, making sure it clearly stated where she would be going and what she would be doing. The final sentence begged Asta to not come after her. If Asta made it back home, Linnea did not want Asta worrying. All they had to do was go to Linnea's old manor and look for the artifacts Queen Else had written about in her journal. It would be quick, and then she could return home.

It wasn't exactly reassuring that Niklas could only find one mention of the Blomvin manor scribbled into a margin, but Linnea would do anything to help Asta after how many years her cousin had looked after her.

If Queen Else had left something behind, it would be in the manor. Queen Else and Linnea's mother had inherited the estate from their father when he passed, so the two sisters had lived there together their whole lives until Else married King Botmar and moved to the capitol. Linnea's mother had lived alone in the manor since Linnea left years ago, since her father passed away when Linnea was young.

The day Linnea's uncle Botmar had come to rescue her was in most ways, the best day of Linnea's life, but in some ways, the worst. Of course, she was eternally grateful for her uncle's interference. However, he had arrived a few hours too late.

That day had been particularly cold, an unforgiving frost settling over the land. Linnea's mother had instructed the servants to stoke the fires as hot as they could go, then dismiss themselves to their quarters to stay warm and she would ring for them as needed. It had been suspiciously kind of her mother to allow the servants to worry about warming their own rooms, but Linnea had a habit of holding out hope that maybe redemption was not lost on her mother.

She had been wrong.

She remembered settling on the sofa with tea and a book, then her memory went completely blank until she had awoken. Linnea will never forget how it felt to wake up to the scent of burning hair, only to realize it was her own. Linnea had jostled herself awake enough to try to put the flames out, only to find that she was shackled to an iron anchor in front of the grand fireplace. She hadn't been standing in the flames, but somehow, her hair had caught fire and she couldn't use her arms to put it out. Linnea had frantically searched for a way to put out the flames, and her stomach had dropped when she saw the steaming bucket of water placed directly in front of the fireplace. It was one of her mother's games.

Linnea had dunked her head into the scalding water, burning her scalp but extinguishing the flames. She'd let out a strangled scream, her scalp stinging as if lava had been poured on top of her. She'd tried to be grateful that her chain was long enough for her to dip her head into the water, but it had all been meticulously planned by her mother. It had not been a coincidence that the only thing Linnea could reach was a bucket of boiling water.

Once she had settled her mind a bit, she was able to think clearly enough to figure out the next part of her mother's plan. The shackles around her wrists were becoming uncomfortably warm, bordering hot. And they would only get hotter had she remained chained in front of the fireplace.

"Linnea?"

She broke from her trance, no longer thinking about the worst day of her mother's abuse. She didn't want to recount what had happened next and she was thankful for Niklas's interruption.

"I'm ready. I was only reading over my letter to Asta again." Linnea smiled softly, but knew she was fooling no one.

Halsten entered Asta's suite and grabbed one of the bags from the floor. "Good morning, Little Flame. We've acquired one more traveler."

Linnea's eyebrows furrowed curiously until she saw Liva enter the room. The female guard grabbed the other bag Linnea had packed, her glowing purple eyes boring into Linnea's.

Liva sighed. "Yes, I'm a sea dragon. No, I'm not going to hurt you. Now, can we get a move on?"

Liva was known for being the "down to business" type, so Linnea was not shocked that this was her approach at confirming the news. To Linnea's surprise, she felt a great deal of comfort knowing the sea dragon would be coming on the journey with them. Aside from the sea beast, she would have Halsten and Gyrial to protect her. Halsten was human, but he was substantially stronger than the average man due to his daily exercising. And Gyrial was a fae, which meant he was stronger than ten Halstens put together.

Even knowing this, Linnea was still uneasy. What if they got separated and her mother locked her away where they couldn't find her? What if, somehow, her mother got to them, too? Her mother was the sneering face she saw in every nightmare, never able to get away from what was done to her. But her worst nightmare would be her new friends enduring exactly the same.

A hand clamped over Linnea's, stopping her from rubbing the scar on her wrist, which she hadn't even realized she was doing. She followed the path of the arm leading to a broad shoulder, up a strong neck and to Halsten's face. His warm brown eyes stared deeply into hers, searching her for something she couldn't quite put a finger on.

Halsten used his grasp on her hand to pull Linnea closer to him until she had to crane her neck back to look up into his face. He placed his other hand on her cheek and whispered, "Nothing will happen to you, Linnea. We may be going with a fae and a sea dragon, but if your mother tries anything, *I'll* be the one she has to worry about. Do you understand?"

Once again, Halsten's tone was firm with her but not in a way that frightened her. Linnea could never be afraid of Halsten.

Linnea shook her head, then took a step back, feeling like all the air had been sucked from her lungs being that close to Halsten. His warm scent lingered on her, a mix of cinnamon and apples. He smelled like home.

Home was not the manor Linnea was returning to. Home was this castle, and her cousin, and her uncle who had rescued her, and the servants she had befriended, and the people standing in this room with her. Home was the produce market on the main road every Sunday. Home was Dyri rubbing his wet, sandy body all over her dress after he had a fun day swimming in the ocean. Home was also Halsten.

Everyone made their way to the stables and loaded up their saddle bags, mounting their horses and departing for Blomvin Manor.

CHAPTER 32

After a week of silent confinement, Kaid was overwhelmed with the havoc happening in the grand hall. Especially since he had woken up so abruptly.

Kaid remembered Maren forcing a sleeping potion down his throat, knowing he wouldn't be able to wake up for many hours. However, he distinctly recalled the moment Asta touched his face and woke him.

His thoughts had been clear enough that he feigned sleep, awaiting the right moment to utilize his unexpected awakening. When he felt Asta surrender her sword and throw it to his bed, he took the opportunity to attack.

Now, he was wide awake, ducking under swinging fists and squeezing between duels all while carrying his chain. There was a tingling sensation shooting through the water surrounding him, which could only mean one thing—the sea witch queen had entered the fight.

Just as the thought processed, she appeared. A circle of snarling, snapping kelpies engulfed her, but with one flick of the sea witch's wrist, all of them were stunned. Her shock currents weren't strong enough to take down the superiorly resilient water horses, but she could certainly stop them in their tracks.

"Round everyone up and let's go!" Asta barked at Soren. The warrior gave a lazy salute and vanished into the disarray.

Kaid was grateful for the rescue, but the finfolk numbers had been clearly underestimated. They simply didn't have enough manpower to keep going.

A finfolk male blazed through the crowd, directly toward Asta, blades cutting down kelpies who entered his path. Asta held off the male, meeting each of his blows with one of her own. Another finfolk came for her back and Kaid threw his chain at it, whipping the creature in the abdomen and causing it to retreat. After a few more strikes to other finfolk, Kaid learned that his chain could be a decent temporary weapon in this fight.

An ear piercing wail echoed off the stone walls, but it wasn't the usual pitch of the finfolk screech. It was a howl of pain coming from the large emerald dragon now facing the sea witch.

The dragon's hide was thick enough to not get stunned like the kelpies, but she was still suffering. Kaid knew the moment Asta had identified the sound based on her warpath through the bombardment of finfolk now swarming the hall. Her blades were cutting a direct path to the sea dragon; her friend in need.

Kaid knew it was a bad idea, but he followed her. Was he a trained warrior like Asta? No. But was he going to let her take on one of the most powerful sea creatures of the Ventarin Sea on her own? Also, no. They only had to distract the queen long enough to get everyone out.

Asta never removed her eyes from the queen the entire time she carved her trail. Kaid didn't care how fucked up it was, seeing her wield a sword with such expert precision was... attractive.

If Asta managed to let a finfolk slip past her defenses—which rarely occurred—Kaid took care of them with his chain. A smug smile formed on his lips. They made quite the team.

As they got closer, Kaid could see that Tova was bleeding profusely from her flank. The wound needed to be packed and sutured. Well, if that's how to repair a sea dragon laceration. Kaid wasn't quite sure.

Queen Yrsa finally acknowledged the blonde wraith coming for her, but a moment too late. Asta was already close enough to swing her sword, aiming directly for the witch's neck. Yrsa blocked the hit with the small dagger she held then latched onto the metal of Asta's blade.

Asta's eyes grew wide, the realization setting in that the finfolk queen could easily shock her through the metal.

Kaid had to think quickly. He only had a millisecond to make a decision. The iron cuff on his wrist inhibited his magic, so if he could just wrap his chain in a complete circle around the queen's arm, he could stop her. Or, at least weaken her enough to lessen the impact of her shock.

He threw his chain, watching it whip around her arm and encase her bicep. His actions were perfectly timed, seeing as a visible strand of lightning wrapped around her wrist and started down the sword, but dissipated by the time it hit the pommel.

Asta yanked the sword back, putrid blood drifting from Yrsa's palm. In the corner of Kaid's vision, he saw Tova slipping out of the gaping hole in the castle's side. Good, at least she was getting herself out.

The kelpies started disappearing after that, then Soren, then Revna. Asta managed to keep the queen busy while Kaid guarded her back. He tapped the back of her fin, signalling it was time to go. Without a word spoken between the two of them, Asta sent her sword careening toward Yrsa's head while the pair made a break for it.

Kaid cleared the path using his chain and they managed to escape through the hole where Thurs and another kelpie were waiting. They each latched onto a mane and the water horses bolted, swimming faster than any of the finfolk—or their vicious allied species—could swim.

CHAPTER 33

The trip back to Naltania was quiet—too quiet. It caused Asta to sleep restlessly each time they stopped for the night. Asta had trouble sleeping the entire trip anyway since she could not perform her hair combing ritual. At this point, they were only a one-day swim away from the siren castle and the crew was starting to run down.

After they had traveled a safe distance from Ryktarva, they had stopped to tend to Tova's wound. Soren had a suture kit in his pack and repaired the laceration with a steady hand as he told Tova a story about a young boy who was playing with a friend on the seashore one day, when a finned creature with pointed ears and fangs crawled from the waves and dragged his companion into the ocean's depths.

The little boy had tried to run, but the creature returned, catching his ankle. He had kicked the beast fiercely—far more ferociously than any child should be capable of—but the finned demon didn't let him go. Its claws dug into his ankle, scraping bone, and he had passed out. When he had awoken, the little boy had been tucked into a soft bed and greeted by a ruby-haired Empress. All the boy had left to remember from that day was a deep scar on his face—from where the finfolk had tried to take his life and failed. The story distracted Tova enough that she hardly flinched during her mending.

Asta had left the subject alone for the days following his story, but knew that was Soren's personal tale. She had so many questions regarding the transformation that she wanted to ask him, but wasn't sure if Soren was the type to share or if he had only wanted to offer Tova reprieve with a diversion.

Can you scent that? The scent of death that will give you life.

The ocean whispered in Asta's ear, caressing her jaw with a wispy current.

Sweet, warm blood. They wait for you above, sea beast. Superior species. They are yours to harvest.

Asta clenched her fists and turned to Kaid who was weaving pieces of seagrass together in a plait. Was he experiencing the same calling she was? How did he always look so calm? They had hardly spoken since escaping the finfolk territory and she was carrying that heavily in her heart.

Asta's gums throbbed as she looked up toward a ship at the surface, its presence so silent underwater. No one else acknowledged the ship, their resistance to cravings much more fortified than hers. That's it, she could not take it anymore.

"Soren, that story was about you, right?" she asked the orange-finned siren who was once again applying salve to the minor abrasions on the kelpies with injuries. It made sense now, why she felt so at ease with Soren. He was turned like her—not a born siren.

Soren nodded, his attention remaining on his wound care. "I know what you're going to ask, Princess."

Asta's back stiffened. His assumption made her defensive. "Oh, and what is it you think I'm going to ask?"

"It's the same question anyone turned siren would ask first," he met her eyes and smiled. "How do you make the cravings stop? Am I correct?"

Her face heated and she began cracking her knuckles. She looked to Kaid who was still focusing on his seagrass but clearly curious. Sirens had preternatural hearing, so there was no way every member of the group wasn't listening.

"Yes," she whispered. "It feels as though someone is digging twigs into my gums; as though I've never eaten once in my lifetime."

Soren chuckled—actually *chuckled* at her suffering and insecurity. She had been starting to like him before this moment; now, she was aggravated. Or was that the intense hunger speaking?

"You'll adjust. You just need to start feeding on other sources and eventually the sea gets the message and stops taunting you. Though, you'll always sense when humans are near. Like right now, I could tell you that there is a crew on the ship above us containing twenty-nine females and thirty-seven males. Eleven are ill in the infirmary and not good feeding sources. Thirty-one are in their prime of life—the ripest harvest for us. A draining of one of them would likely last you weeks. Well, since you're newly turned, maybe about a week as you need to feed more frequently. It never goes away. Your tolerance naturally builds up over time."

Asta blinked hard a few times, her takeaway from this conversation an understanding that she needed to feed soon. Just not from a human.

"And what about…" Asta observed Kaid from the corner of her eye and watched his gaze dart between her face and her cracking knuckles. "Why doesn't he feel the urge?"

Somehow, Asta knew Kaid was awaiting the answer as well.

"I've been pondering that, actually," Soren tapped his index finger to his lips, "and the only answer that makes sense is that it is somehow related to his protection spell he lived under until now. The spell wouldn't have diminished his cravings, but smothered them since his siren side was locked away."

Soren peered around Asta to Kaid, "Were you a particularly fussy baby, Your Highness?"

Kaid's award winning grin appeared for the first time since before his abduction and Asta's stomach flipped. Thank the gods her face was already red, or else her reaction would have been much more noticeable. Kaid was still one of the most frustrating beings Asta had ever met, but something changed after the night they spent in the cave.

"Father said I was the fussiest," Kaid replied with his chest puffed, clearly proud that he had been trouble right from birth.

Soren twisted the cap of the salve back on and stowed it in his pack. "Likely because you were craving blood and all he could give you was milk at first. He likely fed you rare meats when you were old enough to subdue the thirst. Which means, you probably—"

"Have the most obnoxiously fantastic anti-feeding tolerance known to sirenkind," Revna stated plainly as she rolled her eyes.

As if Kaid needed one more thing to inflate his ego.

Asta had barely fallen asleep under the protection of Thurs when Annika let out a low grunt, her head lifting from the sand and observing the dark water surrounding them. Their night vision added with the start of dawn above gave them visibility, but it was extremely limited.

"What do you—" Asta's question was cut off as a massive grouper burst through the kelp beside her, sending herself and Thurs rolling. The fish circled back, massive snapping jaws filled with rows of small pointed teeth coming straight for Asta. She sprung out of the way, the entire camp awake now. Two more of the colossal groupers joined the first and barreled through the camp.

Revna already had her swords, cutting into the fishes' scales with each pass. "Morphling Groupers!" she bellowed.

Kaid floated frozen in fear directly in the path of one of the beasts. Without second thought, Asta grabbed the heavy chain floating at his side and yanked him out of harm's way by the cuff on his wrist. His body slammed into hers but her hands landed on his biceps to soften the collision.

Asta's gums throbbed again. Her hunger was making her weak and she needed *something*.

Kaid snapped out of his frozen state and began using his chain as a weapon, a weapon in which Asta was quite impressed he had learned to control so easily. She scrambled on the seafloor in search of her sword that had been knocked away from her during the first fish's attack. When her hand landed on the grip, she pulled the sword up and turned to swing the blade just in time to slice a deep gash into a grouper's gills.

Black blood eerily similar to that of the finfolk poured into the currents around them. Revna speared a sword between her opponent's eyes and the fish went still. The siren jerked her blade free and the fish floated away in the current. One down, two to go.

Even though Tova was still healing, she was helping Soren with one of the groupers. In her fully-healed state, Asta knew the sea dragon could easily take down one of these fish despite their size, but with one leg being weak, it slowed her.

Kaid continued to swing his chain toward the grouper specifically coming for the pair of them, wrenching scales from the fish's body with the iron links. The creature retreated, but Asta had grown accustomed to its attack pattern by now. Each time it pulled back, it returned by rapidly charging them.

Her hands shook, but it wasn't from nerves. She was starving. There was no time to think about that, however, because she was the only thing standing between herself and Kaid, and death. The male could only do so much with a chain.

The grouper rushed her, its mouth opened wide to strike. The only advantage these creatures had on their crew was the sheer size of them.

Asta held her sword up in front of her, letting the fish come dangerously close.

"Asta! Move!" Kaid roared.

At the last second to spare, Asta dug her sword high into the roof of the grouper's mouth and rolled out of its path. The fish tried to snap its jaw down, but the sword was now lodged into both the roof of its mouth and underneath its tongue.

The fish tried forcing its jaw closed, shaking its head and slamming itself to the sea floor.

Something took over Asta when she saw the beast weak and vulnerable. Her siren nature, her half-finfolk heritage tugging at her.

It is a weakling. Eliminate. Eliminate!

Asta dove forward, sinking her teeth into the side of the grouper. Her siren fangs bore deep into its flesh, striking veins and filling her mouth with warm blood. This was not like the selkie blood she had ingested upon turning. It was gritty and earthy, but not unpleasant. Not like the black color would lead you to believe.

Her entire body relaxed as she drained more and more blood, pulling deeply and feeling the warmth of it slide down her throat like aged wine. Hands gripped her shoulder, squeezing lightly, but not pulling her away. They were comforting.

Asta drained every last drop from the grouper and pulled her face away. Its mottled body was limp and drifted away.

She turned to see who was holding her, but she already knew. Kaid pulled her into a tight hug, stroking a gentle hand down her hair.

Asta was not hungry anymore.

CHAPTER 34

Kaid grew anxious as they approached Naltania. He had been in the Ventarin Sea for over a week now and had not once seen the kingdom that was his. Nor had he met his own mother.

The crew moved quickly after the morphling grouper attack. The final fish had retreated completely once Asta drained its companion, likely frightened to meet the same end.

After an onslaught of questions from Asta, Soren and Revna managed to explain that morphling groupers were actually finfolk. Finfolk all had the option to complete a transformation referred to as the Morph, changing them into beastly, gargantuan groupers. Historically, this form was utilized in battle, seeing as the groupers were incredibly difficult to take down. However, once the Morph was initiated, the finfolk only had three days to live. Again, well utilized in battle as most of those warriors did not expect to make it home anyway. It was a last-ditch effort to fight for their cause.

If the finfolk were dispatching morphlings, they were getting desperate.

Soren did mention that he had never seen anyone drain a morphling grouper in order to defeat them, and he suspected that the one that got away returned to the finfolk kingdom with what little time it had left to report the new weakness that had been discovered. Asta very well could have changed the war in her hunger frenzy, and Kaid was so incredibly mesmerized by her.

He didn't know how to talk to her after the way they had parted on the beach. It did not help that they hadn't had a moment alone since his rescue and he suspected they would not once they arrived in Naltania, either. First things first, he needed to meet his mother—the Empress. That wasn't intimidating at all.

"Just over this embankment," Soren shouted over his shoulder.

Kaid didn't know what to do with his hands. He tightened his fists, then released them. A calloused hand slipped into his and squeezed. Asta gave him a soft smile, her bioluminescent eyes practically glowing in the morning light underwater.

The kelpies rushed over the hill, followed by Annika and Tova. Soren and Revna went up and over together, the tops of their heads disappearing as they went down the slope on the other side.

Kaid saw a tall tower first, pointed and bright. The tower drifted down to shorter belfries, then a full opalescent castle surrounded by a thick coral reef illuminated with every color of the rainbow. It took his breath away.

Asta grinned at Kaid and signed to him. "Welcome home, Lost Prince."

Kaid was quickly whisked through the castle upon entry, more sirens bowing and sea creatures darting out of his path than he could imagine. Kaid and Asta came to a large set of etched pearl double doors, which were pulled open by two siren guards on either side of them. In front of them sat a large golden desk, grand windows made of sea glass shards making up the walls to their left and right.

Behind the desk sat a fire-haired female siren with the same eyes as Kaid.

Queen Arielle rose and Kaid couldn't help but notice they had the same royal blue fins. She clasped her hands together and Kaid swam forward, unsure how to greet the woman who birthed him, but also whom he'd never truly met.

The empress came around her grandiose desk and her breath hitched. She dove forward and pulled Kaid into the warmest embrace he had ever received. His nerves dissipated with each second they held each other. He had a mother.

When Queen Arielle pulled back, she surveyed Kaid's face closely, likely taking him in while also looking for injuries. Her eyes landed on the iron shackle and chain he dragged from his wrist and her brows furrowed.

She quickly signed to Asta and Kaid only knew a few words—*he, stuck, hurt.*

Asta shook her head and signed back—*tried, open, fight, warrior.*

Kaid looked back and forth between the women, wishing someone would include him somehow.

"She asked if you were stuck, and if the cuff hurt. I told her I tried to release you and you were bruised but that's it."

Kaid was new to sign language, but he definitely saw the words fight and warrior thrown in there. Asta was keeping something from him, but his mother read her lips closely and made no objections.

The siren queen signed again and Kaid spoke aloud as he translated. "You are home. You are safe here. My son, I, uh, something?"

Kaid looked at Asta and her cheeks flushed. "I love you."

His heart skipped a beat when she first said it, his breath frozen deep in his lungs momentarily.

Asta shook her head. "That's what she said. 'My son, I love you.'"

"Right, of course," Kaid cleared his throat. She was translating. She had never taught him the word love because he had never asked. It was never in his vocabulary before now.

Kaid signed with his mother, Asta helping with the more complicated words from time to time, but he could get the gist of most of her sentences. The empress of the Ventarin Sea explained that now that the lost prince had returned, the finfolk would be relentless in their quest to dominate the sirens. She could hold them off, as she had been doing for many years, but they would only grow stronger now that they had more motivation. Kaid essentially had a massive "abduct me" sign on his back.

"I do not want you to leave home so soon, but there is work to be done," Arielle signed. "There is a way for us to get the advantage over the finfolk, but it is a mission."

"We will do whatever it takes," Asta signed back.

The siren queen smiled softly. "If you can find the trident, the comb and the mirror, we may be able to end this war. For good."

CHAPTER 35

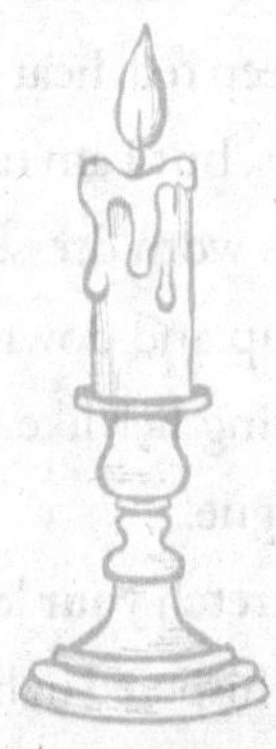

Linnea's legs felt like they were going to fall off after days of riding horseback. She typically traveled by carriage for long distances, but that would have drawn too much attention to them.

The worst part was that Linnea was wearing pants for the first time in her life. The tightness around her lower half made her feel exposed, especially whenever she caught Halsten staring. It always made her search her body, brushing away any dirt or horse hair he may be looking at, which made him laugh and shake his head.

They stopped for the night at an inn about a half a day's ride away from the Blomvin Manor. There was no sense in traveling in the dark when they could rest for the night and eat a good meal, then get an early start in the morning and be to the manor early in the day still.

Gyrial approached the innkeeper to inquire about rooms and Liva rushed over, speaking to him in hushed tones. Gyrial nodded and returned to his conversation with the plump man behind the desk.

Linnea's movements were stiff due to the ache in her limbs, but she concealed it as best as she could.

"Are you walking like that because you are not accustomed to long journeys in the saddle, or because you feel like the entire room is taking in your figure in those trousers?" Halsten jeered.

Linnea's face flushed a deep red, heat creeping up her neck. "I, erm. Mostly because of the soreness, but I am not quite adjusted to my figure being on display. I have always worn dresses."

Halsten looked Linnea up and down, then grabbed her hand and held it above her head, spinning her like a ballet dancing figurine in a music box. He clicked his tongue.

"Take a hot bath, then stretch your legs as much as you can. It will help," he leaned in close and whispered in her ear, so quiet only she could hear. "And to clarify, your figure is drawing the attention of everyone in here. They cannot stop observing your long legs, your rounded behind, or your hourglass shape. The puffy shirt is doing nothing to hide that, by the way."

Linnea's cheeks were now heated for a completely different reason. There was no way that her feeble frame was drawing *that* kind of attention. She always assumed people stared because of how weak she was; how flat and shapeless she was. Though she hadn't really observed herself in the last few months. She had been eating better, taking the long way to any destination in the castle she was heading so she could climb more stairs.

She stepped back quickly so she could no longer feel the heat coming from Halsten's body. She needed to get away before she leaned into it.

The universe was on her side when Gyrial approached with room keys for everyone.

"Three rooms. Niklas, Halsten, and I will take a triple. Liva requested her own room, so Linnea, that means you will be on your own. Is that okay?"

Linnea nodded. She didn't exactly enjoy sharing her space with anyone besides Asta anyway.

"Nothing personal," Liva stated. "I like my privacy."

Linnea didn't doubt that one bit. The sea dragon probably had certain needs to fulfill while they were on a break. She knew that sirens needed to ingest blood, so she assumed sea dragons had similar needs.

The group separated, Niklas and Gyrial heading for the pub under the inn while the other three headed upstairs to get settled into their rooms.

CHAPTER 36

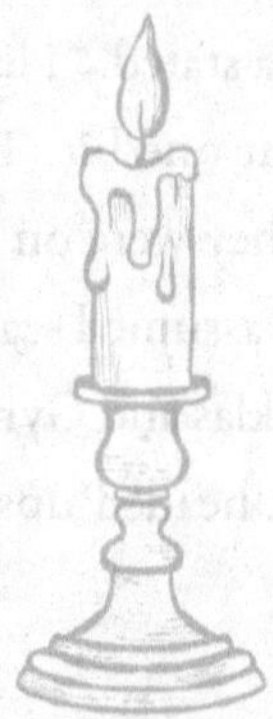

Linnea took a long, searing bath and her muscles unknotted instantly. Heat used to bother her because of her last encounter with her mother, but after years of practice, she could take hot baths again. The sting of warmth on her skin still bothered her sometimes, but that's what permanent scarring from hot coals being shoved down the back of your dress will do to you. They never fully heal.

Sometimes she could still hear her mother's cold laughter, matching the frigid weather of the day she gained her largest scars. Linnea had made the mistake of mentioning it was a tad chilly in the house that morning, which was when her mother formulated the plan to help her "appreciate" the heat that was provided.

What's wrong, dear? I thought you were cold.

Linnea clawed her way out of her downward spiral—working to focus on how wonderful the warmth felt on her aching muscles and not the terrible memories that heat held—and finished her bath.

Halsten was right—as long as she stretched when she got out, she would feel much better. She stepped out and wrapped herself in a towel, digging through her saddlebag for something comfortable to wear. She had been stuck in riding pants and cotton puffy shirts for days now.

Linnea pulled out a multi-layered gossamer nightgown in her favorite color, slate blue. She was not a confident woman, but she always loved how the color accentuated her gray eyes and auburn hair. She stood in the mirror and tied up the decorative strings that sat below her collarbones, leaving a keyhole effect on her chest, and her shoulders exposed.

Her stomach rumbled and she panicked. In her uncomfortable state, her entire focus was on taking a hot bath. She had completely forgotten to go down to eat before she got into her night clothes. Well, she was too tired now, so she would just have to indulge in a large breakfast. She had an apple and a handful of grains in her saddlebag that would hold her over.

She stretched first before her muscles had the opportunity to tighten again. First, standing with a leg on her bed, then she took to the floor and stretched each leg until she could comfortably wrap her palms around the bottoms of her feet again. Lack of body fat growing up had made her flexible, since stretching was the only form of exercise she could endure without becoming winded.

Linnea was about to get up and retrieve the apple from her bag when there was a soft knock at her door.

"Who is it?" she asked through the thick oak door.

"Halsten. Can I come in?"

"I'm not decent. I'll see you in the morning."

"I insist."

Linnea let out a sigh, then glanced around the room for anything to cover herself with. She grabbed a scratchy blanket from the bed and wrapped it around herself before letting him in.

Halsten slipped into the room carrying a tray of food. "I noticed you never came down to eat. I know your legs hurt so I suspected you were protesting the stairway. I figured I would bring the food to you," he said with a goofy smile.

Linnea couldn't help to mirror his facial expression. "Thank you, that's very kind."

Linnea gestured to the small bistro table in the corner and Halsten placed the tray down. To her surprise, he sat himself in one of the chairs. She froze in her tracks, unsure what to do.

"I won't bite, Little Flame. Come, sit with me."

There was that nickname again. He must be jesting at her hair. That had to be it.

"I'm capable of eating by myself, Sir Halsten."

He flinched at the formality but did not budge. She had hoped that would encourage him to leave.

Halsten smiled again, then gestured to the other chair. Linnea cautiously sat down, holding the blanket tight around her chest. She scooped a spoonful of stew with one hand and brought it to her mouth. It was delectable and she let out a soft moan. Halsten's eyes widened as he watched her. She couldn't help but notice his nostrils flaring.

He gestured toward her torso. "Why are you wearing a blanket cape?"

"I'm in my night clothes. It's indecent for a man to see me in them." Linnea gave him a puzzled look as if he should know that.

"Are they... see through?" He raised an eyebrow.

Linnea started. "Of course not! I would not own such scandalous attire!"

Halsten laughed a deep, real laugh. "Then why is it such a secret? Is it not the same as the dresses you usually wear, but less extravagant?"

Damn. He had her with that logic. She held a chunk of baguette in her free hand but hesitated bringing it to her mouth.

"Let go of the blanket, Linnea."

She pulled it tighter. "No."

Halsten pulled the tray to his side of the table. "Then I'll just take this back."

Linnea scoffed. "That's mine!" She reached for the tray, but she had the chunk of bread in her hand so she couldn't grip it.

He dove forward and bit off a large piece of her bread, his mouth now stuffed with it as he laughed.

Linnea gasped, pulling her bread hand back. "Fine!" she shouted as she let go of the blanket. It was making her itchy anyway.

The fabric bunched down at her waist, leaving the upper half of her nightgown exposed. Halsten's eyes wandered up and down her torso multiple times before he slowly slid the tray back to her. There was an odd silence while she finished her stew and bread, but not awkward. When she was done, she dabbed her face with her napkin and stood up, leaving the blanket in the chair behind her. Her legs locked up and she winced.

"Did you stretch?" Halsten asked.

Linnea nodded. "Hot bath and stretched like you said. It was better for a while."

Halsten squinted at her, his chocolate brown eyes glowing in the firelight. "Lie on your stomach on the bed. I can help."

Linnea wanted to protest. That's what any proper lady would do. But he had been sitting here with her in her nightgown and never made her feel unsafe. Now that she thought about it, she had never once felt unsafe in Halsten's presence. If anything, it comforted her more, having him around.

Without a word, but with shaky hands, Linnea laid on her stomach, turning her head to the side so she could see Halsten clearly. He approached the bed and kneeled next to her on the mattress.

"Don't be afraid. I would never hurt you. If you want me to stop, tell me to stop and I will leave. Understood?"

Linnea let out a breathy "yes," unsure of what he was about to do.

Halsten gripped her calf with both hands, working his thumbs in circles starting in the middle and working his way outward. It felt amazing, her muscles relaxing more and more with each stroke of his thumbs.

They sat in comfortable silence while Halsten worked her calves and lower thighs. He never dared approach the hem of her nightgown, which ended mid-thigh. He was being as respectable as a person could be, keeping the massage strictly therapeutic, which Linnea appreciated.

"Why do you call me Little Flame?" Linnea blurted before she could stop herself. She needed to know. "Is it because of my hair?"

"Your—your hair? No, of course not." Halsten's thumbs worked on a particularly difficult knot in the center of her hamstring. "It's just that, since the moment I met you, I knew there was more to you than you let on. You act meager and shy, but I know deep down, you've seen some shit; been through even more. You're tough. You've got a flame in there that you haven't fueled yet."

Linnea nodded, speechless. It wasn't a jest this whole time. She rolled over to her back and looked into his warm eyes, reaching up to rub a thumb over his high cheekbones. He was beautiful.

"Did you mean what you said downstairs?"

"About how irresistible your body is? Yes, Linnea. If we're being honest, it's been a damn struggle to ride behind you the last few days where all I had to look at was your perfect shape."

"I want to try something," Linnea said. "Be patient with me."

Halsten nodded, staying silent. Linnea held the back of his head and dragged it down to hers. When their lips were a breath away, she whispered, "Kiss me."

Halsten did not hesitate. He pressed his mouth to hers and his skin was the softest, most gentle thing she had ever felt. He didn't rush anything, waiting for Linnea to signal she was okay. Refusing to separate their lips, she nodded mid-kiss.

Her body felt hot all over, a warmth she had never experienced before sweeping over her in waves. Every nerve was hypersensitive, so when a lock of Halsten's hair slipped from behind his ear and brushed her neck, she gasped.

Halsten lightly swept against her lips with his tongue and when she did not object, he slipped into her mouth, gingerly knocking at her teeth for entry. Linnea opened to let him in, swirling her tongue around his instinctually.

A low grumble rumbled deep in his chest as Linnea reached for his hips, guiding him so he was kneeling over her. It did nothing to satisfy the heat between her legs, but she wasn't ready for that yet. She had kissed before, so this was not her first time, but she had never felt a need like this.

She trusted Halsten. Maybe she was drunk off everything he had said to her. Maybe she needed to do something risky for once in her life. Maybe, just maybe, he was right—she needed to stoke her fire.

Halsten's kissing became deeper each time he stroked his tongue over hers. "It's my turn to try something. Tell me to stop if you need to, okay?"

Linnea nodded.

"Words, Linnea. I need to hear you say it."

A man being authoritative usually scared Linnea, but Halsten demanding words from her sent pleasant shivers down her spine. "Yes, Halsten. I will stop you if I'm not okay."

Without speaking another word, Halsten dove for her neck. He planted sweet kisses at first and Linnea squirmed under him, her skin growing taut all over. She felt like she was going to burst.

His chest gingerly grazed her breasts as he leaned in and she jumped, the sensation completely new to her. Her mind told her she didn't want it to happen again, because this was far past the point of ladylike behavior, but her body responded to that faint touch by arching. Her nipples brushed his chest again and a small squeak slipped from her throat.

Halsten sat up quickly, surveying her face. When he saw that she was smiling, he smiled as well. "Did you just squeak?"

Linnea playfully slapped his chest. "It wasn't a squeak. It was a high-pitched moan."

"It was a squeak," he said flatly. "But squeak or moan, I want to hear it again."

Linnea closed her eyes when Halsten dipped back down, but she never felt his mouth reconnect with her neck. She opened her eyes to find him hovering over her nipple, clearly visible through the layers of thin gossamer she was wearing. He looked up, making eye contact with her and gliding the flat of his tongue slowly over the nub through the fabric.

Linnea squeaked again, this time louder and longer. Halsten laughed against her chest, causing her to let out a breathy huff of joy with him. He wrapped his entire mouth around her nipple this time, swirling his tongue against the fabric, creating a rough yet warm feeling that made Linnea melt.

There were no nerves. She wanted her fire stoked, and Halsten was volunteering himself as kindling.

He released her nipple and looked up at her. "You know, when your face is flushed, your freckles look a thousand times cuter?" He quickly popped up and kissed the bridge of her nose where her largest cluster of freckles sat. She felt his hand just below her collarbone tugging at the tie there.

His hand slid the material down one of her arms, exposing a breast. She gasped when his palm rested against it, encasing her fully as he squeezed. Linnea pushed on his thighs, making him back up so she could slip her legs out from beneath him and position them on either side of his. Having her legs spread with Halsten kneeling between them made her core throb with need, a feeling she had never felt with any other man.

Linnea's nightgown was still covering her besides her legs and the exposed breast Halsten was kneading. His hips bucked and he closed his eyes, tilting his head toward the ceiling. Linnea didn't know who she was at this moment, but she felt brave. She latched onto the newfound confidence and embraced it, lifting the bottom of her nightgown until her core was exposed, everything on full display since her legs were still spread around Halsten.

He sat back and gripped the sides of her thighs before staring hungrily at her center. He licked his lips and Linnea could see him straining against his trousers.

"Gods, Linnea," Halsten mumbled. "You're fucking perfect. I don't know what I ever did to land myself in this position, but I don't deserve it."

Linnea laughed but it quickly faded as another wave of heat ran through her. The longer he stared, the more she ached for him. "I want to see you," she rushed out.

"You're sure?" he met her gaze, his transfixion with her broken.

She nodded.

"Words," he commanded.

"I'm sure." There was a slight quiver in her voice, but she knew that was more so from how hard she was breathing rather than nerves. Not to say she wasn't nervous. Of course she was. But Halsten was safe.

Halsten untied the knot holding his trousers up and slipped them down his thighs. His member sprang free and Linnea was mesmerized. He kicked his pants off all the way, shoving them off the bed. Linnea reached out, her eyes darting between Halsten's heavy-lidded gaze and his cock. When she delicately wrapped her fingers around it, he hissed.

She let go and ran her fingers up and down him, taking in the soft skin and veins she had never experienced before. Her thumb ran up the slit on the underside of the tip and Halsten bucked in her hand. She quickly realized how addicting this could be. Not sex in general, but sex with this man. The sounds he made and the jerky movements with her slightest of touches made her feel wanted. It made her feel powerful.

She gingerly wrapped her hand around him again and he moaned, gripping her fingers and squeezing to teach her how hard to hold him. Both of their hands stroked him at first until he let go, allowing her to try on her own.

"Can I show you what it feels like to orgasm, Linnea?" he asked. His hands rested at the tops of her thighs, so close to her center that she could hardly stop herself from shifting her body to make his hand land there.

"Please," Linnea whimpered.

"With my hand, my mouth, or—"

"This," Linnea gripped his cock tightly, "and this." She grabbed his hand and rested it on her center.

Halsten hissed out a string of curses that Linnea hoped meant something positive even though they sounded quite filthy. He slipped two fingers into her dripping slit and growled. His fingers brushed over a specific spot and she squeaked again, tingles running all over her body like she had been struck by lightning.

He chuckled. "We'll save that spot for after. I have to get you ready for me."

Halsten slowly slipped a finger into Linnea's opening. At first it was uncomfortable, but after he retracted and reinserted it a few times, she adjusted. He leaned forward and took her pebbled nipple into his mouth again as he eased two fingers into her this time. She hissed and he stopped, allowing her a moment to get used to the feeling. A few flicks of his tongue over her nipple and she relaxed again.

He pushed in further until she felt the pressure of his hand against her, knowing his fingers were as deep as they could go. Linnea let out what she now knew was her signature squeak. He did it twice more, and on the third time, he pushed in quickly, curling his fingers against her walls and she moaned, guttural and completely unfamiliar.

That was the signal Halsten had been waiting for, because he released her breast and sat back, taking hold of his cock and releasing Linnea of the duty. He lined it up with her throbbing center, so wet she was sure she was soaking the sheets.

"Words," he said in a low grumble.

Linnea said the filthiest thing she had ever said, demanding the filthiest thing she had ever desired. "Fuck me, Halsten."

Halsten once again released a steeple-shattering strand of curses as he slowly slid into her. Once he was completely immersed in her, he withdrew slowly and entered again. At first, there was a stinging sensation. Linnea feared she had made a mistake, allowing this to happen. Maybe sex wasn't as enjoyable as everyone made it out to be. Maybe it was only for the men, and this was the pain women had to feel every time it happened.

Halsten's hand returned to its home between her legs and he grazed that spot again. Her clit, the spot that made her see stars the first time he touched it. He pressed the pad of his finger to it at first, allowing her to adjust to the feel of something touching it. When she relaxed and felt herself tightening around his dick, he began to draw large, gentle circles around her clit. His thrusts were small, but the friction made her moan.

She was filled and whatever he was doing was making her pant. After a few more small thrusts, he pulled out almost completely and pushed as far into her as he could go.

Linnea's legs fell further open and she could see Halsten's hand working between her legs. She watched him, her breaths becoming more shallow. A corner of his mouth tilted upward when she looked up at his face.

He leaned in and gave her a deep kiss, his tongue swirling small, tight circles around hers. At that same moment, his finger mimicked his tongue, drawing small, determined circles around her clit. A tingling started low in her stomach, her inner-walls clenching around his cock. Halsten sat back up and thrusted into her, determination etched into his expression. She glanced down to his hand now frantically working her, and that was her undoing. Waves of pleasure washed over her, a shrieking moan tearing from her throat as she realized that Halsten was finding his release as well.

"Little Flame. My good Little fucking Flame," Halsten whispered to himself and closed his eyes.

His Little Flame. He brought one of her arms to his face and kissed the scar on her wrist.

She tightened around him so much that she could distinctly feel the head of his cock flare, and her body tingled all over.

As she came down, Halsten's thrusting slowed to a stop and he pressed his forehead to hers.

"Now *that* was a high-pitched moan."

CHAPTER 37

Nothing felt odd about awakening next to Linnea. Halsten was accustomed to slipping out of bed and sneaking away once the woman he had relations with fell asleep, but he never once felt the urge to do that with this one.

The night before had completely broken him down and rebuilt him as a man. All he desired in life from here on out was the magnificent woman sleeping soundly next to him, her fiery hair a mess and her nightgown disheveled.

These Orntali women were different from any women he or Kaid had encountered before.

He kissed her bare shoulder. "Good morning, sleepy head. It's time to get going."

Linnea groaned, turning over slightly to peek an eye open and look at him. She covered her face with her arms and sighed.

"The men will know what happened since you didn't sleep in the room," she stated.

Halsten's brow furrowed. "If you intended to keep this a secret, you should have told me before we were so loud every room on the floor could hear us."

She blushed a deep beet red. "That bad?"

He swooped in and gave her a peck on the cheek. "Nothing bad about it. And just so we're clear, I never planned on keeping this a secret. I planned on walking out of here holding your hand and never letting go."

The ride from the inn to Blomvin Manor would only take a few hours and they were off to a good start seeing as they were saddled and ready to go by the time the sun came up.

With every hour they rode, Halsten could see Linnea's posture becoming more rigid. This day would not be easy on her. He didn't know the full extent of the abuse she endured in the manor, but he picked up on enough. He had only seen two scars on her, one on each wrist. After last night, he knew her legs did not hold any physical evidence of the worst parts of her life, but that was what strategic abusers did.

If they did leave physical scars, they put them where no one would see them. And that did not even touch on the subject of mental scarring. She had only left those scars on Linnea's wrists because she knew the end was near. She knew Linnea would somehow escape, and she wanted to leave her with a parting "gift" to remember her by.

If her mother even so much as took one step in Linnea's direction, Halsten would end her. Hell, he would have to fight back the urge to do it just from laying eyes on the wretched woman.

Linnea let out a shaky breath. "Just up this path," she gestured by nodding in the direction of the gravel path jutting off the main road.

Halsten did not know what he expected to find at the end of the passage, but it surely wasn't a polished manor with manicured lawns and lion busts. Judging by the confused look on Linnea's face, she hadn't expected it to look so well-kept, either.

"This isn't right. She's not supposed to have anything," she muttered to herself more so than to everyone around her.

Gyrial dismounted his horse, putting a hand out to help Linnea down. Liva stabilized Niklas as he took an uncoordinated leap from his steed, catching his glasses in one hand and grabbing Liva's forearm with a deathgrip in the other.

Before anyone could fully settle from dismounting and tying up their horses, Linnea marched right for the main entryway. Instead of using the knocker, she slammed the side of her fist on the large oak door.

A servant answered, one who clearly did not work in the manor when Linnea lived there, because there was no sense of recognition. Linnea shoved past him, sending him stumbling backward.

"Oh, I'm sorry," she whispered sweetly before turning back and entering the foyer.

Halsten ran in behind her, followed by Gyrial, Liva and Niklas. She was already charging up the stairs, determined to reach a destination no one else knew about.

Following closely behind her, Halsten saw when she threw a door to a room open that was clearly not used often by the amount of dust coating the air.

The entire manor was slightly chilled due to fall beginning, but this room was cold. Beautiful tapestries of what Halsten now knew were sirens and sea dragons were strung on the walls.

Niklas whimpered and squeezed past Halsten. "Queen Else's room," he muttered.

A fascinated Niklas ran his fingers over every surface and fabric he could find while Linnea went straight for the vanity and began digging through drawers.

Halsten stood beside her while Gyrial and Liva guarded the door.

"They've got to be here," Linnea grumbled.

The comb and mirror.

They had traveled all this way in hopes that Queen Else had left the siren artifacts here in her old home, farther away from the sea to protect them. Her small note she had left in a research journal was vague.

<u>Comb and Mirror</u>

Origin: siren

Magic: unknown

Possession: attained

Importance: essential

<u>Greer.</u>

Halsten had never learned what "Greer," meant, but clearly it led them to the Blomvin Manor. It made sense to Niklas and Linnea, but no one else.

Linnea slammed the last vanity drawer closed in frustration. "It's not here."

"It has to be," Niklas declared. "She specifically wrote Greer!"

Linnea closed her eyes and sucked in a deep breath.

"Okay, I'll ask since the two mute guards over there aren't going to," Halsten jested, referencing Gyrial and Liva. "What is Greer?"

"Not what. Who," Linnea said flatly. "My mother."

Niklas pushed past Halsten to investigate the vanity himself. "Nothing in your aunt's journals were wrong. They have to be here."

Halsten had an idea. "Let me check something."

He opened each drawer and knocked on the bottom, closing them when he didn't find what he was looking for. When he got to a bottom drawer, he knocked and a hollow sound reverberated through the vanity.

He ran his fingers along the inside of the drawer until he found a divot. His finger was too big to loop under the indent, so he had Linnea grab it. She pulled, lifting the false bottom out of the drawer.

"You did it," Niklas was hypnotized by what was in the drawer.

Halsten shrugged. "I made a false bottom to hide my rum from my parents when I was younger."

A hand mirror encased in a gold handle covered in ornate carvings sat there, untouched and hidden for decades.

"It's only the mirror, though." Niklas ran a hand through his curls.

Linnea slowly shook her head. "I know exactly where the comb is."

"You do?" Halsten asked. "Where?"

"Hidden in plain sight. Directly on Asta's vanity."

Gyrial stowed the mirror in his pack to keep it safe since he was probably the most lethal of the group. Well, on land, anyway. Get Liva to any body of water and she would take down troops in one swipe.

"How did Queen Else get ahold of such a precious siren artifact?" Liva questioned. "This has been lost for thousands of years. We were always taught that the fae took our most powerful weapons and hid them in an attempt to keep the peace between the two merspecies."

Gyrial shrugged. Halsten always forgot how thick his Spellid mountain accent was until he spoke. The fae was of few words unless he was around Asta.

"No word of your comb and mirror have been passed down to the most recent generations. The first I heard of them was when Niklas mentioned them. The trident, on the other hand, is something any fae will willingly admit we keep hidden. Though the vast majority of fae don't know where it is, we all know we have it."

"Do you know where it is, then?" Liva pressed.

"Of course not, or else I would have retrieved it by now. I would like this war to end once and for all, as well. Asta is not safe until it is." Gyrial challenged the sea dragon with a hard stare.

Either way, the trident was likely not in the Blomvin Manor and they had been blessed by having this much time going undisturbed.

Halsten twirled his finger in a circular motion. "Let's wrap it up. We can rehash century-long feuds on the ride home."

To Halsten's surprise, everyone agreed and emerged from the room. As they came down the stairs, the exit in sight, a figure stepped into their path.

It was a woman, finely dressed in a thick green velvet gown that complemented her auburn hair. A thick smattering of freckles crossed the bridge of her nose, but did nothing to conceal her wrinkles and age spots. Especially her frown lines.

She stood between them and the doorway with a wicked grin on her lips.

Linnea stepped down a few more stairs ahead of the group. "Beautiful dress. Who paid for it? It certainly wasn't the Blomvin trust, seeing as King Botmar is currently storing that until I'm old enough to manage it myself."

Greer smiled sweetly. "Didn't you hear? I remarried after you left me. Duke Tiernan of Besniell. He so graciously repaired the manor you left in shambles after robbing me."

So, that was how she twisted the story. Her evil daughter robbed her blind and ran away with the Blomvin trust, leaving her with nothing.

Greer stopped a servant nervously passing through the foyer. "Be a dear and stoke the fires. It's a bit chilly, and I would hate for my daughter to get cold during her visit."

Judging by the way Linnea's fists balled, Halsten knew Greer struck a nerve. He stepped forward and placed a hand on the small of Linnea's back. She leaned into his touch.

"So you've tricked someone else into your twisted games. Tell me, who do you chain to the grand fireplace now that I'm not here?" Linnea sucked in a shaky breath but concealed it well.

Chained to the grand fireplace? Every muscle in Halsten's body tightened with restraint to stop himself from strangling this woman. The scars on Linnea's wrists were from heated metal. From the corner of his eye, Halsten could see that Gyrial now had his hand on the pommel of his sword, also using an extreme amount of restraint to not slaughter the woman.

A short, stout man with a full face of hair sauntered into the room, a stunned expression on his face when he noticed the crowd on the stairs. "My love, I wasn't aware we had guests coming today."

"They were just leaving," Greer remarked.

"But Mother, you haven't introduced me to my new father yet." A knowing smile spread across Linnea's lips.

Halsten knew that seeing her mother again could either make or break Linnea, and he was amazed at her tenacity despite the jabs Greer had made thus far.

"This is your daughter?" the portly man, Duke Tiernan, asked. "The one who—"

Linnea interrupted. "The one who was mercilessly abused within these walls for years until her uncle, the King of Salendron, came to rescue her and leave her mother with nothing. Yes, I am that daughter."

Linnea raised an eyebrow as Greer scoffed, waving an arm in her direction. "Tiernan, this is all a ruse. They've come here to steal from me. She must have found out about our marriage and come to ransack the manor again."

Linnea stomped down the stairs directly for her mother while Halsten moved to stay with her, just in case. Instead of going to her mother, she marched right up to Duke Tiernan and poked him in the chest. "Duke Tiernan, you should see her artwork. Let me show you."

Linnea bent down and pulled off a boot and sock. "When I was younger, it was easy to blame my cuts and bruises on child's play." She then removed her other boot and sock. "But as I got older, Greer had to get creative." Her mother scoffed at her use of her name instead of parental title. Linnea picked up one foot, presenting the bottom to Duke Tiernan. "Those white speckles are from her making me step on nails. She specially made a board with nails protruding from the back for me to walk on simply because I told her my slippers were becoming worn down and uncomfortable. This taught me to be grateful for my shoes."

It took every single fiber of Halsten's being to let Linnea continue and not make a dive for Greer.

Linnea lifted her other foot and before she could even speak, Halsten's stomach turned. She was barefoot last night, but he hadn't noticed this evidence because he was a tad preoccupied. Now, he wished he had noticed so Linnea could have told him about her scars in a safer environment.

Her second foot that she lifted needed little explanation as to what she was presenting. Her pinky toe was missing.

"This one was innovative as well. You see, she had stepped on my toe and I yelped, which *clearly* meant I was calling her overweight." Linnea rolled her eyes. Duke Tiernan stared in horror as Linnea began putting her socks and boots back on. "She tied a string around my toe so tight that it cut off circulation and shackled me to a bed so I could not reach it and undo the tie. I stayed in that bed for days without food, but she graciously came in and gave me water to sip on. After days of hunger, I passed out."

"*None* of this is true, Tiernan! I swear it!" Greer pleaded.

"Hush now, mother. This is my story," Linnea snapped. "Anyway, once I passed out, she removed the string and called for a mender, telling him she thought my toe was infected and that was why I was in such a state. My toe needed to be amputated."

Halsten had wanted to know her story, but the onslaught of devastation was so intense. "You sadistic bitch," he spat toward Greer. "You never deserved to have a daughter."

Linnea wrapped a hand around his bicep and pulled him back, then rolled up her sleeves. "These white scars are the only ones she left visible, but I think she knew Uncle Botmar was already on the way to get me at that point, so she didn't care anymore. These are from being shackled to the grand fireplace, if you've ever noticed the hook in the molding. The cuffs got so hot that they seared my wrists."

Linnea pulled her sleeves back down, then began untucking her shirt. "Halsten, can you lift the back of my shirt please. I'd like to show Duke Tiernan my mother's finest moment."

It was Halsten's turn to shake. What could possibly be on her back? When he had explored her body last night, she never showed her bare back. He sucked in a deep breath and lifted the fabric, revealing a slew of stark white and deep pink scars, causing unnatural ridges in her skin all over. She turned so her back was to Greer and Duke Tiernan and spoke over her shoulder.

"This was from her pouring hot coals down the back of my dress because I had said it was a bit chilly in the manor that day, to make me appreciate the heat she provided."

Liva gasped. It was rare for the wraith to show emotion.

Halsten let the back of Linnea's shirt fall back down as she turned back to Tiernan.

"Long story short, Duke Tiernan, you have married a monster," Linnea shrugged.

Greer's face was nearly purple, as if her head were about to explode. "You ungrateful, selfish, rotten child! Everything I did was to teach you a lesson! You have always been so unappreciative of what I give you. How else was I supposed to instill proper values into such a distorted mind?"

Duke Tiernan took a step away from Greer. "You admit you've done these things to your own child?"

"Tiernan, dear, you don't understand. She was a terrible child!"

"I highly doubt this brave, young woman was a terrible child. The only thing I am sure of is that you are a terrible parent. And a horrendous person. For her to endure such things and still collect a band of friends clearly committed to her well-being speaks volumes to her character." The duke puffed up his chest, raising his voice. "I will be gone by the morning, Greer, and I am taking my assets with me. I am going to leave you as I found you—poor and alone."

Greer let out a horrific wail, falling to her knees.

Linnea simply stepped around her crumpled mother, not sparing her another glance and left through the front door. When everyone got outside, she was shaking. But she had stayed brave the entire time, and that meant the world to Halsten.

Linnea stared at the manor, inhaling and exhaling deeply multiple times. She turned to Gyrial and whispered in his ear so no one else could hear. He nodded, then jogged off, disappearing behind the manor.

Linnea stood, staring down the manor without a word. Niklas shifted uncomfortably from foot to foot, fiddling with his glasses while Liva stood preternaturally still, staring in the direction that Gyrial disappeared.

When the fae warrior appeared, walking back toward them, a swarm of servants came behind him carrying boxes and luggage. They began loading everything into the various exquisite carriages lined up further down the drive.

There was still not a word spoken between anyone in their group as they watched the servants go back and forth carrying a vast array of expensive items from the manor.

Finally, Duke Tiernan emerged from the main entryway and approached Linnea, placing a gentle hand on her shoulder. Halsten stepped forward to be next to her because he trusted no one associated with this property anymore.

"It's all yours." The duke grinned, then hopped into the nearest carriage and disappeared.

In a flash, Linnea bolted for the front door. Halsten ran in after her, unsure what she was going to do. She ran through the manor with determination and ended in the sitting room where her mother was sobbing on the sofa.

Halsten saw it then, the hook where her mother must have restrained Linnea's chains to the grand fireplace all those years ago. It was covered up by hanging an ash shovel, but Halsten knew what it was immediately.

Linnea marched over to the fireplace and placed the end of the ash broom into the flames.

"What are you doing?" Greer asked, barely audible.

The expression on Linnea's face was less of a full-toothed smile and more of a snarl. "What's wrong, dear? I thought you were cold."

She picked up the flaming ash broom and calmly walked to the curtain nearest to her, resting the flames on the fabric.

"No!" her mother shouted.

But Linnea didn't stop there. She dragged the flaming broom over the armchairs and rug. The smoke inhalation started to sting Halsten's lungs, but he knew Linnea needed a few more minutes. Her mother sat on the sofa in disbelief.

Linnea slowly approached her mother, gently laying the flaming broom on the bottom of her dress skirts. Greer shrieked, but her dress was already going up in flames with her in it.

The smoke was getting too thick now, and the wallpaper was starting to catch and curl. The entire sitting room would be engulfed in flames soon, and the rest of the manor quickly after.

Halsten grabbed Linnea by the bicep and pulled her. She yanked out of his grip, but then grabbed his hand, and they ran out of the burning manor together, fingers interlocked.

When they got outside, Gyrial, Liva, and Niklas were on their horses, the other two horses packed and saddled, awaiting their riders. Halsten hoisted Linnea up onto her horse then jumped onto his as they took off down the path back to the main road.

Linnea looked over her shoulder at the smoke billowing from the open front door and laughed, cheering and whooping as her horse ran at top speed.

"Linnea, I was wrong!" Halsten shouted over the sounds of the wind and galloping hooves. "You're not a little flame. You're a gods-damned wildfire!"

CHAPTER 38

K aid didn't know what he expected his mother to claim was the war-ending weapon, but he never expected it to be a hair comb.

The siren empress had signed fervently back and forth with Asta regarding the missing siren antique. Their pace was so fast that Kaid hardly had time to interpret a sentence before they were already three ahead of him.

Asta summed up their conversation—the sirens have always believed that the fae stole the trident in an attempt to restore peace between the seafolk species. To a degree, the fae had always felt responsible for the ongoing feud between merfolk species since they directly contributed to creating the sirens. However, on a more selfish perspective, they also likely concealed the trident to prevent the sea war from progressing onto land.

Since the comb and mirror had not been recovered in thousands of years, Queen Arielle speculated that the fae had also hidden them in their peace efforts. However, from the selkie reports, there were not even whispered discussions regarding the comb and mirror in fae culture. The items were truly a mystery.

Naturally—and to no surprise to Kaid—Asta saw this as a challenge. She wanted to be the one to return those items to their rightful owners, and he was sure she would succeed in that. Asta was not the type to let anything get in the way of what she wanted.

The next morning, Asta and Kaid prepared to return to Orntali and begin their search. Kaid had his first nights sleep in his true home and he had never slept better. Between the soft glow of the pearlescent walls and gentle sway of the sea sponge bed, mixed with the exhaustion of being abducted for the last few days and also the emotional toll of finally meeting his mother, it was no surprise that Kaid had drifted off easily. Amazingly enough, he started to grow accustomed to the cuff and chain on his arm. They felt like an extension of himself and he no longer felt their presence when he rested.

Asta had slept in the guest suite across the hall and as much as Kaid wanted to protest it, he hadn't had the energy at the time. Now, though, he wished he had. Their only night spent together thus far was spent in pain within a cold, damp cave and Kaid desperately wanted to rectify that. He supposed he would have the rest of his life to do so, but he did not want to waste any more time spent without Asta.

His blonde princess knew how to command a room when she was human, but now that Kaid had seen her siren form, nothing could top that. She wore her fin as if she'd been born with it and moved underwater with such grace. Seeing her as a mythical creature felt so natural that it was odd to think she was originally human.

However, it was time to return to land and complete their mission. Asta packed up her bag and prepared Thurs for the venture. Luckily, the other kelpies were healed from their assistance in Kaid's escape so their herd was full once more.

Kaid hugged his mother farewell and he knew exactly what she had meant when she signed, "See you soon," meaning she would accept no other outcome than Kaid returning to Naltania.

Asta pulled herself up onto Thurs while Kaid accepted the seat offered to him by another kelpie. He knew how important it was that the kelpie had offered him a ride, as the elusive sea horses did not like to be touched or tamed. The reality that Asta had managed to tame Thurs—in the loosest definition of the word—was a testament to her tenacity.

"Your Highness!" Kaid heard a male's voice behind him. "Wait!"

Soren rushed over to them, a pack slung across his torso. Revna swam up behind him, keeping pace but looking far less winded than the orange-finned warrior.

"What's wrong? What's happened?" Asta asked.

Soren grinned. "Nothing is wrong, besides the fact that you lot were attempting to leave us behind."

"Leave you behind?" Kaid shook his head. "You are intending to join us?"

"We are not *intending* to do anything. We *are* coming with you," Revna stated plainly. "You are our prince, who had been lost since his birth. We swear our allegiance and lives to you. We will accompany and protect you, from now until the currents retrieve our drifting corpses."

"To you, and to Princess Asta," Soren added.

Revna sighed, mumbling to herself. "Speak for yourself."

Soren elbowed her in the side, though she did not flinch.

"Very well," Kaid waved a hand. "Find some kelpies willing to offer you rides. If you can each find one, you can come."

When the two siren warriors were offered rides from multiple kelpies, Kaid concluded that they were likely better off taking the warriors anyway. And so, they returned to Orntali.

CHAPTER 39

Asta had not been conscious the first time she had traveled between Orntali and Naltania and she was pleased to find that the trip would take under a day. It was a strange feeling, discovering an undersea kingdom had been so close to her home all this time. However, it made sense as to why Kaid and his father had settled in this half of the country.

Asta leaned down and stroked Thurs's neck, the kelpie whinnying in response. The princess could not wait to tell Linnea everything she had discovered; everything she had done.

"Almost there now," Soren announced to the group. Asta looked at Kaid who nodded his chin to her in response, flashing his rakish smile. She rolled her eyes.

If Asta were being honest, she had been avoiding Kaid since the rescue. Was she a fool for thinking he had meant everything he had said in the cave? He had not done anything to make her believe so since, but with his past behavior...

"Think any harder and bubbles will pour from your ears, blondie," Kaid mocked.

Asta held up a particularly offensive finger and the siren prince chuckled.

Thurs began ascending and their surroundings changed, the sunlight shining brighter through the surface as the water became more and more shallow.

Home.

The kelpie's head broke through the water, drawing in a deep breath through her large nostrils. Asta felt a sharp twinge in her chest before she had the urge to pull in a breath as well. The sea air coated her lungs, transitioning her back to her human form.

Thurs trotted up to the shore, her fish tail disappearing and her color returning to a dapple gray. The other kelpies surrounding them transformed just the same.

Asta wiggled her bare feet as they dangled from the mare. The muscles felt tight, but not sore. It might take her a few laps up and down the beach to adjust to her human figure again.

She jumped down and untied her pack from the horse, the hooved beast darting off down the beach the second she was free. Asta smiled, knowing that Thurs would always remain a free spirit—even though Asta was the leader of the Northern Sea kelpies.

As she watched the kelpies dash away, Asta heard an *oof* from behind her. She turned to see Kaid clumsily dismounting his steed. His sea legs must be worse because he was not only in siren form for many days, but also hardly allowed to leave a bed.

Asta ran over and caught Kaid by his forearm to help him balance.

"Amateurs," Revna mumbled as she steadily marched toward the castle.

"*Amateurs,*" Kaid said in a mocking voice. "I haven't known that one long but somehow, she is more irritating than you."

Asta patted his chest. "Oh shut up. She grows on you."

Kaid grabbed Asta's hand that was resting on his forearm and slid it down toward his hand. Her heart skipped a beat. Was he really about to march into the castle—where he had previously been engaged to one princess— holding the other princess's hand?

Asta's hand slid over his cuff, a piece of the chain still dangling from his wrist. But as her hand passed over the iron, the latch unclasped and the contraption fell to the sand.

Kaid startled. "Did you just—"

"I didn't do anything," Asta shook her head.

She looked down at her hand, flexing her fingers and observing her Blomvin signet ring.

"It couldn't be," she mumbled.

Asta bent down and grabbed the cuff, closing it once again then placing the signet ring against it. The cuff immediately sprang open.

"Where did you get that ring, Asta?" Kaid stared, brows furrowed, at her hand containing the metal band.

Asta averted her gaze to the ring as well, shaking her head. "It was my mother's. I've always had it, just never worn it. I wanted to bring a piece of her with me when I turned in case I never made it back."

The corners of Kaid's mouth pulled back. "I think your mother had a lot more to do with siren affairs than anyone knew."

They had one of the iron keys.

Asta tapped her doorframe then entered her suite to find it empty besides Dyri. The massive canine barreled over to her, slamming his side into her legs so hard that she nearly toppled over. Someone had clearly been taking care of him, seeing as his food dish was full, but Linnea was nowhere to be found.

Once Asta had finished searching all of her rooms, she concluded that Linnea was gone. But where?

Kaid entered her bedroom. "No trace of Halsten. Linnea?"

Asta shook her head.

A piece of parchment on her vanity caught her attention and she immediately recognized her cousin's impeccable penmanship.

The note explained that Linnea, Gyrial, Liva, and Niklas had left for her mother's old manor to search for the comb and mirror. Kaid read over Asta's shoulder and somehow noticed when her heart began to race, based on his comforting hand that came up to rest on her shoulder.

Asta had always pushed her cousin to be more confident, but she never meant for her to go on a quest to the old manor that she had been abused in for the entirety of her adolescence. The last part of the letter blatantly told Asta to not worry, and not come after her. Asta huffed a laugh at Linnea's instinctual knowledge that she would try to chase after her.

Kaid moved to massaging Asta's shoulders. She stiffened, but relaxed once she realized how good it felt.

"She's fine, Princess. She is with a fae and a sea dragon. And Niklas. For whatever that's worth." Kaid's lips lightly grazed the side of her neck. "Relax for a moment. You're home."

Nothing made Asta less relaxed than being told to relax.

She turned toward Kaid to tell him so, but his mouth was already crashing into hers. Their lips moved together and Kaid's arm wrapped around her back to pull her flush with him. He pushed her until the backs of her thighs hit her vanity and she hopped up to sit on it, Kaid settling between her legs.

Kaid broke away from her mouth and his ocean eyes peered into her soul. "I've been waiting days to do that. I missed you."

Asta smiled and caressed his face. "I missed you too."

He dove forward, capturing her mouth again.

"Kaid," Asta whispered between kisses.

He only grunted in response.

"Kaid, the others will come looking for us," Asta managed to rush out.

Kaid pressed his cheek against hers so his lips tickled her ear. "In case you haven't figured it out yet, blondie, I don't give one single *fuck* about the others right now."

A whimper escaped Asta and she cursed herself for letting him make her so weak.

Kaid nipped at her ear before trailing kisses down her neck, toward her chest. One hand gripped her waist while the other traced tantalizing circles on her inner thigh. Her button up shirt only allowed Kaid access to the top of her breasts before he would have to start removing it.

To her surprise, he dipped to the side and caught her pebbled nipple in his mouth, using the friction of her shirt fabric to coax little moans from her.

Asta's hips bucked forward in response and Kaid smiled before returning his mouth to hers. He rolled his hips into her center and her thin cotton pants did nothing to hide how much this brief kissing had affected him.

A knock on the door had them both pausing.

"Asta?" Tova's voice was muffled through the heavy wooden door. "There's something you will want to see."

Kaid sighed. "To be continued."

"Well? What was so important that I couldn't rest for a bit?" Asta scanned the faces of Tova, Soren, and Revna.

Tova muffled a laugh with her hands. "I don't think you were going to get much rest."

Soren turned away so he was no longer making eye contact with the princess and Revna stared at Asta and Kaid in disgust. Having a group of friends with preternatural hearing made it difficult to have any privacy.

Asta's face heated, but she brushed off the comment. "Well?"

The door to the hallway opened and a familiar fae waltzed in, his arms spread wide for his usual greeting.

Asta immediately ran for Gyrial, springing into his arms. He caught her and spun her around. Once she was back on the ground, she pulled back and beamed at him.

"How are you here?"

Gyrial made his way to the sofa and took a seat. He explained that once his crew was about a day's ride home, a familiar gray mare approached them and insisted that Gyrial go with her, nudging him and tugging his shirt sleeves until he mounted her. Thurs ran faster than Gyrial had ever seen a horse ride before. The world around him had turned to a blur, as though they were traveling faster than the speed of sound, returning Gyrial to the castle in a few hours rather than a full day.

Gyrial pulled the mirror from his pack for everyone to observe and Asta could not deny the uncanny resemblance of the hand mirror to her mother's comb on her vanity. That was when Gyrial explained that all these years, Asta had been using a lost siren artifact as her everyday hair comb.

Asta got up and brought the comb out, holding it next to the mirror in Gyrial's hand. The two items hummed, turning warm in their hands and Asta dropped the comb onto the plush chair next to her.

She paced the room, the tension in her chest coiling tighter with each step. How was her mother so involved in the fate of this war and no one knew? It likely hadn't helped that her father's memory had been manipulated by the finfolk queen.

"So, what now?" Tova asked.

"Now, we find the Trident," Kaid stated.

CHAPTER 40

As everyone prepared to leave Orntali for the Spellid Mountains, Kaid couldn't help but watch the ocean waves from his window.

Was it right for him to leave the shoreline? Shouldn't he stay and help protect Naltania?

Kaid had gone from never having responsibilities to being the heir of a siren nation and the Northern Seas.

He turned to the desk and sealed the envelope he had written to his father explaining that he must come to Orntali immediately. Kaid was still processing the news about his family and upbringing, and honestly, talking with his father would help him interpret the gray areas, he hoped.

Kaid brought the letter down to the foyer where an attendant took it to be transported. Everyone else came down shortly after, all with packs in tow.

Asta was in black, wraithlike leathers and Kaid's heart sputtered. She was magnificent. He only hoped that after this was done, they would have their happily ever after.

Soren came trotting over with a kick in his step, grinning. "Ready to leave?"

It was still odd seeing him and Revna with legs instead of fins. Soren could not stop raving about how wonderful it was to be on land for the time being. He had not returned to land since he was turned as a young boy and it was apparent. The male siren had gone around sniffing every flower, every candle, every food dish he could find.

Gyrial grabbed his bag as well as Asta's and stepped out the front door.

"Show off," Kaid grumbled, following the crowd out the door.

Asta rode on Thurs, but the dapple mare was the only kelpie who joined them on the journey. The others would not tolerate a saddle of any sort, which was why they only allowed the sirens to ride them underwater where they could grasp onto their manes for support.

The blonde princess rode at the front with Gyrial which did nothing but grate on Kaid's nerves. Kaid rode next to Soren who had taken to humming cheerful melodies while pointing out every bird and woodland creature he saw. Revna and Tova rode in the back in silence, which Kaid was sure was killing Tova since she was typically quite chatty.

Asta was avoiding Kaid. He just knew it.

This was what she did. Every time they got close, she would pull back. Kaid supposed it was to protect herself due to his dating history, but he had done everything he could think of to prove to her that she was it for him, so what more did she need? Well, he had three long days to think about it while she giggled and joked with her male best friend.

The night was fairly uneventful. Kaid's turn for watch was spent with Revna who occupied her time by carving a thick branch with her dagger until the wood came to a lethal point. As if the siren warrior needed any weapons to kill.

Asta's watch was spent with Soren, who Kaid could hear asking the princess about all of the changes that had happened to the land kingdoms since his departure.

"I'd love to breed someday, so I can take my partner and youngling on land and show them everything that is missing in Naltania. It's wonderful, but not the same. Muted in comparison," Soren whispered.

"We will make that happen for you, Soren," Asta concluded.

Kaid didn't get much sleep. His bed roll was lumpy no matter how many times he punched it and his wool tunic did nothing to keep the night chill away. He would have considered wrapping an arm around Asta while she slept, but she opted to lay her bed roll between Soren and Gyrial. Soren had given Kaid an apologetic look as Asta smoothed out her roll on the ground.

After traveling all day in silence the following day, Kaid couldn't take it anymore. He came up with a plan.

Soren and Gyrial took first watch that night and Kaid knew Asta was next on the rotation with Tova. As difficult as it was after not sleeping the night prior, Kaid forced himself to stay awake and wait for the shift swap. He heard Gyrial wake Asta, and peeking through cracked eyes, saw the fae male gently rub Asta's shoulder as she came to. Their soft, mumbled words were indistinguishable as the blonde princess sat up and stretched her arms above her head.

Tova was already starting to stand when Kaid popped up and tapped her. "I can take this watch. I can't sleep anyway," he told her.

Tova's brow furrowed. "You sure?"

Kaid nodded. "No point in me tossing and turning through an entire shift when someone else could rest instead. Sleep."

The sea dragon did not need any more persuading as she nodded and laid back down.

Kaid stood and brushed the dirt off his pants, then plopped onto the fallen log in front of the small fire. It was mostly embers now, wanting to keep the bright light of a flame away to attract less attention.

Asta sat down next to Kaid, rubbing her eyes and yawning. Hopefully, she was sleeping better than he was.

"Where's Tova?" Asta asked as she poked at the hot coals with a stick.

Kaid shifted his torso to turn toward her. "I told her to keep sleeping. I'm awake anyway."

Asta nodded, keeping her eyes on the fire pit, but Kaid knew she was watching him in her peripheral vision.

"What are we doing, Asta?" Kaid whispered tersely.

She snapped her gaze to his, the corners of her mouth turned down. "You tell me."

Kaid pulled back, confusion etched across his face. "Have I not made it apparent since that night in the cave? Have I not been honest enough with my feelings and intentions? Honestly, Asta, I'm not sure what it is you're holding against me so, please, enlighten me."

"You expect me to believe your word when I've heard the stories about how you are? You come to my home, expecting to marry my sister, and I should believe you with full faith when you say that you are instead interested in me now? Not only that, but you plan on *only* being with me now?"

"I cannot—" Kaid stopped himself, realizing that the volume of his voice was rising. He pulled in a deep breath and released it slowly, this time speaking in a more hushed tone. "I cannot make you believe that I am truly trying if you don't give me a chance. You need to stop shutting me out every time we get close. People can change, Asta."

"People don't change that quickly," she replied curtly.

Kaid scrubbed a hand over his chin. "They do if it matters. They do if everything they have been searching for is within their reach, and it only requires them being a better person in order to grasp it. And as for your sister, I believe it's quite evident that any prior arrangements were nullified when I learned that she was a homicidal fish person that subsequently held me captive."

Asta blinked. "Technically, I'm a homicidal fish person now, too."

"You are. But a very cute, very alluring one," Kaid nudged her shoulder with his and grinned.

Asta's eyes narrowed but the corners of her mouth tilted upward a bit. "Don't be endearing. I'm trying to be serious."

"Oh, I *am* being serious." Asta had begun popping her knuckles and he grabbed her hand. "My seductive, lethal siren princess." He kissed the back of her hand. "My wraith of land and sea." He kissed her wrist. "My everything, from now until the day I drift to the seafloor, never to return."

The princess's breathing hitched and she pulled her wrist away, setting it back in her lap. "I rescued you because I want to believe you. Do not make me a fool for it." She reached up and brushed a piece of his dark hair from his forehead. "Also, I'm not a siren princess. I'm a siren, and also a princess."

"Not yet," Kaid smirked. He planned to change that someday very soon. Yes, he would marry this female and she would join him to rule in his ocean palace.

A branch snapped somewhere in the surrounding forest and Asta was instantaneously at her feet, sword in hand. Kaid slowly stood, observing their surroundings. He could not see anything, but the dense coverage of leaves overhead made it impossible to see very far beyond their camp perimeter. They stood for several moments, not hearing another sound.

"Probably an animal," Kaid whispered.

They both sat down and finished their watch shift in silence.

CHAPTER 41

They were on day two of traveling, which was how long Gyrial had said it would take them to arrive at the fae mountains. So when Gyrial shouted "Just past this hill!" over his shoulder an hour ago, Kaid had never been more happy to hear the fae male's voice.

Gyrial came to a stop in front of two incredibly large boulders at the base of a mountain range. The Spellid Mountains.

Gyrial dismounted his steed and walked between the boulders, shouting in a language Kaid had never heard before, but matched Gyrial's accent.

Two soldiers appeared between the boulders—fae, judging by their pointed ears—clad in golden armor with humongous swords across their backs. They answered Gyrial in their language, the three fae conversing in what sounded like agitated tones.

"They will not let us pass," Gyrial said to the group.

One of the soldiers stepped forward, throwing his long, almond colored braids behind his shoulder. "Tell them what we actually said,

Gyrial Bohr." His accent made him almost impossible to understand and it took Kaid a moment to translate. The soldier spit as if Gyrial's name tasted foul.

Gyrial's face heated. "We cannot pass without a duel. I am not allowed access to fae land until I face the general."

Asta dismounted Thurs and stood next to Gyrial, arms crossed. "Then we duel."

"No," Gyrial protested at the same time the almond-haired soldier asked, "Do we have a volunteer?"

"I will duel with your general if that is what it takes," Asta stated confidently, as if dueling a fae general was a miniscule task.

"Asta, you do not know what you're agreeing to." Gyrial stepped between Asta and the soldiers who were wearing cruel smirks. Kaid dismounted his horse and stood next to Gyrial, as well. If the male was concerned for her safety, so was he. Kaid heard Asta scoff behind him.

The two soldiers laughed as another fae male appeared from behind the boulders. This fae was exceptionally tall, even when compared to the other preternatural beings surrounding him. He moved with the grace of a mountain cat—undetectable and graceful. The gleaming silver sword he held was as long as his body was tall and Soren, Revna, and Tova unsheath their swords in response.

The male had long black hair sectioned into thick locks adorned with beads and jewels, but his dark skin and amber eyes were what Kaid concentrated on as he looked back and forth between the male and Gyrial. They were nearly identical.

"You are the same coward you have always been, Gyrial, if you are willing to let this female do your fighting for you," the fae sneered. His voice was gravelly and rough, a vast contrast to his movements.

"Even worse, General," the almond-haired soldier said, "he is protesting that *anyone* duels."

So this mountain of a male was the general. That made sense. Kaid still found himself comparing Gyrial to the general, and he knew there was only one conclusion to be made.

"He's your father," Kaid said aloud.

The general's eyes jumped to Kaid. "That's right, boy. I'm General Bohr. And the male you're standing next to is my traitorous deserter of a son." The general spat at Gyrial's feet. Kaid was glad that expelling saliva was not a part of any siren traditions that he had observed yet, and hopefully it remained as such.

Gyrial laughed in disbelief. "We have different memories of my departure, Father."

"Then choose your second and duel me, so you may petition the council." General Bohr hardened his stare as he crouched into a fighting stance.

"I am his second," Asta declared as she stepped around Kaid and Gyrial's protection.

Kaid grabbed her forearm. "Asta, there are multiple warriors here that can be his second. You do not have to."

"*I* am a warrior," she replied through gritted teeth, yanking her arm from his grasp and stepping forward.

General Bohr laughed. "Standard duel law. Tap in your second as needed. We go until a forfeit."

Gyrial opened his mouth to reply but Asta beat him to it. "Agreed."

As if someone were dragging a stick through the dirt around them, a circle drew itself around the two fae males, pushing Asta and the almond-haired guard out.

Then, General Bohr lifted his blade and lunged for Gyrial.

Gyrial blocked his father's strike with ease, his feline reflexes allowing him to swiftly duck and swing when necessary. Now that the pair were moving fluidly, it was hard to tell the difference between the males aside from their attire.

The fight went on for some time, Asta and the almond-haired soldier pacing around the fight like caged lions awaiting a meal. Whatever magic had drawn the duel ring prohibited them from stepping over it.

Kaid's heart felt like it would soon beat directly out of his chest. Why would Asta ever involve herself in such a fight? They were accompanied by two siren warriors and a sea dragon, for Knud's sake. Asta was a brilliant fighter, but she was not trained to battle fae warriors.

Or was she? Gyrial had been the one to train her, after all.

Kaid watched as Gyrial raised his sword and came straight down above General Bohr's head, the male barely having enough time to bring his enormous blade up and block the blow, but for the first time, the general stumbled back a step. It was just one step, but it was monumental. Asta shouted encouraging words to Gyrial as the other fae soldier begged to be tapped in.

Gyrial attacked with strike after strike, pushing his father back more with each swing of his blade. Although the general was blocking each, he was wearing down.

"Forfeit!" Gyrial shouted in his father's face. However, his father only answered with a grin before reaching back and tapping the fae soldier's arm. The magic allowed the third male to enter the fight.

The soldier sprung forward, diving for Gyrial. But General Bohr did not back down. He, too, continued toward Gyrial with an onslaught of hits.

Kaid didn't understand. The general had tapped out, so why was he still fighting? Asta was clearly thinking the same thing as she watched, bewildered.

"You cheat!" Gyrial bellowed as he was pushed back by the two opposing fae.

"You were never good with fae wording, son," General Bohr laughed. "I said tap in your second as needed. I never said that meant you tap out."

Kaid then realized what that meant. Even if Gyrial tapped Asta in, it would still be two incredibly powerful fae warriors against an out-of-practice fae soldier and a human-born siren. Kaid only hoped that Asta learned to use her merfolk strength and agility quickly.

Asta reached out her arm multiple times, attempting desperately to reach Gyrial in order to tap in.

"Tap me!" she insisted.

"No!" Gyrial responded.

He would rather lose—or die—then let Asta enter the fight. He never planned on letting Asta duel. Kaid suddenly earned respect for the male, and though they sought after the same woman, he knew that they would both give their lives for her as well.

Gyrial just barely parried a hit to his shoulder—which would have severed his arm—using his short sword as Asta screamed. Her shrill noise caused distraction for a moment, and Kaid's heart stopped as Gyrial's hand connected with hers on his withdrawal from the attack.

It was Asta's turn.

The blonde princess came in like a hurricane made of steel. She did not parry using a short sword, but instead, opted for holding two long swords. Kaid couldn't believe her strength as she battled with two swords that, before his transformation, Kaid could barely hold himself.

Though Gyrial was clearly distraught with her maneuvering her way into the duel, he did not let that stop him from joining her. Together, they moved in unison, pushing the other pair closer and closer to the boulder path.

Asta jumped as Gyrial's father swung for her shins and before her feet landed back on the ground, she struck his exposed elbow with her sword. Blood sprayed from the wound, decorating the warriors and dirt in red. She was the first to draw blood.

Asta hissed, bearing her siren teeth, but Kaid realized before it was too late. A bloodthirsty, newborn siren was like no other creature.

She moved so quickly that she was a blur. The only part of her that was discernable was her blonde tresses. The almond-haired soldier stumbled, falling flat on his back. Gyrial took advantage and kneeled above the male, holding his sword to his throat and pinning his arms to the forest floor with his knees. The soldier let out a grunt, his feet kicking but ineffective.

General Bohr made the mistake of glancing toward his partner for only a millisecond, and that's all the little blonde siren needed. She kicked the male square in his chest, knocking the air from his lungs. He doubled over and she kneed him in the face, his nose making a crunch of defeat. Blood once again sprayed and covered Asta, but she did not stop. She grabbed the male's hand and wrenched the sword from it, tossing it far away from the fight. Then, she grabbed the general by the back of his head and yanked him until his knees hit the ground.

Asta bent down and spoke so closely to the general's face that spit smattered his skin. "Forfeit, or I swear to the gods I will snap your neck and leave you here."

General Bohr swallowed loudly before whispering, "I forfeit."

Soren let out a surprised laugh and Kaid heard Tova whisper, "Fuck yeah, asshole" under her breath.

Asta, however, did not let go of the general's locks. "You will also apologize to your son."

The general's eyes shifted to Gyrial, then met Asta's. "I'm—" he sucked in a breath as Asta's grip tightened, her eyes intently watching the trail of blood dripping from his nose. "I'm sorry."

Asta dove forward and latched onto General Bohr's neck with her mouth and Kaid ran for her.

"No!" he shouted as Asta feasted on the blood that had sent her into a frenzy in the first place. "Asta, no!"

Gyrial got to her first and tried to pull her off the general, but she shoved him so hard that the fae actually flew backward.

Kaid knelt down next to her and petted her matted hair. "Asta, you are not a cold-blooded killer. This is not you. This is your siren."

Her gulping slowed down, but she continued to feed. The general's face was a shade lighter and his eyes fluttered shut.

"Asta," Kaid gently placed a hand on her shoulder. "Stop. You're killing him."

She froze, her feeding paused. She squeezed her eyes shut, and Kaid knew that she was battling the voice in her head that told her to keep feeding. The voice that the sirens had inherited from the finfolk. Her hands shook as she shoved the general to the ground, her mouth disconnecting with a *pop!*

Asta looked to Kaid with blood-stained lips and tears in her eyes, her hands shaking. One of her hands grabbed the other immediately and began cracking various joints in her fingers and all Kaid could do was pull her into a tight embrace until she came back to him.

CHAPTER 42

Asta was still shaken up as the spare fae soldier—the one not involved in the duel—led the group through the boulder gates and into the fae territory.

It was not that she had nearly taken someone's life—especially someone who treated her best friend so poorly—but how little control she had over her actions as she had done so.

Asta always had control. She never allowed anyone else to take charge or guide her actions. Now, an insatiable siren lived within her, able to dominate her thoughts at the first sign of bloodlust. She hated it.

The only person who had been able to reunite her mind with her body time and time again was Kaid. Whenever she fell, he was there to catch her and hold her until she could stand on her own again.

It was a new feeling for Asta, letting someone in. Allowing someone to see her vulnerable sides and not protesting when they tried to help. She did not even allow such a thing with Linnea. But with Kaid, it had happened without her even acknowledging it, and that gave her the answer to a question she had been asking herself for years.

Asta jogged ahead toward Gyrial, who was walking next to the fae soldier.

She tapped him on the shoulder. "Can we talk?" She glanced behind them. "Privately."

Gyrial furrowed a brow but nodded, lightly guiding her by her elbow off the path they were walking on. The group kept walking, clearly taking the hint. Gyrial knew his way around and could lead them to their destination after their conversation.

Gyrial smiled gently and left his hand on her elbow. "What's bothering you?"

Asta did not know how to address the subject she needed to speak about, so she utilized the method she knew best—blunt honesty.

She sucked in a deep breath then blurted, "I love you."

Gyrial's eyes widened, utter confusion emanating from every pore.

"I—oh fuck—no, this isn't coming out the way I need it to," she stammered.

"Asta, breathe. It's me. What are you saying? I need to know *exactly* what you mean." Gyrial's tone was a bit more stern than she was accustomed to.

Asta curled her hands into fists, doing her best to refrain from cracking knuckles. "I love you, but not the way you need me to. And not the way you deserve to be loved. I love you enough to tell you that I'm not *in* love with you, and we have to move on from the 'will-they, won't-they' approach we've always taken. I want to see you happy with someone who feels exactly the same toward you."

The fae male stared at her in silence for many moments, never moving a muscle aside from his eyes searching her face. Then, at last, he let go of her arm and took a step back.

Gyrial cleared his throat before speaking. "Thank you, Asta. Thank you for saying the words I needed to hear aloud to understand." He smiled sweetly, though it did not reflect in his eyes. "It's him, isn't it?"

Asta peered toward the group walking away down the path, her sight set on the deep red-haired male that looked like he had been finely crafted by the greatest sculptor in history.

"It's him, Gyrial."

Asta and Gyrial quickly caught up with their companions, who were being led to the High Fae Lord at their request. Gyrial mentioned many times that he was astonished that the Lord would even grant them visitation, which made Asta nervous.

They arrived at a large structure carved of stone, polished to glisten in the mid-afternoon light, and entered into a large throne room of sorts.

The walls were lined with crackling torches and artwork painted directly on the rock walls, and at the center of the room was a raised dais with multiple seats—also made of stone.

"These fae really love their rocks, hmm?" Tova whispered from the corner of her mouth.

Asta covered her mouth to hide her laughter and Revna glared at the two of them before walking away.

"She must love rocks, too," Asta mumbled. A squeak escaped Tova's lips before she could slap her hand over them, drawing the attention of everyone in the room, including the four fae sitting on the dais.

The fae male sitting in the largest throne stood, his white beard unfurling from his lap and landing mid-thigh on him. His posture was mildly hunched, and Asta concluded that this fae must be *very* old if he looked like an elderly human.

"Is there something amusing regarding our customs, females?" The male's voice boomed through the room, echoing off the hard walls.

Asta's face turned cold, her palms clammy. She didn't dare look at the rest of the group and face their disappointment of her childish behavior. She was raised royal. She knew better. This was worse than being reprimanded during daily lessons with Maren. At least then, the only people she had embarrassed herself in front of were her sister and tutor.

Asta and Tova sheepishly shook their heads.

The old fae gave one sharp nod. "Now that we can move past the jesting, what is the purpose for requesting visitation with the Lords?"

To Asta's surprise, Kaid stepped forward. "I am Prince Kaidian Andreassan, Prince of the Ventarin Sea and heir to the Northern Seas empire. We seek a siren artifact that we believe you possess. I would like to reclaim what was taken."

The elderly fae scoffed. "And I am High Lord Jek Karlana, ruler of the Spellid Mountain fae, and I decline your request to obtain such a destructive object."

Well, that was not exactly how Asta thought that would go. She stepped forward, hands clasped in front of her to subdue her cracking compulsion. "My lord, if I may, we understand that the trident has historically been used recklessly, but that is not our intention. We plan to use it to end this war between the two merspecies once and for all."

Another fae sitting on the dais laughed, a wrinkly elderly female with garish jewelry and deep purple lips. "That's what you lot always claim whenever you seek out that enchanted fork."

Jek held up a hand to cut her off. "What Lady Tressa is trying to say is, why should we trust you more than all the others who have sought out the trident before?"

Gyrial stepped forward this time, crouching down to one knee and facing the floor as he spoke. "Lord Karlana, I can vouch for this group of seafolk, as I have observed them and their intentions intimately, and you know fae word is true."

As Gyrial spoke, Asta noted the way Jek regarded him. The lord's intent gaze made a heavy feeling settle deep in her gut. Jek tapped a finger to his chin. "Ah, Gyrial Bohr. A name I never believed I would speak aloud again. How has exile treated you all these years?"

Exile.

Asta had never put much thought into why Gyrial had left the Spellid Mountains after learning his true heritage. His own father had implied that Gyrial was a traitor who abandoned his clan, not that he had been exiled. Asta searched Gyrial's profile for any indication as to whether the implication was true or not, but the fae never flinched.

"Exile has been nothing but pleasant," he replied simply.

Holy shit, Gyrial really had been exiled by the fae.

Was it even safe for him to return to their territory? What were the repercussions of returning after exile? Asta rested her palm on the hilt of her sword slung at her hip, the uncertainty of the situation making her jittery.

Jek spoke with the other three fae on the dais at a volume that made his words indiscernible. Everyone was on edge, each member of the party fidgeting with their weapons or swaying rhythmically to warm up their muscles.

When the hushed discussion concluded, Jek faced them once more, spreading his arms out wide like a showman revealing his next act.

"The Lords Council has decided to grant you access to the trident..."

Kaid blinked rapidly while Soren's brows furrowed.

"*If?*" Gyrial whispered to himself.

Jek continued. "If each member of your party takes part in thoughtrus and passes."

"Oh fuck me," Gyrial muttered under his breath as he ran a hand down his face.

"What's thoughtrus?" Asta murmured to him.

"To answer your question, siren," Lord Karlana sneered, "we borrow your mind to ensure your intentions are true to your word."

Asta didn't quite understand what "borrowing your mind" meant, but she knew it likely wasn't pleasant based on the menacing smirks each fae lord and lady wore. But they had made it this far, and Asta was not one to quit so easily. They needed this trident. There was no other option.

CHAPTER 43

The group was rushed to the edge of the dais while they awaited the thoughtrus fae. Asta risked a glance at Kaid, who returned her stare with a look steeped in worry.

Gyrial turned to everyone and rattled out few but important words. "The thoughtrus magic will penetrate your mind and examine your deepest thoughts. Do not fight it—this could cause brain damage. Do not try to hide anything from it—this will cause it to draw more atten-tion to that part of your mind. We have nothing to hide. Do not make it seem like we do."

"Wise words for a male who abandoned his kind," Jek interrupted.

Asta did not like this particular male, whether he was powerful or not. *She* was powerful, too.

A female fae with silver hair floated into the room as if she hovered on a cloud. She stopped at the edge of the platform and held out a hand to Lady Tressa, who had shuffled to the side of the dais. The lady took the female's hand and examined it as a soft glow emitted from her fingertips.

"She is she," Tressa declared.

So the white glow was a type of identification magic. The silver-haired female approached the group now and Asta could see that her irises were so silver they were nearly indiscernible from the whites of her eyes—very similar to the traitor siren from the village, but far less menacing.

Gyrial stepped forward, the willing volunteer. Asta was uncomfortable with her best friend going first, but she could not think of anyone else she would have wanted to take his place. She had grown to care for everyone here, and they were all in danger.

"Hello, Gyrial Bohr. You return to us at last. I've been waiting," the female said.

"I planned to prolong my return indefinitely, but desperate times—you know. It is lovely to see you, Sabella." Gyrial got down on his knees in front of Sabella and averted his eyes to the floor.

Sabella placed her hand on Gyrial's head, her fingertips sifting through his braids and caressing his scalp. As she closed her eyes, the air in the room became thick with something unfamiliar to Asta. It smelled sweet and savory at the same time and the sensation in the air caused the hairs on her arms to stand erect.

Asta didn't dare move, didn't dare breathe while Gyrial withstood the thoughtrus. She didn't know much about magic, but she suspected one distracted thought, one hostile emotion and Gyrial would be done. It seemed as though everyone else in their band of misfits did not dare disturb the process either.

After what felt like an eternity, Sabella released Gyrial's scalp and stumbled backward, disbelief overtaking her every pore.

"His intentions are pure. But his exile…" Sabella covered her mouth with a shaky hand.

"Enough of your dramatics, mindwalker. Onto the next candidate," Jek shouted dismissively.

Sabella stared at Gyrial with—was it pity?

She seemed to be the one selecting candidates, and when she approached Revna, Asta did not worry. If there was one singular person of their group who was guaranteed to pass this test, it was Revna.

The silver-haired fae plunged her digits into Revna's ice-blue hair until the tips disappeared. It took the fae half the time to search Revna's mind compared to Gyrial's. She steadily stepped back and nodded toward the fae council on the dais. "Pure," Sabella stated, then stood in front of Kaid. Asta's heart skipped a beat. Before she knew what she was doing, Asta pushed her way between Kaid and the female.

"Eager, are we?" Lady Tressa suggested with an eyebrow raised.

Asta mimicked a curtsey, though she ignored the usual mannerisms of a proper dip. "Eager to prove to you all that there is no need for such interrogation. Eager to prove to you all that you are delaying aid to the ones who wish to end a war."

Lady Tressa scrunched her nose, but did not object.

Asta did as the two before her had done and sunk down to her knees. However, she did not avert her eyes to the floor. She stared deeply into Sabella's mirrorlike gaze, and Sabella stared back.

Sabella smirked, one corner of her mouth turning up obscurely. A sign of respect.

The fae female gave a jerky nod, then pushed her fingers through Asta's hair. The moment she felt the pads of Sabella's fingers graze her scalp, the female's eyes became blurry, then completely clouded over with depictions from her own conscience.

Images of Asta's father flashed quickly, as though Sabella was flipping through her memories until she found something of interest. The mindwalker moved onto Maren, forcing Asta to relive the images of her sister bearing skin shredding teeth and pointed ears. These memories lingered longer, as if Sabella was investigating the details more closely.

Anything Asta had pushed to the edge of her memory, Sabella dragged back front and center. She saw her moments in her suite with her friends, the times she daydreamed with Linnea, the moment she found Thurs.

Then, every memory with Kaid resurfaced in a beautiful montage of hate and want. First, they met in the hall outside of the party the first day he had arrived. The scene quickly changed to the beach where she kicked a bit of water at him. Asta would always feel guilt for that—for reigniting the beacon of his princedom. Then they were in her dimly lit bedroom, his palm resting on her stomach. Then they were in the cave and—no, no. These memories were for *Asta*, not some fae she had just met.

Instinctively, she pushed. The thoughtrus lunged at her like a cobra, its fangs penetrating her protective shield around her memory. Asta felt a dull ache with every blow the cobra struck, the tattered shield still holding, but not for long.

Asta knew her defenses would only withstand a handful more hits before coming down. She knew that if that happened, she risked memory damage. She knew that it was silly to hide such a thing; to sacrifice so much for one small private memory. But she could not stop.

As the cobra reared back for the final, mind melting blow, it retreated, disappearing back toward the infiltrative mass in Asta's mind. Toward Sabella.

Then, an image that wasn't true but could very well become a reality poured through Asta, bleeding into every crevice and congealing.

Asta saw herself, hunched over something wrapped in a tattered blanket. She rocked rhythmically, counting aloud.

"Twenty-six, twenty-seven, twenty-eight. One, two, three..."

The counting continued in a loop as Asta rocked a newborn child. The baby screamed in her arms, but she was too lost to the counting. Too lost to her ritual. The only indication that this alternate-reality "Asta" acknowledged the child was the crinkle of her crow's feet at the corners of her eyes. But she could not stop. She must count, and count, and count.

Not only that. She must produce child, after child, after child. One heir was not enough. One heir was not enough. One heir was not enough. Birth the children, raise them, marry them off. That was her purpose. And it drove her mad. She watched as the elder Asta lightly tapped the edge of the blanket—tapping, tapping, tapping. Rocking and counting. Tapping. The screaming persisted from the baby.

It was her own personal Hell. It was her greatest fear.

That was what thoughtrus was intended for. Through her greatest fears, Sabella could determine her greatest desires.

Sabella withdrew, the tendrils she had wrapped around Asta's brain retracting with a tickling sensation. When Asta returned to the throne room, she was still staring deeply into Sabella's silver gaze. The female gently smiled at her, her cheeks flushed and a sheen of sweat on her brow.

Was thoughtrus draining? Had Asta's been difficult? She did not see the fae female look so drained until she completed Asta's assessment. Her stomach churned with nausea from both living through her worst nightmare paired with Sabella's pending result.

The blonde princess dared a glance at Kaid, who was breathing heavily in anticipation. She wondered if her thoughtrus was longer, like Gyrial's, or shorter, like Revna's. Either way, Asta had pushed against the magic, which Gyrial had specifically instructed she not do.

"I need... time," Sabella announced over her shoulder toward the dais. "Let me gather my thoughts while I continue assessments."

Jek stood up, his hands fisted into tight balls. "I demand you report whether she is a threat or not. Your council demands answers!"

Sabella snapped her gaze to Jek, baring her elongated fangs with a hiss. "You will not rush me. Am I not your only mindwalker? Am I not the only one who understands what this power requires? Magic does not abide by our rules. We abide by the laws of magic."

To Asta's surprise, Lord Karlana sat back on his throne without another word, his face deep crimson.

Sabella quickly worked through her assessment of Soren. Moving onto Kaid, Asta's chest tightened. The thought that continuously gave Asta comfort was that she knew, beyond a shadow of a doubt, that Kaid's intentions were pure in wanting to help the sirens bring peace to the Ventarin Seas.

The siren prince's assessment was swift, Sabella hardly touching Kaid's head before she determined that he was trustworthy.

They only had one more person—Tova. The sea dragon shifter was shaking like a leaf, her usual carefree demeanor buried with worry and anticipation. Asta did not know what she had to worry about. She wanted the sirens to be free of war as much as everyone else here.

As the thoughtrus fae approached Tova, the sea dragon glanced toward Asta and shook her head before averting her gaze.

Sabella grabbed Tova's head and jerked, her arm stiffening and her fingers grasping roughly at Tova's scalp. The females breathed heavily in unison, their bodies shaking. Before long, Sabella released her grasp and fell backward onto her rump. Tova fell to the side, convulsing and foaming at the mouth.

Asta rushed to her friend's side. "What have you done?" she shouted through gritted teeth. "What is wrong with her?"

"She resisted," Sabella crawled back, awestruck. "I could still see her memories through her fight. She had no reason to push me."

Asta brushed Tova's hair from her face as her eyes lolled back and her convulsions subsided. She was still breathing, but what the fuck was wrong with her?

"Tova? Tova! You need to wake up!" She shook her friend's body.

Asta felt a hand on her shoulder and looked up to see Kaid, lips turned in and sympathy in his gaze. "She resisted, Asta. She knew the risks. There isn't—" He shook his head. "We will take her home with us. Maybe being in a familiar setting will help."

Lord Karlana clapped slowly, dramatically, as he stood once again. "A traitor in our midst, as we expected. And what of the blonde creature?"

Asta instinctually hissed at him, her siren at wits end with this fae council after losing her friend.

Sabella gestured toward Asta. "She is of pure intent with the trident. She is of pure intent of anything she sets her mind to." The silver-haired fae faced Asta and continued speaking in hushed tones. "I worried, regarding your relationship with your sister, that you may wish to use the trident to reconcile with her somehow. But I see now that you are one who says what you feel, and acts on how you feel. And above all else, you covet the moments you share with others when you are acting on your emotions. I cannot fault you for such a thing. Truthfully, I commend you on your willingness to risk your wellbeing to protect those moments. You are not your fears. You are not a vessel for breeding. Your rituals do not make you mad. You are you, and that is valuable. You are you, and you should not question your worth because of habits you cannot control. They do not define you. Do not let them."

Asta, grateful to the mindwalker, bowed her head—an action a princess should perform for no one besides kings and queens. She was forever indebted to the female for respecting something she coveted so dearly even though she could have snapped her mind in two for harboring a memory. Through it all, her honorable intention was clear and allowed her to pass the thoughtrus test.

CHAPTER 44

Kaid grabbed Asta by the hand. It was not the time, nor place, to show such a weakness to the high fae, but he needed the small comfort. He needed something to ground him—to remind him that the fears he envisioned were not real and never would be.

If Kaid had been subjected to thoughtrus a few months ago, his greatest fears would likely have been misfortune, being tied down to one woman, and—materialistically—never ingesting a drop of liquor again.

However, Kaid's life had changed drastically since he arrived in Orntali. And so, it made perfect sense that the lost siren prince would fear loneliness. Not only loneliness, but losing Asta and his parents. Kaid saw himself in the dining hall of his Haalberg estate, a feast laid out with no one to share it with. They had lost the war. Kaid had lost his parents. Asta had sacrificed herself. He heard the empty echo of the home while he cut into his meal, the metal on porcelain scraping the silence like nails on granite.

Kaid found it somewhat amusing, how his greatest fears had changed so quickly. Now, he did not care for riches. He did not care for parties, royalty, or philandering. He cared for Asta and his family. He could lose everything, but if he still had them, he had everything. More than everything.

Asta's gentle squeeze on his hand broke Kaid from reliving his nightmares over and over again. He wondered what she had seen. He couldn't hear what Sabella had whispered to her after her assessment, but he was glad the fae's words brought her comfort, as Asta's shoulders had relaxed gradually during their interaction.

The air in the room felt stagnant as Lord Karlana and the other council members evaluated them. They all passed, so what was the delay?

"We've passed. Give us the trident," Kaid said, growing more impatient by the second. The fate of his family and kingdom laid in the hands of these cunning fae.

Lord Karlana balled his hands into fists so tight that his knuckles turned white. "The agreement was that if you all passed the thoughtrus magic, you would receive the trident. Well, you did not all pass." Karlana gestured to Tova, who was sitting on the ground at Gyrial's feet as he supported her weight with his legs. "How do I know there aren't more traitors waiting for you back home? How am I to know that you won't simply take the relic and pass it to the wrong hands?"

The room fell silent again. The bouts of stillness were wearing on Kaid. He was tired of wasting time, which was exactly what these fae were trying to achieve.

"Give us a blood oath," Gyrial's deep voice boomed off the stone walls, demanding attention from everyone in the room.

The council snickered, exchanging hushed words. However, one face remained like stone. Lady Tressa approached the edge of the dais where Gyrial waited with squared shoulders and an unrelenting gaze.

"You would swear a blood oath for these creatures? For those who are not fae?"

Lady Tressa stood so still that the light reflecting off her gaudy jewelry did not waver. Though he knew what she meant by her referring to him as a "creature," it still rubbed him the wrong way. Afterall, sirens were half fae. They only existed because the fae placed their trust in the wrong "creatures" to begin with.

Gyrial's eye contact never broke as he responded. "I would give my life for any member of this group, as they are the most trustworthy beings I have ever met." Which was saying a lot, since Gyrial had lived such a long life thus far. "So yes, my Lady, I would take a blood oath ten times over for anyone standing beside me now."

The other council members laughed again, but Lady Tressa remained still. She assessed each and every one of them, and for the first time, Kaid acknowledged how truly predatory fae were. Being a siren, he was a predator too, but he was still not accustomed to thinking in such a way.

"Everyone step forward. I will do it," Lady Tressa gestured to the foot of the dais.

Kaid had not expected the stone-faced, unreadable council member to be the one to put her trust in them, but then he turned to Asta and it made more sense. Asta had an incredibly hard exterior and even harder, fortified mental walls, but she gave everyone a chance. One chance. Then, if you failed her, you were banished from her life. This female fae must operate similarly.

Kaid approached the dais while still holding Asta's hand, followed by Soren, Revna, and Gyrial who guided Tova's steps. They followed the Lady's instructions to add a pool of their blood to the large golden bowl that was passed around. They each sliced their palms using their own blades and watched the crimson red splash into the bowl below.

When they were done, Lady Tressa gave three drops of her own blood. Then, she trained them on what words to say once she performed the oath. Kaid's palms were sweating profusely. Luckily, the small incision he had made on his palm was already a faint pink scar thanks to his siren magic.

"I will now state the terms of the oath," Lady Tressa announced to the rock ceiling as though she were speaking directly to the goddesses and gods above. "These beings swear to use the sacred siren trident for the greater good. They swear that the trident will not be gifted to those who wish to use it for tyranny. They swear that the trident will be concealed when its use is complete. On their lives, they make this promise."

Kaid knew that once he responded, his life would be tied to the trident. It was one thing to give your life for someone you cared about, but to willingly shackle your future to an inanimate object felt irresponsible. Still, it was the only way the sirens could ever win this war.

"On our lives, we make this promise," they all responded in unison.

Then, the bowl was passed down, everyone taking a sip of the blood mixture. Kaid let the warm, thick liquid slide down his throat and resisted the urge to gulp down the entire dish. His bloodlust was finely tuned without him ever intending it to be, but drinking pure blood like this made him second guess his will power.

With that thought, he passed the bowl to Asta, whose hands shook uncontrollably. Unlike everyone else here, Asta's bloodlust was still new. "It's only a sip," Kaid whispered in her ear and she nodded in return. The princess lifted the bowl to her lips and ever so slightly tipped it. Something about seeing the red liquid smooth over her lips sent shivers down Kaid's spine.

Drink, drink, drink. Drink until only residue remains.
Drink from the bowl while I drink from you.

Kaid closed his eyes tightly, willing the siren voice in his head to silence.

When Kaid noticed Asta had drunk a little more than the rest of them, he pulled the bowl away, leaving a dribble of blood at the corner of her mouth, which she wiped away with her sleeve. He knew he was fucked when he wished he could have licked it off her himself.

Lady Tressa retrieved the bowl and drank what little was left. Kaid felt a jolt run through his body for a fraction of a second, then it was over.

Lord Karlana caught everyone's attention as he approached the edge of the dais holding a golden, glinting object. The trident. He held it out begrudgingly while glaring at Lady Tressa, who watched the exchange carefully.

Kaid reached forward and wrapped his fingers around the cool metal staff that held a three-pronged fork at the end. A gentle glow emanated between his fingers, then drifted down the rest of the relic, the metal humming and warming under his touch. A familiar song infiltrated Kaid's thoughts, the trident singing to him the way the ocean did, but with no distinguishable lyrics. It was the symphony of the sea—the smooth waves, the stirring currents, the sharp edges of the rocks below, all blending together to sing him a song of home.

The light traveled up Kaid's trident tattoo on his hand, extending up his arm and illuminating the fine lines of the mark. It was like being reunited with an old, dear friend.

As if the journey to the Spellid Mountains hadn't been hard enough, the journey back posed to be that much more difficult now that they were transporting a massive relic—and a heavy one at that.

Kaid took the first turn, strapping the trident to his back the way a warrior would secure a sword. Everyone rode in silence for the first day, likely reflecting on everything they endured during their thoughtrus assessments.

Everyone was also taking turns having Tova ride with them, as she was not fit to lead her own horse. She stared blankly ahead, every so often blurting out gibberish. Every time it happened, Asta would hold Tova's hand, offering soothing words and cooing her back to silence.

During the second day of travel, the mood was a bit lighter. Soren began his usual storytelling while Gyrial mumbled softly to Revna regarding travel and battle plans. Kaid could not decipher if Asta was truly enthralled by Soren's tales or if she was simply using them as an escape from their current situation. At the end of it all, they were preparing for war.

With one more day of travel ahead, they stopped a little earlier in the evening to enjoy a proper meal and good rest before the last leg of the journey. Revna and Gyrial took off to hunt for any form of meat while Soren began building a fire.

"Help me forage?" Asta asked Kaid, nodding her chin to some prickly bushes a little further into the woods.

They walked in comfortable silence until they got to the blackberry bushes and began picking. "Do you think you can wield it? The trident?" Her eyes flashed to the golden prongs sticking up from behind Kaid's head.

Kaid shook his head. "I'm not sure. All I know is that it feels right, having it in my hands. Like it belongs with me."

"That's because it does. You're the long lost siren prince, remember?"

Kaid grinned. "And don't you forget it."

Asta rolled her eyes and dropped some berries into the small satchel they were putting them into. Kaid held up a plump blackberry between two fingers. "This one looks particularly juicy. Here, for you." He held it forward and Asta went to grab it, but Kaid snatched it away. "*Ah ah ah. No hands.*"

Asta scowled, realizing how close to each other they had drifted, then opened her mouth enough to wrap her lips around the tips of his thumb and index finger, flicking her tongue over them before pulling the berry into her mouth.

Kaid's breathing hitched and he dropped the handful of berries, letting them softly thump on the forest floor, before pulling Asta to him and crashing his lips to hers.

Kaid swept his tongue into her mouth tasting a mix of Asta and the blackberry. His arms wrapped around her, while hers brushed his face, his chest, his arms. *Fuck* she tasted so good mixed with berries. Kaid wished they weren't in the middle of the woods. He wished they were back in Orntali, locked in Asta's suite where he could show her how intoxicating he thought she was. It was better than any black-out night he'd ever had.

"*Ugh,* go find another cave."

The voice behind Kaid made his back stiffen, ice solidifying his veins. He knew that voice.

Asta backed away from Kaid, who turned around to look at Maren. Asta dropped the satchel of berries and pulled her sword from its sheath.

"Hi sissy. Miss me?" Maren asked. Svanhild stood next to her, sword aimed at Asta.

Kaid pulled his dagger from his hip, not entirely sure what he could do with it in a sword fight, but he would try. Maren stepped with slow, feline grace toward Asta. "I was here to deliver a message, but if you want a repeat of our last fight, I would be more than happy to oblige."

"What do you want, Maren?" Asta's eyes followed every move Maren made, so Kaid focused on Svanhild.

"Just checking in to see if you know where your sweet cousin is," Maren smiled. "Because I know, and I also know exactly where a pack of Ryktarvans are headed right now. Funny, I think they might share the same location."

The air left Kaid's lungs. *Halsten.* He feared for everyone in the group, but Halsten was his best friend, his partner in crime. He couldn't lose him. And Kaid knew that Asta felt the same about Linnea.

"What the fuck did you do, Maren?" Asta shouted, lunging forward and swinging for her sister's throat.

CHAPTER 45

Grateful for his sword training, Halsten blocked the Ryktarvan warriors' attacks. He had never had to use these skills in a real fight and practice meant nothing compared to the real thing.

When the traitor siren soldiers had first attacked, Halsten had shoved Linnea behind him and so far, he had been able to protect her. Liva was beside him guarding Niklas. If only Gyrial hadn't left them—they would have stood a far better chance with a fae warrior here.

There were five grunts in total. Halsten knew it was unrealistic for him to think he could kill them all, but he had to at least try to run them off. Did the enemy know that they possessed the mirror? Was that why they were here?

They were so damned close to home. So close to making it out of the journey unscathed. If they hadn't been held back by a dangerous storm for almost a full day, they would be in Orntali right now.

Halsten's arm muscles burned, but he couldn't stop fighting. Linnea was behind him, and he would not let any harm come to her.

Liva plunged her sword through one of the siren's hearts and he toppled to the ground in a heap. One of the merfolk hissed, fangs glinting in the fading sun. One down, four to go.

Though Halsten could not distinguish what they were saying, he could hear Linnea and Niklas speaking behind him. There was a terrible screech, and another siren went down under Liva's blade.

Come on, Halsten. Don't let Liva do all the work!

Halsten had never actually been in battle before, nevermind kill someone, but he needed to try. If they lost, it meant Linnea would be injured—or worse—and he could not let that happen.

The thought of Linnea getting hurt started the rage within him, and the memory of how her own mother treated her back at the estate sent the fury pumping throughout his entire body.

How could someone hurt Linnea? *Strike.* How could her own mother starve her? *Strike.* How could anyone look at this marvelous, strong woman and want to do anything to dim her light? *Strike.* How could Halsten even let these soldiers get within ten feet of her?

Halsten purposely left his ribs open, enticing the soldier to step forward for a killing strike and at the last moment, he twisted forward and let his blade spin with him, aiming right for the siren's neck. Halsten didn't feel the impact of the steel on skin, didn't feel the resistance of slicing through muscle and bone. Didn't feel remorse as the siren's head came clean off and rolled away.

So that was Halsten's motivation—Linnea.

He moved onto the next soldier, trying the same method, but this warrior was stronger and faster than the last. The creature met each of Halsten's strikes with a block no matter what training strategy he used. Then, the soldier started fighting back. Each swing of her blade came quickly and Halsten was barely stopping them inches before impact.

Halsten's first kill had made him cocky. Realistically, he knew he had never fought before and likely got lucky. Now, he was paying the price. He aimed low, trying to slow the siren down by injuring a leg, but the creature jumped, her boots landing directly on Halsten's blade and ripping it from his hands. He stumbled back, but could not retreat because Linnea was behind him and he would not expose her.

The female siren spun and threw a short sword, which speared through Halsten's thigh like a warm knife through butter.

For a few seconds, he couldn't feel the pain, and in those few seconds, he watched as Linnea plunged a dagger into the gloating siren's jugular. Then, the world went black.

The world was still dark, but Halsten could feel his body slightly jostling and hear the sound of hooves hitting dirt. At his first attempt to move, pain like he'd never experienced seared through him emanating from his thigh.

Forcing his eyes to open, he found himself riding a horse backwards, his back leaning against the other rider who was leading the horse. His leg was stretched out in front of him, his ankle and foot dangling off the horse's rump. His pant leg had been cut off very high up on his limb, dangerously close to revealing his manhood. The fabric from his pant leg was then used to secure a thick patch of white—now covered in blood—cotton to what Halsten knew was a life threatening injury.

White flashed in his vision but he eventually turned his head enough to see who he was leaning against, shocked when auburn hair blew in his face and tangled with his own black locks.

"Oh! You're awake!" Linnea exclaimed, the horse slowing down and the hoof clapping sounds ahead of them stopping as well. "Help me get him down."

Liva and Niklas came into Halsten's view and they eased him down off the side of the horse. He would never tell them how painful it was for them to move him since they took such intensive care of his injured leg, but the throbbing made him want to vomit.

Halsten sat on the ground, injured leg stretched in front of him. Linnea sat down next to him, holding a square of cotton. "We have to change your bandage. You should drink some water and try to eat something, too." Linnea offered him a waterskin and a handful of dried apple slices.

Halsten drank the water as Linnea watched intently. When he was done, she encouraged him to nibble on the apple slices while she changed his bandage. She warned him that releasing the pressure of the bandage temporarily will likely hurt, and he did not have the heart to tell her how much agony he was in already. He tore off a very small piece of the dried apple slice and nearly heaved. A cold sweat spread across his forehead and his palms became clammy. When Linnea untied the fabric and released the pressure, Halsten turned to the side, vomiting all of the water back up. Again, the world faded to nothing.

Halsten stirred in bed, listening to birds chirping through the window beside him. Wait—in bed.

He opened his eyes and looked around, surprised to find himself in his suite back in the Orntali castle. The warmth of the sun beat down on him while he laid tucked safely under a heavy comforter. No one else was in the room, so he peeled the blankets back to investigate further and found his leg to be splinted and heavily bandaged. At least this time, there was no strikethrough.

A woman came bustling in with a tray. "Oh, Sir Halsten, you're awake!" The woman rushed over and dropped the tray onto his bedside table. She grabbed the blanket and placed it back over him. "Best you don't get up yet. You're not quite ready for that yet. Here, try to drink something. I've also brought some broth in hopes that you would be awake enough to try eating."

Halsten heard a gasp near the door and all sounds faded, all scents dissipated, as Linnea stepped into the room, her fiery hair illuminated by the golden sunlight. Her expression changed from shock to relief, a soft smile tugging the corners of her mouth up ever so slightly.

"I'll excuse myself. Call if you need anything," the woman said before stepping around Linnea and closing the door behind her.

Linnea slowly approached the bed, perching herself on the edge near Halsten's hip, and laid a hand on his chest. "Don't you ever scare me like that again, Halsten Seung, you stupidly brave man."

Halsten smiled, "Do you think I'll have an impressive battle scar?"

Linnea lightly pushed on his chest. "And who will be looking at your thigh so intimately that you'll have the chance to impress them?"

"Just you, Little Flame."

Linnea blushed, then reached for the bowl of broth. Halsten sat up slowly, the world slightly spinning as he did. He must have lost a lot of blood from his wound.

He reached forward to grab the bowl from her and she pulled it away, holding up a finger. "You're still recovering."

She held out the spoon to him and he begrudgingly swallowed down the broth. "Lin, my hands aren't wounded. Solely my leg."

She didn't care. She sat there and spoon fed him the entire bowl of broth, then watched as he drank down the water that the nurse had brought. Halsten had never been taken care of like this by anyone, not even when he was sick as a child. Linnea was a caretaker, so he let her do what she did best.

Linnea rested a hand on his chest again and he grabbed her wrist, pulling her down so they were face-to-face. Halsten leaned forward, pressing his lips to hers and she gingerly moved hers in response.

He backed away, eyebrow raised. "My lips aren't broken, love."

He kissed her again, and this time, she kissed him back. An unfamiliar warmth grew from the center of his chest, overtaking his entire body and he knew what it meant. Halsten knew that he was falling for Linnea.

She kissed him more passionately then, her chest resting on his, her tongue sweeping into his mouth playfully, and he was incredibly proud of her for taking control. It was a bloom of confidence he wanted to nurture in her and watch grow over time. Over their time together. Forever.

Linnea suddenly backed away. "I should go. You need rest."

"I am resting," Halsten protested, pulling her back to him. "I don't need to get out of bed to do what I want to do to you right now."

Linnea blushed again, a little giggle escaping her. Halsten guided her hand that was previously resting on his chest down his body slowly, setting it on his hardness. "That's not broken either, my wildfire."

Halsten did not leave bed that afternoon, but he certainly did not get any rest.

CHAPTER 46

Either Asta's fighting techniques had improved substantially in a matter of days, or Maren was holding back. But Asta knew her sister. Maren *never* held back. Even if her blows—verbal or physical—were subtle, they were always impactful.

It was almost as though Maren was lazily swinging her sword around. The same went for Svanhild, from what Asta could observe in one second spurts between swings. Kaid was holding his own against the siren warrior, which was impossible. Asta loved Kaid, but there was no way in Gylla's hell that he was giving Svanhild a fair fight.

Oh goddesses, she loved him. She *loved* him.

She ground her teeth together and snarled. "What did you do to Linnea?" Asta asked as she spun, her long sword poised to take off Maren's head if she didn't move out of the way in time.

Maren ducked, rolling to her side and getting back to her feet before stabbing her sword at Asta's exposed abdomen. "I thought you ought to know that your little band of fake warriors are experiencing their first battle. The sweet babies, all grown up. I wonder how our meager cousin is fairing." Maren tapped a finger to her chin as if in thought, letting her guard down. "Oh, and what a nice little trinket you're bringing back with you. Too bad the trident doesn't actually work anymore."

A rustle of leaves to Asta's right caught her attention and she dared a look, seeing Gyrial and Revna barrelling toward them. While she was distracted by the interruption, Maren looped Asta's sword with her own and unarmed her, sending her sword careening through the air.

"See you next time, sister," Maren waved, then she and Svanhild took off through the forest in the direction that Asta's sword had landed.

"Are you okay? What did they want?" Gyrial surveyed Asta and Kaid, searching for any injuries.

"We're fine now. It was an ambush." Asta picked up the small satchel of berries from the ground and handed it to Kaid. "They know we have the trident now, although my sister is under the impression that it can't be wielded anymore. But I'm sure they will prepare a tactic to use against it now. We've lost our upperhand." Asta sighed and walked in the direction that her weapon was thrown. "I have to go find my sword."

Kaid silently walked alongside Asta as they approached the area where she remembered the blade landing. With the sunset glowing golden around them, finding the shiny metal was easy, and Asta offered a silent prayer of thanks to Absolon above.

The blonde princess bent down and picked up her sword, inspecting it for any damage. Pleased that nothing was scuffed or scratched, she put it back into the holster at her hip. As she turned to walk away, something glistened on the forest floor. She bent down, looking closely at the decaying leaves, trying to find the source. When Kaid tried to ask what she was doing, she silenced him.

Asta sifted through the pile of leaves. She knew she saw something. She knew that she was not making it up.

As she was about to give up, she saw the glint again and scooped up the leaves in the exact location. Whatever it was, it was small enough to hide in the palm of her hand. She carefully picked away the leaves until a small ring rolled in her palm. Upon closer observation, she realized it was a signet ring. But not just any signet ring. It was an exact replica of her mother's ring, which also doubled as an iron key.

Asta showed Kaid, holding the new ring up next to the one she already wore.

"How the hell did a Blomvin signet ring end up in the middle of the forest, exactly where we set up camp for the night?" Kaid took the ring and held it up toward the fading sun, surveying every crevice of it as though it would reveal how it got there.

Did the ring happen to be there, or did someone put it there? Asta, again, thought about how easy it was to hold off Maren and Svanhild. How odd that the ring was exactly where Maren had flung her sword. Come to think of it, this was also the direction that they had fled to.

If Maren had left Asta the ring, what was the purpose? Should she not be touching it? Was the metal filled with poison somehow? Asta grabbed the ring from Kaid, panicking that it was bewitched or cursed. She slipped it into a small leather pouch, then put the pouch in her pocket. They wouldn't touch it any further until Queen Arielle could look at it.

Aside from the run-in with Maren, the travel home was uneventful. Everyone was supposed to take turns bearing the trident or helping Tova, but Kaid elected to hold the trident the entire journey. Asta could see how connected he was to the relic, as though they called to each other and now that they were reunited, they would not be separated. She did not dare break the bond.

Finally, the seaside castle was in front of them. They brought their horses to the stables, then headed home. By the time Asta and Kaid got to the west wing, they were practically running. They checked Asta's suite first, finding it empty. Then Kaid's. Then Linnea's.

They were outside of Halsten's suite when they heard a cacophony of familiar voices within. The pair grinned at each other, then flung the double doors wide open.

Asta didn't see anything besides a flash of red before she was being squeezed so tightly her air was cut off. Dyri was jumping around her and Linnea, barking while his ears bounced around goofily.

She knelt down and hugged Dyri next, the canine covering her face in sloppy kisses. Niklas smiled at Asta warmly but Liva remained straight-faced, awaiting her twin's arrival. Asta pulled her aside. "Gyrial is with Tova in the infirmary." Liva's eye widened and moved to push past Asta, but she caught her arm, stopping her. "She's not physically injured. It's... I'm not really sure what it is. She's not quite herself, so be prepared. Okay?"

Liva nodded, sprinting from the room.

Asta was glad to be home, but worried about Tova's recovery. She wasn't even sure if recovery from such a condition was possible. They would try anything, including asking the sirens for guidance. She would get her friend back to health, no matter the cost.

Kaid hugged Linnea and gave Dyri the attention he deserved before forcing a hug onto Niklas. "Where's Halsten? Training on the beach?"

Asta watched Linnea's posture stiffen. Her cousin sucked in a deep breath before she gestured to the bedroom door. "He's in his room."

Kaid and Asta opened the door, seeing Halsten sitting against the headboard of his bed. He spread his arms wide, grinning like a fiend. He still acted like typical Halsten, but why was he bed-ridden?

Kaid approached the bed but did not say anything, only stared at Halsten in bewilderment. Asta cleared her throat, urging Kaid to speak.

Kaid sat on the bedside table. "What happened?"

Halsten looked to Linnea, who was now standing in the doorway. She explained what happened with the Ryktarvan soldiers, how Halsten got injured, how he had an infection that made its way to his bloodstream but he was recovering, now waiting for his leg to finish healing.

"She's leaving out the parts where she was a total badass." Halsten crossed his arms. "Like when she basically burned her mother's estate down, or stabbed a siren in the neck, or stitched up my leg in the middle of the woods using a dress pin and thread."

Asta turned to her cousin, eyes wide. Linnea—the woman who was always so reserved. A twinge of guilt struck Asta, wondering if by protecting her cousin all these years, she had diminished her ability to fight for herself. Although she never wanted her cousin in danger, she was oddly glad they had this adventure to the Blomvin estate so Linnea could find confidence in herself. However, she was going to need *a lot* more details regarding these heroic events.

"She's also leaving out the part where we're going to live happily ever after, so we're basically cousins now, Asta." Halsten winked at her and Asta shook her head, again turning to Linnea wide-eyed in disbelief. What the fuck happened on this trip? "Now, if you'll excuse us, I need a proper reunion with my best friend without your judgement."

Asta and Linnea doubled over laughing when they exited the room and heard Kaid say "I'm not kissing you," flatly before the door closed behind them.

CHAPTER 47

ALTERNATE CHAPTER AVAILABLE

"All right, now that Linnea isn't here, how do you really feel?" Kaid leaned against the closed door, folding his arms over his chest.

Halsten sighed and ran his fingers through his hair. "The mender said there's nerve damage, as well as a muscular tear. She told me she could try to repair the muscles surgically, but it was risky and I still would most likely come out of the surgery in the same condition."

"And what is that condition, Halsten? Why are you in bed?"

"Because of the nerve damage, I can't exactly feel my foot sometimes. It's like it's there, because I can feel the pressure of it touching something, but I can't feel the sensation on my skin, if that makes sense. And then," Halsten leaned off the side of his bed, pulling out a stick from underneath it. "I have to walk with this. Probably forever. Like some old goat, waving his cane around yelling at kids to not trample his flowerbeds."

Kaid laughed despite the devastation he felt. "I've seen a lot of young dukes using canes as a fashion statement. Own it, brother."

They dove into telling the tales of their journeys. Kaid never wanted to be separated from his best friend like that again. He knew that if the sirens won the war, he would likely figure out a way to spend his time in both kingdoms, but he wouldn't be leaving his best friend in perilous situations every time he departed, so that was different. He also would not be leaving his friend alone any longer, now that Linnea was around. He could never repay Linnea for the care and love she provided for his best friend the last few days.

Kaid poured a glass of water from the pitcher and handed it to Halsten. "So, you *had* to claim the other Blomvin woman, hmm?"

"You know I've always had a thing for redheads," Halsten laughed. "But seriously. I know how we used to be. But we've got these two amazing, fierce women in our lives now and I have no interest in that anymore."

Kaid sighed. He had been so wrapped up with Asta that he never even saw the relationship blooming between Halsten and Linnea. What was confusing to Kaid was how easily Halsten fell into step with Linnea, how quickly he put his past behind him. "How do you know you're not going to fuck it up? We've never done this before."

"I'm not saying I'll never do something wrong, but I'm devoted to her. If I wrong her, it will be bringing her the wrong tea in the morning, or wearing a color that clashes with her dress to a party. It won't be anything involving another woman. *Ever*. It's okay to let go and enjoy the free fall. I have been."

That was exactly what Kaid wanted, too. To free fall with Asta. But they each had a habit of protecting themselves above all else, even if it led to their demise. "I'm not entirely sure how to do that. Every time I feel like we're making progress, something sets us back and we're arguing again."

Halsten started laughing and Kaid couldn't for the life of him figure out what he had said that was so funny.

His best friend took a deep breath to stop himself from cackling. "Do you not remember how you two met? You've always been good at challenging one another. You're just challenging each other on the wrong things right now. Show her how serious you are and make her step up. You know she'll want to one-up you simply to prove to you that she can love you more. Eventually, it will even out. That's how you two function."

This was why Halsten was Kaid's best friend. Above all else, he knew how Kaid's brain worked—even when Kaid couldn't quite figure it out himself. He was right. If he wanted to free fall with Asta, he had to grab her arm on the way down and race her to the bottom.

Kaid left Halsten's suite with a spring in his step, feeling lighter than he had in weeks. He and Asta didn't have some deeply rooted problem, destined to never work out. They needed to give in to what they both felt and call each other to rise to the occasion.

He marched to Asta's suite, letting himself in and sitting on the couch next to her. Dyri curled up at his feet while he and Asta watched the calming crackle of the fireplace in front of them. She was wearing a dark blue, silk night dress that left nothing to the imagination, and it drove Kaid mad.

He didn't avert his gaze from the flames as he spoke, scared that looking into Asta's intense stare would cause him to stutter. "I've meant everything I've said to you, you know." Asta did not respond, so Kaid continued. "I need you. I need you to point out my flaws and guide me when I feel lost. I need you to knock me down a peg sometimes."

"I do enjoy doing that," Asta mumbled playfully.

Kaid faced her and grabbed her hand. "Let's wear matching outfits and break protection spells together, forever."

Asta laughed, rolling her eyes. "Let's actually do neither of those things again. I can't believe I had to be the one to introduce myself to your mother. You didn't even have the sense to do it yourself."

Kaid was the one laughing now. Asta had actually met his own mother before he even had. Well, aside from when he was born.

He gripped Asta's waist and pulled her onto him, her legs straddling his lap and her night dress riding up her thighs. One of Kaid's hands gently caressed her thigh while the other wrapped around her back, pulling her face down to his.

"Do you still hate me, my love?" Kaid asked, his lips inches from Asta's.

"Until the end of time." Her lips crashed into his with a world-shattering kiss.

He knew what she meant. Until the end of time, she would hate that she fell for the man she was never supposed to love. But she would love him with everything she had.

Kaid reached up and wrapped his hand in her vicious curls, yanking her head back until she let out a moan.

Taste her. Taste her blood. Let her essence infiltrate your very being.

Kaid's siren hissed at him, forcefully urging him to feed. He pushed the feeling away, knowing that sirens did not typically feed from each other. He wasn't sure what it meant.

He kissed down the side of her neck, sucking on the sensitive spot where her neck met her shoulder, eliciting a whispered string of curses from her lips. He ran his other hand around the back of her thigh, slipping his fingers under her silk garment to grip her full ass. He pulled her forward, pressing her center against his lap and she gasped. It was a sound he wanted to hear again. Kaid moved Asta back then slid her against his lap again, stealing another gasp from her.

"Keep making that sound, Princess, and this night dress won't be in one piece much longer."

Asta took control and ground herself against him. "That's the plan, *Prince*."

Kaid grazed his thumbs over her peaked nipples through the silky fabric. They hardened even more under his touch and there was something about knowing that his hands could bring that kind of physical reaction out of her that made him take pause.

"I love you," he admitted.

"I love you, too," she whispered back.

Kaid stilled, not expecting her to so readily say it back, but ecstatic that neither of them were afraid to admit it any longer.

Then, she reached down and palmed his cock through his trousers, causing him to buck into her hand.

> *Bite. Bite. Lick her blood from her body like the starving beast you are.*

Kaid's eyes closed, fighting off his siren, while he also avoided coming in his pants from her light massaging. Never in his life had he been this close from a gentle touch.

He pulled her hand away before it happened, then leaned forward and pulled one of her nipples into his mouth through the fabric of her night dress. He was careful to avoid his siren fangs that were out due to his apparent thirst for her blood. He instinctively latched onto her peak, biting harder than he intended. As he went to apologize, she let out a deep moan not of pain, but pleasure. *Interesting.*

Kaid bit down harder on her nipple while pinching the other between his fingers and Asta began panting. He was moaning too, finding pleasure in how vulnerable she was being with him. His cock was the hardest it had ever been.

Kaid stood up, wrapping Asta's legs around him and leaving his shirt behind. It would be a good warning sign for anyone who may come in and try to disturb them, anyway.

He walked to the bedroom, shutting a pouting Dyri out before laying Asta on her plush bed. Her golden hair glowed in the firelight, which turned her green eyes to an amber color.

"This is familiar," Kaid chuckled before kneeling on the bed between her legs.

Asta spread her legs so Kaid could see that she was not wearing any undergarments. "I think it's a little different than last time."

Oh, yes it is. This time, Kaid would kiss Asta, would touch Asta, would fuck Asta with no remorse.

Kaid slid a hand up the inside of Asta's thigh, over her exposed pussy, then back down the inside of her other thigh. She whimpered, frustrated at the lack of contact, but she didn't try to take control, which Kaid found peculiar.

"Tell me what you want, Asta."

"I want you to touch me." She sounded like she was in pain, her hips ever so slightly lifting, searching for friction and only finding air.

"Then show me how you like it." Kaid palmed his dick through his trousers, his erection begging for something to wrap around it. Asta's eyes went wide and she shook her head slightly. "Haven't you ever pleasured yourself before, Princess?" She nodded. "Do you want to show me what you did?"

"Yes," she whispered between pants. "I've just never..."

She had never shown anyone how she liked to be touched, and that made Kaid furious. Not at her, but *for* her, because he knew she had likely never experienced a proper ravishing before, the way *she* liked it.

"I'll help you," he groaned as he unbuttoned his trousers and freed his member. He wrapped his hand around it, slowly pumping from base to tip. "That night, when I fell asleep here after my lesson, did you slip your fingers between your legs?" Asta nodded. "Good. Show me how you slid your hand down your body and I'll show you how I gripped my cock that night, still thinking about your soft lips and your perfect breasts." Asta's hand cautiously slipped down her stomach and landed incredibly close to her pussy. Kaid's eyes did not leave her fingers and they ever so slowly dipped down between her lips and she sucked in a sharp breath.

Kaid swirled his thumb through the bead of moisture leaking from the head of his cock. "Do you want to see what I did next?" Asta feverishly nodded, her fingers finally finding her swollen clitoris and tracing soft circles around it. Kaid took his free hand and gently massaged his balls while still pumping himself.

Asta swiftly pulled herself up and kneeled in front of him, tugging his trousers down. Kaid took the hint, slipping off the bed to pull his pants off fully. Asta waited on her hands and knees and when he turned back to the bed, she did not hesitate to pull him to her by the base of his cock. She wrapped her lips around him, using one hand to massage his balls while the other stabilized her torso.

Her velvet tongue flicked against the head of Kaid's member and he wasn't sure what heaven was truly like, but he hoped it was this. Forever, with Asta, where they can laugh and cry and explore each other's bodies for all eternity.

Her blood is yours.

Asta pulled off him suddenly, looking confused as she ran her tongue across her teeth, revealing her siren fangs on full display.

"It's okay. It's happening to me, too." Kaid gently pushed her onto her back, peppering her collarbone with kisses. His dick grazed her slick center and twitched hungrily. He bit the top of her night dress, using his fangs to pierce holes in the fabric. Then, he savagely ripped down using only his teeth and the dress ripped in two.

Asta smiled devilishly as she shucked away the remnants of the slip. Then, Kaid leaned down and trapped her lips with his, whispering to her between kisses. "My wraith." *Kiss.* "My pretty little demon." *Kiss.* "My siren of death."

Kaid lined himself up with her center, looking into her eyes one more time for any sign to stop. When she bit her lip and nodded, he slipped into her. He met some resistance, but it was not for lack of lubrication. She needed to adjust to his size.

Once he was fully seated, he pulled out almost to the tip then slowly pushed back in again and it took everything in him to hold back an animalistic growl, his siren needing to make itself known. Asta's inner walls contracted around him, gripping his cock and pulling him in deeper. Her hips pulled up off the bed in small thrusts, begging for movement.

He took her in fully—hardened nipples, wild curls spread behind her, grinding up onto him without a care. No rituals, no impending war. Just the two of them, their bodies connected physically and emotionally. Kaid had been intimate with women before, but he had never made love. Now, he knew there really was a difference.

As Kaid set a slow pace of thrusts, he pulled her nipple into his mouth once again. He tested out biting down harder, and each time he tried a little more intensely, Asta bucked wildly beneath him and whispered expletives to herself, asking the gods and goddesses to help her. Kaid smiled around her nipple and she smacked the top of his head, knowing he was enjoying dragging this out.

Something deep within him awoke, his body moving of its own accord. He circled a fang around her peak, applying enough pressure that the sharp point left behind a red circle. Asta's nipple was at full attention and she watched in curiosity, then realization overcame her. "Do it," she grumbled. "I think we're supposed to. It feels right."

Kaid opened his mouth wide and clamped down around her areola, his fangs piercing her skin and blood flowing into his mouth. Her blood tasted like a blend of floral teas, and it was the most addicting thing Kaid had ever savored.

As the blood coated his throat, it was as if it was traveling straight to his cock, which was still buried in Asta to the hilt. Kaid soothed the sharp sting of his feeding by swirling his tongue around her nipple. He fed on her and thrust into her, drawing out guttural moans from his princess, but once the feeding frenzy slowed, his thoughts cleared. He didn't know what this feeding meant, but he knew it was Asta's turn.

She knew that as well, judging by how she slowly pulled herself from beneath Kaid and pushed him into a sitting position. Asta climbed onto his lap, grabbing his cock and guiding it back into her. From this angle, Kaid could feel himself reaching the end of her passage, no more of him able to fit inside her. Asta's pussy throbbed as she stared down at where they were connected.

Kaid tucked her hair behind her ear. "You focus on your feeding, blondie. I'll take care of everything else."

Asta traced a delicate finger all over Kaid's body, clearly choosing where to mark him. He shivered when the pad of her finger tickled his jugular and she grinned. She still had newborn bloodlust, but he trusted her. This feeding felt different.

She dipped forward and licked the spot that made him shiver before lightly pressing her fangs to his throbbing vein. He felt her hesitate, her hot breath dancing across his skin. Every nerve ending on his body was on fire.

"I trust you. You'll be able to stop. I trust *you*." Kaid reassured her.

Kaid lifted her hips, sliding himself out some, then slammed her back down onto his lap. Asta bit down and the pain was blinding at first, but quickly turned to a pleasant ache. She ground into him as she fed and Kaid used one hand to help guide her hips while he slipped the other between her legs and found her swollen, pulsing clit. He traced circles around it, matching his tempo to the pace she set.

The room began to blur, all of his focus on the two points where their bodies connected. Her pussy tightened around him, strangling the life from his cock, causing his balls to tighten in response. If she didn't stop soon, he was going to explode.

Her breathing became labored, but she did not stop feeding. Her grinding intensified, the headboard slamming into the wall while she moaned into the crook of his neck. Asta fell apart on top of him, her mouth disconnecting from his neck and blood dripping down her chin.

She threw her head back as he tugged her nipple and rubbed her clit. Asta screamed and her pussy clamped down onto him. Kaid couldn't hold back any longer and he came along with her, growling so loudly the entire castle likely heard. He slammed into her multiple times, her walls rippling around him as he filled her with his come.

When they both fell from their high, Asta slowly pulled herself off him and they went into the washroom together, helping each other clean up. Neither of them yet to acknowledge what they intrinsically knew, that the bite marks were some sort of bond, and they had finalized it.

CHAPTER 48

A soft knock on the door pulled Kaid from the best sleep he had ever had. He grumbled, burying his face deeper into Asta's hair and pulling her tighter against his chest. Frustratingly, the knock came again.

"Umh, I'm so sorry, but we need you in the foyer," Niklas's voice was hardly above a whisper. Clearly, Kaid's shirt on the couch had not scared him off, so it must be important.

Kaid slid out of bed, pulling on his trousers and sauntering over to the door. He slipped out, gently closing it behind him so as to not wake Asta. Judging by the lack of sunlight, it was either very late at night or very early in the morning.

"What could be so important that you've dragged me from bed, Niklas?" Kaid leaned against the threshold with his arms crossed.

Niklas pushed his glasses up his nose and smiled. "There is someone here. Someone I think you will not care to wait until daylight to see."

Was it his mother? Or some other siren? Who even knew where he was?

Kaid told Niklas that he would come down in a few minutes after he had time to fix his appearance. He went back into the bedroom, waking Asta by peppering her face with kisses. Another night spent together where Asta had completely forgotten about her hair combing ritual and fallen asleep with no reluctance. Though, after the journey home then everything they had done last night, Kaid was not surprised that she was able to fall asleep immediately.

He righted his hair and cleaned his teeth, then sat on the couch while Asta did the same. Hand-in-hand, they walked to the entry hall.

As they descended the stairs, Kaid caught a glimpse of the top of his visitor's head. He immediately knew who it was and began running down the stairs.

Kaid reached the bottom and sprinted directly into his father's open arms. He didn't care how childish it looked for a grown man to run to his father. This man had sacrificed more than Kaid had ever known and all he had given him in return was headaches over the years.

He pulled away and Duke Aerik—well, King Aerik—clapped a hand on his son's shoulder. "It sounds to me like you have had quite the adventure since arriving in Orntali, son."

Kaid laughed, because that was the shortest, most pleasant way to word it. "How did you get here?"

King Aerik delved into the story of how Annika—in her human form—had arrived in Haalberg to retrieve him. He mentioned how fortuitous it was that she was the one sent to brief him, as he likely would not have believed anyone else aside from Arielle herself. It had been a risk, all these years concealing a lost prince and he dreaded the day a half-finfolk came knocking at his door, blades at the ready. Luckily, that day never came.

Kaid grinned widely as he asked, "Father, are you ready to see your wife?"

The look of excitement and longing on Aerik's face was indescribable, pouring off him and filling the air with hope and love and an aching need. He had not seen his soulmate—his bonded—in over twenty years, and it was time for Kaid to bring his father home.

The room was somber as everyone who was departing for Naltania hoisted their bags onto their shoulders, ensuring their blades were strapped properly and they had everything they needed. Kaid once again secured the trident to his back and it hummed against him, like the purr of a delighted house cat.

Liva knelt in front of Tova and whispered to her, though her sister was unresponsive. Tova would be staying here under the protection of Gyrial so she was not in harm's way in Naltania. Kaid was grateful that Liva had agreed to join them in battle, knowing that having even one sea dragon was better than none.

Kaid watched Asta hug Niklas, then Gyrial, then Dyri, then finally, Linnea. She squeezed her cousin so tightly that Kaid was afraid she would snap her in half from her siren strength.

"Good luck out there, brother. See you on the other side." Halsten held out his free hand for a shake while the other stabilized him using his cane. Kaid pulled his best friend into a tight hug, similar to the one he had witnessed between Asta and Linnea. This could very well be the last time he sees his best friend.

"Get that leg better, and take care of your girl. If I don't make it back—" Kaid was shoved backward by Halsten, cutting him off.

"You're making it back. We're all making it back. And then we're going to have a joint wedding and marry these ridiculous women and be happy once and for all. Got it?"

Kaid had no idea when his best friend had turned into such a sap, but it was a side of him Kaid was glad to see. Linnea was changing Halsten for the better like Asta was changing him.

Kaid nodded, then everyone stepped out onto the shore and mounted their kelpies, Asta giving Thurs affectionate pats before nudging her with her heels.

The kelpies rode into the waves, their colors morphing from dapple gray to emerald green, and their tails transforming into powerful fins. Once Kaid was up to his chest in water, he felt a warm sensation through his body, and once he was fully underwater, his royal blue fin hung off the side of his kelpie steed.

Kaid turned around and observed his father in his siren form for the first time. His face and torso looked the same, but it was incredibly odd to see him with a silvery gray tail fluttering in the current. King Aerik sucked in a deep lung full of water and Kaid could see the tension in his body dissipate. He had been a siren for over eighty years before he banished himself to land for his son. The deprivation of his true self for so long must have been tormenting, and Kaid felt a pang of guilt in his chest even though he didn't exactly have a say in the matter.

The kelpies traveled at the speed of light, making Kaid's stomach roil. He had never traveled this fast before and he could tell they were exerting themselves, but understood the importance of getting to Naltania quickly. Traveling at this pace had left Liva and Annika behind, but they could take care of themselves. Every so often, Kaid reached back to ensure the trident was still secured, yet he always knew it was there from the fervid vibrations against his skin.

Kaid let out a sigh of relief when the pearlescent castle came into view. However, the setting was not like last time. The light did not reflect onto the castle in a playful manner, no colorful fish danced between the coral, and come to think of it, the coral itself looked more dull. The somber mood of leaving Orntali had traveled with them. Everyone and everything knew that a battle was coming.

The kelpies dropped them at the gates, which swung open. Asta and Kaid moved aside, letting King Aerik be the first to enter. Liva, Revna, and Soren bowed their heads as Kaid's father slowly swam into the castle. Through the doors, they could see the fiery-haired siren queen sobbing.

CHAPTER 49

Asta knocked on the door to Queen Arielle's office a fair amount of time after her reunion with King Aerik. She wanted them to have a proper homecoming, but also knew how precious time really was given the current situation.

Kaid tagged along, peering over Asta's shoulder as she opened the door and the king and queen waved her in. Asta tapped the door frame as she entered, then she and Kaid both sat in the moss covered seats across the desk from them.

Arielle signed, addressing them both. "I am forever indebted for what you two have done for us. We now stand a fair chance against the finfolk and may be able to end this once and for all." Arielle's eyes latched onto the trident that Kaid started carrying everywhere. "I can feel it, humming. But it does not call to me as it should. It seems it recognizes a different ruler of Naltania as its owner. But there is something else in the room with us, isn't there?"

With shaky hands, Asta removed the items she had stowed away in her bag, safely wrapped in multiple layers of cloth to keep them safe. She laid the comb and mirror on the desk and the relics slid closer to each other without anyone touching them.

Queen Else had taken a great risk by hiding the comb in plain sight where it could have fallen into the wrong hands, but she trusted that her daughter would grow up to be someone who coveted things that belonged to her mother.

Arielle inspected the pieces, turning them over in her palms multiple times. Her brow furrowed, lips turning down. "I wish I could be the one to use these to their full potential, but a voice is required. It seems that these will be better in your hands," she gestured to Kaid and Asta.

"Your Highness, can you—do you know anything about how my family is connected to all of this?" Asta was hopeful that the empress knew something, as she seemed to know everything.

Arielle nodded, a soft smile on her lips as she reached across the desk and grabbed Asta's hand. Then, she let go and began.

The siren explained that Asta's mother, Else Blomvin, came from a long line of Blomvins. The family had always been involved in magical affairs even though they held no magic any longer.

Blomvins, along with many other old family names in the western parts of Salendron, once belonged to a fae clan in the western mountains. The clan was incredibly docile compared to its neighbors, which led to frequent attacks from other clans wanting to acquire their land. The western mountains held the finest soil for crops, the most intricate cave tunnel systems for travel and homes, and the area in general was a hot spot for magic.

Asta's ancestors, to her surprise, were the clan leaders, similar to the fae council in the Spellid Mountains. Asta supposed that was where all of their generational wealth came from.

Over time, the fae clan of the western mountains grew tired with never feeling safe and constantly needing to defend their homes. They dismantled, and each fae went their own way, some joining the neighboring clans and others removing themselves from the fae affairs completely.

The Blomvins chose peace—to settle and live a calm life. And after so many generations of marrying and reproducing with humankind, their fae heritage became so diluted that they were nearly full human. However, all members of the Blomvin line had an affinity for magic due to their bloodline.

Asta asked how it was possible that her family possessed the comb and mirror, and how her mother knew so much. Queen Arielle did not have an answer for Queen Else's knowledge, suspecting that she had discovered old family journals or some form of record keeping from centuries ago.

As for the comb and mirror, the western mountain clan was one of the clans that helped create the sirens, so naturally, they would have helped conceal any of the relics that could potentially be used as weapons for sirens looking to cause trouble. Many generations of Blomvins likely did not know what they were passing down, only assuming that they were family heirlooms. But Queen Else knew, and made sure to strategically separate the items.

It was funny, Asta thought, how Else's own daughter would be someone involved in reuniting the relics and planning to harness them. Even though she did not know her mother, she knew she would approve of Asta's determination to end the violence.

Asta had watched the villages surrounding the castle be tortured for years, not knowing that it was finfolk causing the distress. Now that she knew, she would avenge all those taken from her kingdom.

"I have something else for you to look at," Asta signed before pulling the second signet ring from her pouch and placing it on the desk. "Can you tell if this is cursed in any way?"

Arielle inspected the piece of metal through squinted eyes for several moments before placing it back on the desk. "I sense nothing sinister within. However, I do believe that this is an iron key."

A knock on the door startled Asta, and a scout swam in, handing a seaweed scroll to Queen Arielle. Asta and Kaid stood up to remove themselves, but the queen gestured for them to remain seated. She unrolled the seaweed and read silently, her face never changing. King Aerik read next, scrubbing a hand over his chin.

The king cleared his throat as he rested the scroll on the desk. "Ryktarva is coming."

CHAPTER 50

The scroll contained information from various siren scouts calculating the largest band of finfolk troops they had ever seen. They would arrive in a day's time.

The castle was in complete chaos, sirens speeding past in every direction. Shouting erupted around every corner as generals instructed troops and prepared for the onslaught. Windows were being reinforced with driftwood and doors were being barricaded.

Asta watched the pandemonium from atop the grand stairs, her hands shaking as she remembered the battle she had fought to free Kaid. At least this time, she would have him by her side. Asta felt that familiar tightening in her chest and she wrapped one hand with the other, cracking her knuckles one-by-one.

Your friends will die. Crack. *Kaid will be forced to marry Maren.* Crack. *The sirens will be slaughtered.* Crack.

With every terrible thought, Asta cracked a knuckle, and eventually they stopped. With one final pop, the tension in her chest dissipated and she could breathe again. Kaid, noting Asta's fidgeting hands, moved closer to her.

"Son!" King Aerik called for Kaid, speeding in their direction. "Your mother. She's asked to borrow your trident."

Kaid stared at the golden staff in his hand, confused. "It's not mine. It's the royal sirens."

Aerik chuckled. "There is no denying that it calls to you. And although it will work in any royal siren's hands, it seems destined to be its most powerful in yours."

Then why are you taking it elsewhere? Asta thought, but did not intervene.

Kaid handed over the trident, his hold lingering on the metal before his father pulled it away. Even with her limited knowledge in magical affairs, Asta could see that the trident had chosen Kaid above all else.

Asta followed Aerik, Kaid swimming up beside them. Kaid's father darted out of the castle, meeting with Arielle at the gates where she took the trident from her bonded.

Queen Arielle raised the gleaming pitchfork far above her head, aiming it at the sky beyond the sea. The golden metal began glowing, the water around them charged with a strange feeling Asta had never experienced, heavy with magic.

Above the water, Asta could see the sky darkening, laying an eerie gray blanket over the castle and surrounding coral. The surface of the water became so choppy that she couldn't make out anything above, only the faint light of a stormy sky. Around the underwater fortress, massive water funnels started to form, pulling sand from the seafloor up with them. The funnels hovered in place, as if on guard for the arrival of the finfolk troops.

King Aerik handed the comb and mirror to Asta. "Keep them safe. You will know when the time is right." Asta nodded, somewhat confused by his ambiguity, tucking the relics into her satchel and securing the latch. "Now go get some rest. We don't have long, but the scouts will alert us."

Asta turned to leave but the sight of Thurs zooming past caught her attention. She then noticed the flashes of emerald surrounding the castle, the entire herd on patrol. Asta flagged down her kelpie, the temperamental mare stopping before her.

"You don't need to be here. This isn't your war." Asta ran a hand down the bridge of the kelpie's nose. "Go to shore and be safe. Keep your herd safe."

Thurs whinnied, nudging Asta's hand away. She stomped a hoof into the pearlescent tiles of the balcony in protest. Asta knew the kelpies would not leave her even though it was for the good of the herd. Asta was the leader of northern kelpies, tamer of the alpha. They would fight fiercely beside her until the very end, whatever that end may be.

Thurs swam off, assisting the siren soldiers in their patrol as hundreds of emerald water horses joined in.

Kaid pulled Asta away and back into the castle. They needed to prepare.

CHAPTER 51

Kaid stirred on the sofa where he had fallen asleep, opening his eyes to faint light creeping in between the pillars. It should have been dawn by then, but the impending storm above had darkened the skies so much that it was impossible to tell exactly what time of day it was.

He felt the room shake before he heard the explosive boom from somewhere outside of the castle, followed by shouting. Asta sat straight up on the chaise she had been napping on, startled by the rumbling.

The door to the sitting room flung open and a siren scout shouted "Finfolk battalion approaching!" before rushing away. Kaid grabbed his sword, feeling empty without the trident, but he knew that his mother was the better wielder for the time-being. She needed to control their surroundings and had a plan, likely one she'd thought over for many years while she was searching for the lost trident.

Asta double-checked the latches on her satchel, holding a longsword and short sword, and swam through the door and into the havoc.

The front lines swam past the reef where they clashed with the finfolk, the sound of metal-on-metal slicing through the water and echoing off the castle walls behind them. Since they were royalty, Kaid, Asta, and his parents waited on the balcony inside of the gates. As badly as he wanted to dive into battle, he knew that they only fought in hand-to-hand if completely necessary.

Wretched morphling groupers weaved between the battle, taking out sirens as they went—most of the time swallowing them whole. There must have been a call for volunteers to make the morph—to give the finfolk the upperhand in brute force.

Kaid could hardly distinguish Soren's shouts of instruction over the clamorous mob, telling the Naltanians to feed from the groupers in order to defeat them.

On the other hand, it seemed as though the rest of the sea was on the siren's side. Selkies charged through lines of finfolk, knocking them off balance and giving their siren opponents the advantage. Sharks clamped onto enemy shoulders and fins. Kaid's stomach churned when he witnessed a dolphin playing with a finfolk's decapitated head.

"They're getting closer," Asta whispered. "I love you, Kaidian."

His full name. He hated how official it sounded; how final it sounded. He turned to her, kissing her deeply then gripping the nape of her neck. "Whatever happens today, Asta, we *will* have a happy ending. If we get separated, you make sure you come back to me, okay?"

"Okay," his blonde princess nodded, the whites of her eyes reddened.

Arielle swung the trident around her, commanding all elements in the water. The stagnant water funnels moved, quickly reaching the battle grounds and pulling hoards of finfolk to the surface. If they went above water when it wasn't their time to mate or birth, they would not survive. The funnels were picking off entire troops at a time, but so many remained.

Strong currents started whipping past them, shoving the finfolk troops back. Although the currents were not depleting the number of enemy soldiers, they were at least giving the siren warriors enough time to collect themselves between attacks.

Asta shouted indistinguishable words and pointed ahead to something behind the front lines. Kaid narrowed his eyes, locking in on what Asta saw. Within the secondary line, three figures broke through and were emerging toward the battle—Maren, Svanhild, and Queen Yrsa herself.

The finfolk queen was accompanied by a swarm of wretched eels wrapping around her body and swimming between her arms and torso. Each time she raised an arm, multiple siren soldiers quivered. The sea witch was using the electric currents from the eels to amplify her static magic to stun their soldiers.

Once stunned, Maren and Svanhild sliced through the front lines with ease. They looked unphased as they cut down sirens and animals, no evidence of remorse for their life ending blows.

Asta grabbed Kaid's hand, squeezing tightly before letting go and adjusting her grip on her blades. If the finfolk wanted a fight, they would get a fight. Kaid wished desperately that he had his trident, but his mother was so far from them now that he would have to use his blades.

The golden trident is yours. Yours to command, yours to control. Seize it, and end them all. Seize it, and show them what power truly means.

His siren itched to use the trident, which he knew was dangerous. He resisted, lifting his blade as his ex-fiancé came barreling toward them, her face twisted into a scowl.

CHAPTER 52

It was as if Asta's life was happening in slow-motion. She watched as her sister cut down the siren lines like a large ship through ocean waves. It was then that Asta accepted that her sister must truly be her enemy.

Svanhild made it through first, sword poised to slice Asta in half diagonally from shoulder to hip and Asta blocked too late. She was able to parry, but her arms quivered on impact. In her peripherals, she saw the blue-hued finfolk queen approaching Kaid.

Asta strategically retreated in order to position herself next to him. He may be a siren prince, but he was not trained in combat, nor did he hold the one weapon that truly called to him.

"Oh princeling, your new family has come to bring you home!" Queen Yrsa jeered. Her disgusting, pointed teeth made Asta's stomach turn sour.

Asta held off Svanhild, the finfolk female's hits becoming incredibly hard to block when only half her attention was on them. Maren swam between her lady-in-waiting and her mother, approaching Kaid. He slashed his blade at her in defense and she jumped back and gasped, the metal grazing her stomach and leaving a shallow red mark.

"Husband!" Maren shouted, observing her stomach. "Save our disputes for behind closed doors."

Kaid's face turned to disgust. "The only closed door that we will be observing together is when I put you behind bars for the rest of your miserable life while you rot away in a cell."

Asta knew that there was no way they could ever end this war with any of this trio alive, but she did not have the heart to tell Kaid this. She also knew that it was something she was not ready to admit aloud just yet.

Svanhild summoned her full attention as she let out a feral shriek, bringing both her long and short swords up to strike. Asta flicked her tail, allowing her to swim out of the danger of the short sword, and twisted her blade down to block the long sword coming for her chest. The sound of metal-on-metal was deafening, causing her ears to ring. Even though her arms shook, Asta twisted her blade around Svanhild's and ripped the grip from her hands. The sword went gliding through the water toward the reef in the distance.

Asta heaved from the exertion. The finfolk female's power was unmatched compared to anyone she had ever scrimmaged. Just as she started to let her small victory sink in, Queen Yrsa was before her.

The finfolk queen held out her hand, blue streaks of lightning flashing between her fingers. The eels hissed and snapped in her direction. Then, the currents moved through the water and connected with Asta. The shock flattened her to the seafloor, convulsing as every nerve in her body felt like it was on fire.

"Asta!" Kaid shouted as he swung his blade toward the queen. She easily summoned a small yet forceful sea current to push him back.

Queen Yrsa let go of her hold on Asta, but she was too weak to move. Her blonde hair settled on the sand around her, tickling her face, but she had nothing left in her to push the strands away.

Kaid attempted to help her multiple times, each time getting pushed away as if he were nothing to fight off. Queen Yrsa stretched out her arm once more and Asta's body convulsed with the shock, then locked frozen. All Asta could do was observe her surroundings. Kaid's face was twisted with rage and desperation as he exhausted himself by trying to defend her. Svanhild circled, occasionally exchanging glances with Maren who stood next to her mother and watched with a blank stare.

The finfolk queen let go again, releasing Asta from the numbing sensation. Her limbs barely began regaining feeling when the queen approached her, lifting her head by gripping her chin, forcing Asta to look at her. The queen's eels slithered around Asta's body, their slippery skin causing gooseflesh to rise on her arms.

"Weak, just like your mother." Yrsa let go of Asta's chin. "But since you've been such a nuisance, I thought I would remind you how insignificant you are in this fight."

Maren continued staring blankly, but something about her posture made her seem frozen in time.

Asta dug her palms into the sand beneath her and pushed her torso up. If the finfolk queen wanted to deem her insignificant, she would use any strength she could muster to prove to her how wrong she was. Yrsa could strike her with lightning. She could let her daughter do her dirty work and end her with a blade. She could feed her to her warriors. But Asta would not endure any of those things without putting up a fight.

Although Asta's arms shook, although her elbows buckled, although her shoulders strained, she lifted herself off the ground and locked eyes with the finfolk queen.

Queen Yrsa flashed a devious grin. "Oh, I will not further torture *you*. I did, however, send some of my favorite warriors to the surface."

To the surface. Where Asta's friends and family were.

Asta pushed off the sand and careened her body toward the finfolk queen, hands outstretched. Before she could wrap her grip around the queen's throat, a flash of red barreled through the finfolk female.

She observed as Liva—in her terrifying red sea dragon form—dragged the finfolk queen across the seafloor effortlessly. Shock waves flickered between them, but the dragonhide was too thick for the currents to break through without significant force.

Maren and Svanhild took off after the sea dragon, likely to free the queen from being pummeled into the ground.

Kaid gripped Asta by her elbows and she was thankful for the support. He stared off into the distance and Asta followed his gaze, landing on his parents on the veranda.

Asta brushed a lock of hair from his forehead. "Go to them. I'll be fine."

"No," he shook his head. "I can't let you face that alone."

"And I will never forgive myself and if you come with me and something happens to your parents while you're gone. You just got them back, Kaid. Make sure you don't lose them."

Kaid rested his forehead against Asta's. "I love you. Release my pretty little wraith on them."

Despite the current situation, a laugh bubbled up from Asta's chest. "I love you too."

Kaid's lips were on hers in an instant, and just as quickly removed. He squeezed her hand, then swam for his parents.

CHAPTER 53

"On your right!" Gyrial shouted as a siren dove at Linnea. She spun, the merfolk barely missing her. A swarm of sirens had breached the ocean's surface not long ago and came for the castle. Gyrial, being the ever-diligent male he was, took notice right away and kept the battle on the beach. If anything, they could protect the staff within.

Linnea had never even held a knife until a few days ago, let alone been trained in hand-to-hand combat. But after bringing a siren down by stabbing it in the neck, Linnea figured she could be of use.

The traitor sirens sent to attack them were anarchic. They had little regard for their own lives, which made their tactics that much more terrifying and unhinged. They quite literally had nothing to lose.

A siren female unsheathed her fangs and snapped at any limb she could get her mouth near. One male summoned long, glistening claws and slashed furiously at anything that moved. Altogether, the twenty-or-so traitorous sirens were a maelstrom of mayhem.

Linnea may not have been trained, but she was smart. When the male using his claws as a windmill of death approached her, she ducked, then used the force of her entire body to throw him sideways into another siren. He shredded them to pieces.

She figured out that some of the hoard must be half finfolk, as they had finfolk features—elongated ears and tinted skin—when they first popped out of the water and were able to walk on land. She didn't know enough of the logistics of these merspecies, but she had received a crash course on the basics by being catapulted into the middle of a centuries-long war.

A female half-finfolk latched onto Niklas and screeched in his face, the high-pitched sound making everyone's ears ring. Instinctually, Niklas screeched back—in fear, not a strategic attack—and the female released him in surprise. Linnea used the opportunity to shove the female toward Windmill Arms, who was still swinging. Another one down.

Halsten was not great with sword work, but his hand-to-hand was impressive, even with the nerve damage in his leg. Luckily, none of the merfolk had brought weapons. They were cocky enough that they thought they didn't need them.

Linnea and her friends were weak, useless humans, right? Wrong. Even though they were the inferior species, they would not be underestimated.

The suicidal approach of the warriors let them keep the upperhand for an extended period of time. Gyrial, being preternatural, moved quickly through the crowd, cutting down the enemies in a blur. But no matter how many sirens and finfolk mutts they terminated, more came to the surface.

Linnea gasped as one of them latched onto her shoulder and shredded it with their fangs. She shoved them away, leaving long tooth scrapes visible through the ripped fabric of her tunic.

You've endured worse.

She had, sadly. The cruel reality of the situation was that it didn't bother Linnea. At the end of the day, this was still easier to handle than her childhood.

A metal clink caught her attention and she turned to see Gyrial falling to his knees. She ran to him, her heart dropping into her stomach from the look of devastation on him.

Gyrial was invincible. She didn't worry about him. He was supposed to be safe—the one who stood a chance. So why was he the only one falling?

Linnea had never been particularly close to the male, but over the years, they became friends. Even though she knew he was not the right match for Asta, she still loved the way he cared for her. It made her realize that males who worship their females were real. She had a great respect for the male who was brought to his knees by iron chains wrapped around his wrists.

Gyrial knelt as the cuffs clicked, weakening him to the point of submission.

Linnea knew that iron made sirens unable to use their magic and weakened them a bit, but the effects must be much stronger on fae.

Linnea knelt beside Gyrial, her knees sinking into the soft sand. If they hadn't been in the midst of war, it would have been the perfect day for a walk on the beach.

She slipped her fingers under the cuffs, attempting to release the fae male, but it was no use.

"Can you get up?" Her voice was breathy as she tugged at the unforgivable metal.

Gyrial planted one foot on the ground, then the other, Linnea helping him by lifting under his arms as best as she could.

She guided him to the brambles near the terrace. "Stay here until I can figure this out,"

Linnea said. "We will be okay."

She may have lied.

The onslaught of merfolk kept coming, Halsten and Niklas doing what they could to hold them off. But that was all they were doing—holding them off. What if help never came? Halsten was hardly maintaining balance without his cane. If they were required to run, he would need to be left behind or carried.

Linnea raced back into the fight, though all she held was a dagger she grabbed from Gyrial's belt. Sirens and finfolk came for the fallen fae hiding in the bushes and Linnea used them against each other as best as she could. Windmill Arms truly made for the best secret weapon. She kept feeding him more victims as he shredded through them. His bloodlust was blinding at this point, and he had no idea who he was harming. Other than that, Linnea had no strategy.

Halsten and Niklas moved their fights to stand next to Linnea, guarding Gyrial. He had protected them every step of the way. It was their turn to show the fae loyalty.

Linnea wished, more than anything, that Tova was well enough to help them. Even though she could not use her sea dragon on land, having a siren warrior next to them would surely give them a greater advantage. For now, the sea dragon was being cared for in the infirmary by the very staff they were trying to protect.

The sea spawn came with attacks so brutal that Linnea questioned if they were simply prolonging defeat. She could only shove so many warriors toward Windmill Arms before they caught on.

As the hoard began closing in on them, a ring of metal caught everyone's attention. They all turned to see King Botmar unsheath a sword.

The king of Salendron swung a dark-metaled blade and cut down three merfolk at a time, shrieks carrying through the air and bouncing off the stone castle walls to double back as a reminder of the violence.

Linnea watched as her uncle, her savior, brought down their enemies with ease. Though he was making great work of it, they kept multiplying as they emerged from the sea.

King Botmar's sword seemed to bring down the beasts with a greater force than she had seen previously.

"What is that?" she shouted. She kicked out a leg, pushing a finfolk back into a siren looming behind them.

"Iron sword!" King Botmar responded.

Iron. The one thing Linnea figured out had subdued magical species.

She grabbed Gyrial by the chain between his cuffs and dragged him from the brambles, leading him to the king. Gyrial stumbled but jogged behind her, clearly understanding her thoughts.

She approached Botmar and pushed Gyrial toward him, who held out his arms as best as he could. Between cutting down groups of warriors, King Botmar turned and struck through the iron chain. And though Gyrial still wore iron cuffs that weakened him, breaking the connection between limbs freed him.

CHAPTER 54

Asta glided through the water on the back of Thurs, who appeared the moment she began her journey to Orntali. The mare always knew when she needed her.

Her satchel felt heavy, still containing the comb and mirror. If she had to use them, she would. But the siren artifacts were destructive and unforgivable.

To Asta's surprise, Revna appeared next to her, riding a subordinate kelpie.

"Where you go, I go," the siren warrior shouted over the noise of sea currents in Asta's ears.

She didn't know she had earned such loyalty from Revna, but she was honored. For fear of spooking off the siren, Asta bit her tongue to hold back that thought.

The kelpies rode at preternatural speed—the kind that made Asta nauseous—but she held on. Every second gained was a second closer to rescuing her friends and Linnea.

Their heads breached open air as the kelpies rose to the surface and Salendron was in sight.

Asta gripped the reins, giving them a flick. "Go, Thurs! Go!"

Asta's purple fin tingled, morphing back into her familiar human legs. She risked a glance toward Revna, who was also transformed into her land form.

As they approached the shore, the familiar sounds of battle overpowered the sounds of the waves around them. Asta's grip on the reins tightened.

After what felt like an eternity, they hit sand, the kelpies transforming to their dapple gray and galloping toward the chaos.

Asta jumped from her mare, rolling to absorb the impact and landing back on her feet like a feline. She ran, slashing her blade through any unrecognizable face she saw.

To her surprise, Gyrial and Linnea seemed to be a team, throwing opponents at each other and letting them be their own demise. Then, Asta saw the chains on Gyrial.

"Linnea!" Asta shouted as she threw the second signet ring toward her cousin.

At the last possible second, Linnea reached a hand up and snatched the ring midair. Linnea pressed the ring into the iron cuff at Gyrial's wrist. It broke into two pieces and plummeted to the sand below while Linnea freed the other wrist.

"Keep that in case you have more trouble! It's ours, anyway," Asta shouted through the surrounding shrieks and grunts.

Gyrial dove in front of a finfolk holding an obsidian dagger aimed for Halsten's chest, blocking the blow and shoving the merfolk back. Revna immediately jumped into battle the moment her feet touched sand, slicing down anyone within her radius.

A shriek startled Asta, a finfolk with black rotten teeth running for her with outstretched, tattered claws. Asta ducked and a flash of silver cut through the finfolk mutt.

"You shouldn't be here!" Asta shouted at her father.

King Botmar wobbled. He held an iron sword, perfect for defeating the creatures before him, but he was struggling. He was not the soldier he had once been.

"I am right where I need to be, love!" King Botmar shouted as he used the metal in his hand to cut a siren in two.

Barking caught Asta's attention and she saw Dyri barreling toward the beach from the terrace. The canine had never been brave once in his life, and she wished he had remained a coward.

She sprinted for the dog, diving under claws and jumping over fallen corpses. For four humans and a fae, her friends had really held their own.

Dyri barked and howled, bee lining it for Linnea who was fighting off a female half-finfolk. The female dug her claws into Linnea's thighs and Asta's cousin screamed. The dog made it to them before Asta did and muckled onto the finfolk's neck, dragging the being down to the sand in a splash of granules. The finfolk thrashed under Dyri's bite, but the canine didn't let go. He pushed the creature to the ground by her throat as she lashed out with her arms and legs.

Asta watched in horror as she sprinted for her dog. He was not supposed to be here. None of her friends or family were supposed to be here. It was not their fight.

The finfolk that Dyri was pinning down grabbed one of his hind limbs, sinking her claws in and shredding through muscle and bone.

The canine whimpered, but never let go of his grip. He bit tighter, until the finfolk went limp and her limbs dropped to the ground in a thud.

After a moment of stillness, the dog fell, his blood staining the sand red.

CHAPTER 55

"Can you fix it?" Halsten shouted over the eruption of battle cries that carried across the shore. He shoved a finfolk back, guarding Linnea as she observed Dyri's injuries.

Halsten hadn't seen the pup get injured, but he knew it was a driving point for Asta now. The second Dyri had cried out in pain, the blonde princess had cut clean through two finfolk at once, stepping through their spliced bodies as they fell and targeting her next victim.

"He's bleeding so much. I don't know what to do!" Linnea had tears streaming down her face as she tried to staunch the bleeding with a wad of cloth ripped from Halsten's shirt. "He saved me! I need to save him!"

A hissing siren swiped at Halsten's chest, leaving claw marks in his shirt but luckily not making contact with skin. His movements were incredibly slow due to his leg injury, so he focused on holding his ground. The Ryktarvan warriors were multiplying at a concerning rate, more of them slithering up from the shoreline every minute.

Halsten did his best to keep them away from Linnea while she worked on Dyri, but it was not easy. His leg throbbed, hardly able to withhold weight. Even with Asta, Revna, and King Botmar joining the fight, and Gyrial being freed from his iron, the odds were not in their favor.

A gray mass stepped next to Halsten and held the line. Thurs, the alpha of the northern kelpies, had come to help him.

The mare kicked and bit the approaching opponents, her teeth terrifyingly sharp and definitely not horselike. She frequently checked behind her and Halsten was positive she was checking on Dyri's condition. After all the times the dog had attempted to befriend the kelpie, something must have made an impact on her.

Halsten and Thurs worked in tandem to guard Linnea and Dyri, the mare's help being the advantage they needed. If anyone had told Halsten two months ago that he would be fighting merfolk next to a gigantic flesh-shredding horse someday, he would have asked them what was in their glass—and if he could have some.

He also never thought that Niklas would be a "below the belt" fighter—both literally and figuratively. The man had no problem kicking the beings between their legs, pulling hair, or throwing sand in their eyes. Halsten supposed he had likely never been in a fight before. Even worse, he had likely never been trained in combat even once. So the fact that Niklas was holding his own against individuals with preternatural speed and strength was really quite impressive.

"Incoming!" Asta bellowed, pointing toward the shoreline.

Another hoard of Ryktarvans were crawling out of the waves, hissing and snapping at the air. The sea witch must have sent her most deranged soldiers to take care of them, and likely to also lure Asta away from the bigger fight.

Halsten knew that the sooner they were safe, the sooner Asta could return to Naltania and protect his best friend. He knew that the Salendronean princess would do anything to keep Kaid safe—something she had proved time and time again.

The onslaught of extra soldiers was their downfall. The line they had made to guard the castle, as well as Linnea and Dyri, was being pushed further and further back.

"We can't hold them off forever!" Gyrial yelled down the line.

Halsten knew he needed to ensure Linnea's safety, but he also knew that she would not leave Dyri. As if reading his mind, Thurs broke from the line at the same time Halsten did, sprinting back for the pair they were protecting. Halsten apologized to Dyri, only taking a moment to observe the mangled limb dangling from the canine, before hoisting him up over his shoulder and laying him on Thurs's back. It was a testament to the pup's demeanor that even in such pain, he never once lashed out or tried to bite.

Halsten yanked Linnea to his chest by her wrist, planting a powerful kiss on her lips, then lifted her up onto Thurs behind Dyri. The mare took off toward the castle and Halsten knew that it could very well be the last time he saw Linnea. Even though his leg was going numb, he turned and dove back into the fight.

King Botmar's iron sword left sizzling corpses in its wake and Halsten wished they had more than one iron blade. They needed something—anything—to give them an advantage.

An outbreak of shrieks and hisses sounded from the forest before a swarm of people appeared, running through the underbrush toward the beach.

Was it just Halsten, or were the people all very short?

No, they were not short people. They were children. At least twenty of them.

The deafening screeches were not human sounds, and Halsten panicked. How was he supposed to justify fighting children, even if they were dangerous ocean dwellers?

This was how he would die. Halsten couldn't fight children. Kaid, maybe, if he were here. Kaid punched first then asked questions later. Halsten, though? Halsten at least put some thought into what he punched before he did it. And he would not be punching youth.

He braced himself as the children approached and closed his eyes, flinching when he felt them brushing past him. When he opened his eyes, he realized they had run around him and were fighting beside Asta. Fighting *against* the Ryktarvans.

They were vicious little things, using their razor sharp teeth to latch onto the warriors. It took two-to-three of them to take down one warrior, but the extra hands were helpful.

As thankful as Halsten was for the children, a shiver ran down his spine as he watched them. There was something very terrifying about watching murderous children. Halsten may have developed a new fear of youth in general now.

Either way, the new arrivals were not enough, and Halsten and his friends were fighting a losing battle.

CHAPTER 56

Tears threatened to fall from Asta's eyes as she continued fighting.

Her orphans had come. They had come to help her. Some of them were hardly old enough to form a fist, but they knew that Asta was their friend and she needed their help.

In a normal situation, she would have demanded they return to the safety of the orphanage, but this was not a normal situation. These orphans were abandoned by the creatures they were attacking. Birthed and planted to be used later when it was convenient. This fight was as much for them as it was for Asta and her friends and family. She couldn't take that from them.

However, they still needed something more to give them the upperhand. They were not getting pushed back as quickly now because of the orphans, but they were still being herded toward the castle.

"Asta! Behind you!" her father howled.

She spun, swiping her blade out in front of her to stop whatever was coming her way.

Maren was charging her, causing Asta to do a double-take. Asta's sword did not strike, her sister being far more skilled than the warriors that were sent. Maren rolled out of the way and once she was back on her feet, she sprang into the air. Asta raised her sword to block what she anticipated was coming her way, but Maren jumped over her, landing behind her and plunging her sword into a Ryktarvan warrior's chest.

Maren withdrew her blade and locked eyes with Asta. "Mother's comb! Asta, use it!"

Asta froze, baffled. What was she seeing right now?

Maren spun, slashing her blade and cutting down her own soldiers, her red hair flaring out like an inferno ring around her.

"Asta!" Maren gritted her teeth. "Listen to me for once in your life!"

Was this some form of a trick? Was Maren manipulating her somehow, coaxing her to reveal the comb and mirror for some nefarious reason?

But what good would the siren artifacts be to a finfolk princess? Unlike the trident, the comb and mirror could only be used by sirens.

Asta's father continued his fight, but watched his daughters closely. Would he intervene if something happened? How would he choose a side?

There was one thought that brought Asta comfort—if she used the comb and mirror and Maren attempted any sort of trick, Asta could use the artifacts to control her sister. But would she be able to go through with it, if it came down to it?

Fuck it.

Asta pulled the comb and mirror from her satchel. She had always felt connected to her mother when she combed her hair with the piece of metal in her hand. Her mother. Maren had called her mother, also. What did she mean by that?

Everyone had naturally encompassed Asta in a circle of safety so she could use the items. Would there be any repercussions from using the magic within? She supposed she would find out.

The metal heated as Asta held the mirror before her, staring at her reflection. She was covered in dirt and blood splatter, her blonde curls a tangled mess. She brought the comb up and gently ran it through her hair slowly.

Her siren awoke within her, clawing its way to the surface. The voice that came from her lips was not her own.

Asta sang her siren song.

Listen, all who are near, Your leader is here

Do as I say, And it will only be play

Disobey, And it will be your final day

Though my song is done, It cannot be unsung

So long as I wield, You all will yield

Every Ryktarvan stood at attention, awaiting Asta's command—apart from the orphans and Maren. Asta had been sure that her intentions as she sang were to only control those who were attacking them, which meant Maren must truly be fighting *with* her, not against her.

Halsten's chest heaved as he caught his breath. King Botmar's arms quivered from wielding the iron sword. Niklas shook, clasping his hands together. And Revna, ice warrior, was on one knee, her head down, bowing to Asta.

She lowered the mirror, being sure to not let go of either item. From her song, she understood that once she let go of the artifacts, her control over them would break.

"Return to your kingdom and withdraw from the war!" she commanded.

A handful of warriors immediately turned toward the sea and walked in, transforming and disappearing within the waves.

Well, that was easy, Asta thought.

But why were the rest of them not moving?

"They are disobeying," Maren stated, reading Asta's thoughts.

Right. *Disobey, And it will be your final day.* Would they all truly rather die than admit defeat?

The more Asta thought about that, the more she realized she would likely choose that option as well.

Asta waved to her orphans to look at her, then signed. "Close your eyes, little ones. Count to ten, then you can open them."

The children nodded, closing their eyes. Asta knew that each and every one of them had killed today—that it was in their nature to kill—but they did not need to bear witness to this.

"I'm sorry," Asta whispered, more so to herself than the Ryktarvans. "You have disobeyed. Today is your final day."

With pained expressions, the remaining enemy warriors wrapped their fingers around their own necks, digging their claws into their jugular veins, gripping, and pulling.

The Ryktarvans dropped, the gaping holes in their throats leaking pools of blood into the sand.

Death's kiss had returned, ready to release her fury on the world.

CHAPTER 57

After making sure the orphans returned to the safety of the village, Asta told her friends and father to take care of themselves and Dyri. She prayed to any god or goddess that would listen to save the pup.

Thurs returned not long after the Ryktarvans fell, nudging Asta with her muzzle.

"Only *one*," Asta said, and Thurs nudged her again. "Fine. One *each*."

The Salendronean princess turned away as the kelpies made a meal of the fallen enemies. The rest would be pulled away by the rising tide where they would return to sea.

"We have to go, sister." Maren kept her distance as she spoke, her grip remaining tight on her sword.

Revna eyed her menacingly, the ice in her gaze sending a chill through Asta.

She had not heard such a pleasant tone from Maren in years.

Asta stormed toward Maren, her sword pointed at her sister's throat. "What's your game? What do you want from me?"

Maren did not flinch. "I cannot tell you until this is over. There's too much at stake. I know I have done everything to make you distrust me, but understand it was not real. I need you to have faith in me."

"That's a big ask from the princess of our enemy kingdom," Revna seethed.

"I'm not the enemy." Maren's gaze switched between Asta and Revna, before settling back on Asta. "I'm not your enemy, Asta. I'm your sister. The one who played sirens with you. The one who would hide under buffet tables at balls with you. The one who needed to push you away to keep you safe—though that did not work the way I hoped it would. Of course, I never suspected that the lost prince would end up moving in with us by sheer happenstance. That changed the trajectory of my plans. Especially since you had grown to care for him by the time I confirmed who he was."

Asta shook her head. "I don't understand. Why did you push me away?"

"You won't understand until we've won."

Revna pointed her jagged dagger at Maren now. "Define 'we.'"

"I cannot," Maren sighed. "Trust me, or don't. Either way, no harm will come to you by my blade." She dropped her sword into the sand at Asta's feet.

Asta knew that her sister didn't need a sword to be lethal, but she also knew the significance of giving up your weapon when two are pointed at you.

She lowered her weapon and picked up Maren's, turning and mounting Thurs who had finished her feeding. Revna mounted another kelpie, and Asta pointed at a third. "Get on, before I change my mind." Maren climbed onto a kelpie with ease. She was always better at riding than Asta was. Asta tossed Maren's sword back to her. "You'll need that. Don't force me to kill you, sister."

And then they rode like three merfolk had never ridden before, returning to battle. When they got there, would they be fighting against or with each other? Asta did not know.

Maren yipped as the kelpies approached Naltania, her warrior cries bouncing off the reef below. Something in Asta's chest tightened and she cracked her knuckles. She saw Maren watching her and hid her hands. Her sister lifted her arms above her head, her red hair billowing in the currents around them, and let out a finfolk shriek. Asta couldn't tell if it was camaraderie, or hope, or a final goodbye between them, but she, too, raised her arms and released a siren scream.

Once they crossed over the reef, the battlegrounds were in sight. Revna dove off her kelpie and disappeared into the front lines while Asta searched the chaos for Kaid.

Maren hovered next to her, also searching the mayhem, but for who? Her sister's brow furrowed and worry crept across her features.

A water funnel the size of a hurricane approached and Asta and Maren steered their kelpies away from its path of destruction. Ryktarvans were pulled into the funnel and sent flying up into the skies above. Trails of blood drifted heavily throughout the water and soldiers bellowing commands to their inferiors echoed all around.

A flash of gold caught Asta's attention and she followed the light, her eyes landing on Kaid and his parents, Arielle still wielding the trident.

Asta turned to show Maren where to follow her to, but her sister was already guiding her kelpie straight into battle. Asta quickly realized that Svanhild was within the group that Maren was approaching and once she got there, Svanhild hugged her tightly. Maren shouted indiscernible words and the Ryktarvan warriors surrounding them stopped fighting the Naltanians, instead turning their blades on other Ryktarvans.

Asta frantically reached into her satchel to ensure the comb and mirror were still there and when her hands wrapped around the handles of each artifact, she let out a breath of relief. But how was Maren making the Ryktarvans turn on each other? It wasn't something she had time to ponder right now. All she knew was that Maren had secured a fraction of trust within her.

CHAPTER 58

Kaid fought with his back to his father's as they protected his mother. Queen Arielle wielded the trident as though she had used it every day for the last one hundred years, her strikes precise and effective. Not only was she controlling the currents below and weather above, she was also tracing paths through the battlefield using the trident to take down Ryktarvans with a vaporizing magic.

Asta came swooping in on Thurs, who dropped the princess at Kaid's side then disappeared into battle.

"You made it." Despite the war surrounding them, Kaid's voice was warm and happy.

Asta smiled before plunging her sword into a finfolk's chest. "I will always make it back to you."

Kaid did not doubt that.

"The sea witch is approaching!" Aerik alerted them.

Kaid's vision locked onto the dark-haired demon as she sent a jolt of lightning so strong through the water that multiple sirens fell to the seafloor, never to get back up.

"We can't fight her and these soldiers at the same time," Kaid hollered. "We need to clear the field."

Aerik grunted as he heaved a brawny finfolk off himself. "I'm open to any suggestions on how to do that!"

Asta started digging through her bag, then pulled out the comb and mirror. "This is war. No one comes out with their hands clean. Protect your people."

If he'd had any question regarding using the comb and mirror before, they vanished. Asta was right. Kaid had a duty to withhold.

Kaid took the artifacts and felt them warm in his hands, his siren form taking over as he sang a song of undeniable command, promises of violence, and clarity of intent. A large portion of the finfolk surrounding them ceased fighting, dropping their weapons, and those who did not slit their own throats. Though the comb and mirror could not control the whole battlefield, they had cleared the diameter surrounding the royal family.

Queen Yrsa broke through the clean line where the comb and mirror's reach ended, a wicked grin revealing her mouthful of fangs. Arielle pushed between Kaid and Aerik, meeting the sea witch halfway.

CHAPTER 59

Asta watched in horror as Arielle grabbed the sea witch by the wrist and used the trident to propel them to a tower on the castle. As angry as Asta was that Arielle chose to isolate the dangerous fight, she could not truly be upset, as it was exactly what she would have done.

The advantage of being a siren any other time was that they could simply swim up to the tower, but with the turbulent currents, water funnels, and rows of archers releasing arrows tipped with cerith shells toward anyone who appears above the battleground, simply swimming up to the tower was unachievable.

Flashes of gold and blue light came from the top of the tower where the queens fought and Asta knew she needed to get up there to help. They all did.

Soren broke from the lines of finfolk warriors closing in, filling the gap from where the comb and mirror had cleared the field. "I've got your back! Go!"

Asta did not waste time. She grabbed Kaid's wrist, the siren prince shouting to his father to follow, and they made a dash for the castle. Soren swam backward and fought off anyone coming for them. It wasn't long before Revna found them, joining Soren to hold back the enemy.

When they got inside, they found another battle happening within. Asta hadn't even noticed that the battle had infiltrated the castle walls.

The approaching finfolk bottlenecked at the castle doorway but fanned out as soon as they entered. Asta stopped to slash her sword at a few of them who had slipped past Soren and Revna.

"Can you use the comb and mirror again?" Asta asked Kaid while he helped fight off the beasts.

He shook his head. "I think the repercussion of the magic is that you can only use it once and then have to wait a bit. Now that I let go of them, I lost my chance."

"Asta! Behind!"

Asta turned in time to find that Soren was the one who shouted to her, but it was too late. He dove in front of her, the spear aimed for her heart claiming his instead.

Soren slowly fell to the iridescent floor, blood pouring from his wound around the spearhead.

"No!" Asta screamed. She threw her short sword, the weapon cutting through the water so quickly that it was a silver flash, before it embedded itself into the spear-thrower's skull.

She got down to Soren's level and ran her fingers over his scarred face and he smiled at her. "Listen to me, before I run out of time."

"You're *not* running out of time, Soren. Hold on until the mender can help."

"Ever the dreamer, like me," Soren laughed. "I know you're going to be the siren queen someday, but don't forget your human side like I did. And one more thing…"

Asta held back a sob as she squeezed his hand. "Anything."

"Tell my story someday."

And then, Soren's grip loosened, his eyes no longer searching Asta's face but looking through it. He was gone.

She would tell his story, always. She would tell the story of the male whose life was taken from him before it began, who rose from the ashes and made a name for himself, who taught those around him to be compassionate and caring, who taught her that not everyone's journey took the same route, who loved telling tales and painting pictures with words. Soren would live on through Asta.

A gentle hand landed on Asta's shoulder. "We have to go," Kaid whispered.

The sounds of their surroundings rushed back into Asta and she was once again back on the battlefield, leaving her friend behind.

Maren and Svanhild were waiting at the mouth of the ramp to the tower and Asta hesitated. "Follow us!" Maren shouted over the chaos. Her sister then turned and started making her way up the ramp.

Asta approached cautiously, but when she looked around the curve of the ramp and saw Maren and Svanhild carving a path through the mayhem, she followed. Kaid, Aerik, and Revna followed closely behind, holding off the Ryktarvans coming up the ramp.

When they reached the top of the tower, King Aerik burst through the door and swam to his wife's side. Arielle had a large gash on the side of her head and swayed slightly. Something was wrong.

Kaid pushed past Asta, pulling the trident from his mother's grip and aiming it at the sea witch. "Get her to the mender!"

Revna grabbed one side of Queen Arielle while King Aerik grabbed the other. However, they had nowhere to go. It had taken all of them to fight through the enemy warriors to get here. There was no way they could fight their way back down while supporting the queen as well. It all had to end here.

Asta inspected Queen Yrsa, spotting only minor abrasions. How had she harmed Arielle so badly when the siren queen held the trident?

Kaid raised the trident, pointing the prongs at Yrsa, teeth bared. His trident tattoo illuminated the same gold that the trident was made of. "Now it's a fair fight, witch."

The finfolk queen cackled. "What makes you think you're superior to your mother in battle? You couldn't even escape my castle without your girlfriend rescuing you."

"You misunderstand. I would never dare say I surpass my mother's greatness. However, you were fighting her when she was at a disadvantage." Kaid gripped the pronged staff tighter, sending a humming glow through the metal. "The trident will respond to any merfolk using it, but it only recognizes one owner at a time."

Queen Yrsa's eyes flicked to Maren, a flash of confusion appearing and vanishing rapidly. "And that is not the all-powerful Empress Arielle?"

"No. It's me." Kaid sent a blast of magic from the tip of the trident careening toward the finfolk queen.

CHAPTER 60

The trident took over for Kaid, trapping Queen Yrsa in small water funnels and disorienting her, wrapping currents around her throat, countering her scattered lightning blasts with its own.

Yet, it could not directly end her. Kaid understood that now, being the true owner.

The magic of the trident maintained balance by not allowing itself to take the life of a merspecies leader.

Aside from that, the trident's magic was stretched thin as it controlled the surrounding elements, protecting as many Naltanians as it could.

Meaning, Kaid needed to get close enough to the queen to kill her himself. Trapped on a tower, ideally, would be the easiest way to corner someone. But when that someone had lightning magic that could end opponents without the wielder even needing to lift a finger, that posed a conundrum.

While Kaid attempted to formulate a plan, Asta, Maren, and Svanhild kept the doorway clear. Kaid had no idea when Maren and Svanhild had swapped kingdoms, but he was not going to argue against having such skilled beings on their side.

Now that Asta and Maren weren't fighting against each other, they actually worked quite well together. It was uncanny how similar their combat styles were, which was probably why they were always fair opponents for each other.

Queen Yrsa began firing off uncontrolled lightning currents, charring the colorful walls surrounding them. The blue streaks slithered through the water, but everyone managed to dodge them—though Kaid could have sworn one struck Maren. Seeing as she hadn't fallen, he must have been wrong.

The sea witch growled in frustration, sending a second wave of frenzied lightning currents toward them. Everyone scattered, but Asta cried out, falling to the floor.

Kaid rushed to her side, keeping the trident aimed at the finfolk queen as she maniacally laughed. A streak of black, charred hair cut through her signature blonde and her eyes fluttered as she struggled to keep them open.

Maren was next to Asta in an instant, inspecting the damage, but nothing was visible besides the black hair. "She must have been grazed on her head," Maren told Kaid. "If she's fighting passing out, it wasn't a full hit. She will be okay, but she needs a mender to diffuse any lingering currents within her."

Kaid stood back up to his full height, understanding that both his mother's and Asta's lives relied on him ending this quickly. He used the trident to bring on currents, pushing Queen Yrsa back and pinning her against the wall. Lightning still blasted from her fingertips, scattering along the walls and floor. How was Kaid going to get close enough to kill her?

Maren calmly swam up to Kaid. "I can do this."

Without another word, Maren wrapped her fingers around the trident. Kaid didn't let go at first, pondering. He had sworn a blood oath to not give the relic to anyone seeking tyranny. If he let Maren take it, and she turned on him, he and everyone he loved would drop dead.

Something in his chest told him to let go. Maren held the trident as she swam toward her mother. Lightning currents flickered through the water, wrapping themselves around Maren and the golden staff, but not harming her.

Maren was truly on their side.

At first, Kaid thought that maybe Queen Yrsa could control who the lightning harmed, but once he saw the expression of astonishment on the finfolk queen's face, he knew that was not the case.

The finfolk princess stopped in front of her mother, observing the dark-haired beast pinned to the wall.

"Maren, my precious heir. You never told me that you—"

"No one cares what you have to say, *Mother*," Maren cut her off. "I will no longer be your pawn."

Maren held up the trident, the prongs dancing with lightning. Then, Kaid saw it. Purple bolts danced around her claws, down the pole, and encompassed the trident. Maren was a sea witch.

"Don't. We can rule together," Queen Yrsa shook her head, her limbs still pinned to the wall.

Maren laughed. "If you had ever shown me a scrap of love, I may have considered such an offer a long time ago. It's too late now."

Yrsa gasped. "*Love?* Love makes you weak!"

The finfolk princess swam up so her face was just inches from her mother's. "Everything I have ever done has been for love. And I am not weak."

Maren plunged the lightning-charged trident clean through the queen of Ryktarva's chest, then withdrew the prongs with the queen's heart speared at the end. Maren shook the staff, and her mother's heart drifted to the floor.

EPILOGUE 1

Asta and Kaid walked up the beach, entering the castle from the terrace, where Linnea greeted them with a hug.

"It's only been two days, Lin," Asta laughed.

"I know, but I'll always be happy to see you two walking up that beach." Linnea stepped back and grabbed Halsten's hand while his other held him steady with a cane.

Asta and Kaid had been traveling back and forth between Naltania and Orntali every few days while they prepared for Kaid's coronation. Queen Arielle was more than ready to retire from the role since Kaid had returned. After being separated from King Aerik for so long, Kaid's parents could not wait to live a life of few responsibilities together.

Dyri came barreling down the hall, barking and panting, his hind end extra springy due to only having one rear limb now. Asta could never thank the medical staff enough for saving his life, even if it meant removing his mangled leg in order to do so. She knelt down and squeezed him tightly while Kaid patted his head.

"How is she?" Asta asked Linnea.

Her cousin smiled softly. "Go see for yourself."

Asta made her way to the infirmary, sucking in a deep breath before entering. Two dark-haired twins sat on the crisp, flat sheets, laughing and speaking in hushed tones.

"Tova?"

The twin with longer hair turned around, her bright smile the same one Asta remembered from before the thoughtrus incident.

Kaid excused himself to spend time with Halsten while Asta stayed with the twins. Tova explained that she had not meant to resist the thoughtrus; she only wanted to repress any thoughts of Liva in case the situation escalated. She would never do anything to endanger her sister, and Asta understood completely. Now that Tova was better, she would join her sea dragon twin in their joint position of emissaries between the Ventarin territories and Orntali.

The finfolk and siren kingdoms were no longer at war. Actually, it was quite the opposite. After the fall of Yrsa, Maren stepped into the role of queen of the finfolk. She had been working with the sirens to help the finfolk adjust to the new feeding arrangement they had made.

Understandably, once there was a merfolk war both underwater and on land, it was difficult to hide the existence of the species from the villagers of Orntali. And so, finfolk and sirens were Orntali's little secret. The humans knowing about the species made life easier for everyone.

The finfolk were required to help the fishermen meet their quota, guiding whichever fish species was overpopulated at that time into their nets. In exchange for their help, the humans had volunteered to let the finfolk sustainably feed from them.

This was where the sirens had to step in to help—training the finfolk when to stop feeding so they did not take a human's life. No finfolk was allowed to feed unless a siren spectator was with them.

Maren was working diligently to civilize the finfolk species, including putting an end to abandoning their children on the shore.

During battle, the new finfolk queen had revealed that she turned on her mother for love, but Asta learned what she truly meant a few weeks after the war ended.

Maren had lied—a lot—in order to accomplish everything she had. Her end goal, however, was protecting Asta and living a life of blissful peace with her wife, Svanhild.

Queen Yrsa had been so wrapped up in a strategic merspecies marriage that she had never noticed that her daughter had fallen in love with her lady-in-waiting. The moment Maren understood what her mother's extensive plan was, she began undermining it.

Maren had left Asta the extra iron key in the forest on purpose. She had led Asta's friends to reunite the comb and mirror by placing Queen Else's informative journal out in the open of the archives. She had pushed Asta away so she would not get involved in a war she knew nothing about—though that did not work out. The night that Kaid and Asta hid in the cave, Maren and Svanhild held off the search by swearing up and down that they had seen them continue running down the beach. Maren had even convinced her mother to send the most feral warriors to the shore to attack Asta's friends and family, knowing that they would likely be able to out-smart them.

Everything Maren had done had been driven by her love for Svanhild and Asta. She even explained that though she did not live with Queen Else—Asta's mother—for long, she knew that Else loved her more than her birth mother ever would, so she did this for her as well. And their father.

Out of everyone, Maren deserved a happy ending the most.

Asta returned to her suite to find a letter from Gyrial, updating her on his latest patrol. The fae male had returned to the Spellid Mountains after the council lifted his banishment. Once Sabella had helped reveal the truth about Gyrial's parents—how his father had murdered his mother and that was the reason he attacked his father—the council issued a formal apology and offered Gyrial an officer position in their army. Before he left, the fae male explained that he was leaving because even though he valued the friendships he had made in Orntali, it was time for him to find his happy ending, too. Asta could not argue with that.

She folded up the letter and placed it on her vanity before looking out the window and watching a herd of wild, dapple gray horses galloping and bucking down the beach. The kelpies made regular appearances now, traveling freely between the ocean kingdoms and Orntali. Though the villagers didn't exactly know the truth regarding them, they understood enough to give the horses their space. However, they left troughs of freshly killed hare out each night and were pleased to discover the rabbits were gone each morning.

"Niklas is in heaven," Kaid said as he entered the bedroom, wrapping his arms around Asta from behind. She stared at herself in the mirror, observing the streak of black hair that remained from Yrsa's attack. "Allowing him to open the archives to the public was the best thing you could have done for him."

After learning about all of the historical pieces that had been shoved down into the archives to collect dust, Asta knew that giving that knowledge back to her people was the best way to ensure history would not repeat itself. The legends needed to live on. It was also the best way for her to confirm with her villagers that their suspicions regarding preternatural beings' existence were real without outright saying so.

"So, when can we tell your father?" Kaid kissed Asta's neck playfully.

She laughed. "Let's not spring this on him when he's planning my coronation. We have two major ceremonies coming up. We don't need to inform him that we may have skipped over a third and took the easy way out."

"You think fighting a war, managing two kingdoms, finding peace between merspecies, and revealing the existence of magical beings to an entire village was the easy way out?"

"Well, it was easier than planning a wedding, I would bet," Asta grinned.

"Asta Blomvin Enrathi Andreassan, you really are the most infuriatingly intriguing female I have ever met."

Their secret wedding had taken place in front of their cave—their only witnesses being the priest, Linnea, and Halsten.

The sunlight had filtered through the cave's tree root ceiling, illuminating the spot they had both realized what they meant to each other. The gulls squawked from above. The scent of briny water and fragrant evergreens engulfed them. It was perfect. So perfect that Halsten had asked Linnea to marry him in that exact spot, and she excitedly said yes.

Kaid kissed her deeply, and they fell into bed, and Asta did not need to comb her hair, or crack her knuckles, or tap her doorway, or swing her sword in order to fall asleep. At least, not tonight.

EPILOGUE II

Congratulations on the dual birth of <u>Prince Soren Botmar Blomvin Enrathi Andreassan SIREN</u> and <u>Princess Else Maren Blomvin Enrathi Andreassan SIREN</u> of the Ventarin Sea.

Born to Emperor Kaidian Blomvin Enrathi Andreassan SIREN of the Ventarin Sea and Queen Asta Blomvin Enrathi Andreassan SIREN of Salendron.

May the gods and goddesses watch over them.

ALTERNATE CHAPTER 19

A sta stretched and let out a yawn. The tourniquet had done its job and stopped the bleeding. Her injuries were not deep, but certainly had made an impact. Figuring the cloth had been tied on for multiple hours now, Asta released the knot and let it fall. The bleeding didn't seem to start again.

Kaid watched her and did the same with the tie he had made above his thigh wound. In her daze, she hadn't remembered to ask him about his injuries, but he had remembered and treated hers, and guilt bloomed on her cheeks. To her relief, his leg injury seemed to be clotted now as well, no thanks to her.

"I can't sleep sitting up like this," Asta said.

Immediately, Kaid took off his fur-lined cloak and laid it on the ground, patting it down.

Asta unbuttoned her cloak and slipped it off. "We can use this as a blanket," she murmured as she laid down between layers.

"We?" Kaid asked.

Asta huffed a laugh, amazed that she could smile even under such circumstances. "We. I need you down here with me. For warmth purposes."

It wasn't a lie. It was autumn now and there was a brisk, salty breeze coming off the sea and making its way into the cave. They would freeze to death before the night was through if they didn't use each other to stay warm.

Kaid didn't object and slid between the cloaks, lying close but not touching her. His breath wheezed slightly as he settled.

"Do you have to breathe like that?" Asta huffed. He drove her mad.

"Oh, sorry, Princess. I'll just stop breathing to please you," Kaid quipped.

Asta hid her faint smile. "That would please me very much, thank you."

They rested in silence, Asta trying to not think about how cold she truly was. She couldn't stop her body from trembling, between the cold air and the last of her adrenaline draining from her.

Kaid's closeness became very apparent to her, and she remembered that the last time they were in such tight proximity was that night in her bedroom. The night where he kissed her as a part of his torment.

His warmth slid closer to her, forming to the shape of her body. The heat he was letting off instantaneously made her shivering stop. The cold was still nipping at her, but it was much more bearable.

"For warmth purposes," Kaid mumbled.

Asta tried to push away how right it felt to be up against him like this. How she wished he would wrap his arms around her and pull her in snugly.

A familiar, tight ball formed in her chest.

Kaid's fingers dove into Asta's hair, brushing downward to the tips and starting back at the top.

One, two, three…

"What are you doing?" she snapped, but couldn't stop her instinctive counting.

Eight, nine, ten…

He chuckled. "Relax, Princess. I know you can't sleep without."

Fifteen, sixteen, seventeen…

Asta had been subconsciously counting his strokes already, but now she was focusing on them, hoping they would help relieve some of the tension in her chest.

Twenty-two, twenty-three, twenty-four…

Four more. Four more strokes and she could breathe. Four more strokes and she would be able to focus on the world around her again.

Twenty-eight.

Twenty-eight. The age my mother was when she died. When I killed her.

The ball in her chest released its grip on her thoughts. She didn't know why it worked when Kaid did it, but she couldn't help but let a tear slip from the corner of her eye at the thought. They had just been through something terrible and he still remembered. He remembered her ritual and didn't tell her to forget about it for a night; to let it go. He didn't remind her that it wasn't important in comparison to the current danger they were in. He helped her.

Asta closed her eyes, wishing away the comfort it brought. She shouldn't feel this way. Not about him.

A strong arm wrapped around her abdomen while another nudged her head to lift off the cave floor. When she set it back down, she realized that Kaid was providing her with a pillow using his own arm.

The emotions were undeniable now. There was no stopping them. At least not tonight.

Asta allowed her courage to take one final stand before it disappeared completely. "Was it all a game? Was *I* a game?"

Kaid's body went rigid, his voice unsteady. "You're the first thing in my life that hasn't been."

Asta swallowed loudly and scooted back so her body was pressed against Kaid's. At first, he didn't react to her movement and she worried that she had crossed a boundary. But his fingers start brushing against the fabric of her shirt, tracing lazy circles across her torso.

Kaid respectfully avoided any intimate areas within his path. He traced a long line starting at her hip, gliding up her side, breezing past the side of her chest, tracing her collarbone, and running up the corner of her jaw. Asta's breathing hitched under his touch, all thoughts leaving her mind besides him. He continued to trace the contours of her body, dipping his hand down to outline her thighs.

She backed into Kaid as hard as she could, unable to stop her hips from moving. What did it matter? They may die, anyway.

At first, Kaid paused when he felt her hips rocking, but then his fingers continued their circles with more purpose.

He leaned down, his warm breath coating the skin of Asta's ear. "You're safe," he whispered.

Asta let out a small laugh, her skin mottling with raised bumps. "That simply can't be true when I'm stuck in a cave with my greatest enemy."

Her proclamation didn't stop him from pressing his lips to her neck, each kiss deeper than the last. Asta craned her neck to allow him more access and he chuckled.

Kaid's teeth grazed Asta's earlobe before he asked, "Do you still hate me?"

"Yes," Asta replied breathlessly.

She realized that was the answer he had wanted when Kaid's lazy circles quickly turned to a grip on her abdomen.

"Tell me why," he growled.

What was the reason? Because of his reputation? Because of his uncanny ability to show up everywhere she was? Because he matched her challenges and pushed back?

There was only one real answer which summed everything up.

"Because, Kaid, you are... insufferable. You drive me absolutely mad. And I *hate* that I enjoy it."

Asta concluded that the sentiment was reciprocated when Kaid slipped his hand under her shirt and began palming her chest. She rolled onto her back and captured his mouth with hers, their kissing feverish and determined, much different than the kissing they had done in her bed.

Gods, she had wanted this for so long and refused to admit it. She might be able to tolerate him if he never spoke again and they lived in this moment for eternity.

One of Kaid's fingers lightly brushed under Asta's waistband and he pulled his mouth away from her, looking into her eyes with his turquoise gaze glistening in the moonlight, glowing like the bioluminescence of the sea.

"Will you hate me more if I keep going?" His finger continued tracing a line across her abdomen, back and forth.

"Yes," Asta replied.

Kaid's too-perfect-for-this-world smile slid across his lips and Asta nearly passed out from the sight of it.

He pressed a kiss to the corner of her mouth before asking, "May I proceed anyway?"

Asta didn't need a moment to think about her answer. She knew what she wanted. Damn the consequences—she would deal with them in the morning.

Her voice was hardly more than a whisper. "Yes."

Kaid kissed her ferociously, his chest rumbling. He removed her trousers and tossed them aside.

"You wickedly cruel, beautiful thing. Please, hate me forever," Kaid whispered.

She could hate him forever if this was what it meant. If this was what it led to.

Kaid dove between her legs, remaining there until waves of pleasure came over her.

She could do this every day. That was, if her sister wasn't set to marry this man in less than a week.

Now that the lust was leaving her body, her mind cleared and reminded her of that. But in that moment, she didn't care. Kaid helped her get dressed, knowing her arm was still sore from its injuries, and then nestled in next to her.

Tomorrow, she would be the pretty princess in the seaside castle who was happy for her sister for finding a husband.

Tonight, she was the warrior, fighting for what she wanted and seizing it.

ALTERNATE CHAPTER 36

L innea took a long, searing bath and her muscles unknotted instant-ly. Heat used to bother her because of her last encounter with her mother, but after years of practice, she could take hot baths again. The sting of warmth on her skin still bothered her sometimes, but that's what permanent scarring from hot coals being shoved down the back of your dress will do to you. They never fully heal.

Sometimes she could still hear her mother's cold laughter, matching the frigid weather of the day she gained her largest scars. Linnea had made the mistake of mentioning it was a tad chilly in the house that morning, which was when her mother formulated the plan to help her "appreciate" the heat that was provided.

What's wrong, dear? I thought you were cold.

Linnea clawed her way out of her downward spiral—working to focus on how wonderful the warmth felt on her aching muscles and not the terrible memories that heat held—and finished her bath.

Halsten was right—as long as she stretched when she got out, she would feel much better. She stepped out and wrapped herself in a towel, digging through her saddlebag for something comfortable to wear. She had been stuck in riding pants and cotton puffy shirts for days now.

Linnea pulled out a multi-layered gossamer nightgown in her favorite color, slate blue. She was not a confident woman, but she always loved how the color accentuated her gray eyes and auburn hair. She stood in the mirror and tied up the decorative strings that sat below her collarbones, leaving a keyhole effect on her chest, and her shoulders exposed.

Her stomach rumbled and she panicked. In her uncomfortable state, her entire focus was on taking a hot bath. She had completely forgotten to go down to eat before she got into her night clothes. Well, she was too tired now, so she would just have to indulge in a large breakfast. She had an apple and a handful of grains in her saddlebag that would hold her over.

She stretched first before her muscles had the opportunity to tighten again. First, standing with a leg on her bed, then she took to the floor and stretched each leg until she could comfortably wrap her palms around the bottoms of her feet again. Lack of body fat growing up had made her flexible, since stretching was the only form of exercise she could endure without becoming winded.

Linnea was about to get up and retrieve the apple from her bag when there was a soft knock at her door.

"Who is it?" she asked through the thick oak door.

"Halsten. Can I come in?"

"I'm not decent. I'll see you in the morning."

"I insist."

Linnea let out a sigh, then glanced around the room for anything to cover herself with. She grabbed a scratchy blanket from the bed and wrapped it around herself before letting him in.

Halsten slipped into the room carrying a tray of food. "I noticed you never came down to eat. I know your legs hurt so I suspected you were protesting the stairway. I figured I would bring the food to you," he said with a goofy smile.

Linnea couldn't help to mirror his facial expression. "Thank you, that's very kind."

Linnea gestured to the small bistro table in the corner and Halsten placed the tray down. To her surprise, he sat himself in one of the chairs. She froze in her tracks, unsure what to do.

"I won't bite, Little Flame. Come, sit with me."

There was that nickname again. He must be jesting at her hair. That had to be it.

"I'm capable of eating by myself, Sir Halsten."

He flinched at the formality but did not budge. She had hoped that would encourage him to leave.

Halsten smiled again, then gestured to the other chair. Linnea cautiously sat down, holding the blanket tight around her chest. She scooped a spoonful of stew with one hand and brought it to her mouth. It was delectable and she let out a soft moan. Halsten's eyes widened as he watched her. She couldn't help but notice his nostrils flaring.

He gestured toward her torso. "Why are you wearing a blanket cape?"

"I'm in my night clothes. It's indecent for a man to see me in them." Linnea gave him a puzzled look as if he should know that.

"Are they... see through?" He raised an eyebrow.

Linnea started. "Of course not! I would not own such scandalous attire!"

Halsten laughed a deep, real laugh. "Then why is it such a secret? Is it not the same as the dresses you usually wear, but less extravagant?"

Damn. He had her with that logic. She held a chunk of baguette in her free hand but hesitated bringing it to her mouth.

"Let go of the blanket, Linnea."

She pulled it tighter. "No."

Halsten pulled the tray to his side of the table. "Then I'll just take this back."

Linnea scoffed. "That's mine!" She reached for the tray, but she had the chunk of bread in her hand so she couldn't grip it.

He dove forward and bit off a large piece of her bread, his mouth now stuffed with it as he laughed.

Linnea gasped, pulling her bread hand back. "Fine!" she shouted as she let go of the blanket. It was making her itchy anyway.

The fabric bunched down at her waist, leaving the upper half of her nightgown exposed. Halsten's eyes wandered up and down her torso multiple times before he slowly slid the tray back to her. There was an odd silence while she finished her stew and bread, but not awkward. When she was done, she dabbed her face with her napkin and stood up, leaving the blanket in the chair behind her. Her legs locked up and she winced.

"Did you stretch?" Halsten asked.

Linnea nodded. "Hot bath and stretched like you said. It was better for a while."

Halsten squinted at her, his chocolate brown eyes glowing in the firelight. "Lie on your stomach on the bed. I can help."

Linnea wanted to protest. That's what any proper lady would do. But he had been sitting here with her in her nightgown and never made her feel unsafe. Now that she thought about it, she had never once felt unsafe in Halsten's presence. If anything, it comforted her more, having him around.

Without a word, but with shaky hands, Linnea laid on her stomach, turning her head to the side so she could see Halsten clearly. He approached the bed and kneeled next to her on the mattress.

"Don't be afraid. I would never hurt you. If you want me to stop, tell me to stop and I will leave. Understood?"

Linnea let out a breathy "yes," unsure of what he was about to do.

Halsten gripped her calf with both hands, working his thumbs in circles starting in the middle and working his way outward. It felt amazing, her muscles relaxing more and more with each stroke of his thumbs.

They sat in comfortable silence while Halsten worked her calves and lower thighs. He never dared approach the hem of her nightgown, which ended mid-thigh. He was being as respectable as a person could be, keeping the massage strictly therapeutic, which Linnea appreciated.

"Why do you call me Little Flame?" Linnea blurted before she could stop herself. She needed to know. "Is it because of my hair?"

"Your—your hair? No, of course not." Halsten's thumbs worked on a particularly difficult knot in the center of her hamstring. "It's just that, since the moment I met you, I knew there was more to you than you let on. You act meager and shy, but I know deep down, you've seen some shit; been through even more. You're tough. You've got a flame in there that you haven't fueled yet."

Linnea nodded, speechless. It wasn't a jest this whole time. She rolled over to her back and looked into his warm eyes, reaching up to rub a thumb over his high cheekbones. He was beautiful.

"Did you mean what you said downstairs?"

"About how irresistible your body is? Yes, Linnea. If we're being honest, it's been a damn struggle to ride behind you the last few days where all I had to look at was your perfect shape."

"I want to try something," Linnea said. "Be patient with me."

Halsten nodded, staying silent. Linnea held the back of his head and dragged it down to hers. When their lips were a breath away, she whispered, "Kiss me."

Halsten did not hesitate. He pressed his mouth to hers and his skin was the softest, most gentle thing she had ever felt. He didn't rush anything, waiting for Linnea to signal she was okay. Refusing to separate their lips, she nodded mid-kiss.

Her body felt hot all over, a warmth she had never experienced before sweeping over her in waves. Every nerve was hypersensitive, so when a lock of Halsten's hair slipped from behind his ear and brushed her neck, she gasped.

Halsten lightly swept against her lips with his tongue and when she did not object, he slipped into her mouth, gingerly knocking at her teeth for entry. Linnea opened to let him in, swirling her tongue around his instinctually.

A low grumble rumbled deep in his chest as Linnea reached for his hips, guiding him so he was kneeling over her. It did nothing to satisfy the heat within her. She had kissed before, so this was not her first time, but she had never felt a need like this.

She trusted Halsten. Maybe she was drunk off everything he had said to her. Maybe she needed to do something risky for once in her life. Maybe, just maybe, he was right—she needed to stoke her fire.

Halsten's kissing became deeper each time he stroked his tongue over hers. "It's my turn to try something. Tell me to stop if you need to, okay?"

Linnea nodded.

"Words, Linnea. I need to hear you say it."

A man being authoritative usually scared Linnea, but Halsten demanding words from her sent pleasant shivers down her spine. "Yes, Halsten. I will stop you if I'm not okay."

Without speaking another word, Halsten dove for her neck. He planted sweet kisses at first and Linnea squirmed under him, her skin growing taut all over. She felt like she was going to burst.

His chest gingerly grazed hers as he leaned in and she jumped, the sensation completely new to her. Her mind told her she didn't want it to happen again, because this was far past the point of ladylike behavior, but her body responded to that faint touch by arching. Her chest brushed his again and a small squeak slipped from her throat.

Halsten sat up quickly, surveying her face. When he saw that she was smiling, he smiled as well. "Did you just squeak?"

Linnea playfully slapped his chest. "It wasn't a squeak. It was a high-pitched moan."

"It was a squeak," he said flatly. "But squeak or moan, I want to hear it again."

Linnea closed her eyes when Halsten dipped back down and latched onto her neck. Linnea squeaked again, this time louder and longer. Halsten laughed against her, causing her to let out a breathy huff of joy with him.

There were no nerves. She wanted her fire stoked, and Halsten was volunteering himself as kindling.

"You know, when your face is flushed, your freckles look a thousand times cuter?" He quickly popped up and kissed the bridge of her nose where her largest cluster of freckles sat. She felt his hand just below her collarbone tugging at the tie there.

His hand slid the material down one of her arms, exposing her chest. She gasped when his palm rested against it, encasing her fully as he squeezed. Linnea pushed on his thighs, making him back up so she could slip her legs out from beneath him and position them on either side of his. Having her legs spread with Halsten kneeling between them made her squirm, a feeling she had never felt with any other man.

He sat back and gripped the sides of her thighs before staring hungrily at her. He licked his lips and Linnea could see him straining against his trousers.

"Gods, Linnea," Halsten mumbled. "You're fucking perfect. I don't know what I ever did to land myself in this position, but I don't deserve it."

Linnea laughed but it quickly faded as another wave of heat ran through her. The longer he stared, the more she ached for him.

Halsten gripped the waistband of his bands before asking, "You're sure?"

She nodded.

His brows furrowed. "Words," he commanded.

"I'm sure," Linnea responded breathily. She was nervous, but Halsten was safe.

Halsten untied the knot holding his trousers up and slipped them down his thighs and Linnea was mesmerized. She quickly realized how addicting this could be. Not sex in general, but sex with this man. The sounds he made and the jerky movements with her slightest of touches made her feel wanted. It made her feel powerful.

Linnea lifted her nightgown in confidence, and Halsten let out a string of curses that she hoped meant something positive even though they sounded quite filthy.

Halsten ran a hand over her and she writhed. She wanted him to take her right here in this dirty inn.

"Please," Linnea whimpered.

"Words," he said in a low growl.

Linnea said the filthiest thing she had ever said, demanding the filthiest thing she had ever desired. "Fuck me, Halsten."

Halsten once again released a steeple-shattering strand of curses as he slowly slid into her. While he was completely immersed in her, he worked her center with his hand.

"Little Flame. My good Little fucking Flame," Halsten whispered to himself and closed his eyes.

His Little Flame. He brought one of her arms to his face and kissed the scar on her wrist.

Stars danced across Linnea's vision as Halsten ground into her and her body broke out in a tingling sensation.

As she came down, Halsten's movements slowed to a stop and he pressed his forehead to hers.

"Now *that* was a high-pitched moan."

ALTERNATE CHAPTER 47

"All right, now that Linnea isn't here, how do you really feel?" Kaid leaned against the closed door, folding his arms over his chest.

Halsten sighed and ran his fingers through his hair. "The mender said there's nerve damage, as well as a muscular tear. She told me she could try to repair the muscles surgically, but it was risky and I still would most likely come out of the surgery in the same condition."

"And what is that condition, Halsten? Why are you in bed?"

"Because of the nerve damage, I can't exactly feel my foot sometimes. It's like it's there, because I can feel the pressure of it touching something, but I can't feel the sensation on my skin, if that makes sense. And then," Halsten leaned off the side of his bed, pulling out a stick from underneath it. "I have to walk with this. Probably forever. Like some old goat, waving his cane around yelling at kids to not trample his flowerbeds."

Kaid laughed despite the devastation he felt. "I've seen a lot of young dukes using canes as a fashion statement. Own it, brother."

They dove into telling the tales of their journeys. Kaid never wanted to be separated from his best friend like that again. He knew that if the sirens won the war, he would likely figure out a way to spend his time in both kingdoms, but he wouldn't be leaving his best friend in perilous situations every time he departed, so that was different. He also would not be leaving his friend alone any longer, now that Linnea was around. He could never repay Linnea for the care and love she provided for his best friend the last few days.

Kaid poured a glass of water from the pitcher and handed it to Halsten. "So, you *had* to claim the other Blomvin woman, hmm?"

"You know I've always had a thing for redheads," Halsten laughed. "But seriously. I know how we used to be. But we've got these two amazing, fierce women in our lives now and I have no interest in that anymore."

Kaid sighed. He had been so wrapped up with Asta that he never even saw the relationship blooming between Halsten and Linnea. What was confusing to Kaid was how easily Halsten fell into step with Linnea, how quickly he put his past behind him. "How do you know you're not going to fuck it up? We've never done this before."

"I'm not saying I'll never do something wrong, but I'm devoted to her. If I wrong her, it will be bringing her the wrong tea in the morning, or wearing a color that clashes with her dress to a party. It won't be anything involving another woman. *Ever.* It's okay to let go and enjoy the free fall. I have been."

That was exactly what Kaid wanted, too. To free fall with Asta. But they each had a habit of protecting themselves above all else, even if it led to their demise. "I'm not entirely sure how to do that. Every time I feel like we're making progress, something sets us back and we're arguing again."

Halsten started laughing and Kaid couldn't for the life of him figure out what he had said that was so funny.

His best friend took a deep breath to stop himself from cackling. "Do you not remember how you two met? You've always been good at challenging one another. You're just challenging each other on the wrong things right now. Show her how serious you are and make her step up. You know she'll want to one-up you simply to prove to you that she can love you more. Eventually, it will even out. That's how you two function."

This was why Halsten was Kaid's best friend. Above all else, he knew how Kaid's brain worked—even when Kaid couldn't quite figure it out himself. He was right. If he wanted to free fall with Asta, he had to grab her arm on the way down and race her to the bottom.

Kaid left Halsten's suite with a spring in his step, feeling lighter than he had in weeks. He and Asta didn't have some deeply rooted problem, destined to never work out. They needed to give in to what they both felt and call each other to rise to the occasion.

He marched to Asta's suite, letting himself in and sitting on the couch next to her. Dyri curled up at his feet while he and Asta watched the calming crackle of the fireplace in front of them. She was wearing a dark blue, silk night dress that left nothing to the imagination, and it drove Kaid mad.

He didn't avert his gaze from the flames as he spoke, scared that looking into Asta's intense stare would cause him to stutter. "I've meant everything I've said to you, you know." Asta did not respond, so Kaid continued. "I need you. I need you to point out my flaws and guide me when I feel lost. I need you to knock me down a peg sometimes."

"I do enjoy doing that," Asta mumbled playfully.

Kaid faced her and grabbed her hand. "Let's wear matching outfits and break protection spells together, forever."

Asta laughed, rolling her eyes. "Let's actually do neither of those things again. I can't believe I had to be the one to introduce myself to your mother. You didn't even have the sense to do it yourself."

Kaid was the one laughing now. Asta had actually met his own mother before he even had. Well, aside from when he was born.

He gripped Asta's waist and pulled her onto him, her legs straddling his lap and her night dress riding up her thighs. One of Kaid's hands gently caressed her thigh while the other wrapped around her back, pulling her face down to his.

"Do you still hate me, my love?" Kaid asked, his lips inches from Asta's.

"Until the end of time." Her lips crashed into his with a world-shattering kiss.

He knew what she meant. Until the end of time, she would hate that she fell for the man she was never supposed to love. But she would love him with everything she had.

Kaid reached up and wrapped his hand in her vicious curls, yanking her head back until she let out a moan.

> *Taste her. Taste her blood. Let her essence infiltrate your very being.*

Kaid's siren hissed at him, forcefully urging him to feed. He pushed the feeling away, knowing that sirens did not typically feed from each other. He wasn't sure what it meant.

He kissed down the side of her neck, sucking on the sensitive spot where her neck met her shoulder, eliciting a whispered string of curses from her lips. He ran his other hand around the back of her thigh, slipping his fingers under her silk garment to grip her full ass. He pulled her forward, pressing her against his lap and she gasped.

"Keep making that sound, Princess, and this night dress won't be in one piece much longer."

Asta moved against him. "That's the plan, *Prince*."

Kaid grazed his thumbs over her chest through the silky fabric.

"I love you," he admitted.

"I love you, too," she whispered back.

Kaid stilled, not expecting her to so readily say it back, but ecstatic that neither of them were afraid to admit it any longer.

Bite. Bite. Lick her blood from her body like the starving beast you are.

Kaid's eyes closed, fighting off his siren.

He kissed down her chest, careful to avoid his siren fangs that were out due to his apparent thirst for her blood. He instinctively latched onto her, biting harder than he intended. As he went to apologize, she let out a deep moan not of pain, but pleasure. *Interesting.*

Kaid stood up, wrapping Asta's legs around him and leaving his shirt behind. It would be a good warning sign for anyone who may come in and try to disturb them, anyway.

He walked to the bedroom, shutting a pouting Dyri out before laying Asta on her plush bed. Her golden hair glowed in the firelight, which turned her green eyes to an amber color.

"This is familiar," Kaid chuckled before back away from her slightly.

Asta spread her legs so Kaid could see that she was not wearing any undergarments. "I think it's a little different than last time."

Oh, yes it is. This time, Kaid would kiss Asta, would touch Asta, would fuck Asta with no remorse.

Asta whimpered, frustrated at the lack of contact, but she didn't try to take control, which Kaid found peculiar.

"Tell me what you want, Asta."

"I want you to touch me." She sounded like she was in pain, her hips ever so slightly lifting, searching for friction and only finding air.

"Then show me how you like it," Kaid demanded.

Asta shook her hand. "I don't know."

She had never been touched the way she wanted, and that made Kaid furious. Not at her, but *for* her, because he knew she had likely never experienced a proper ravishing before, the way *she* liked it.

Kaid bent over and kissed her, hungry for more.

Her blood is yours.

Asta pulled off him suddenly, looking confused as she ran her tongue across her teeth, revealing her siren fangs on full display.

"It's okay. It's happening to me, too." Kaid gently pushed her onto her back, peppering her collarbone with kisses, whispering to her. "My wraith." *Kiss.* "My pretty little demon." *Kiss.* "My siren of death."

Kaid aligned himself with her center, waiting for her nod of confirmation before thrusting in. He took her in fully—wild curls spread behind her and legs spread without a care. No rituals, no impending war. Just the two of them, their bodies connected physically and emotionally. Kaid had been intimate with women before, but he had never made love. Now, he knew there really was a difference.

He bit her breast and she moaned. "Do it," she grumbled. "I think we're supposed to. It feels right."

Kaid opened his mouth wide and clamped down on her breast, his fangs piercing her skin and blood flowing into his mouth. Her blood tasted like a blend of floral teas, and it was the most addicting thing Kaid had ever savored.

He fed on her while still seated in her, drawing guttural sounds from his princess. Once the feeding frenzy slowed, his thoughts cleared. He didn't know what this feeding meant, but he knew it was Asta's turn.

She knew that as well, judging by how she slowly pulled herself from beneath Kaid and pushed him into a sitting position. Asta climbed onto his lap and reinserted Kaid's member.

Kaid tucked her hair behind her ear. "You focus on your feeding, blondie. I'll take care of everything else."

Asta traced a delicate finger all over Kaid's body, clearly choosing where to mark him. He shivered when the pad of her finger tickled his jugular and she grinned. She still had newborn bloodlust, but he trusted her. This feeding felt different.

She dipped forward and licked the spot that made him shiver before lightly pressing her fangs to his throbbing vein. He felt her hesitate, her hot breath dancing across his skin. Every nerve ending on his body was on fire.

"I trust you. You'll be able to stop. I trust *you*." Kaid reassured her.

Asta bit down and the pain was blinding at first, but quickly turned to a pleasant ache. The room began to blur, all of his focus on the two points where their bodies connected. If she didn't stop soon, he was going to explode.

Her breathing became labored, but she did not stop feeding. Asta fell apart on top of him, her mouth disconnecting from his neck and blood dripping down her chin, the sight causing Kaid to come undone with her.

When they both fell from their high, Asta slowly pulled herself off him and they went into the washroom together, helping each other clean up. Neither of them yet to acknowledge what they intrinsically knew, that the bite marks were some sort of bond, and they had finalized it.

THANK YOU!

I have a long list of people to thank. When I showed up to work one day and said, "I think I'm going to write a book," not a single person told me I couldn't. Thank you to those coworkers I no longer have the pleasure of seeing everyday but will always remember. Thank you to the current coworkers I do have for taking their place and always believing in me. Thank you to the friends that stuck by me through the ups and downs of publishing, always being my shoulders to cry on and my biggest cheerleaders. Thank you to my family who, when I told them I was publishing a book, asked "How can we help?" Thank you, thank you, thank you to my alpha, beta, and ARC readers. Thank you to my supportive boyfriend, who didn't always understand what was going on, but always understood when to comfort or congratulate me. Thank you all, from the bottom of my heart.

AUTHOR'S BIO

Stacey Foss is a multi-subgenre romance author who can't resist writing–or reading–a good enemies-to-lovers storyline. As a lifetime New Englander, Stacey's favorite seasons are the ones where the bugs disappear. When she isn't hurting her own feelings with her writing, you can find Stacey curled up with her cats (Cobweb, Terrasen, Bellatrix and Andromeda), a good book, and a warm coffee.